# EXOGENE

Vhat do you mean when you say there isn't enough
ne? To live, you mean? You want to live longer, to
come a..." He stopped and turned, looking at one of
e soldiers. "What is it you call them, Sergeant, the
es who run, who want to live?"

"Satos," one of them said.

"That's it. Sato. You want to become a sato?"

I shook my head. "I want more time to kill."

He punched at the tablet more quickly now, leaning
er the desk until I could have grabbed his throat.
ill the enemy, you mean."

"Kill anyone."

BY T. C. McCARTHY

*The Subterrene War*

Germline

Exogene

# EXOGENE

## The Subterrene War: Book 2

## T. C. McCARTHY

orbit

www.orbitbooks.net

ORBIT

First published in Great Britain in 2012 by Orbit

A CIP catalogue record for this book
is available from the British Library.

ISBN 978-0-356-50042-3

Printed and bound by CPI Group (UK) Ltd, Croydon, CR0 4YY

Papers used by Orbit are from well-managed forests
and other responsible sources.

MIX
Paper from
responsible sources
FSC® C104740

Orbit
An imprint of
Little, Brown Book Group
100 Victoria Embankment
London EC4Y 0DY

An Hachette UK Company
www.hachette.co.uk

www.orbitbooks.net

*For Josh and Conor*

# PROLOGUE

*You* told me they'd welcome suicide," General Urqhart said. "That once their service term expired, Germline units would march in like virgins, ready for their own sacrifice. But that's not happening."

His audience was silent. The general's aides stood along the edges of a conference room while a group of scientists sat around a long table, and he stared at the holo-map that rotated overhead to show allied lines in blue, Russian in red. Nothing on the map moved; he didn't expect it to. For now it was static, a car stuck in a ditch that they hadn't yet figured out how to dislodge and with no sign of a tow truck. A disaster. If Urqhart didn't retake the mines within six months, and hold them for at least three, the war would be a financial catastrophe and that was the problem with his scientists: they didn't "get" war. Winning didn't depend on holding territory anymore, it hinged on pulling as much metal from the ground as you could and then leaving at the right time, a strategy that depended on having every tool working. And now he had to reassign Special Forces when he needed them the most.

"We're hemorrhaging genetics," he continued. "The first fielded units reached the end of their term, and of those, sixty percent are going AWOL. Heading west into Europe."

One of the scientists cleared his throat. "General, we already have reports of escaped Germline units dying before they can get too far. We just don't see this as a crisis; safeguards are working."

The rest of them nodded and some of the scientists even smiled, which made Urqhart furious. He pounded the table.

"Really? You don't think there's a problem? How do you think it looks to the public when news reports show disfigured girls in Amsterdam, Ankara, even Norfolk? What do you think the public sees? Not the military. They see *you*, but instead of geniuses you look like monsters. The news shows our genetic units with gangrene, their flesh rotting off, eyes milky white and blind, and most of the girls are crazy, drooling too much to even say a word. *Then* the public asks one question: how can we do this to human beings—to girls? People don't see them as things, as tools; they see them as people like you and me, and now they think we've murdered children in the most horrific ways possible: with war and disease."

The general paused to light his cigar, puffing until the end glowed and thick smoke coiled around his head, floating through the hologram. One of the scientists coughed. *Fuck him*, thought Urqhart, and he puffed a cloud in the man's direction, wishing the scientist would die on the spot, enjoying, for a moment, the thought of drawing his pistol and firing into the man's head to get everyone's attention—to show this wasn't an academic exercise.

The scientist who had spoken before nodded and folded his hands. "We think the problem lies in their psychological conditioning—while the girls are growing in the tanks. Apparently faith wasn't the answer our psychiatrists assured us it would be."

"Where are they now?" asked Urqhart, looking around the room. "Are there any shrinks here?"

The man shook his head. "No, General. We contracted psychiatric efforts to Hamilton Diversified, who refused to let their people attend this meeting without the company attorneys."

"Typical."

"But I spoke with one of their junior psychiatrists, a bright kid named Alderson, assigned to one of the deployed observation and maintenance teams. He had an interesting insight. Alderson thinks that experience plays a greater role in the girls' emotional development than was previously modeled, and that the problem is one of contradiction. Somehow realities at the front undermine their belief in God and the afterlife—make them doubt faith is the answer. And we don't know why."

The general's anger faded. Maybe he had misjudged this particular scientist; it wasn't the answer he wanted, wasn't a roadmap to a solution, but it was enough to seed an idea in Urqhart's mind, a notion that made him shiver with a sense that one day he and every man in the room would wind up in hell.

"I think I know why." His scientists turned their attention back to him and the general sensed in them a kind of skeptical amusement. "You people are idiots. Psychiatrists. Biologists. Fucking hell," he shouted now, his teeth almost biting through the cigar, *this is war!* I can't believe *I* can see the problem, and yet we pay you people millions each year to figure these things out for us. What the hell are we paying you for? *I shouldn't have to fix this.*"

He paused, scanning the room slowly, enjoying the moment for what it was and noticing sweat had appeared on some of their foreheads as he pulled deeply at the cigar.

"General," someone said, "what's your idea?"

"None of you have been in combat. And yet here you are, psychologically programming these girls for a combat environment, using religion not to infuse a sense of faith and duty, but to make them fearless. They *know* that if they die in war they go straight to heaven. It's a start, but here's the problem: it doesn't mesh. Down in the tunnels, once your friends start dying and the shit hits the fan, reality is a whole different thing from what these girls are being taught. Faith is a funny concept—either you have it or you don't—and war tends to mess with whatever scrap of it you might have."

He stubbed out the cigar on the scientists' table, leaving a black mark on its lacquered surface. "So, for now we do nothing. I have to reassign Special Forces units to their new mission, hunting down your mistakes, but the second batch of girls, the newer models, is almost in position for our counterattack. In a few weeks we retake the mines and hold as best we can. In the meantime we wait."

As he headed for the door, his aides holding it open, the scientist who had done most of the talking called after him.

"General, I'm lost. Wait for what?"

"The girls," said General Urqhart. "They sense that

what they're taught about faith is bullshit, that it all came from someone who doesn't know war, a bunch of four-eyed eggheads with no balls to speak of and even less experience. We need them to learn from someone who speaks their language, one of their own, someone who's seen the ass-end of humanity and still reported for discharge.

"So keep the psychiatrists in the field, conducting interviews, and assign this guy Alderson to watch the most promising girls, to look out for one that seems better than the rest. We're looking for someone who can tell the story of faith and war in a way that rings true for all the others, and we'll record every single thing she says about it, incorporate it into our future mental conditioning packages.

"We're waiting for a genetically engineered saint. And more than that, we need what the Greeks used to call a Psychopomp." Before anyone could ask he gritted his teeth and said, *"Look it up, assholes."*

# ONE

# Spoiling

*And you will come upon a city cursed, and
everything that festers in its midst will be as
a disease; nothing will be worthy of pity, not
insects, animals or even men.*

MODERN COMBAT MANUAL
JOSHUA 6:17

*live forever.* The thought lingered like an annoying dog,
to which I had handed a few scraps.

I felt Megan's fingers against my skin, and smelled the
paste—breathed the fumes gratefully for it reminded me
that I wouldn't have to wear my helmet. Soon, but not
now. The lessons taught this, described the first symptom
of spoiling: When the helmet no longer felt safe, a sign of
claustrophobia. As my troop train rumbled northward, I
couldn't tell if I shook from eagerness or from the railcar's jolting, and gave up trying to distinguish between
the two possibilities. It was not an *either-or* day; it was a
day of simultaneity.

*Deliver me from myself*, I prayed, *and help me to
accept tomorrow's end.*

Almost a hundred of my sisters filled the railcar, in a
train consisting of three hundred carriages, each one packed
with the same cargo. My newer sisters—replacements

with childlike faces—were of lesser importance. Megan counted for everything. She smiled as she stroked my forehead, which made me so drowsy that my eyes flickered shut with a memory, the image of an atelier, of a technician brushing fingers across my cheek as he cooed from outside the tank. I liked those memories. They weren't like the ones acquired more recently, and once upon a time everything had been that way. Sterile. Days in the atelier had been clean and warm—not like this.

"Everything was so white then," I said, "like a lily."

Megan nodded and kissed me. "It was closer to perfect, not a hint of filth. Do not be angry today, Catherine. It's counterproductive. Kill with detachment, with the greater plan."

I closed my eyes and leaned forward so Megan could work more easily, and so she wouldn't see my smile while smearing paste on my scalp, the thin layer of green thermal block that would dry into a latexlike coating, blocking my heat. The replacements all stared.

"Do you know what to expect in Uchkuduk?" one of them asked. "It's my first time—the first time for most of us. They mustered us a month ago from the Winchester atelier, near West Virginia. How should we prepare?"

"It's simple," I said. "There's one thing they don't teach in the atelier: *Bleeznyetzi.*"

Several of them leaned closer.

*"Bleeznyetzi?"*

I nodded. "It's Russian for twins."

"You are an older version," one said. "We speak multiple languages, including Russian and Kazakh, and we know the word."

"Then you know what our forces call us—the humans."

"No. What?"

The train squealed around a sudden bend, pushing me further against the wall. I braced a boot against Megan, who had just fallen asleep, to keep her from slumping over.

"Bitches and sluts. The tanks taught English too, right?"

They left me alone after that. It was no surprise—we all learned the same lesson: *"Watch out for defeatists, the ones near the end of their terms. Defeatism festers in those who approach the age. Ignore their voices. Learn from their actions but do not listen to their words. When you and your sisters reach eighteen, a spoiling sets in, so pray for deliverance from defeatism and you will be discharged. Honorably. Only then will you ascend to be seated at His right hand."* The replacements wouldn't associate themselves with me for fear that I would rub off on them, the spoiling a contagion, and for some reason it made me feel warm to think I had that kind of power.

"You're incorrigible," I whispered to Megan. "It is *not* your turn for rest," but she didn't hear and exhaustion showed on her face while she slept, in thin lines that I hadn't noticed before. "I'll tell you a secret: Hatred is the only thing keeping me from spoiling, the only thing I have left, the only thing I do well."


The armored personnel carrier's compartment felt like a steam bath. Heat acted as a catalyst, lowering the amount of energy it took for the phantom dead to invade my mind, and I focused on my hands, thinking that concentration would keep the hallucination at bay. It was no use. The APC engine roared like a call from the past, and Megan melted away to be replaced by the dusty outskirts of

Pavlodar, a bird jibbering overhead as we jumped off from the river. Five Kazakhs stood in an alley. They looked at me as if I were an anomaly, a dripping fish that had just stood up on two legs to walk from the Irtysh, and they failed to recognize the danger. Our girl named Majda moved first. She sprayed the women—who began to scream—with flechettes, her stream of needles cutting some of them in half as she laughed. Majda wouldn't laugh for much longer. A rocket went through her, leaving only a pair of twitching legs…

Megan was shouting at me when the vision evaporated.

*"Catherine!"*

The APC compartment reappeared. We sat encased in a tiny ceramic cubicle, strapped into our seats and struggling to breathe alcohol-contaminated air as the vehicle idled.

"You're spoiling," she said. "You were laughing."

I nodded and tongued another tranq tab—my third in the last hour.

"It's an insanity," Megan continued, "I worry. The spoiling seems to be worse in you than in any other and someone will report it. One of the new girls."

"It doesn't matter. Soon we will kill again and then it will be as if nothing was ever wrong, as if destruction was a meal, maybe toast and honey."

The turbine for the plasma cannon buzzed throughout the vehicle, vibrating the twenty cubicles like ours along each side, and three large ones down the vehicle's spine. We had two ways out. The normal way, a tiny hatch in the floor where we would come out underneath and roll from between the APC's huge wheels, and an escape hatch in the roof where we could pop out in an emergency. It wouldn't be long before everything stopped and time would dilate with excitement, with the freedom of movement and a sudden breakout into the open where one could find targets among men.

The turbines went quiet and I saw a tear on Megan's cheek.

"It doesn't matter," I explained, "not because I don't care about you. I do. It doesn't matter because we're dead anyway tomorrow. And I don't *want* to die."

"Don't."

"I don't want to be discharged."

"You speak like them, like the nonbred."

I shook my head, ignoring the insult, and placed a hand on her shoulder. "Haven't you ever wondered what it would be like to live past the age? Maybe the spoiling goes away. *Fades.* I have more killing to do, and they will rob me of it at eighteen."

Megan shook her head. She turned and I saw from the movement of her neck that she had begun sobbing, which made me feel even worse because my actions ruined the moment. This was to have been a sacred time. It was said that in quiet seconds during battle, when the firing paused as it sometimes did without explanation, one heard His voice in the wind or in the silence of the suit, His hand on your heart to let you know that you were a sacred thing among the corrupt. So the time before an engagement was to be used for reflection, to prepare for glory in an hour of meditation that climaxed with a flash of anticipation, of wanting to prove one's worthiness. But words ruined everything.

There were plans and strategies, mapped out in advance by semiaware computers and human generals to calculate just how far we could go before our systems reached their limit. It was a ritual beyond us—the way our leaders communicated with God and channeled His will. Nobody gave us the details. For the past two years neither Megan nor I knew why the war existed, except what we had caught in passing during interactions with men, with human forces, the nonbred. But those were glimpses. They weren't enough to answer all the questions, and soon we stopped asking because it was enough to know that we fought Russian men, and we prayed that God would make the war last forever. A feeling of satisfaction filled me as I thought about it, as if knowing that God was a part of the plan was enough, something that made us invincible because He trusted us to cleanse this part of the world, to allow a Lily like Megan to exercise her will.

We would move out soon. Far below us, the advance shock wave of our sisters was already attacking, underground, pushing into Russian tunnel positions and killing as many as they could before we followed with the main force—a mixed army of humans and my sisters, exposed aboveground for the greater glory. Our attack would make Megan feel better, I was certain. Waiting never helped, but war?

*War made us feel fifteen again.*

They played it over the speakers when we were born at fifteen-equivalent—the hymn, a prayer known only by the faithful, our first lesson and a call to the faithful:

*"This is my Maxwell. It was invented over a century before I was born but this one is new, this one is mine. The barrel of my Maxwell consists of an alloy tube,*

*encased by ring after ring of superconducting magnets. I am shielded from the flux by ceramic and alloy barrel wraps, which join to the fuel cell, the fuel cell to the stock. My Maxwell Carbine has no kick, my carbine has a flinch. It is my friend, my mother. My carbine propels its children, the flechettes, down its length, rapidly accelerating them to speeds ranging from subsonic to hypersonic. It depends on what I choose.*

*"My carbine is an instrument of God. I am an instrument of God. Unlike ancient firearms, the flechettes have no integral chemical propellant and are therefore tiny, allowing me to fill a shoulder hopper with almost ten thousand at a time. Ten thousand chances to kill. My flechettes are messengers of God. My flechettes are killers. The material and shape of my killers makes them superior armor penetrators. But my killers are not perfect. I am not perfect. My killers are too small to work alone and must function as a family. But I shall not worry. My Maxwell will fire fifty flechettes per second, and fifty is a family. With my Maxwell I can liberate a man of his head or limbs. With my Maxwell I will kill until there is nothing left alive.*

*"With my Maxwell, I am perfect."*

It was then, at fifteen, when Megan and I met our first humans. Until that point the technicians kept us in atelier tanks—alive and conscious, fed information and nutrients through a series of cables and tubes. The tanks gave us freedom of motion so we could put movement to combat scenarios played out in our heads, lending our muscles the same memories fed to our brains. Fifteen-equivalent was our birthday, when we became the biological equal to a fifteen-year-old human and slid from the growth tanks to feel cold air bring goose bumps and, along with them, a sense that the world was both a hostile and a promising place, full of danger but also the opportunity for redemption.

First steps were awkward. Megan had stumbled when trying to stand and crashed into me, sending us both to the cold floor in a heap. We giggled. *I'm Megan*, she had said, and I told her my name, after which we looked into a mirror and I thought, *She looks just like me*—skinny girls, with leg and arm muscles that flexed like pistons under gravity, and which I knew could be used to kill the human technicians around us in hundreds of different ways. They had hair. Our heads had been shaved perfectly smooth and Megan and I sat there, on the floor, rubbing the tops of them and tracing our fingers over the scabs where only a few days before, cables had penetrated, and the thought occurred to me that if I killed one of the humans we could take his hair, to glue it onto our heads just to feel what it was like. But the technicians were kind. They helped us both up, guiding us to the dressing area where they gave us our first uniforms, orange and bright enough that their color glowed under fluorescent lights; and the sounds—unmuffled by the gallons of thick fluid that normally surrounded us in the tanks—were enough to make me dizzy. I vomited on the floor.

A new voice spoke through the speakers while we organized. "Glory unto the faithful. On this, the day of your birth, a choir of angels sings your praise in heaven, telling God that he should watch for the time when you join him, to sit at His side after serving mankind. This you *shall* do, in honor of your creators.

"It is said that 'all the earth shall be devoured in fire. For then I will restore to the peoples a pure language, which they will serve my Masters with one accord. From beyond the rivers the daughters of His dispersed ones shall bring offering. On that day I will not be ashamed for any of my deeds in which I transgressed against God; for then he will take away from our midst those who spoiled, and they shall no longer be haughty in His holy mountain. He will leave in our midst a meek and humble people, and we shall trust in the word of our Creators.'

"Rejoice, for *you* are His daughters and ours, a holy Germline, Germline-one-A, and you will bring to Him eternal glory through death and with sacrifice. So sayeth the *Modern Combat Manual*."

While the voice read passage after passage, Megan helped me into my orange jumpsuit and when we looked at each other I knew she was the one.

It didn't matter now, in Kazakhstan, that those memories were old; it was the same look I gave her on that afternoon, when we slid from the bottom hatch of our compartment and stretched outside the APC under a dim sun. We smiled. I didn't need to say it to her: it was an amazing day, cold and bright like on the day we were born, and we would be together when the enemy turned to face us. My hatred burned with an intensity it hadn't mustered since the day before and both legs trembled, wanting to move out regardless of whether or not the others were ready.

Our APCs had stopped across the border, west of Keriz and inside Kazakhstan where vehicles spread across the countryside. To our north, contrails marked the passage of autonomous fighters, semiaware drones that calculated probabilities in less than a second, twisting through the sky in patterns like braided white ropes. Russian ground-attack craft tried to cross south, the APC's making an attractive target as they stopped in the open to assemble, but so far our fighters had kept the aircraft away. Every once in a while you saw a black streamer fall, followed by a cloud of fire and then a distant thud.

"It is here," said Megan, "in the air."

I nodded. "Death and faith."

"I will kill all I see."

"And we will bathe in the blood of mankind, washing ourselves of their sins."

She said, "Let it go. Detach."

But I didn't answer.

You can tell a battlefield from its smell. Burned metal tinged with rot, acrid enough so that it felt like the tissue in your nose would singe, foreign enough that it made you clench fists with the impatience to wade in. Only about half of us remained. Many of my sisters—the ones who had led the shock assault earlier that day, underground— had partially melted armor, bubbled from plasma attacks. Several were absent an arm or a hand. Despite the wounds, they would feel nothing because the nerves would have shut down, and blood vessels had sealed themselves to prevent further fluid loss. A plug of ceramic—locked in place with quick paste—would seal the suit breach and maintain thermal integrity. I felt proud. This was *my* unit, and none of us had spoiled to the point of being combat ineffective, so that our dead now looked down from heaven with the same sense of pride. Our wounded were the new girls, the replacements, and before they helmeted you saw that their faces still glowed, but now it wasn't the glow of nervous expectation; it was the glow from having killed, of *knowing.*

We began our advance, following on foot behind APCs that moved at jogging pace, sending sheets of mud and snow into the air and coating our suits in a dripping mess. Our feet made sucking sounds as we plodded. On either side of us, a full Division of Foreign Legion and Marines advanced at our flanks. *Human.*

There were no words to describe it, no way to understand except through experience. Trudging. Fighting against the mud with every step so that within five minutes your muscles screamed, and then having to continue like that for thirty minutes, an hour, two. I was near the edge of our formation, close to a group of Marines. You could see some of them, their armor almost new, as they twitched with every explosion or dropped to the earth at the first hint of tracer-flechettes. Many of them began stumbling and barely lifted themselves, falling behind as we continued. Nobody cared. The exhaustion got so thick, so fast, that it was all anyone could do to keep one's eyes open, let alone pull a straggler from the mud. I could have blocked the pain, willed it away the same way I twitched a finger, but the sensations reminded me that I hadn't been discharged yet and so they became comforting things, reminders there was more killing. Pain was familiar now. Welcome.

At times a walking plasma barrage moved ahead of us so that we moved faster, jogging over a crust of hard glass. It was a Godsend, and I heard Megan whisper her thanks. We spent the whole first day of the advance like that, walking then jogging, and soon I remembered that distances in Kazakhstan killed resolve almost as easily as the spoil. A tree on the horizon might look close. But as you walked through the day, it barely changed position, and was enough to drive you mad with the feeling that you would never reach it.

Then, at last, contact. Close to sundown, Megan and I found ourselves in a hole with three Marines. One of them screamed as Russian grenades cracked on every side, sending sprays of thermal gel over our position to hiss and smoke as the droplets melted whatever they touched. The other two men were hardly better. Both huddled at the bottom of the crater, screaming to us that we had encountered the outermost positions of a Russian defensive line.

I kicked one. "How can you aim from there?"

*"Get up and fight,"* said Megan, but the men cursed at her.

She grabbed the grenade launcher from one and peered over the lip of the hole. I fell beside her. A hundred yards away, behind a small rise, tiny flashes marked the position of a Russian grenadier whose helmet and shoulders the low sun outlined, and we had to duck when a spray of white tracer-flechettes kicked up the dirt around us. Megan dialed in the range. At the same moment she popped back up and fired, I sprinted from the hole, doing my best to zigzag through the mud toward the Russian position, not able to think through the haze of fatigue.

We continued like that for a few minutes. I would drop to the ground when she stopped firing, until her grenades started detonating ahead of me again—my sign to get up, keep going. Finally, I got close. I waited for her to stop and almost immediately saw the shape of a Russian behind the edge of a fighting position. His helmet was black, with paired, round, blue vision ports instead of a single slit like ours, and a series of cables connected the outside of the helmet to a power pack, so that they draped over the man's shoulders like thick strands of hair. You almost forgot why you were there, transfixed by the realization that he was so close, his proximity releasing an influx of hatred that made you want to scream. The man shimmered in the light. I saw all of them then, the ones who jeered at us as we waited for the cars in the railyard, who pelted us with empty food packs, but especially the ones in white lab coats, always there when we returned from the front, eager to punch data into their tablets as they forced us to answer questions. This was a man. It was rare to get this close, and it made you want to savor the moment, to get even closer and rip his helmet off so you could watch his expression change with death.

I slipped a grenade from my harness, hit the button, and waited for its detonation before rolling into the hole to push aside the dead Russians. "Check fire, Megan. Clear."

A set of three shafts led straight down in the center of the hole, the only way the Russians could have survived our plasma barrages. I tossed in grenades to make sure the shafts were empty, and then let the exhaustion wash over in a warm tide, numbing my muscles and nearly sending me to sleep. The sun set at that very moment and according to our locators we had made it to a point west of Karatobe. *They* were in Karatobe. The Russians had retreated there to establish a major defensive line on either side of the Syr Darya River, with Shymkent well to the south.

*Tomorrow*, I thought with a shiver. *Tomorrow is our day.*

Megan flopped down next to me and yanked off her helmet. She laughed. I removed mine before kissing her, after which we lay against the dirt wall of the hole and stared up—the sky turning an unbelievable reddish orange as the sun's light faded—waiting for the stars, something we never got tired of seeing. Megan especially loved stars, and they always brought wonder to her face. Soon I would dream. Sleep was a thing feared, something that resurrected buried memories and then twisted them into nightmares, a time to avoid. But you couldn't evade sleep any more than you could avoid the men in white coats.

"I count seconds as if they were hours," I said to him, "minutes like days."

"Explain that."

"What is there to explain?"

A man in a white coat sat on the other side of the table. He punched his computer screen with a shaking finger, and every once in a while glanced at me, then to the side to make sure the better men were still there, still keeping him safe. From me. The room shifted and my head hurt, a stabbing pain that shot through my spine and blurred my vision.

"I mean let's go further, and I'd like it if you'd elaborate on why you count seconds as if they were hours."

"*Sava, nie toma Meg. Sava.*"

"What language is that?" he asked.

"What?"

"What you just said. I didn't follow, was that Serbian?"

I shook my head. The better men stared at me, not even blinking, and looked as though they'd be more of a challenge than a typical soldier; they wore Special Forces desert hats in a way that spoke of ease. Familiarity. The stocks on their carbines were worn, and when my focus returned I counted the screws on their sights, custom ones, but each spaced a little differently from the other's, maybe due to one of them experiencing the onset of near-sightedness or ocular injury.

"It's not Serbian, is it?" He continued. "Is that the language of your sisters? The secret language, tongue of the bred?"

I stared at him and said nothing.

"I thought they cured all of you, in training. Thought that the punishments were so severe that even nerve override wouldn't work, that Germline units knew better than to keep speaking that crap." He smiled as he punched something else into his tablet. Data. This one had never *seen*.

"You're not the usual one we meet after battle," I said, "not the white coat I'm used to. *Bentley.* I think that was his name."

He wiped his forehead with an arm. "Insurgents killed Bentley on his way in from Bandar Abbas. I'm Alderson, new to the team from MIT, and here to replace him... Catherine, is it? Germline-One-A, Unit oh-five-seven-triple-one?" When I nodded, he tapped his foot on the floor. "Why do seconds seem like hours?"

"We don't have enough time." It should have been obvious, and a feeling of pity took the edge off my hatred, the realization that this one would never know God. "He put us on this Earth to serve. Death and Faith. Anyone who doesn't believe this, anyone like you, will never cross over into heaven. It is in the manual for all the faithful to study. You should taste a war, Alderson, or at least read about one."

"What do you mean when you say there isn't enough time? To live, you mean? You want to live longer, to become a..." He stopped and turned, looking at one of the soldiers. "What is it you call them, Sergeant, the ones who run, who want to live?"

"Satos," one of them said.

"That's it. Sato. You want to become a sato?"

I shook my head. "I want more time to kill."

He punched at the tablet more quickly now, leaning over the desk until I could have grabbed his throat. "Kill the enemy, you mean."

"Kill anyone."

Megan shook me awake, ripping me from my dream so that I found myself in Kazakhstan again, in the hole, wanting to finish what I was about to say. But the white coat had vanished. In the darkness light amplification made everything green and I waited for Megan to inspect my armor, to finish the routine. She checked for leaks. Our armor was designed the same way as human armor, sealed tight except for air intakes and exhaust, so that minimal thermal emissions would escape and no chemical or biological agents could penetrate. I checked my heads-up display, made sure that I had enough power and that the chill can, which would cool my exhaust to ambient temperatures, functioned.

"Clear," said Megan.

"*Sava*."

"What?"

"The language," I explained. "I remembered it in a dream."

She laughed and touched a gauntlet to the side of my head, and I imagined a smile on her face.

"You are different than the rest. Better. I had forgotten it, and don't know if I could remember much, not when we're this old."

But by then I was fully awake and the dream had begun to unravel, clarity taking hold and convincing the conscious part of my mind that nothing had happened while I slept. It had all dissolved.

"I have trouble remembering everything these days. Contact?" I asked.

"No. I patrolled for four hours. It's your turn, and I uploaded the path into your computer. Do you have enough of a charge in your fuel cells?"

"Yes." I flicked the forearm button and watched as my suit transformed, taking on the same colors and texture as my surroundings to the point where I couldn't see my own hand unless I moved it, and only then as a hint, a distortion in the air. I crawled slowly over the hole's edge and moved out.

There were four more hours until sunrise.


By the next morning, ten of us occupied the hole, Megan, me, and eight Marines. The ground shook with the explosions of a plasma barrage, as shells rained down over enemy positions a few kilometers away. I peered over the edge and watched. The clouds of gas—born from magnetic containment shells—expanded in brightly colored bubbles that hypnotized, their edges melting into hot tendrils that disappeared almost instantly. We'd move out soon. I felt it. The plasma wouldn't kill many Russians but it would keep their heads down and eventually we would jog across the open fields, behind the APCs, advancing toward the explosions to get as close as we could before the barrage ended. I lowered my helmet and slid the locking ring shut with a hiss.

It was almost unbearable. The ceramic threatened to collapse onto my face, to close over my mouth and nose in a suffocating mass and—*this isn't real*, I told myself, *this is the spoiling. My helmet is fine…* I tongued a tranq tab and shook my arms. While I waited for the tablet to dissolve, orders crawled across my heads-up display and crackled over the headset: *Prepare for jump off. Move bearing zero-nine-zero, neutralize all enemy positions and hold on east side of Syr Darya River. Jump at code sign Bravo.*

Megan flicked her safety off.

"You guys hear about Shymkent?" one of the Marines asked.

Another one answered, "Messed up."

"Shymkent?" asked Megan.

At first, the Marines didn't say anything, and although helmets hid their expressions I guessed what their faces looked like—what these men felt. Revulsion. *Do we have to talk to these things?* They were all men in white coats.

"Russian genetics pulled out of Shymkent last night, took positions in front of us to reinforce against you guys. *Thanks.*"

"Then we shall destroy them all," I said. "This is a *good* thing. They will be a challenge, a means to prove your faith."

"Jee-zus," the Marine said. "*Whacked-out* G's."

It wouldn't change our plans. Unless the reinforcement had been enough of a concern to change the overall strategy, we would attack the same way we always did, regardless of opposition. I glanced at Megan and saw her cradling her left arm with a free hand, shaking it up and down to get the blood flowing, and bringing back to me a flood of memories.

On our first exercise outside the atelier, Megan had broken her arm. A concussion training grenade had landed in our position and rolled close to her side before it blew, shattering her upper arm in ten places because we hadn't been wearing full armor. As soon as she tied it off with her belt, we rose to advance through the forest.

A bot popped from the ground. I raised my carbine and fired, the weapon dialed down to the point where the flechettes barely had enough energy to leave the barrel, and a few of them bounced off the thing's metallic skin, enough to alert it that it had been hit and should deactivate—but not before it lobbed several grenades in our direction. When one of them detonated behind us, someone screamed.

Megan and I crawled and then stood when we realized the exercise was over, so that we walked a few meters through tangled brush into the clearing from where the noise had come. The girl screamed again. A grenade had detonated on her back, carving out a crater so that we saw portions of her spine, but by the time we got to her side, she had silenced the pain and smiled at us.

"My name is Sarah," she said. "I think my back is broken, paralyzed."

"Does it hurt?" asked Megan.

"Not anymore. I am so lucky—to be the first from our unit."

Megan nodded. She dialed up her carbine's muzzle velocity, aimed, and fired into Sarah's head. A few minutes later we had reached a nondescript hill, our objective, and waited for our trainers to arrive, but the image of Sarah wouldn't leave me. *It should have left me.*

"What do you think it's like to die?" I asked Megan. She leaned against my back so that we wouldn't have to lie on the ground.

"We have simulated it. You know what it is like, an instant of pain and then darkness."

"Not the actual moment," I explained. "I mean afterward. On the other side."

Megan thought for a moment. "It is glory."

"Yes," I said, "of *course* it is glory, but what happens? How do we get to *His* side, what is *He* like?"

"These are questions for our mothers, not questions for us," Megan said angrily. "Leave it alone."

I thought it was odd—to have remembered that moment while we waited in the Kazakh steppes for our attack. But it struck me. Megan hadn't answered my question back then because she couldn't. Who could? And since we hadn't simulated the other sided of death, I began to wonder. We simulated everything else, over and over; why not the aftermath of death? How would we know how to reach His side; would there be enemies between us and Him, trying to keep us from reaching His position? Then I thought, *Maybe we didn't simulate it because* nobody *knows what happens after death, not even men.* I didn't know how to process the possibilities, and in the end put aside the thought because it made me uneasy.

*More waiting.* After ten minutes I suspected something was wrong and after half an hour the Marines got jittery, talking to one another in whispers. The sun peeked over the horizon and began melting the ice that had formed overnight, turning the fields ahead of us from a semisolid mass into a sea of mud. Then we heard it. Incoming plasma rounds, when they came close, sounded like someone ripping open the sky, and Megan and I shouted at the same time.

*"Into the holes!"*

We didn't have time to use the hand holds. I slid into the closest shaft feet first, and fell almost thirty feet straight down, pressing my knees against each concrete wall so that the ceramic of my armor would slow me. The shaft was tight, with barely enough room for my shoulders, and Megan came down on top, her weight pushing down until my legs locked against the walls. I braced myself and waited for the Marines to land on top of her, but it didn't happen.

Something made me laugh. The temperature on my heads-up climbed and the low oxygen warning light blinked on, but the sensation of being in the middle of it all, of the realization that in a moment it could all be over, brought happiness. For the moment it didn't matter that we might not know what it was like to die—to transit into His house. A plasma strike would be quick and I'd find out for sure. For myself. The rounds exploding overhead ripped the air from our hole so that as I waited for my emergency oxygen valve to open, it felt as though I would suffocate, and I prayed for an honorable exit, but soon the small tank hissed and filled my suit with air.

The booming of plasma sent me into a place of semi-awareness, where the walls melted to be replaced by the faces of my sisters, writhing in agony next to me as they burned and fused and I cursed them for looking so scared, which made me laugh all the harder until I wanted to choke them. But they stayed out of reach. The blasts vibrated everything to the point where my jaw refused to clench no matter how hard I tried, teeth rattling against each other as if shivering. The temperature inched higher. Our indicator readouts had been designed to shift from blue, to green, to yellow, and then to red—when the heat was within fifty degrees of damaging armor systems— and mine had gone red some time ago, making me wonder how Megan was doing since she was that much closer to the barrage, closer to glory.

I realized it stopped when all of a sudden I heard my own laughter, echoing inside the helmet. Megan began climbing. We made it to the top and stepped onto a sheet of glass, the ground crunching under our feet as clouds of steam shot from the cracks, and a pair of Marines climbed from the shaft next to us. The rest of them were gone, transformed into black lumps. Our headsets crackled to life and a single word blared over the net three times.

"Zebra, zebra, zebra."

Megan and I glanced at each other. Around us lay the ruined hulks of APCs, most of the closest ones cracked open and sending columns of smoke skyward as they burned. We slung our carbines and motioned for the remaining Marines to follow as we climbed from one crater to the next, moving westward as quickly as we could, in retreat. The hair on my neck stood up, skin tingling.

The Russians were on their way. You couldn't see them yet, or hear them, but you felt them and knew it had gone horribly wrong because "zebra" was a retreat code.

*   *   *

The route brought us to the rally point outside Keriz, where we sat, and where a flood of memories entered my mind along with exhaustion.

Our first combat advisor had a kind of look, like his soul had already left his body, an empty shell similar to the orphans I had seen in Tashkent on my push up from Iran, children whom the world had changed so they looked only at their feet. He sensed things. I never forgot the first time the man stared at me, with eyes that had stopped recognizing anything of this world, and if anyone knew what happened after death, I realized later, it would have been him. I should have asked. Among all men, this one we considered a brother, someone who understood what it meant to kill and how to do it, not a white coat, but a guide who had been tasked to show us the way north because he spoke Russian. Sisters that came after us spoke a hundred languages and had local geography vision-imprinted in their memories, but we didn't. We had only this broken human. On his last day of life, we all sat in the back of an APC, in one of the large main compartments surrounded by flechette hoppers and boxes of grenade magazines, waiting for the orders to hit Shymkent prior to pushing northward.

"You have been in more than one war?" someone asked him. When he nodded, Megan and I scooted forward on our seats. "We have not. This is our first one, I mean. It is good that you will be with us."

He leaned against a bulkhead and looked at the ceiling. "Why?"

"Because prior to this," said Megan, "in training, we only killed convicts and the insane. After the landing in

Bandar, on the push north from Iran, they all ran away and it didn't feel like combat, like it wasn't a *real* war; those men almost never returned fire."

"That's great," he said. "I'm so glad that you at least have experience with killing the mentally ill."

"I agree," I said. "It was an excellent training method."

When the APC ground to a halt, we slid from the rear hatch and followed him into ruins, a playground of tactical possibilities. The suburbs of Shymkent had been leveled. Fields of concrete rubble lay in a jagged landscape that seemed impassable but to us the area spoke of prospects, and Megan and I crouched as we followed the man through the wreckage, tracing the movement of our sisters on either side. Thousands of us filtered silently through the city.

Our advisor held up his hand and the word passed instantly to hold in place, drop to the ground. It went wrong a moment later. The Russians had placed plasma mines in the rubble, waiting for us to get within range, and when the man turned to run, explosions lit up the fields, blinded me for a split-second before my goggles frosted over. A pocket in the rubble protected Megan and me from the blast, but when it ended we heard nothing. I peered out. The blackened hulks of our sisters littered the concrete, and the ones closest to the plasma mine had fused to the soil, but there was no sign of our advisor. He had vaporized. Megan and I moved forward with the remaining survivors and attacked. I leapt into an enemy hole and flechetted the closest Russians, grabbing one who tried to run so that his helmet ring cracked when I snapped his neck. I twisted it further. Megan laughed with me and we pushed forward.

I didn't need tranq tabs back then. But after that initial battle, when it was over and we all sat amidst the concrete blocks to eat, I cried. It seemed strange. There was no sadness, just some need to release tears as if my eyes had become a kind of safety valve for an unfamiliar pressure in my chest.

And while we sat there now, near Keriz after our retreat, I saw myself in them—in the new ones, the replacements who had just survived their first battles only to run. Megan saw it too. Some of them took off their helmets, then their vision hoods with goggles, and showed their faces, which just a day ago had looked fresh but which now showed dirt and burn marks, their eyes empty so that you would have thought they had been fashioned from black glass, lifeless.

"Where is the Second Division?" Megan asked. "Our reinforcements?"

I shook my head. She didn't really expect an answer, but I gave one anyway. "I don't know. I worry more about what will happen next; the Russians might come before we can load into our own vehicles."

You still felt the Russians, out there. The horizon to our east had turned a reddish brown with the exhaust and dust from their vehicles, and I had taken off my helmet to feel the mild chill of a windy spring morning and to hear the enemy's vehicles if they got close enough. We had run all the way to the rally point. At least a hundred of our APCs were moving in from the west, reserve vehicles from Keriz that the Marines and Foreign Legion had sent to pull us back to a defensive line, and now it was a race to see who would get to us first—our forces or theirs.

Ten minutes later, we heard our rescue vehicles. It took

some time, but eventually they sped into our position and began the process of loading the wounded. I put on my helmet. Megan looked at me as though it were odd, which it was; there was no need for a helmet inside the APC, but I didn't want her to see me cry or suspect what I already knew—that I was crumbling faster than anyone realized.

I cried because another thought had occurred to me: I didn't want to disappear like our first advisor had. As if he never existed.

Even the bouncing motion of the APC—my head slapping against the ceramic bulkhead—couldn't pull me from the hallucination. The real world didn't exist. It took Megan some time to reach me, and I didn't notice her efforts until she had removed my helmet and poured a packet of water over my head.

"Come back," she said, crying.

I stroked her cheek. "I'm here."

"Where do you go?"

"Everywhere," I said. "And nowhere. Sometimes it's like being in darkness until something brings me back. Other times I walk through our past, unable to change anything."

Megan grabbed my hand and squeezed it. "Please stay with me. We still have today."

"Death and faith."

We had to stop talking when the whine of the turbines rose. The vehicle angled upward, climbing a small slope. If you hadn't been in an APC before, it would make you wonder how long it would take to suffocate, which, in turn, opened the door to hundreds of additional death thoughts. Alcohol fumes made it difficult to breathe. Behind my head the motors of the plasma turret screamed as it rotated back and forth, and I felt the throb of the compact fusion reactor that took up the center of the vehicle, its sole purpose to generate hot gas so it would be a race if they hit us. When enemy rockets struck an APC's reactor, a bloom of plasma might melt the passenger compartments before its energy dissipated, or the rocket might penetrate into troop sections, where its overpressure and flames combined to liquefy the occupants.

Those kinds of thoughts had never been a concern. But as we sat there, listening to the vehicle communications, I began to shake.

"Contact," a voice said. "Enemy APC columns, moving toward Keriz, over three thousand vehicles."

Megan and I glanced at each other and shifted closer, our hips touching.

"New contacts, airborne—bearing oh-one-five, oh-twenty three, and oh-five-two. Speed, six hundred. Distance, three hundred klicks. Forty thousand targets. Computer solution in ten seconds."

"Roger that," another voice responded, "Proceed to Papa-Golf-three-four-nine-two-four-one, offload and hold. Orders being distributed."

Megan and I checked the maps. Tamdybulak. We waited, until a few seconds later the orders crawled in green letters across our goggles' heads-up displays: *Reform at Tamdybulak and prepare defenses.* I couldn't swallow. The anticipation became palpable, an electricity that ran from my feet to my scalp, cold with the certainty of war and the equal certainty that there would be nothing to shoot at, that we'd be targets for Russian auto-drones.

"And the time will come for a reckoning," said Megan. "When God's final test will be laid upon you in a blanket of fire and chaos. We will know then the true purpose of our existence—the meaning of death and faith."

A short time later, the APC screeched to a halt and the floor dropped out beneath us, a Marine commander's voice coming over the intercom. "Everybody out. Inbound, E-T-A two minutes." Already the plasma turret spun slowly as it tracked its first target, still not visible over the horizon.

Megan's voice clicked over the headset. "Button up. Take cover."

I glanced to the side as we sprinted. There were still at least a thousand of my sisters and three times as many Marines, but we had begun the day before with more than twenty thousand girls, and I wondered how many more we'd lose in the next few minutes. Tamdybulak swallowed us in its rubble. Megan and I spotted a gap between two overturned slabs of crumbling concrete and dove in, just as the APCs opened fire.

"I will be as a viper," I whispered, "hidden until the time is right. I will melt my enemies from the earth, and slaughter his family so that none may take up arms again. Each death is a trophy for my Lord, a testament to my willingness. This is a test of faith." The pulsing of plasma cannons shook the ground so that dust and pebbles pattered on my helmet like rain.

Like most of the settlements you encountered in Kazakhstan or Uzbekistan, Tamdybulak had been reduced to a sea of blackened rubble, pockmarked by thousands of craters, and the inhabitants had long since fled or been killed. Dust coursed around us as a strong wind blew through the ruins.

A factory once stood nearby, its iron girders still poking up vertically among the wreckage, and two storage silos managed to hold on to their concrete sheathing, which had been riddled with shrapnel and partially melted by the heat of plasma. "Look," said Megan, pointing to an APC that sat in the factory's center.

We saw a Marine. The man jumped from the APC and scrambled over a pile of rubble, searching for a hole large enough to hide in, but all of them had been taken and the man began to curse.

"A fool," I said.

"Fire, fire, fire," someone announced over my headset, "eighty thousand inbound."

Through a crack between concrete blocks, we saw thousands of rocket trails crest the horizon. The first missile hit the APC directly in the crew compartment and blew the front half into a cloud of ceramic, catapulting the vehicle ten meters into the air. When it landed the wheels popped off, one of them rolling directly toward our position while three missiles homed in on the movement. They struck simultaneously. I was closer than Megan, and screamed when the explosions blew me upward several feet, the huge concrete slabs flipping aside as if they had been feathers. Once I collected myself, Megan and I crawled into a new position, scurrying under one of the slabs that had been tossed over.

The attack ended quickly, and we waited for the next volley. But before the remaining Russian drones could fire another salvo, a squadron of Marine fighters roared overhead, forcing the enemy aircraft to flee, after which I looked down again to see the man who had been trying to find cover; he pulled himself along the ground, with both his legs now missing. We watched, until a few minutes later he lay still.

Megan must have noticed something in me—despite the fact that I was still fully suited. "What's wrong?" she asked.

I pulled my helmet off and vomited; it surprised me more than it did her, and my scalp grew hotter until it felt as though the branding scar, on the back of my head, had ignited into flame.


After training they branded a lily on Megan's head and epoxied a white enamel lily on each shoulder of her armor, symbols which meant that she could be followed, the purest among pure. It seemed like yesterday, but in a different world.

Our final atelier test had nothing to do with military training, but everything to do with faith. The unit Mother, Sister Miriam Anne, would conduct it. Atelier technicians assigned a hundred of us to each family, crammed into a small barracks with our mother's apartment at the far end where she watched over her daughters. The mothers were all bald, but much older than us, and had their own uniform—a clean white dress, white shoes, and a white scarf that they tied over their heads to protect themselves from the sun. Of all of them, only Sister Miriam carried a rattan cane. Of all of them, Sister Miriam knew how to use the cane best.

On the evening before our final exam, we returned from field exercises exhausted, mud covering every inch of our orange uniforms and caking the partial armor and combat kits that now felt a hundred pounds heavier. Megan and I always grinned. In those days it felt exhilarating, because as we mentally shut off each twinge of pain, it reminded us that we had almost made it, that soon we would be accepted into the sisterhood of warfare. Sister Miriam waited for us on the barracks steps, and frowned when she saw my arm draped over Megan's shoulder.

"Miss Megan," she said. "A *word*."

Megan pushed me away and gave me her look, *I'll catch up with you inside*, but after moving through the door I stopped to watch through a narrow window. Sister Miriam waited. When Megan got close to her, she lifted her cane and swung it over and over, until a spray of blood came from Megan's mouth and spattered Sister Miriam's dress. The red looked brilliant against the white. When Megan finally collapsed onto the ground, her bald scalp lacerated in several places, the beating stopped and Sister Miriam lowered herself to whisper something. Megan began sobbing.

After she finally returned to the barracks I tried to hug her, but Megan stepped back. "Don't touch me."

"Why? What did Mother say?"

She shrugged and removed the first aid kit from her pack. "They worry about us. You and me. They have seen us together."

"So what?" I asked. "It matters for nothing, we are not the only ones who love each other."

*"It matters for everything!"* Several of the other girls stopped what they were doing and stared. Megan lowered her voice. "Tomorrow is our final exam. I *want* the lily, can't you understand that? To be one among a hundred is a great honor. *Second only to death*. Our feelings make us less efficient, get in the way of duty, make us impure."

I felt as though she had knocked the wind out of me,

and said nothing. *I wanted the lily too.* We showered in silence and walked through the mess line without speaking to each other, not even saying good night when the lights went out. The carbine kept me awake. Its cold barrel poked me in the cheek, and wouldn't let me drift off, making me more and more nervous so that I forgot about Megan as the next day approached. *The day of our final test.* Reveille sounded before sunrise, and we rolled from our racks, dressing in fresh uniforms and boots. I had never been that nervous. But we were so ready—all of us—that they could have put us in a cage with a thousand lions and we would have leapt at them, shredding with our bare hands anything stupid enough to resist us.

Instead of lions, however, they gave us kittens. Our mothers issued them soon after we reached fifteen-equivalent and ordered us to care for the animals, to play with them several times a day. Mine I had named Megan, and Megan had called hers Catherine, and as we waited on the cold morning of our final exam, Sister Miriam stood in front of a row of APCs on the parade ground, where she pointed at stacks of small animal cages. You heard the kittens—now full-grown cats—mewling, and I felt something then, but didn't know what to call it, didn't recognize horror until later.

"Good morning, my daughters," she said.

We answered in unison. "Good morning, Blessed Mother."

"My people were created in God's image, and you were created in ours. Facsimiles, identical to each other in every way, close to perfection. Serve humanity loyally and without question and, like us, you will earn a seat at His right hand.

"Today you become women. Perfection. The first of your kind were male, Germline-A, a failed experiment who turned on their creators, their aggression untamable, their bravery so psychotic that they became strategic liabilities and tactical failures. Not so with you. Today you are sixteen-equivalent. For the next two years you will kill at every turn, and the sight of fallen enemies will warm your hearts. Across the atelier right now, there are hundreds of ceremonies like this one, all of you destined for eternal glory, but within this group, in my family, there is one. One among a hundred. One Lily, pure and without sign of spoil."

Megan shifted beside me.

"Megan. Step forward." When she approached, Sister Miriam placed her hand on Megan's shoulder and handed her the cat, Catherine. Then she attached a series of sensors to Megan's forehead and stepped back. "When I give the command," Sister Miriam said, "snap its neck."

I didn't know if anyone else saw it, but I did. Muscles tightened on Megan's jaw and she cocked her head forward, signs of sadness that I recognized instantly. Even *I* felt something, a whisper, like someone had sent an invisible message that what was about to happen was *more* than just wrong. *Evil.* In the aftermath of the test and by the time we landed in combat, the sensation had gone, burrowed into the darkest parts of my mind where I never thought I'd see it again, but on that day it was clear.

"Now," said Sister Miriam. Megan didn't hesitate. She twisted the cat's neck and Sister Miriam watched the screen on her palm computer, hit a few keys, and then smiled. She pulled a small metal rod from her dress and pushed a button; the end of the rod glowed white a few seconds later as she walked behind Megan. "Lean forward," she said.

Sister Miriam turned to us then and raised her voice. "This is your Lily. Follow her and listen to her words, for in them there will never be spoil, never a taint. She speaks for us, for the ateliers, and for God."

Megan never flinched. Her skin smoldered, a quiet hiss as the brand melted the thin layer of flesh at the back of her scalp. We all lined up then, one by one slaughtering our cats. But a few of the girls must have done something wrong because technicians led them away and we never saw them again.

Where Megan had been branded a Lily, on the head, we also received the brand, a single mark on our skin, mine identical to all others: the number "1."

I saw the lily on Megan's head now, as the sun set over Tamdybulak. The scar had blended into her skin and one of the two enamel flowers on her armor had lost its petals; the other had completely broken off, and I wondered if she still felt the same about the honor—if time altered a Lily the same way it had spoiled me—but there wasn't a chance to finish the thought. We had finished digging defensive positions and stared to the northeast when she pointed. A lone Russian in combat armor had crawled to the edge of a distant rubble field.

"Contact," Megan said over the net. "Enemy scout sighted. *Catherine*."

I wrapped my finger around the trigger, bringing up the sighting reticle, and slowly rested the carbine on a rock to wait for the feeling of joy that always preceded a kill. But it didn't come. Instead the reticle trembled, its crosshairs bouncing around until I tongued another tranq tab, waiting for it to dissolve and cool me with a promise of control. The trigger pulled, a burst of a hundred flechettes impacted against the Russian's faceplate, and he fell back to disappear in the wreckage.

"Clear," said Megan, and she placed her helmet against mine so nobody else would hear. "Why did it take so long?"

But there was no answer to give. Something had shifted in me, perhaps during the plasma shelling east of Keriz, or in the APC as we fled in the face of advancing Russian forces; I didn't know. But whatever it was felt like a betrayal of the mind, a mutiny of the limbs, and when the truth materialized it hit me in the chest so that my breathing quickened to the point where my bio-readout blinked yellow in warning: I was hyperventilating. The spoiling had finally reached my core. It was fear.

"I wanted to take my time," I lied, "to enjoy it."

Megan laughed. "There will truly be a special place for you. In heaven. Because in hell they are all too scared of you."

# TWO

# Birthdays

*For sinners, there is only destruction at the
hands of My enemies, for they have taken
of an accursed thing and have stolen.*
MODERN COMBAT MANUAL
JOSHUA 7:13

The Marine commander clicked in. He had surveyed the
defensive line an hour before and I recognized his
voice because he sounded musical, like someone who had
once sung hymns to us in the tank, and for a few seconds
it made me wonder if this was all a simulation—that an
hour from now I would be born again, new and fifteen.

"Marine and Foreign Legion forces," he said, "are
ordered to retreat and reform at Uchkuduk. Genetic orders
incoming."

Megan and I heard men shouting and we rolled over to
watch while Marines, some of them tossing their weapons
into the rubble so they could run more quickly, retreated
into their APCs, and when the vehicles had finished
on-loading, the wheels turned slowly, rumbling southward in clouds of dust. *Abandoning us.*

One of the Marines shouted as his APC hatch swung
shut. "See ya, *bitches*!"

And time stopped. My hands trembled in their gauntlets in a way that was noticeable only if you looked closely and the suit air had turned rank, forcing me to endure the smell of terror, a sweat that wouldn't stop although it was cold enough inside the carapace to make me shiver. The newness of the sensation fed on itself, made the fear grow in my chest until I clenched my teeth so that they wouldn't betray my anxiousness with chattering. *Concentrate on the sky,* I thought, *the ground, anything,* until finally I saw a single clover that had survived the trampling, plasma, and digging that Tamdybulak had suffered for the last several years. The thing was new. Green, and it waved in a breeze. I was about to look away when the realization hit that it had survived everything, without a display of emotion and without fear, so that I slammed my fist against the plant until it collapsed into the dirt, buried under concrete and rock.

Orders eventually popped up on our displays: *Enemy attack expected within ten to twenty-four hours. Hold Tamdybulak. No relief expected. Maintain as high a kill-loss ratio as possible.*


"We need to increase the kill-loss ratio for series one," said Alderson. He sat across from me, wearing the same white coat as always but this time he had come closer to the lines, underground, where wet air draped everything in a thick and invisible mantle. The atmosphere was steamy, and surrounding rock hummed with the sound of ventilation as a hundred pumps fought to bring cooler stuff from several kilometers above and force hot airborne waste—along with its scent of decay, sweat, and burning ceramic—into the alleyways of Shymkent, into the sky, into the lungs of Kazakhs. And there were other sounds. Plasma shells pounded the rock above and my ears noted the vibrations, sending data to my mind where neurons converted frequencies into probabilities in less than a microsecond: these were Russian shells intended to deny the topside while their infiltrators crawled into our lines. Soon I would move upward. We would meet them, the Russian nonbred who had overcome fear and so deserved my attention, had earned more than an average death from heart disease, or old age, or cancer. Our humans called them Popovs. But the word didn't fit and felt too demeaning, for even though the Russians *were* nonbred, at least they showed a kind of dignity in their efforts to die rather than fade off, showed fiber in a world of rubble and cowardice.

Then there was Alderson, trying to hand me something. My vision didn't register on what he held but instead on the tremble in his fingers, a shakiness that infected the man's throat so that when he spoke, his words vibrated like the walls.

"... so take this."

"What's wrong with you?" I asked, not moving for the packet he offered.

"Never mind me, you're sixteen and a half. Equivalent. And according to our data your group has the highest kill rate, and the other genetics in your outfit call you 'the Little Murderer.' We like this. So you have to take this medicine. It will help with our research."

"But you shake. Why? The only thing that could possibly reach us here is a deep penetrator and the Russian attack suggests they want our underground positions intact, not collapsed. Even if they did penetrate, we would be invincible in glory. Death and life are not the same; death is better. And Bentley was a better man than you. Even though you've done the right thing by coming here, to where it all could end, I still think he was more like us."

"I don't have to ask for you to take it. I could call my Special Forces escort and have them force you. An injection."

"Why don't you?"

Alderson didn't say anything at first, and tapped the table.

"Because you are almost perfect at killing. Better than even the current crop of Lilies. The most promising prototype we've seen, an operational example of what we intended when designing genetic units. So we thought you should be asked. That maybe you'd take the agent willingly. We were being *nice,* Catherine."

I grabbed the packet and ripped open the top before he could flinch. *Better than the Lilies, even Megan?* "What is it? A lie?"

"A psychotropic cocktail. Multiple pharmaceuticals designed to shut down portions of your nervous system, depriving the brain of certain signal pathways. A few months ago my research team in Bethesda found studies that had been conducted over two centuries ago; when taken in the correct doses, *low* doses, the treatment can stimulate creativity. It opens new neural connections. As a result, we think an appropriate regime could result in your brain generating new ideas that otherwise would remain buried, making you a better, more inventive soldier."

"You want me to find new ways to kill."

Alderson shrugged. "Let's say we want you to be creative. Artistic."

The liquid tasted slightly metallic, like our recycled water, and I squeezed the packet as hard as I could, tilting my head back to shake out the last droplets. After a few minutes I shook my head.

"It doesn't work."

"Give it time," he said. "Sometimes these types of drugs don't kick in for an hour, or their effects are so subtle that you don't even notice. In the meantime our recon drones suggest that the Russians are attempting another infiltration topside, but the data is inconclusive. If they come, we want you and the other Germline-Ones to meet them. Sentry bots will be deactivated and your mission will be to stop the attack with no support."

"All of us have been given this treatment?"

He grinned and took out his computer. "Just you. We'll follow your progress via drone, documenting changes to your effectiveness."

"Then I should rejoin my sisters."

"No." Alderson motioned for me to stay in my seat and began typing. "There's time for that still. Right now I need to ask you some questions."

And then I noticed. The vibrations of plasma impacts moved through the rock and into my body so the energy became a living thing, communicating anger, whispering about the plasma shells' rage at having been denied real tissue, which I understood and which made me sympathetic to them, made me want to bring Alderson topside. They needed a sacrifice. If the rounds consumed him they would have at least something for their troubles and the shells showed more bravery in their short existence than he had in an entire nonbred life. But then it changed again. Alderson's coat shone brightly, even in dim combat lamps that should have made it seem blue, but instead the garment became so brilliant that I could only stand to look at him for a moment. Each thread came into focus— as if my vision had reached a new level of acuity, perfectly tuned.

"And now for the last question," he said.

"What? I thought you had a lot of questions for me."

Alderson laughed. "I did. You've answered most of them for me already. It's been…illuminating. You don't remember?"

"How much time has elapsed?"

But I already knew from my chronometer, and Alderson confirmed it. An hour had gone by and I didn't remember a thing. It underscored the sensation that had already seeped in, soaking into my brain the same way blood sank into the ground, slowly and quietly: the world had changed, along with my perception of it.

"Are these effects permanent?" I asked.

"The sensations the drugs bring on are not, but over time, as you grow accustomed to the treatments, we predict that new neural pathways will likely be established to the point where you can access them without treatments. If this works, it should make you sharper and keep you there, until you're discharged. Shall we continue?"

I nodded.

"Have you ever been afraid?"

"I don't understand." My mind raced at the thought, and the room shifted sideways, replaced by the vision of our mother beating Megan, the cane whistling as it arced downward. "I fear nothing."

"Good. Then get back to your sisters. We've just gotten word that Popov will be here in twenty-four hours."

\*     \*     \*

It was almost exactly twenty-four hours between the time our humans abandoned us at Tamdybulak and the moment the Russians arrived. Marines had left us three broken-down but semi-serviceable APCs, and we did our best to camouflage them beneath dirt and concrete blocks, after which there was nothing to do but wait. It only took an hour for the silence to make me tremble.

"Alderson said that I killed better than the rest," I said to Megan, just to break the monotony. "Even better than the Lilies."

"What are you talking about? What made you think of him?"

"When I blinked out a little while ago, it's what I saw: one of my interviews with him. He said that I was the best killer in Germline-One and better at it than the Lilies."

Megan shifted, and I sensed her staring at me, but my eyes didn't move.

"We call you the Little Murderer. That was after Majda was taken, when the killing really started, and I think Petra thought of it, started the name behind your back. You were always better than me at killing. Better than anyone."

"He told me that too. The inside of my head feels cold now, Megan."

I got tired of scanning the horizon and slipped deeper into the hole, letting Megan handle the watch as I spoke. "It's not so easy anymore. Do you remember the name of our first Special Forces escort? When they assigned them to us, before their mission changed to hunting us down?"

"No."

"I see him sometimes too, and it's always the same dream, always takes place during our first advance into Shymkent. Sunrobe. His last name was Sunrobe. What do you think it means? In my visions you can always see it clearly, stenciled on his armor in yellow, the way Special Forces liked it instead of black. But I think that is a strange name to have."

"I think they're all strange. All the nonbreds."

I shook my head and knocked dust from my carbine's breach. "I want a last name too, Megan."

"Why?"

"Because they're important."

She snorted. The helmet speakers amplified it, made it sound like a burst of static. "Important to the nonbred. To the soft. But not to us."

"The soft created us. And Special Forces are so much like the Germline, worthy. Be smart. If it's important to them to have names, than it must be so for a reason. What if last names are the secret to heaven—not glory? What if our mothers lied to us?"

But she didn't say anything. My chronometer read oh-one-hundred, and in the green of night vision Tamdybulak had begun to look like a moss-covered boulder field, with half-ruined structure after half-ruined structure stretching beyond the goggles' range, and in the silence that had fallen between me and Megan, Tamdybulak's ruin became more inviting. It called to me. In retrospect it could have been the tranq tablets but they had long since ceased to have any dramatic effects, so it seemed unlikely they were the cause, but I thought that the ruins had signaled for someone, invited and welcomed me because they understood the importance of naming, refused to give up their own name of *Tamdybulak* even though nobody had lived there for years. To this city, I was a native. Anyone could be a native in an empty city.

"I'm going hunting," I said.

"There's nothing out there. We've seen no movement since you shot their first scout and I can't risk losing you in a collapse. Or you could fall into a hidden substructure; there may be tunnels all over."

"Megan. I have to go."

"Why?"

I thought for a second, remembering Alderson. "It's because I'm an artist. The Little Murderer. And because it's after midnight, and the order for discharge could come through at any time so this may be my last chance."

"The orders already did come," said Megan, "but not the way you think. They sent word while you were hallucinating, that we're not to be discharged until after the engagement is over."

"If we survive," I said.

"Fuel cells?"

"There's enough."

Megan brushed the side of my helmet with her hand. "OK. Go hunting and be the Little Murderer while you have the chance. I love you."

And so the city took me in, swallowed me into its green on black within gray, and for the first time I could remember it felt good to be away from Megan. For now she wouldn't see that I was terrified.


The combat suit was home. A temple. Its ceramic carapace had flexible joints and the body section opened like a clamshell from waist to shoulder so that once you slid in, getting out was almost impossible. Between me and the shell was an undersuit—a synthetic one-piece garment through which tubes and hoses circulated cooling fluids or carried away excess energy. Heat. Without a way to remove it, it would have killed me. A computer system, communications equipment, sensors, vision hood with goggles, and me, all of these things generated energy, and fluids shunted it off to a backpack heat-exchanger before it could accumulate, then blew it through a pair of ports at my lower back where a secondary coolant system, aerosol, lowered the thermal bloom's temperature to almost ambient. Systems created a slow and steady power drain, but with chameleon skin activated, the drain became more noticeable.

"But I am invisible," I whispered, "an artist," and my power indicator had almost reached null by the time I found one of them. "I am Catherine Little Murderer."

A Russian genetic had buried himself under rubble about three hundred meters from our perimeter, leaving only the tip of a collector exposed, which I wouldn't have noticed except that he must have adjusted himself and caused the rubble to shift, showing the man's entire device. A new idea popped into my head, but there was a problem. I had frozen. Sweat ran down my face despite the suit's coolant and my mouth dried to the point where swallowing became impossible. I prayed that a series of violent shakes wouldn't make any noise as I lay there. It took three more tablets and ten minutes to force my hands still, and tears fogged the goggles while my arms and legs worked to bring me closer to my target.

Collectors like this one were designed to gather

information sent to them by microbots, which would be fired onto our positions just prior to their assault. The tactic would give the Russians our exact positions. But that was hours from now, an eternity that might never arrive, because what mattered more was that if this one had a collector then the microbot launcher would be somewhere else, with one of his brothers, also hidden in the rubble— not too close, but out here. Still. I ignored the thought that another Russian might be watching as I shifted pieces of rubble, one at a time, from the place where it seemed this one's chest should have been. Soon a small pit formed. Into this I carefully placed three thermal grenades and after another three minutes I had replaced the rubble in a way that left the arming switches exposed.

*Three flicks and three seconds to run.* My finger shook as I quietly typed a message to Megan, telling her of my plan and asking her to inform the others to get ready; there was a chance the other Russian would fire at me when I ran, giving away his position too. As soon as she acknowledged me, I acted.

Three seconds passed as I sprinted parallel to our line. Behind me I heard the pops of my grenades, followed by a muffled shout and then all around me Russians seemed to sprout from the ground. There was no time to fear. Tracer fire erupted from Megan and the others, pinging the rocks to form flickering sparks that made it hard to see through night vision and I dropped to the ground, trying to stay as low as possible. One of the Russians dove next to me, his chameleon skin deactivated by a series of hits that had ruptured his fuel cell. He cursed. Bringing my carbine around, I placed it against his temple and squeezed the trigger, watching in fascination as the man tried to bring his weapon to bear so that in the end I had to squeeze three times to take his life, three times that ended in a rage. I ripped his helmet off and began slamming the butt of my carbine against his head, and sensed it when bits of him flew against my faceplate and chest.

Within moments it had ended, and as I crawled back to Megan, the field had gone quiet again.

"You have the enemy on your suit," she said.

"How can you tell in night vision?"

"I turned it off."

I sighed and slumped to the bottom of our hole, pulling off my helmet. "He angered me. There were nine more out there."

"Eleven. They will come in force tomorrow." She helped me wipe the Russian's blood and tissue off my armor and popped her helmet to kiss me. "Little Murderer."

At sunset the next day the booming of plasma cannons sounded well to our southeast, and we didn't know what to make of it because there shouldn't have been fighting in that direction. Megan shrugged. Our light amplification kicked in after the sun went down and the landscape again turned varying shades of green, the only sound coming from a light breeze that moaned as it blew through crevices in the debris fields. I shivered. I knew they would come, and still had not gotten used to waiting, defending, having time to ponder the fact that within hours we would both be discharged and gone. Megan wrote with a finger in the dirt. *I love you.*

Movement from the distant rubble caught my eye and I

watched as a line of about a hundred Russians crawled toward us, keeping to cover as much as possible. *Finally it had begun,* I thought. Either way, it will all be over soon.

"Contact," I said. "Approximately one hundred infantry, northeast."

Megan clicked in. "Grenadiers. Faith."

The popping of grenade launchers broke the stillness and flashes blossomed in the rubble, sending flechettes to scatter among the advancing enemy. One of the Russians screamed as his armor smoked under thermal gel and he rose to charge our line. Megan cut him down.

The Russians yelled then, rising from their cover to sprint forward in a mass. "*Pobieda! Ooo-Rah!*" And all of us opened up.

When it was over, Megan slapped my shoulder and I crept from my hole, crouch-walking through the rubble. I drew my pistol. The bodies were easy to see, their dying warmth forcing my vision kit to switch to infrared, and I stopped to pump a single flechette into the head of each one. An hour later I crawled back into my hole, exhausted.

"I can't see anymore, Megan. I am so tired."

But before she answered we both heard a rumbling—faint at first, then growing louder by the second.

"APC's moving up the main road from the north," a voice announced. One of our sisters had volunteered to man a forward outpost, hidden in a mound of rubble. "Ten of them. Multiple infant—" An explosion lit the distant sky, cutting her transmission short.

"Rocket teams on the line," said Megan. "Disperse in forward positions then hold for the order. When I give it, APC's and rockets open fire."

"Ten isn't right," I said to Megan.

"I know."

"Where are the rest? There should be over ten thousand infantry, and thousands of vehicles." Fear had almost overwhelmed me by then, forcing my voice to crack and making me wonder how much longer it would be before I ran.

"I know," Megan repeated. "It makes no sense. The rest may be moving on our flanks. We'll know soon, Catherine."

We watched as almost a hundred of our sisters whispered past in groups of two or three, heading northeast, each of them carrying a three-shot antitank weapon. The weapons could penetrate APC frontal armor—as long as they were fired within eight hundred meters of their target. *It was suicide*, I thought, *but these girls were new, hadn't spoiled.* Anyone who waited until an armored vehicle was within eight hundred meters and fired a rocket would announce to the enemy, "Here I am, shoot back at me." Anyone who got that close could die before they got a chance to fire; I found myself happy I wasn't sixteen again, glad to not be a fearless idiot who hadn't learned the real lessons of the field, an idiot who hadn't been called the Little Murderer and who hadn't learned not to volunteer to hunt vehicles.

"Contact," one of them reported. "APC's sighted, about two thousand enemy infantry dispersed behind them. Range, nine hundred meters."

Megan clicked off her safety.

"Seven hundred meters," the same voice announced. But we saw the vehicles now, lumbering things, whose wheels mesmerized as they bounced up and down to trace a path over chunks of concrete and boulders, their turrets moving back and forth like a single eye, searching. Megan waited a few minutes and before the girl announced the five-hundred-meter mark, she gave the order.

"Faith."

Our APCs lit the night with plasma cannons, and I flinched when antitank rockets shrieked toward their targets. The Russians returned fire instantly. Plasma clouds expanded over the area where our rocket teams had hidden and to me it looked like only a few of them had managed to get off a shot.

"God..." said Megan.

"Five APC's wiped," someone else announced, "Five inbound."

A pink ball of plasma engulfed one of our broken-down APCs and my suit temperature jumped.

"APC one, *out*."

Suddenly, a final rocket screamed from the rubble in front of us and slammed into the glacis of the lead Russian vehicle, the missile's shaped charge steaming through its armor in a jet of molten metal. The vehicle shuddered and then exploded.

We cheered at the sight and Megan gave the signal, laughing. All of us opened fire. My tracers streaked out in bright flashes, and I guided them into pockets of the enemy while tears of panic streamed down my face. The Russians fell. At first we held them in place, their vehicles pulling behind ruined structures and their soldiers hugging whatever cover they could. But then we heard the deeper rumble of approaching armor, a basso throbbing that reached a crescendo when two Russian tanks crested the rubble in front of us.

Our second APC disappeared in a cloud of plasma, and with a scream, the Russians charged.

"Fall back," said Megan.

I leapt from the hole and began zigzagging rearward. Before they left, the men had dug a second perimeter farther to the rear, which covered the Tamdybulak road intersection where our last APC hid under thermal tarps and camouflage netting. I made it to the next hole and jumped in. After taking the time to reload, Megan checked her status board.

"Three hundred of us left."

I grunted and snapped a new hopper onto my shoulder, trying not to show my terror. "These are *tanks*, Megan."

The Russians pushed toward us again and I screamed. There were no shafts for us to drop into and I heard the armor of my sisters pop loudly when plasma bloomed around them. None of the Russian troops were visible. Only the two tanks advanced, crunching over the wreckage of our previous positions and firing plasma bursts. Suddenly, a pair of rockets jumped from the ruins of a house near the closest tank and hit the vehicle's turret. The impact caused a release of plasma, which melted it from the inside out, but which also consumed the area from where the shot had come. There was no cheering that time.

*"Fall back,"* I pleaded with Megan.

She slapped on a new hopper and ducked when a plasma shell screamed over our hole. "That is not permitted."

*"I don't care!"* The terror had begun to consume me. I couldn't think anymore, except that it was time to run— run *with* her while we still had the chance. There would be no discharge for me; I had decided it in that moment, knew that something in me had broken so that even if my

mind wanted the end, wanted the honor of a quick death, my body would have rebelled and done whatever it could to evade the inevitable, and that in such a struggle there would be no overcoming instinct; instinct would win. Life, for whatever reason, was now too important.

"No." Megan pointed her carbine at me, and when she spoke her voice shook. "I will kill you, Catherine. Do not spoil here, we need you."

Somehow, I turned to face the line again and raised my carbine slowly, the barrel clicking against blocks of concrete as my hands shook. The remaining tank headed straight for us. Both of us aimed for its sensors or any exposed system, and squeezed off several bursts before Megan gave our last APC the signal.

"APC three," she said.

The Russian tank erupted in flame when our APC scored a direct plasma hit, and we waited, expecting the rest of their forces to charge. Then we waited some more. A haze covered the battlefield, obscuring everything beyond a hundred meters out, and it felt as though the universe had transformed around us, bringing us to a place that wasn't Earth at all but some other planet where fog ruled everything. Only the burning tank made noise, its expanding ceramic plates popping off one at a time and water lines hissing as their fluid drained to the ground. But eventually even those noises stopped. Everything had gone quiet. None of my sisters spoke over the net and when I poked my head up there was no sign of movement from the positions around us. Still we waited, as the silence fed me with the thoughts of terror, until I was at the point of jumping from the hole, screaming with rage because there was nothing I could do to stop the whispering, a voice assuring me that something was wrong and that this was all a trick. When the sound of Russian APCs came faintly from the northeast, I cringed; half of me expected them to open fire at any moment, but they didn't and the noise faded until eventually it vanished.

Megan stood and I shouted. *"Get down!"*

"I'm getting a transmission—on command net," she said. "Our sisters, the Second Elite Division is pushing northward, Shymkent retaken with no resistance, forces pushing toward Karatobe, to our east. Enemy air-cover nil. Russian units routing en masse."

We flinched at the sonic boom of aircraft as they flew close overhead, toward the retreating Russians.

"That's what happened to our reinforcements," I said. "Our second division moved back to Shymkent to attack from there rather than come to *us* when we retreated two days ago. They surprised the Russian flank."

Megan nodded and motioned for me to be quiet. "It's much bigger than that, Catherine. Division estimates that Tenth Mountain will be back in Astana within a month, in Pavlodar to retake the mines a month after that. Third Marine, Eighty-Second Airborne and One Hundred and First Airborne will be pulled off the line for refit in Bandar as Spanish and French units move up."

"And us?" I asked.

"We hold here."

She popped her helmet with a hiss. I didn't know what to say, and popped mine, my tears now a reflection more of relief than fear. Wind blew the smell of battle away from us and I almost didn't notice it when the three-girl APC crew joined us to begin searching among the wreckage for survivors. It didn't take long. All our sisters were dead and Megan and I dove to the ground when a last Russian soldier detonated a plasma mine, its blast catching the other three girls to incinerate them in an instant.

I had never seen Megan lose control, but when the field had gone quiet again she dropped to her knees and screamed. I couldn't get her to stop. Her body shook in my hands as she kept yelling until finally her voice died with the effort, fading into sobs so that finally I understood what she was saying, over and over. *Nonsense.*

Before I could respond, new orders crawled across my display. *Surviving Elements of First Elite fall back to Uchkuduk for reassignment or discharge.*

I didn't know if Megan saw them. "They want us to fall back to Uchkuduk," I said. "It is our time. I will not go, Megan. I won't die."

"I don't want this anymore," she said, nodding. "Don't want the Lily."

At first the words were a shock, and the thought that I should kill her for cowardice popped into my mind. Instead I grinned. "Come with me."

"Wait," said Megan, just before she started laughing.

"What's so funny?"

She wiped a tear from her cheek. "They never told us—told us what this war was about. And we never asked."

"It was not our place," I said. "We do not need to know."

"No," said Megan, "we do not need to know. But we *deserve* to. We know how you earned your name, but don't you want to know why? It can be your last name: Catherine Murderer. Why did we murder, was it for the mines alone? What could have been the calculus behind that kind of decision?"

I began to feel uncomfortable, not knowing where she was going. This was a new Megan. She spoke of things forbidden and of not wanting to be a Lily, and I sensed that I needed to choose my words carefully, unsure of what they would do because I had begun to wonder, what effect would the spoil have on *her*? "I don't understand."

Megan grinned and reached out, sliding her fingers over my neck ring. She kissed me. "You have hair now— growing through the remains of your thermal block."

"We have not had time for a cut," I said.

"It's beautiful." She looked westward and sighed when a red message flashed over our display, Division demanding an immediate response to their order. "They'll find us. We can't run forever, it is not permitted and they hunt down anyone who refuses their discharge. I love you."

"I still don't understand. What are you saying?"

"I want to run with you. West. I want to live, because I have no more faith—no faith in war and no faith that we'll make it. But maybe *you* do. Now you can be the Lily. I never told you what Mother said to me that day in training, when she struck me with her cane.

Megan sighed. "She said that one of us, either you or me, were to be the group's Lily. But she also said that the feelings you and I had for each other were an abomination, an insult to the Lord, and that one of us had to pay; if *I* paid the price, she said I could be the Lily. And that is why I took the punishment, Catherine, why I promised to end things between us. It wasn't to protect you, it was so that I could have the honor, that I could be the one. A Lily. A mark. I took it from you, and I'm sorry."

And for the first time, I didn't mind the cold, didn't feel the dust as it blew against my face and found its way into my mouth so that no amount of water washed it from my tongue. I felt something. It took me some time to name it and I really didn't know the word's meaning, but it *seemed* to be the right one for that particular sensation. Not anger or resentment. It didn't matter that Megan had stolen the role from me, taken a thing that once I might have wanted more than anything else in the world, because what value did the Lily have now? There were no Lilies among the dishonored and living. This new feeling was better than being honored, better than all I had felt for the past two years, and certainly better than what had washed over me for the last two days, and when the name for it finally crystallized, I smiled at her and said the words.

"Hope. It's *hope* and faith. I became the Little Murderer to show everyone that I was better than the Lilies, better than you. And better than man. So we're even."

# THREE

# Hatred

*When the time comes, baptize yourself and
cleanse the soul. Do this, and you will know
only victory.*

MODERN COMBAT MANUAL
JOSHUA 7:13

One heard things in the tank. It started on training day,
incipience, the day they inserted cables to shock us into
a mental birth. The teachings raced through our minds in
real time—small unit tactics, weapons, history, and
devotions—on a six-hours-on, six-hours-off schedule, but
to us hours meant nothing since we hadn't yet been
decanted and knew nothing but sleep and training.

My world outside of simulations was a deep orange, a
thick gel which enveloped and kept me warm and which
prevented me from seeing the atelier. But I *heard*. Voices
surrounded the tank with song, a choir whose words were
just loud enough to hear, and which swelled with promise
until one day, after a rest period, I heard a different voice.

"Die," it said.

My eyes popped open, met by the orange glow. At first
I thought I had been dreaming.

"You are an abomination."

*Who are you*, I thought.

It sounded angry, and moved around me, never coming from the same direction. "I am an embodiment of hatred—of those you serve. You will be our tool, a thing, one pharmacon among many, to be exiled and spent so the rest of us can live. We will use you until you are withered and then nothing will be left except waste. You are the discarded."

*I have been chosen. To serve Him and there is no greater honor.*

"You have been chosen to learn the bare minimum."

With that I felt a jolt of electricity, a moment of burn that shot through my brain and into my spine, forcing my back to arch until the electron flow normalized. The tank melted away. A classroom, in which my sisters surrounded me, replaced it and in front of us stood a new instructor whose face alternated between that of an old man and that of a grinning skull; none of my sisters seemed to notice.

The man's voice was the same one I had just heard. "Combat suits will protect you in most environments. Embedded detectors will signal your heads-up display should the enemy try a micro-robotic, chemical, or biological attack. In the event of a micro attack, the ceramic and joint materials will provide you with at least ten minutes of protection, giving enough time for electronic countermeasures. In the event of chem-bio warfare, it doesn't really matter. Your biochemistry is such that your immune system will almost instantly deploy enzymes or killer cells to neutralize harmful agents. If they don't, the carapace is sealed anyway, and the filters will keep out anything bigger than molecules normally found in breathable air.

"That's the good news." The man turned from his holo-display and stared at me, a pair of horns sprouting from the thick bone of his head. I tried turning away but something prevented it, forcing my eyes to look in his direction. "The bad news is that our intelligence reports indicate the Russians may have developed something new—an agent we haven't yet been able to counter, and which they inject via special flechettes. It's a full cell, synthetic, and is too big to pose an inhalation or percutaneous threat. The pathogen is capable of changing at will, overcoming any new defense your body develops, and eventually causes your flesh to rot, your internal organs to hemorrhage. So one piece of advice: try not to get shot. If you do, at the first sign of infection, amputate at least a foot above the wound site because we think for now that the organism spreads slowly.

The man smiled, and I sensed that his next message came only to me. *"If you ever run from us,"* he said, *"we will find you."*

A distant boom of thunder yanked me from the memory, pulled me back to the Uzbek reality, and I gently traced a gauntleted finger across the back of Megan's neck. I had noticed it yesterday. She tried to hide what had happened, but during the Tamdybulak engagement, several flechettes had pierced Megan's right hand and now it gave more trouble than it should have. When a fresh drop of blood fell from a tiny hole in her gauntlet, I worried—that maybe she had been infected.

"What do you think?" she asked. "Should we go in?"

I shrugged, fingering the zoom control outward to get a better view. "I don't know."

Prefab ceramic slabs and domes formed the farmhouse's main structure, lending it an Arabic appearance. Its roof glinted white in the sun. Around the building, tufts of tan grass swayed, and I realized as we stood there that it had already gotten warm, that for a moment spring had arrived so the grass reached a height of almost one and a half meters, rising to our chests and forcing us to stand for an unobstructed view.

Megan kept her attention on the sky while I focused on the farmhouse again, a gray trail of smoke rising from its chimney.

"It's been days since we've seen any sign of our forces or theirs," she said.

"I know."

Megan cleared her throat. "You are worried. Why?"

"It's not right. Everything else in the area is destroyed, why not this?" The static from my headset clicked off and on as my computer scanned the frequencies. "And who's jamming us?"

"Shut it off and conserve power. Communications aren't necessary anyway, not for us."

We watched the house for another ten minutes and saw nothing.

"Let's go," said Megan.

It took five minutes to crawl to the farmhouse, and I looked around before Megan rose to approach the door. She cocked her head when it opened. Two Uzbek farmers—a man and his wife—hung from the ceiling by the neck, their tongues blue from suffocation, strings of mucous swaying in a breeze that we had let in through the doorway. Behind the farmers, the house had been ransacked. Tables and chairs lay smashed and it looked as if several waste pouches had been emptied over the wreckage, along with pieces of Russian armor and empty ration packs.

"Russian genetics?" Megan asked.

I popped my helmet to get a better view, and saw that boot prints had smeared a patch of dirt at the front door; I knelt to examine it. "We did this. Those are from our Special Forces."

"Then they are looking." Megan removed her gauntlet and I saw the red skin of her hand, streaked with white.

"You are infected?" I asked. "With the organism?"

Megan nodded, and threw her gauntlet to the floor.


The view from the windows showed nothing, except that desert and square plots of switchgrass surrounded us on all sides, and for the moment I felt exposed. *Obvious.* We shouldn't have been there—anyone searching for us would naturally focus on the farmhouse—but I saw in Megan's face that the infection had gotten worse and she needed rest indoors, out of the elements and without having to wear a helmet.

We didn't bother to cut down the corpses.

"I thought a lot about what you asked me once," said Megan, pointing at the swinging bodies. "About death."

"What about it?"

Megan said nothing and began taking off her armor. When she had finished, she slid her combat knife from its sheath, handed it to me, and rolled up the sleeve of her undersuit. "That this is no way to find out what waits on the other side. Take care of my infection."

The knife handle felt cold at first. Megan lay on the floor and shut her eyes, extending her arm toward me. The infection had begun to spread to her wrist, and I saw that portions of her fingertips had gone black, a whiff of rot making the threat more real.

There was no reason to hesitate. I chopped and she whimpered for only a moment before gaining control of the pain reflex, her blood clotting instantly.

Megan tied off the undersuit's sleeve below the elbow. "Thank you," she said. "I'm so tired."

I picked up my carbine and headed for a small ladder that led to a hatch near the ceiling. "Lay down, you need rest. I will watch from above."

I pushed through the hatch and secured it behind me before stepping onto the roof.

The sun had almost disappeared over the horizon, and its fading light cast a pink glow across the fields. As a wave of delirium washed over, it occurred to me that the countryside was beautiful, but the sight lasted only a few moments. Soon, a moonless night threw its dark shroud over us, and in the stillness I heard Megan snoring.

A distant formation of more than a hundred burning lights—white hot on my infrared sensors—streaked eastward, sending sonic booms to roll over the field. I almost woke Megan. But the aircraft passed well to our north before cutting sharply northeast, toward Kazakhstan, and disappeared quickly over the horizon. The moment of fear brought with it a memory of footprints and of the swinging bodies. I considered the explanations, calculating the probabilities before arriving at an answer. *"If you ever run from us, we will find you."*

We were being tracked. But for now there was nothing to do except wait, so that Megan could get some rest.

I hadn't had time to enjoy the fact that she had changed. All night, while I stood watch, I kept smiling, unable to believe that if we made it to safety we'd be able to stay together. Focusing on any one thing became difficult. Megan and I had taken the first step, running west, away from the war and away from our family so part of me felt happy—like there was nothing but hope and I couldn't keep from laughing—but another part couldn't fathom it. How would we survive? What would we do and where would we go? What else was life *but* war? For the time being my hatred and terror had subsided, had seeped deeper into my subconscious where I knew they both waited for the right moment to emerge—the correct conditions, their infinite patience providing them with a capsule that would never mold over or rust into impotence. And I wanted it to stay there, never wished for it to leave. They called me Little Murderer. It wasn't just a name, it was me, an immutable fact of my existence and the substance of who I was, and no matter where we wound up, in war or peace, that was my purpose, my talent, and the only available vocation; it was an identity that *needed* hatred, and besides, the thought of getting rid of it never occurred to me because it was a leviathan, a thing that could at times be pushed aside momentarily, but never eradicated. How did you sweep away an elephant? To destroy it would require something momentous, a realization like this—that a Lily had fled from discharge. Such a world had never before existed and my darkest moments on the line had always been staved off by a recollection of immutable facts that any one of us could have recited, even when nearest to death. Lilies never spoiled, Lilies never faltered, Lilies were the purest among the pure, the trusted among the honorable, and so I had always thought Megan sure to die whether anyone wanted her to or not.

Corruption had never been a contingency. Yet even as my thoughts orbited this, began to spiral around the puzzle of how this could have ever happened, I set it all aside; the realization that she was with me pulled me back into the present and I hugged my chest with happiness, having to fight the urge to abandon my post and hold her. And hatred? *I would hold onto it too,* I decided.

Then the sun made the sky lighten. My muscles ached, and a lack of sleep had rendered me so tired that I almost missed it when a pair of lights flickered into view on the southern horizon, but my goggles zoomed in, forcing me to watch for a few seconds before I got up and ran toward the hatch. It took less than a second to slide down the ladder.

*"They're coming!"*

Megan jumped up and began pulling on her armor with one hand. By the time we got her helmet on, the sonic boom shook the windows and both of us dove to the floor.

"There," said Megan, pointing to a trapdoor in the kitchen.

Everything moved in slow motion. There wasn't enough time for fear, and once we pried the door open, we had less than a moment to drop through the dark hole and land in a concrete basement.

A roar tripped the cutoff for my helmet pickups. Overhead the kitchen floor rumbled and a huge crack appeared without warning, dropping chunks of cement on top of us—until the trapdoor disappeared. I screamed. A jet of plasma shot down through the narrow hole and spread out over the floor, its tendrils snaking toward us as our temperature indicators shot upward, but the things dissipated before reaching us.

We huddled in a corner for what seemed an eternity. Drones screamed overhead in multiple passes and dropped a variety of ordnance on our position so that eventually, thermal gel ate through the basement roof to sprinkle around us like drops of hissing acid. By the time it got quiet, the sound of jets fading in the distance, we saw morning sunlight stream through the trapdoor opening and I shook with relief.

"We must move," said Megan.

"Wait." I pulled my helmet off and removed the vision hood, careful to make sure that its power cables stayed connected, and then activated my receiver.

"What are you doing?" asked Megan.

"Shh," I said.

Megan stood so that I could move the headset over her armor. At a point close to the back of her neck, the sound of static swelled in pulses, and I waved it over once more to make sure before trying it on myself.

"It's in our necks," I said, "some kind of tracking device that must be millimeters below the skin. I would guess it began transmitting on our eighteenth birthday."

Megan handed me her knife. I dug the thing from her neck, wiped the blade clean, and then waited for her to do the same to me. The transponders looked like black capsules, each of them marked with tiny red lettering, and we crushed them with a chunk of concrete before sweeping ourselves one more time and resuiting.

"They will still know the direction we're taking," said Megan.

"Vaguely, but we have no choice. If we move south to change direction we'll approach our forces in Iran, and if we head north wc'll run into the Russian lines."

Megan checked her carbine before shouldering it, and muttered as we crept upward, back into the farmhouse. " 'Without the conviction of a killer, it is impossible to please Him. For she who comes to God must believe that she is death embodied, and that He is the reward for those who massacre.' "

"Amen," I whispered.

There was nothing left. The ceramic structure had melted and shattered to its foundations, and all around us lay a bumpy field of dark glass, which reflected the sunlight with such intensity that our goggles frosted into near obscurity. We sprinted to the edge of the destruction, where we dove into the switchgrass, crawling westward with the sun at our backs.

Beyond the farm we moved into an abandoned mining area that transformed the Uzbek flatlands into an unfamiliar terrain, pockmarked by tiered pits that stretched for miles to end in aqua-colored lakes. Our chemical sensors tripped on multiple occasions. It occurred to me then that these weren't simply water bodies, man-made or natural, but that they were the refuse of a generation's worth of digging for metals, of extraction, and that although to me the greens and blues mixed with brown seemed beautiful and intense, they were equally lethal, the liquids comprised of water, weak acids, and cyanide. Nobody would ever live here again—if they ever did in the first place.

And fear had made its return. What before had been the terror of dying mutated to form a knot in my stomach, a paranoia insisting that Special Forces waited behind every rock or lay waiting among the huge piles of dirt. Within an hour it exhausted me. Both feet had gone numb and no matter how hard I tried, efforts to cut off my nerves, which had been so easy the day before, now didn't work at all so that above the numb area both sets of calf muscles cramped in nearly paralyzing spasms. We collapsed every hour, unable to move until we had rested for a few moments. I couldn't imagine Megan's suffering as she struggled forward using only one arm, her breathing shallow and rapid with the effort to drag herself along while ignoring the loss of a limb. Despite the suit's climate control, sweat coursed down my back and soaked into the undersuit. By the time we broke for lunch we had made it only a few kilometers; it seemed as though we hadn't moved at all.

"Something is wrong with me," I said, and described the numbing, the pain.

Megan nodded. "I have it too, in my legs and in my arm. It is the spoiling."

"The spoiling is a mental thing, doesn't cause physical pain."

"I don't know that anymore. Take off your suit."

"In the open? Now? I'll be visible." But I did it anyway, sensing that she was right. Once I was free of the carapace and disconnected, Megan pulled off the thick socks of my undersuit to expose both feet. I gasped; the tips of my toes had gone black. Dead.

"It is the spoiling. You weren't wounded during the last two days?" When I shook my head she continued. "Then they lied to us. The rotting isn't from Russian organisms; it is within us."

"They wouldn't lie," I insisted. "Not our mothers."

"Maybe. And yet there are your feet, dying, like mine."

She replaced my socks and once I finished squeezing

into my armor we sat, pushing food from our pouches into our mouths but not tasting anything, and I barely noticed when a second flight of drones screamed to deliver new ordnance on what used to be the farmhouse. There could be no plan now. Our creators had a plan, and it took care of everything, made me wonder why they bothered to chase us at all when our very bodies formed the pieces of a bomb, slow fused, decaying at an unknown rate in both mind and tissue so that soon—maybe in weeks—we would be gone. By comparison, a quick discharge seemed... humane. *Humane.* The word stuck in my mind and slowly fear turned back into hatred, worse than it had ever been before and I grabbed hold of it to stroke the sensation, encouraged it to grow into visions of what I would do to the next nonbred I found, any nonbred, and before I realized it, my arms and legs had begun carrying me westward again, crawling with the hope of finding someone to kill. I would take as many with me as I could now.

I elbowed Megan as I left, but she didn't move at first. A few seconds later she screamed and I froze, waiting for a drone or patrol to zero in. When nothing happened, I turned to face her.

"What's wrong?"

"They come frequently now," she said.

"You've had hallucinations?" When she nodded I sighed and pulled her by the neck ring, helping her forward. "Don't be afraid. They can't hurt you and soon you will see everything as I do."

Megan laughed. "That doesn't comfort me; I am not accustomed to this, Catherine."

"Accustomed to what?" I asked. "The spoiling, or to *me* taking care of *you*?"

"*You* telling me what to do. With confidence. You even *sound* like a Lily."

"It's not confidence. It's hatred. There are ways to punish them, and we may as well find revenge to our west. I can feel my mind wander and want to move from here, put more distance between us and the farm before my dreams come, and before I'm the onc screaming."

I had fallen asleep without knowing it, allowing the dream to invade.

Megan and I sprinted through the forest, our half-armor clicking as we went. With one hand motion, she gave me an order. I dropped to the ground and covered myself with leaves, dirt, anything I could find including the corpse of a fox—half eaten. Nothing moved. I peered out from between two rocks and fingered the trigger, bringing up my sighting reticle as I waited. Megan had long since disappeared but her voice crackled in my ear.

"I'm chasing him to you; we'll be there in thirty seconds."

You couldn't see them yet, or hear them, but Megan knew the woods and remembered exactly where she left me. The man we chased wouldn't have realized that she was forcing him into a trap.

"One hundred meters," she said.

I heard them now, some distance away in the underbrush, and nearly froze when I saw that the man carried a wcapon. They had given him a carbine—not fully automatic, but capable of firing single shots. He paused and dropped to one knee, squeezing off several flechettes, and then rolled down a short slopc bcfore rising to his feet.

"He's been trained," I whispered to Megan. "This one knows." I had already made up my mind when I saw him, knew that the carbine would be unsporting, unfair.

I removed my finger from the trigger.

"Now!" said Megan.

*Not yet*, I thought, *let him come...*

Megan sounded panicked. "We will *lose him*!"

The man was close, and I saw that his head had been shaven poorly, someone cutting it in the process so that dark scabs covered parts of his scalp. I jumped to my feet. His eyes went wide and when my four fingertips slammed straight into his windpipe, so hard that I felt and heard the crunch of his throat simultaneously, the man gurgled a word, maybe "please". He dropped his carbine, fell to his knees, and grasped his neck with both hands.

"Go with God," I said to him, my mouth next to his ear. "You are worthy, on the path, and so shall be forgiven. I am that path."

I woke then, before reliving the next few moments—when Megan and I had beheaded him.

Uzbekistan reminded me of those days, of hunting convicts in the forest so that we could learn the feeling of a kill. But this time, *we* were the hunted. Megan had let me sleep in a stand of tall grass and after I finished wiping the dirt from my faceplate she pointed at a pair of dust clouds, small and distant.

"Scout cars," I said. "One, maybe two of them."

Megan nodded and fingered her forearm zoom control. "I see one now, no sign of a recon drone, but they might be dispersing micros. The winds are coming this way."

"Special Forces?" I asked.

"Probably," said Megan. "They're the only ones who would risk searching for us in small numbers. It's getting dark, we need to keep moving."

"We will have to kill them, Megan. We can't just run."

She stopped. Her back was to me but even in the armor I could sense that Megan's shoulders had slumped. "I know. And it is wrong for me to think that way. I am not on the path anymore, Catherine, I can't see it. To kill men, those who created us..."

"Wrong has nothing to do with it. They will kill us from afar; they have already killed us with spoil, and are cowards. *They* should serve *us*." The words startled me, ones I had never uttered before, and the idea, now that it was voiced, sounded to me exactly like heresy should: like thunder. I waited for Megan to strike me but she didn't.

"Maybe they do deserve that." She moved down the dune on which we now stood, and headed back toward our hide in the grass. "But it *feels* wrong. Running is one thing but these taught us about our God, showed us the way. To kill *them* is saying to heaven that it does not exist; will you tell God that He means nothing?"

I followed her, nearly slipping in the loose sand. "I think now that this *is* God's will."

And I believed it. This was not a joyful time, not like the feeling I got from slaughtering Russians, but it didn't feel as if it were wrong because it did nothing to abate my hatred. The moment excited and terrified me at the same time. To be pitted against Special Forces, real men who had trained even longer than we had, who were genuine warriors...this was a blessing; it *had* to be. God tested all of us, deciding who was worthy of the kingdom, and for the first time ever *we* were choosing our own path with no orders crawling across the heads-up, no semi-aware computer calculating the best way to use us, where to throw our sisters against some hole in our line or the Russian's'. For a second my fears, all of them, evaporated. *God had given me my first choice.*

I slapped Megan on the back and helped her lie down. "We will kill them and you will feel whole again. The border can't be far now."

Our hole was shallow, just barely deep enough so that when we lay down our bodies would be even with the surrounding desert. It was our only chance. After lying flush with the lip, Megan unrolled a thin sheet of copper mesh, so fine that she had to be careful or it would rip, and spread it across us.

Somewhere from behind came the roar of engines. Over them echoed a loud pop and I felt Megan tense when a few seconds later we heard something that sounded like sand sprinkling on the copper blanket. I couldn't see them, but they were there. You imagined the microbots, tiny spheres too small to power their own motion, as they floated on the wind and began collecting and transmitting data the moment they landed—but only as long as their power lasted, only for a few minutes. The blanket would shield our electronic emissions and block their motion trackers, keep us invisible.

A short time later, we heard the engines fade. I lifted the sheet, rolled it up carefully, and helped Megan sling her carbine so that she could fire it with one hand. When she was ready I grinned. We sprinted, almost silent except for the sound of my breathing while we struggled up the side of a dune and then slid down the other. Their tracks

were clear, in shades of light-amplified green. Once we no
longer heard the engines, we slowed to a march.

"They will stop soon," Megan said, "to sleep."

I checked my computer. "And now the wind is at our
backs."

" 'Remember the former things of old,' " said Megan,
" 'for I am God's messenger, and we are many.' "

I smiled at the words, felt the warmth of doing what
we had been born to do. " 'And there are many like me,
declaring the end from the beginning, and from ancient
times the things that are not yet done, saying, His counsel
shall stand.' "

" 'And we will do what we please, for we know all
before it happens,' " Megan finished. " 'God gave us the
foresight, and from His judgment no man can hide. Death
will teach some everything, but it will be too late; these
lessons do no good in hell.' "

She adjusted her carbine and flicked off the safety.

The men had camped in front of us, in a flat area of
desert where they had parked three vehicles and arranged
a ring of sentry bots. A dead soldier lay beside us, my
combat knife still embedded in his throat. We knew
they'd be there. Megan and I never talked about how we
knew these things but we did, always, as if it were a sixth
sense or maybe more simple like knowing there would be
air when you took a breath. While Megan had disabled
the closest sentry bots, I had killed their watchman.

And I felt good again.

Megan let me lead because with only one hand she
couldn't give commands, but I would have led anyway; now

that I was half-dead, I felt alive at last, a Lily who moved under God's hand, which guided everything as if the world had revealed itself to be an intricate clockwork—everything in place, everything with a purpose, but, ironically, a world in which now I had a will. One could walk into the camp loudly, spraying flechettes as one screamed, or crawl up silently and break each neck, one at a time, grinning more widely with each snap. I crouched and moved in slowly. Three of them rested next to the scout car closest to me and I motioned for Megan to take them, holding up two fingers so she would give me time to reach the others.

There were four near the second scout car. One of them stirred, rolling over with a cough, and it occurred to me that they had been sloppy—that they had bunched up.

Two minutes came. The first one died instantly, with only a slight twitch when I slammed the knife through his armored neck joint. The others heard it. Within a second, I had sprayed them with my carbine, the sound of flechettes snapping loudly across the dunes, a continuous zipperlike noise that ceased only when everything became still again.

"Come here," Megan said.

I approached and saw one of them propped against the scout car, his helmet off, the man struggling to breathe. "Please," he said.

I pushed the barrel of my carbine against his forehead. "Deactivate the remaining sentry bots, so we can leave your perimeter."

The man's hand shook and blood trickled from his mouth as he punched at his forearm controls.

"Who are you looking for?" Megan asked.

He stared. "For *you*. Our guys didn't know if you were

killed in the airstrike. We lost your transponder signal and they sent us to do a sweep—to make sure."

I felt like smashing his face, like slamming my carbine into it. "Why can't you just let us go?"

"There have been so many lost. We don't know where they are, and Command ordered us to hunt you all the way to the Turkmeni border."

Megan dropped to her knees and grabbed his neck ring. "There are others of us?"

He nodded. "Yes. I don't know how many."

"What about Turkmenistan?" I asked. "Can you hunt us there?"

"Not in all areas," he said, "because we don't occupy most of western Turkmenistan. Some of us operate out there anyway, but at risk of getting shot by the Turkmen Army. Please, let me go."

I slit his throat without thinking and wiped my knife clean while he slumped to the sand. "There are *others*."

Megan popped her helmet and grinned. "Turkmenistan."

We took a few minutes to gather ration packs, water, and fuel cells before moving out again. There would be no rest—not that night. In the morning, someone would come looking for them and we needed to put as much distance between the men and us as possible. At one point I checked the computer map and laughed out loud.

"What?" asked Megan.

"We will be at Druzhba in a few days. Then across into Turkmenistan. Free, in a way."

"Yes," she asked, "but then what?"

It was a good question, one that we both had been asking ourselves since setting out, and neither of us had an answer. Not yet.

\* \* \*

We traveled by night. The days had gotten warm—warm enough that Megan and I grew concerned about our suits' ability to maintain temperature without straining climate control—so we slept during the day, buried under sand.

At night, waking dreams and hallucinations always came. We tied a long piece of webbing to connect us, so that if we both fell into a dream state we at least wouldn't get separated. The wind howled in my helmet pickups and both legs felt like lead as we moved slowly up the side of one dune, sliding down the other, over and over, until collapsing at first light. There were no landmarks, just sand. You couldn't have known where to go and how to navigate without computers and suit guidance software, the thin blue line of the Amu Darya, the border, edging closer to us with the arrival of each day.

We were still a day or so from the river when Megan heard it, just before sunrise.

"Down," she said.

I flattened into the sand as the noise of jet engines grew. Three aircraft, painted a flat gray almost impossible to see in the dim light, flew slowly overhead and turned in wide, lazy curves as the vehicles scanned the ground. Eventually the planes passed overhead, their roar fading to a groan as they increased their distance.

"They know we're heading for Turkmenistan," I said. "Those were recon drones."

Megan nodded and rose to her knees so she could dig a shallow hole. I joined her. When we were done we lay down, and began scooping the sand, pushing it onto us so that it covered everything except one air intake port.

"Rest," said Megan. "I'll get up in a little while and stand watch."

"Did they see us?" I asked. But she was already asleep, and my eyes fluttered shut.

When Megan finally woke me the sun had gone down, and I sat up to grab my carbine.

She waved me silent. All I could hear was the sound of an owl, screeching as it looked for prey under the moon—a thin sliver that had just risen above the horizon. She pointed south, toward an open salt pan and held up four fingers. I crawled slowly to the edge of a tuft of switch-grass and peered out.

My night vision cast its green pall over the scenery, making it hard to distinguish between shapes, and at first I didn't see them. Then they moved. Four shapes rose from the ground to form the vague outlines of men in combat armor, their chameleon skin activated, all of them crouch-walking slowly toward us.

Megan motioned for me to raise my carbine. We turned our Maxwells over and dialed down the power, to ensure that the rounds would fly at less than supersonic velocities. *Silent.* When she signaled, I extended my barrel from the dry grass and touched the trigger lightly, steadying my aim. The trigger clicked shut. With a noise that resembled a spray bottle, flechettes sprang from my carbine and punched through the first one's face-plate so that he collapsed to the ground, a puff of blood settling gently on the sand as I moved my reticle to the next one and steadied my aim.

It was over in three seconds, but we waited for a few minutes to make sure they were dead.

"Get up," said Megan, "it's not good to stay here anymore."

We crouched, walking slowly southward across the salt flat.

The wind came and went, howling across the desert in a gale for one minute, falling the next to embed us in a layer of silence. Megan dropped to the ground at the sign of anything unusual and twice we had to wait for aircraft to wander across the sky and out of sight while my muscles screamed at me to stay in place, not to move. *Rest.* The numbness had moved upward now, separating the top of my foot from the shin in a sharp line of burning agony that I tried to ignore but couldn't. In three hours, we advanced only about five kilometers, and after another flight of aircraft I was about to suggest we stop when my silent alarm activated, filling my helmet with red light.

"The drones dropped *Micros.*" I swatted at my forearm computer, popping the cover off with a single motion, and began punching the keys.

"Hurry," said Megan, "I can't use my computer with only one arm."

As soon as I hit the final key, a blue web of crackling static electricity ran over the outside of my armor, frying any bots that had adhered to its shell. I grabbed Megan's arm. But by the time I finished activating her countermeasures, we both saw the heads-up display.

"It's too late," I said. The computer flashed a yellow indicator. "They transmitted."

Megan dropped her carbine and snapped off the hopper, tossing it to the ground before we switched on our skins. "*Run.*"

The sand gave, our feet slipping with each step as we tried to put as much distance between us and our previous position as possible. Once we had moved what seemed like a hundred meters, we dove into a depression between two low dunes and stayed still. The growing rumble of jets came from the southwest.

An attack drone passed overhead, scanning the ground for heat and movement. A second came in much lower and I braced myself. The plane sprinkled the dunes around us with flechette and thermal gel cluster bombs, their detonations making the ground tremble, and at one point the aircraft came so close that I heard the wind whistle over its skin. We lay on the edge of the beaten zone. The overpressure of multiple explosions flattened the mounds of sand in front of me and droplets of thermal gel hissed all around, sending up tiny streamers of smoke while we braced for the third plane. It came in low, but further west of our position, all its ordinance wasted on an empty section of desert. Finally, the first aircraft looped back. It screamed straight over us, so that we heard explosive bolts pop when the plane dropped its munitions.

Megan shouted at first, but then laughed when she saw what had happened. Four cluster bombs detonated a hundred meters away, well behind us, and I laughed too when I realized just how badly the plane had overshot. With their wing loads expended, the craft turned and sped away.

"They'll send another patrol," Megan said. "We have to move, *now*."

So eventually I stood, wincing with the agony of each step as we ran westward, while my suit discarded its waste down the side of my leg.

Time had almost stopped. As I stared at the map, showing the Amu Darya so close that my dot had merged with it, our day disappeared behind clouds and the temperature dropped to below freezing. A thick snowfall prevented us from seeing anything except the insides of our helmets. Megan popped hers first and then I slowly removed mine. Although we had fought in snow, neither she nor I had actually experienced a storm like this, where we had the time to think about the stuff and contemplate it for what it was—instead of for tactical considerations. For the moment, we were safe. Sensors wouldn't penetrate the low clouds, so there was no worry about being spotted from above or of having to stay still. The bitter cold seeped into my suit from the neck, snaking its way down to my waist, where it felt clean and dry against the sweat-soaked undersuit. I let flakes melt on my tongue and then found Megan by touch before noticing that she had collected some snow in her good hand, placing it inches from her eyes where she could examine individual flakes.

"It's beautiful," I said.

She shook her hand clean. "It's just snow."

"How can you say that? It's so clean. The flakes look like feathers, white from a distance and clear up close. You saw it yourself. Perfect."

"And why should *that* be beautiful?" I heard her anger clearly now, and wondered if her mind had spoiled in a different direction than mine; I had never seen her so enraged.

*"Answer me!"* she screamed.

"I don't know. It just is."

"That isn't a good enough answer. Not nearly. Look at us: *we're* perfect. Perfectly designed to fight, to kill, to live in a combat environment and take orders. Perfect slaves. But snow has an advantage over us, something that makes it better, closer to God. Do you know what that is?"

"No."

Megan slammed the back of her hand into my face. The impact jarred my teeth and I felt the sting when my lip split, sending the taste of blood and the incredible sensation of pain throughout my mouth. Now it was certain; all of my ability to control nerve impulses had vanished, and tears welled in my eyes before I could stop them.

"What is wrong with you?" I asked.

"*Snow* was made by God. That's what's wrong with me. And you. *We* were made by men, and those men were probably cowards, soft like the ones in white coats, scientists and intellectuals, the same types we've despised ever since I've known you. Since we first stepped onto the field. What does that mean, Catherine?"

"Tell me."

"It means that we are impure. Flawed. One step removed from God, and abominations that He probably despises—despite what our mothers said."

Her words made me tremble. The cold that a few minutes ago had transformed me into something new now felt hostile, and I snapped my helmet back on, afraid, as if somehow anything created directly from God may have been intended to destroy me, that the cold could carry with it some form of disease or weapon, there to specifically target not just Germline units, but me. Why hadn't it occurred to me before? The sense that I was on the path, and its assurance that everything I did was according to some greater plan, evaporated, replaced by a new kind of terror: that I would only feel safe underground, surrounded by thousands of sentry bots and encased in my carapace, forever, because not only men hunted us now; God might be helping them, helping them to eradicate alien things in a for-human world.

"That would change everything," I said.

"It changes nothing. It just shows the same things in a different light."

"How, Megan?"

She snapped her helmet in place, so that now her voice came through the speakers, changing her into what I felt like: a machine.

"How what?"

"How did you come to this knowledge? How did you figure it out?"

"I have a computer."

"So do I," I pointed out. "But this…"

"Not in my suit, Little Murderer. In my head. On the ship when the men first delivered us to Iran, they gathered all the Lilies while you trained, and cut into our skulls, replacing the backs of them with a computer, wired into our very brains. We were warned never to mention them or it would be death for us and whomever we told. It talks to me even now, tells me we will die soon, suggests that we would do better to give up. And I can't shut it off."

There were no words, nothing in my vocabulary to make such a horror seem positive, and so I said nothing. Instead I held her hand.

"I didn't figure it out, Catherine. The computer told me this just now, knew I was enjoying the snow and let me know how much we don't belong here. Or anywhere. You might get away, find someplace quiet, but not me. How do you escape your own brain?"

"Could it be sending signals? To track us?"

Megan shook her head, her helmet barely swiveling. "I don't think so or they wouldn't have needed the one you found in my neck. Maybe there wasn't enough space to add a tracking function, or maybe they didn't think it was necessary."

"If they could install such a device," I said, "someone could take it out. You never know what we'll find in the world, Megan."

But before she responded, we heard shouts. Men. Somewhere to our east a group of them laughed and the whine of a scout car rose and fell as it crawled among snow-covered dunes, so that we couldn't tell if they moved closer to us or not. We froze at the sound of a loud pop, and waited for the patter of microbots as they fell on us with the snow. But none came. I imagined the tiny spheres with their microcarbon propellers floating among the flakes and wondered if they could be aware, if they knew that they didn't belong or if maybe they thought they *were* snow, one flake among millions and oblivious to the fact that their makeup fundamentally differed from those all around them. Megan pulled me from my thoughts and pointed. Less than a foot away, a dark shadow formed the shape of man; he walked past silently, not noticing the two girls half buried at his feet, and it wasn't until ten minutes after he passed that we dared move again.

"The snow protected us from them, Megan."

"So?"

I pulled my knees to my chest and glanced at the time, wondering if night would ever come. "So it matters. I can't believe that God is against us simply because a thing in your head told you so. That thing, the computer, is of man. The snow *is* beautiful."

"It's just snow. And soon we'll find out whose side he's on. It can't snow forever."

As the night wore on, someone observing us would have seen the signs. Megan and I stumbled, and the careful crouch-walking had long since been replaced by tired, upright shambling through a mixture of snow and sand, and I slapped the Maxwell over my left shoulder, holding the barrel and letting the stock swing freely to help with balance. We stopped once to eat and fell asleep, ration packs dangling from our feeding tubes, but Megan prevented catastrophe when she awoke from a nightmare. An observer would have identified us immediately: *the walking dead.*

At about one a.m., I heard something and stopped. Megan looked at me.

"I hear it too," she said.

We ran up the side of a dune, the sand shifting underfoot to taunt us, two steps forward, one step back. Eventually we made it to the top and peered down.

"Druzhba," I said. Megan wrapped her good arm around me, unable or unwilling to talk.

In front of us, the Amu Darya rolled over hidden rocks, its water thick with runoff from the spring thaw, despite the fact that it had turned cold again. The water sounded angry. Great waves surged over submerged obstacles and the whole thing roared as if shouting obscenities at the world, for having forced it to navigate such a horrible place, as the border between two slices of hell. On the far banks lay the large town of Druzhba; its lights gleamed like white stars on the green backdrop of our night vision, and I wondered how we would cross, trying not to get excited about the prospect of reaching the other side. Just past Druzhba was the Turkmeni border.

"I will help you across," I said, gesturing to Megan's severed arm, but she started down the dune face before I could stop her.

"Let's *go.*"

The sand slid underneath as I jogged to catch up, unable to stop smiling. Megan paused at the river's edge and popped her helmet, throwing it to the side so that it landed in a puddle with a splash.

"I will never wear armor again," she said.

*Hair.* She had hair too. It was short, only a few centimeters, but I hadn't noticed it before, and for some reason the sight shocked me.

"What?" she asked.

I pulled my helmet off and grabbed a tuft of my own. "Your hair must be more beautiful than mine."

"This is beautiful," said Megan, running her hand across my head. "More than the snow. Yours is longer than it was in Tamdybulak; does mine look like yours?"

"How should I know?" I asked. "I have no mirror."

"You're so . . ." Megan started.

"What?"

She kissed me deeply, pawing at the latches on my carapace. "Different."

"They are out here somewhere and there's no time."

"I don't *care,* Catherine."

We were out of our armor in minutes, too tired and excited at the same time to think about the danger while we rolled in the wet sand near the river, the cold slamming into us with a strong wind, and light snow still falling all around. *She* kept me warm. When we had finished, Megan lay her head on my chest and looked up.

"We have no plan."

"Stop it," I said.

"What?"

"You. Stop it. You're not the Lily anymore, Megan. We don't need a plan all the time. Once we swim over to the far bank and cross into Turkmenistan, they won't be able to hunt us and we'll get a chance to think things through. We can plan as we go."

"I know, it's just that—"

Red tracer flechettes streaked by, snapping past us to hit the dunes with tiny puffs of sand and cutting her off midsentence. Megan rolled to the side. I went in the other direction and grabbed my carbine, searching for a target before I realized I couldn't see anything without my vision hood and that the carbine was still attached to my suit by its flexi. Someone fired another round of tracers and I aimed at the source, squeezing off a few bursts before I heard her.

"Catherine, *please*."

I knew from her voice, and my chest felt like it was about to explode as I tried to find her in the darkness. I sensed everything before seeing a line of flechette wounds running almost the entire length of her leg, the blood pumping out from an artery wound—or several of them.

"It's not important after all." Another burst snapped over our heads, one of them nicking my shoulder, and Megan continued. "Forget what I said about the snow."

"Fine," I said.

She was heavy, and I was tired. With my legs buckling at first, it took a moment to stand, and I must have looked like a monster, naked, carrying an impossible load toward the river. What would I do once we were in it? We had almost reached the nearest bank when a red line of tracers stitched its way toward me through the sand, slamming through my legs at the same moment we splashed into the water. At first I swam, tugging Megan by her arm. She screamed. It wasn't long before the current took its toll and my legs stopped working the way they should have, sending me down into the muddy waves, which pulled her from me at the same time my strength vanished.

The men had a spotlight. After submerging I opened my eyes and saw the water above illuminated in an orange glow: *It looked just like the atelier tank, warm and inviting.* But there was nothing warm after Megan went under and the feeling of her hand had been branded into my palm. Before I blacked out, the cold water sucked the air from my lungs, forcing me to inhale it in a twisted reflex that first prevented me from going after her, then prevented me from breathing.

It was the last time I ever saw Megan.

# FOUR

# Traitors

*For it will come to pass that some of you may find yourself cut off from Him, and at that moment you will be lost forever, to wander alone. Death delivers.*

MODERN COMBAT MANUAL
JOSHUA 22:11

The first things I noticed were whistles. One was low, a single tone that I had heard before but which didn't register as a train-whistle until I noticed the clanking of wheels beneath me, the shaking of a railcar. But there were other whistles. High-pitched ones. And although cold drafts pushed up through the carriage floorboards, what I eventually determined was music brushed the chill aside with a tune that disturbed and comforted simultaneously; the song was sad. Someone whispered into my ear afterward and his plucking a fiddle as he spoke made me smile.

"*Cherniy Voron, dyedushka*, a little music for death, the only warm place in winter. We've *all* seen the raven, but maybe none so closely as you, and it's supposed to be spring and yet everyone freezes in this crappy railcar. A hundred years ago and Russia would have been thawed, but now? Now winter lasts six months, sometimes eight, and the nonbred all wish for those days when *warming* was a threat. Let me tell you something else..." But before he finished, pain rushed upward from my legs, forcing me back into unconsciousness.

Who knew how much time passed before I finally woke? When I did the sight of them didn't shock me; to the contrary, it made me feel secure. These were Russian genetics. The wounded and maimed and the dying, maybe at the end of their service term. All of them were boys about the same age as me, and when my eyes opened to see how we had been arranged, in bunks stacked to the ceiling with about half a meter of space that left barely enough room to breathe, and with hot vents doing their best to keep the chill off, it felt safe in an inevitable sort of way. If they killed me, so what? The Amu Darya had already taken Megan so that whatever existence remained was more than I should have been allowed—more than I wanted since it would be spent alone—and my desire to run had vanished. Death would be a way to join her.

The music had gone, but when they saw me awake they all shouted something—those that were conscious— and then laughed, one of them leaning down from the bunk above to offer a cigarette, an act of kindness that I never would have expected.

"I don't smoke," I said. But he insisted, and so I took it and inhaled, coughing to the point where the pain in my legs revived, reminding me of what had happened. I started crying. Of course they were happy; these ones still had their families.

Someone said something but then another cut him off.

"She speaks English. Only English, so be fucking polite for once."

"Play her another song."

"*Brodyaga*?"

A number of the boys groaned, and the one above me spoke up. "Not that one again. Play us something really strange. That Jew song, that one you played a long time ago."

The boys hushed then, and I heard several of them get off their bunks to sit on the floor next to me, and a few seconds later another song filled the railcar. I had to look. They grinned as they played, five boys, as identical to each other as Megan and I had been, and so I asked because they had gone to the trouble to play.

"What song is that?"

"The Jew song," the one above me said.

I shook my head. "No, I mean what is its name?"

"That's what I said, the Jew song. We don't know its name, so we call it that, and none of us even know what a Jew is. It's as good a name as any other, who cares about a name? Do you have a name?"

"Catherine."

"Katarina?" he asked. The song stopped then, and at first I thought I'd said something wrong when a discussion broke out in Russian, but then the boys with instruments arranged themselves again, preparing. "Not Catherine. Not on this trip. While you're with us, your name is Katyusha."

Everyone screamed "*Katyusha!*" and the boys played a new song, faster than the last.

The boy above me leaned over and smiled. Now I saw that his left hand was severed at the wrist, the wound still open and raw but without losing blood, and many of his teeth had broken to make his grin a jagged, but friendly one.

"Katyusha is an old song. Very old. The first one we

learn in training; it's about a girl who sends her lover off to war and promises to wait for his return."

"Why are you being…" I searched for the right word but couldn't find it. "Why am I alive?"

"Why haven't we killed you?"

I nodded.

"Orders. We found you on the river bank, in Dargan Ata where we had been sent to scout American movements in Uzbekistan. Across the river. The American Specials came and didn't know we were there. They were looking for you, and so we let them have it, but they called in an airstrike, which is when we all got wounded. The doctor took care of you while you were out, and your wounds aren't bad, a few flechette hits, but we know what happens to you after two years in war. He says you're dying anyway so why *should* we go to all the trouble of killing you when nature will handle it soon herself? Besides, we've been told to take as many of our sisters alive, whenever we can. Orders."

If it were possible, his grin got even wider, so wide that it made me forget my legs.

I said, "We assumed all of you hated us."

"Why?"

"Because we're enemies."

"That's the difference between you and us, the American synthetics and Russian ones: we don't have enemies, we only have missions. It's just a job, Katyusha. Some of us might hate you, but most of us don't care about those we kill and when you think of it we both have the same mission, the same parents. Hatred, amidst all that, is just too tiring."

My limbs went slack and the cigarette fell to the floor

in a shower of sparks as another wave of exhaustion hit, forcing the room to go dark. The last thing I heard was the boy.

"Hatred is an obscurant."


My dreams traced a path of hatred.

Time and repetition should have illuminated its genesis sooner, but I suspected that constant fatigue had kept me blind, or maybe there was something about being wounded that clarified it, brought the reasons for my hatred into focus. Whatever the reason, they came. Faces, Marines with whom my unit had always been attached, and their thousands of expressions played out in my subconscious, laughing, and I couldn't blame them for it, wondering at my own stupidity and that of my sisters—especially of Megan and the Lilies. For having served without question.

There was the Marine leaning out of the APC and waving good-bye—*see ya, bitches*—just before the image faded, transformed into another where a supply depot near the town of Yangiyul' stretched out as far as we could see, the detritus of war mingled with the lifeblood of its participants. Piles of crates and shipping containers formed massive square structures. In places these had been hit by enemy air attacks, and cranes moved in to salvage the containers that were intact, discard those beyond salvage, which sometimes, when lifted, spewed their contents—usually helmets, rations, or spare parts—onto the ground like a bursting piñata. On the northern side of the depot, three massive portals lay open. Dark. The entrances led to tunnels so wide that vehicles could pass in either direction for front-line supply runs, but one of them had been targeted, its mouth filled with concrete rubble that I saw, when I zoomed in, also held mangled bodies of those unfortunate enough to have been caught in the blast.

*Yangiyul' was a wreck*, I realized.

Marines scrambled over rubble and slid down into plasma craters while we climbed from the flat cars, and from the open platform we could see more of what remained of the Tashkent-Shymkent sector's main depot. Point defense towers lay flat on the ground where an aborted Russian advance had destroyed them, and new towers stretched upward. When Russian drones approached there wasn't an alarm. Instead, almost as soon as we had assembled, the Yangiyul' plasma defenses thumped like a chorus of tympanis and Marines sprinted to any cover they could—rubble, bomb shelters, or the bottoms of craters. We just stood there. Then we shrugged when the drones and missiles never came, having been driven off by defensive fire.

After the all clear, a group of men closest to us complained of the heat but they returned to their work, lifting sections of magnetic containment coils to place them on cargo crawlers—huge flatbed tracked vehicles that artillery units used to transport reactor equipment, which would provide power and deuterium for our plasma cannons. The coil-pipes were flexible ceramic-and-alloy tubes roughly one meter across, about a metric ton per section, and would line narrow rock channels that had been drilled from the rear into our main underground positions. That way, if the enemy took a section of our line, artillery units could pipe super hot gas into our abandoned tunnel; many

Russians had been cooked this way. The coils themselves would be electrified, creating a charge that prevented the gas from making contact with the pipe-walls, ensuring that the plasma was still hot when it arrived.

The men moving the coil-pipes didn't actually *do* any lifting, but merely had to guide them to make sure they didn't rotate out of alignment as the crawler's crane carefully lowered them to its deck. Our orders had not yet arrived, so Megan and the rest of us squatted on the platform to watch the work. We had been there almost an hour when it happened.

"McTear!" an officer shouted, "Get out from under that coil-pipe."

The man shuffled out and waved. "Sorry."

"Listen up." The officer stood at the bottom of a crater and observed as they loaded the last section onto a carrier at the crater's lip, above him. "When we're done with this one, y'all can have a half-hour break. Chow's inside entrance four."

The Marines gave a half-hearted cheer and the one named McTear rested his hands on the nearby coil and pushed, his expression turning immediately into one of horror. "Shugart, get out of the way, it's swinging wide!" But the warning came too late. The section was on its way down and started to rotate in the direction of another man, who stood on the edge of the flatbed. His back was to the coil, and he stared off with a blank expression as if he didn't hear the shouts. *"Get out of the way!"*

Before it could strike him, the section's straps snapped and the thing crashed against the edge of the carrier, catapulting the man, Shugart, twenty meters into the rubble. His officer, who had begun his way up the crater, stopped to look. Three coil sections tumbled off the carrier and slid down the sloping side of the pit in slow motion, rolling over him before they stopped with a groan. He never had time to even scream. A smear that looked like raspberry jam had been wiped against the glassy crater side, all that remained of the officer, a message spelled out in dead tissue, that war could touch you anywhere, anytime. Even the rear could be a dangerous place.

*"Corpsman!"* one of them yelled.

*What would a corpsman do?* I wondered, glancing at Megan. You could see she was thinking the same thing.

"Someone fucking *do something*. Goddamn it!" The Marine named McTear slid to the bottom of the crater and pulled at the edge of one of the pipes, a tiny pool of blood collecting next to his boots as Shugart stood to shake his head clear.

Someone said, "Get outta there, McTear; he's gone. The coils might shift again."

But none of the other Marines moved except for Shugart. He had finished dusting himself off and started sobbing. Eventually, after he dropped to his knees, a sergeant arrived and the men began the slow process of pulling out the sections, one by one until they reached the officer, who had been crushed so badly that all that remained was a pile of ceramic shards, meat, and intestines, collected in a pool of blood at the crater base. I zoomed into it, fascinated by the realization that on the inside we looked the same.

McTear saw me watching. "What the hell are you looking at?"

Then he threw up and my thoughts cleared. Some of these men cared about each other and couldn't stomach death, especially not when it was one they knew. I wanted to see more, to stay there and hold hands with Megan, but the play faded, beyond my control, and I felt a sense of blind acceleration until another scene crystallized.

It was the first time we had seen real human cruelty. I don't know why it affected me the way it did, but even Megan had trouble on that day.

"Jesus," a Marine Lieutenant said, "*look* at that, Top. Bunch of animals."

It had turned into a surreal morning for me, as soon as Megan and I came topside to a clear day, in which the sky seemed a lazy blue. There were no contrails, no plasma bursts, and no whining APCs—just a breeze that teased one with the thought of unsuiting, so you could feel and smell what the world was really like, and it was so clear that if you zoomed far enough, you could almost imagine seeing the ruins of Pavlodar, thousands of kilometers away.

The lieutenant had called us up to join him and the Top Sergeant in an above-ground observation post, where the four of us now crouched in a shallow bunker, its thick ceramic walls capped with a three-foot concrete slab. A mound of rubble covered the position and narrow slits allowed us to see in every direction. After we waited for a few minutes, Megan cleared her throat to let them know we were there.

"Oh, hello ladies," said the lieutenant, "glad you could join us."

Megan asked, "You called for us, so what do you need?"

He motioned for his sergeant to move, so we could get closer to the vision slit. "Look out there, about eight hundred meters, eleven o'clock."

I fingered the zoom controls and scanned the snow-covered fields, moving back and forth until I saw it. It took a moment for my goggles to autofocus, but when they did it took another for my mind to process what I saw, for the sight to register as something horrific, even for someone who didn't fear dying. Megan tensed next to me.

"Well?" The lieutenant asked. There was laughter in his voice and the sergeant nearly shook with the trouble of controlling a giggle. "What do you see?"

At the enemy lines, Russians lifted four women in black undersuits, their arms and legs lashed around steel poles. Eight soldiers secured the poles with rubble and concrete and when they had finished, raised their arms, a single word drifting across no man's land. *"Pobieda!"*

"The ones on the poles are our sisters," Megan said. "Probably captured in our last action."

"You don't say," said the lieutenant. "Wow."

The sergeant burst out laughing. "Looks to me like they're having a barbecue."

"You want to call in the fire mission, ladies, or should I?" the lieutenant asked.

Megan keyed into tac-net. "Fire mission, pre-established coordinates zebra-seven-seven. Fire for effect."

Thin wisps of smoke floated up under the girls, and we watched four separate sets of flame blossom. Within seconds, our sisters' high-pitched screams echoed over the empty fields, forcing me to manually shut off helmet pickups. The artillery unit wasn't far to our rear, and we felt the vibrations of our guns at about the same time we heard them, followed by the roaring containment shells. The Russians disappeared into their airlock. Our sisters kept writhing atop the poles until blue plasma enveloped them in a flash, blackening them into charred hulks.

"Check fire," Megan whispered into her radio. "Is that all, Lieutenant?"

The two men looked at each other and the sergeant gave her a thumbs-up. "Man, they're cold, L-T. Cold-ass *bitches*. They'll wipe their own friends and then go on like nothing happened."

"Yeah, Top," said the lieutenant, "watch out for these ones." He waited for a full minute, not looking at us before he waved Megan away. "OK," he said, "that's all."

There my dreams ended. I felt a tingling on my skin, not in my dreams but for real, and a bright glow forced me to raise a hand to my eyes, the air suddenly colder than it should have been. *Freezing.* I remembered then, that I was on a train.

A few of the boys said something in Russian, which sounded like curses, and then the door to our car slammed shut, returning the warmth slowly.

"Easy, now," a man said. I didn't recognize the voice, didn't want to pull my hand away because this wasn't a boy's voice; it was a man's, a human's. "We're heading north now, back to Russia, where we can take care of your infections, try to save what's left of your feet and legs." The man touched me and I nearly screamed, wishing I had a knife to slam into his throat. My dreams had shown me everything—convinced me that for the rest of my life, whenever I encountered humans, they would die. It was a *new* kind of faith. But when I finally looked at him, my hatred softened, because if this was a human it was a type I had never seen before, one damaged and then redamaged, and a feeling crept in, one that almost never materialized: pity.

"Boys are in a good mood, I think." The man's left eye

had gone almost white, its pupil more of a milky gray, and above and below it a long scar ran from the edge of his hair to his chin. The other side was worse. His good eye stared out from a pocket, around which the skin had melted into scar tissue so it looked as though someone had dropped a black marble into molten plastic, allowing the stuff to congeal around it. I let him work. The way he spoke, softly, and a glint from his good eye conveyed a sense of caring and suggested that he had found his vocation—that being a doctor was perfect for someone like him. Because he was so gentle.

"What happened to you?" I asked.

"To me?" He wore a combat suit, the bulk of which made it hard to fit in the narrow space between bunk rows, forcing him to shift. "My face, you mean. Plasma. Now let's have a look at those legs. Do they hurt?"

"When I move them."

He lifted the blanket and spent a minute examining me, lowering the blanket softly once he'd finished. "They're bad. Not as bad as some I've seen but we'll have to get there quickly to save them."

"Where?"

"Zeya," he said. The boys who had been talking quietly hushed when they heard the name.

"Zeya?" one asked. He said something in Russian then and the doctor glared, silencing him with one look from that eye.

"Zeya."

I shook my head, confused. "Where is Zeya, and what do you mean, 'save them'? You can't save my legs, they're spoiling along with the rest of me."

The doctor didn't respond as he pulled out a box and

opened it; the Russian medical kits were similar to ours, and I watched as a droplet of gray microbots disappeared into my arm to check blood pressure and take other readings, sending the data back to his suit.

"Zeya is where we take some of your kind, and we can save you, since it looks like you are an early model. Americans. Always the first, and look at you; you're beautiful, almost perfect, and they overlook one basic feature."

"I *am* perfect," I said, "better than *you*. They call me the Little Murderer."

"Ha!" He turned and spoke in Russian to the others, and the room erupted with laughter. The doctor must have seen my face because he raised both hands to surrender. "No, no, you misunderstand. They laugh because they like the name. In Russian, you are Malenkiy Ubitza; it's a good name for a genetic soldier."

"Then how am I not perfect?"

"You are as perfect as they could make you. Like my boys. But the early American models lack one important thing and I do not blame them, your creators, for their lack of foresight. I mean look what they accomplished anyway. Manufacturing a human being is no easy feat; one mistimed gene activation here and a minor mistake there, and boom, your liver grows too soon, too late, or worse, it grows right out of your forehead. No, your scientists, they did OK. The only thing they got wrong were the security features, which depend on your immune system failing at exactly the right time, when it stops telling the difference between foreign matter and your own tissue. You are a ticking immuno-bomb. That is why your flesh is dying. To add insult to injury, your immune system already destroyed the very thing that makes you fearless, perfect: your ability to block pain."

"I know," he went on, pulling the blanket up to my neck, "it sounds like there is no mistake but think; they didn't take away your chromosomal repair genes. Every one of us normal humans has a set of genes whose job it is to identify and locate material that has, well... malfunctioned. So that the body can produce materials to repair the damage. A long time ago we figured out that a little dose of radiation activates these genes and the good news is that someone forgot this when they designed you. So, boom. A little radiation, and your genes kick in and there you go, most everything back to normal. Your parents never accepted the fact that there is such a thing as a *healthy* dose of radiation, and that was their mistake, one that will save you—one that has already saved many of your kind."

"*Most* everything?" I asked.

"Your mind is what it is, there's nothing we can do for it except give you psycho-active drugs at Zeya. And your body, well, you'll never be as good as you *were*, Ubitza, never the same. I'm sorry. But we have a surprise, one that will take your mind off things." He clapped his hands and the boys stared, hanging on every Russian word he spoke, before the doctor turned back to pat my shoulder. "I can't stay for this. It's too grotesque, even for someone as ugly as me, but you'll be fine in Zeya. Trust an old doctor."

As soon as he left I closed my eyes again.

The anger forced tears, which rolled down the side of my face and onto the pillow. It wasn't a surprise; what the doctor had told me I already suspected, even knew, but his confirmation made me realize that I didn't just hate humans, I hated myself—for having been made. Perfection had never existed and it was true that my genes were flawed, that now I was worse than a nonbred; I was a defective who felt pain and shame, and death was once a welcome destination but now my fear of it intensified to a point where it forced me to grip the blankets as hard as I could, trying my best to ignore the fact that Megan was really gone, but worse, that maybe I *didn't* want to join her. Hallucinations would come next. With no tranq tabs, time began to slip first as if gravity in the railcar had ceased to exist and once the sensation solidified to the point where I no longer heard the boys, one last thought occurred to me.

God had betrayed us both. Me and Megan.

"God doesn't exist," said our Special Forces advisor. Megan and the rest of us had been dropped into Mashhad to cover the highway north and prevent Iranian guerillas from infiltrating the city, where behind us, engineers had begun their work on widening the roads, preparing the way for a main advance into far-eastern Turkmenistan. They worked in the open, exposed, we as their only protection. The group of us had been flown in, in pairs, by carrier auto-drones that landed us along the road, which doubled as a runway so the aircraft could offload before self-destructing once we'd cleared. After the last one detonated, the night went still. It was summer and even without the sun, heat radiated from the road's surface and gave the asphalt a gentle glow on thermal sensors so that it appeared to be magic, a white ribbon that stretched out forever; you wondered what lay at the end of the road, maybe some forgotten place with plenty of targets, untouched and pristine, so that I had to fight the urge to stand up and run toward them. As if reading my mind, Megan put her hand on my shoulder, pulling me back to reality. A hundred of us lay invisible in the sand on either side of the highway, forming a wide L-shaped ambush, where Megan and I rested at the corner, looking straight down the road.

*How could he say that God didn't exist? He is here, around us, and on the highway.*

"That's blasphemy," Megan said to him.

"Seriously. You chicks wouldn't know any better, but he's a myth. Doesn't exist."

"What are our orders?" I asked, wanting to change the subject. That early in the war, orders were still transmitted to our handlers first and then disseminated to our unit, until someone later realized that if the special advisor got hit—before telling us what to do—we would take the initiative.

He cleared his throat. "An insurgent unit regrouped in Chenaran and will hit our engineers from the north tonight, to slow our advance over the Turkmeni border. Our sources say they'll be driving white electro-plus vans."

"Electro-plus?" I asked.

"Just shoot at any vans that come down the road. But don't shoot until I do."

While Megan relayed the orders to everyone the curiosity became too great to ignore and I whispered to him. "How do you know they're regrouping? Where does this information come from, and who fights in vans? Surely they know they'll die."

"Baby, you don't know these guys. Nut jobs. But brave

ones, they believe in God, just as much as you do and if you were to ask any one of them who had God on their side, they'd tell you it was them—and they'd be sure of it. They're just as sure of him as you are. And you don't need to know how I know they're regrouping. I just do."

The wind picked up and a weather alert crawled across our heads-up, warning of a dust storm that would arrive within ten minutes. We made sure our pouches were shut, covered anything that we didn't want filled with sand, and waited, my mind going into high gear. The storm was a sign. It could only help the insurgents since it meant that our thermal and night vision would be as useless as normal sight, and the only warning we'd get would be from the sound of their engines since we'd be unable to see the vehicles until they had drawn alongside our position. But back then I was fearless. Whatever uncertainty had begun to bud did so deep inside, too small to even make itself felt because it lay buried under hatred, a foundation of knowing that killing was my life and that it had been too long since the last engagement, the boredom in between almost too much to handle. I *wanted* a fight.

Hours crawled by. By three a.m. my position had filled with so much sand that I must have looked like a dune among dunes, the road was a river of sand with curtains that blew across to pile up on either side, and the drifts threatened to block the passage of anything, which only made me angrier. I prayed they would come soon. If the road filled with too much sand the mission would be called off and we'd be forced to walk south to the city, at least a three-kilometer march through loose grit with nothing to show for our efforts.

And the storm blinded us, filling our intake vents so

that we had to clear them regularly or risk asphyxiation while ignoring gusts that made the particles hiss when they struck my ceramic helmet; after a while the noise formed nonsensical sentences like, *death sleeves seem selfless*. The sand triggered an irrational feeling of thirst, so that before long I had worked through half my ration of water packets, each mouthful containing tiny granules. Sand crunched between my teeth as if taunting me that no matter the precautions, no matter how fast I opened the packets and inserted the tube, there weren't any measures that could keep the stuff out. This land belonged to the sand. It wasn't long before my dedication eroded under the onslaught, my determination to fight shifting slowly into a desire for it to end, for the monotony to cease and the sand to leave us or die for just a moment so that I could see more than a foot away.

I was about to shout in frustration when they came. Our forward-most position reported lights and my thoughts went still as calmness took hold, rooted in the knowledge that soon we'd be free.

"Hold your fire," our advisor whispered over the headset.

We saw the first set of yellow headlights as a large van navigated slowly through the dunes, silently. Its electric engine made almost no noise. The vehicle passed our first position and had almost reached us when Megan moved beside me.

"We should fire," she said.

"I can't make out their color; we have to make sure they're white. Hold your fire."

A second vehicle appeared in the distance, the first one almost past us now.

"I'm going to open fire," said Megan.

"Hold your fire," our advisor insisted. "Or so help me—"

But Megan had already relayed the order. Instantly the first van blew into pieces when three grenades impacted on its side, forcing jets of hot gas into the interior; its doors whizzed overhead and I smiled, pulling the trigger at dark shapes that leaped from the wreckage, humans trying to escape in our direction. The second van stopped and began to reverse, but someone had snuck into the road and placed a mine so that the van jumped into the air and flipped, landing upside down on a drift. A group of grenadiers targeted it then, blowing holes in the side and turning the vehicle into a blackened pile within seconds. All night it went on. The storm's intensity prevented the convoy members from seeing what had happened to their vehicles in the front, and one by one they crept toward our position without knowing what waited for them. Soon the road became impassable. Wrecked vans collected to form a kind of dam and we shifted our position northward, not bothering with stealth because whoever occupied the vehicles seemed incapable of resistance, and we wanted to get into position before the next one saw us and reversed. And then it started again.

By the time morning had arrived, the storm lifted and we saw the results. A mixture of sand piles and wreckage stretched out for over a kilometer, winding through the dunes, which hundreds of bodies decorated in daylight so their clothes looked like scraps of colorful paper that flapped in the breeze. Our advisor jumped from our hole. He ran from body to body, checking each one and then looked inside the vehicles that hadn't been completely destroyed by our ambush. After an hour he returned and slid into the sand, popping his helmet.

"Congratulations."

"Thank you," Megan said.

"Yep. You just took out half of the Red Crescent volunteers operating in this area."

"That is their name?" I asked. "The insurgent group's?"

"No, you stupid sack." He threw his helmet at me, and the thing slammed into my faceplate, knocking my head back so that I almost shot him in anger. "They're freakin' *aid workers*. Do you know what those are? Aid workers? Nurses, doctors, people who go through war zones and take care of wounded civilians?"

"We have no need for aid," said Megan, but the words made his face go red, and the man raised his carbine to point it her.

"You're a bunch of psychos."

Megan's hand blurred and slapped his weapon aside before she jumped, ramming the butt of her carbine into his windpipe.

"And *you* are distressed," she said. "Something is wrong with you and I relieve you of command."

"Something is wrong with me? With *me*?"

"The dead are with God," she continued, "and they have no more worries in this life."

But by now we had seen the same thing happen with other units, as we sped northward from Bandar Abbas, and we already knew that the nonbred looked on civilians differently so that the thought of Megan killing him seemed excessive. It didn't feel right. This one had spoken with us as equals, always taking the time to find out how we worked, how we fought, and how we thought, and I didn't realize that within a few weeks a plasma mine would swallow him for us anyway, because until now we had been invincible and had not lost a single sister in the long fight north. It seemed like maybe this man would guide us through the world until our end; he was a good one, perhaps sent by Him to show us the way.

So I pulled her rifle away. "Not this one, Megan."

"Why?"

He coughed when his breath returned, and the man spat blood onto the sand.

"Because he has been chosen. It's not right."

Megan yanked her helmet off and nodded.

While we watched, our advisor crawled to the far side of the hole and pulled his helmet back on, speaking in a low voice into the radio, reporting what had happened. When he finished, he turned back to us.

"Pickup is in one hour. We move southwest on the road and meet the APCs, to take up defensive positions closer to the engineers."

"They died quickly," I said to him, "the Red Crescents." Other girls had begun gathering around us now, but said nothing.

"They didn't die quickly. They died terrified."

"But we thought they were insurgents," said Megan, "and it would have been wrong to let them by, to let them get close to the engineers."

"Someday you'll get it," he said, grabbing his carbine and reattaching the flexi so he could move out. We followed him, pushing through the sand, and headed southwest. "Someday you'll know and by then this war will be over."

His words changed our mood. It didn't matter to me if he was right, that one day I'd understand how he felt, because I didn't *believe* he was right about that, but the thought that the war might end sent a chill through me, made me want to sit down and think. War without end— this was to be our destiny and at that early age, to think otherwise required a fundamental shift in belief, one that we had just enough experience to know could happen, but not enough experience to actually imagine, let alone handle. As we marched I prayed, and decided it then: God would grant me death before the end, because after all, who wanted the end of war?

"We want the war to end," the boy in the bunk over me said, his head and shoulders visible as he hung down. When he saw my confusion, he frowned. "You were talking in your sleep and you asked who would want it to end. We do. In the meantime, we brought something for you to play with."

The car had dimmed since the doctor left and on the other side of a narrow window near the closest door, snowflakes streaked past in a wall of gray that made everything darker, the only light provided by alcohol lamps lit at either end of our car. A biting wind roared down the narrow aisle. From where the boy pointed I heard the other car door slam shut, and then curses in English, so I gathered the blanket around my neck and strained to lift myself a few inches and look at a man. Human.

They dragged him forward by a rope that had been tied around his neck, and if it weren't for the fact that he stood on two legs I wouldn't have recognized him as man. Both arms were gone at the shoulder. What stumps remained had been charred black, cauterized so that he'd live for a few moments longer, and his face had been beaten to the point where it ballooned into something like a bizarre collection of grapes, forcing both eyes shut so he bumped into the bunks, blind. The boys spat at him. By the time he stumbled to my side his face ran with spit, both cheeks sparkling with the boys' hatred, and the man collapsed to his knees, grunting when he fell because he had no hands to catch himself. The boy above me handed down a knife, double edged and bright.

"We captured him after we pulled you from the river," the boy said. "He's the one who shot your sister."

"How do you know?" I asked, taking the knife without thinking.

"He told us. And we saw it all."

Megan. I remembered her then, saw her, and recalled the last moments we shared along with the feeling of hope. She had been new. Changed from a Lily into a thing that neither of us recognized, but which had embraced uncertainty, given up on control or trust because nobody could really tell the future, and this was part of what made our escape so wonderful: doubt. Responsibility. Without orders *we* would have decided what to do next, and Megan had transformed with the burden into a girl who seemed more beautiful now, dead, than she ever had in life, so that when the man coughed and said something, I ignored the pain, shifting to the side and sitting up, my legs visible for the first time. The Russians had dressed me in a gown. Both feet hung in the cold, exposed, and the toes had turned black, sending red streaks of infection upward.

"Who are you?" the man said. His words slurred and when my foot brushed his face he screamed.

"I'm a Germline unit. Catherine. You took something from me."

"She is Ubitza," someone else said.

The man started laughing. "She's a whore. And so was her sister."

I recall doing it, but not why. He said other things, words which didn't matter, things that all of them knew because the special forces had been briefed by the white coats, the ones who picked at our minds when our minds wanted to rest along with our bodies, but there wasn't any rest and so it made no difference how many of them knew my secrets. This one had to die. It was a clinical decision and my knife went smoothly into his eye, sliding all the way until it cracked through the back of his skull, nailing his head to the car's floor planks; but still it wasn't enough so I stood and grabbed one of the boy's boots, which hung by its laces from the bunk. The heel hammered on the knife, drove it deeper into the floor so that the man jerked in reflex, his body flopping, swinging back and forth on the pivot point of its head until even the reflex left him. Empty. I remember the boys yanking the knife out and lifting his corpse while one of them lowered me back into bed, pulling the blanket up; another one cautioned to throw the body clear and make sure it didn't derail the train, but that was in Russian so I wasn't sure if it was actually what they said. Maybe it was my imagination. By the time the car had gotten warm again someone dimmed the lamps and a group of them gathered next to me, including the one from overhead, his good hand lifting another cigarette to my lips. The flame from a lighter turned their smiling faces orange and made me feel warm.

"It was a good kill," the one said. "Faster than he deserved, but I liked the ending."

"The ending?"

"Every kill is a story. A tale with a beginning, a middle, and an end."

"We know the ending now. Tell us the beginning and the middle."

"Tell us yours, Ubitza," another one whispered, "and we'll tell you ours."

I shook my head, and pointed at my bunkmate. "Wait. You said that you wanted the war to end. Why? Now you say you like killing. How can you believe both at once?"

"It's true, Ubitza. We like killing. I would kill you if they told me to but they didn't. But that doesn't mean we want the war to go on forever."

"She doesn't know," another one urged. "Tell her."

"Tell me what?"

The boy leaned over and kissed me on the cheek, wiping the knife clean on his pajamas and then placing it in my palm. He used his one good hand to curl my fingers around the grip. "We don't die like you, in two years. They gave us a full life. And land, an open place in Siberia, hell on earth with a winter that lasts ten months and nothing but mining spoil and shit for miles around. But ours. Our brothers before us work it now, the ones who completed their duty, and they're waiting for us, the new crop of broken soldiers to arrive and help with the work. This train stops at Zeya, for you and us. They gave us Zeya. So we rumble northward to our destination because we completed our service term and now we muster out, each of us in their own way."

"What is your service term?"

Another one, behind him, answered. "We serve until we die or become too wounded, too broken to be of use in war. That's how it ends for us. And now we can go home."

I noticed it then, and thought it ironic. When the lamps were brighter it hadn't been obvious, except for the missing hand of my bunkmate, but now that the lights were low and they surrounded me in a throng of glowing cigarettes I saw that all of them had been shattered. Each of them lacked at least one body part, and most were missing two. Yet all of them grinned. One with no eyes smiled the most and I wondered what job they would give him, what work he could do for their farm, and as if in answer one of them slapped the blind boy's shoulder and insisted that he'd make a great snow shoveler because it didn't matter where the snow went, there wasn't any place to put it anyway, and although I should have felt nothing, I felt everything at once. Tears streamed from both eyes. I tried to grin but my mouth wouldn't work that way, and instead twisted into something that I'm sure they didn't recognize because they looked surprised and one of them asked if he'd said something wrong.

"You didn't say anything wrong," I said, struggling to speak around the cigarette, "it's because I'm broken."

My bunkmate shook his head. "You'll be fine. Maybe lose a couple of toes or your feet, but that's it."

"I'm not broken there. My mind is cracked. They gave us medicine for it, but I don't have any now. I might start telling you my story and then go blank, and you never know when they come, when the dreams take over and turn everything into nightmare. It's called the spoiling. And I don't even know if any of you are real or if I can remember the beginning of my story anymore. The men in white took everything."

"We're real," he said, "as real as you. And tell us any story because we're all going to Zeya together, you and us, and we need to know our neighbors. Tell us about these men in white."

We walked back to the main advance-force, our unit missing three girls—three who had been unlucky enough to encounter a Turkmeni anti-aircraft unit. Nobody had seen them. The men had used the hulk of a burned-out bus to conceal both their thermal signatures and an ancient auto-cannon whose chemical rounds—forty-millimeter shells—ripped the air, smashed through the girls' ceramic armor, and shattered bones before the rounds exited the other side. The gunner walked his shells across our line. He started with the closest girl and took out two more before we slaughtered him and his loaders in place, leaving our dead where they lay. There was never a burial for the dead; we said thank-you and smiled, for they had been given a gift and we had to move out. In the wake of the battle came a quiet day, and while we pushed forward over a semi-arid landscape, scrub plants dotting it with patches of green, it had seemed there was no war, that with the exception of us and an occasional rabbit nothing else existed and that the target village was still too far to even imagine let alone see, and so might have vanished into thin air.

What remained of our patrol assignment passed uneventfully when after another hour we reached our destination, a blurred scene of moving through the village—

a house by house clearing operation in which one door seemed like the next, one wall an exact duplicate of the thousands we had broken through already, so that the only difference between this and Mashhad, Bandar, or any other town were its inhabitants. The women threw themselves at us with knives, which, in retrospect seemed more brave than stupid. Staying there had been their end. Then again, running after we arrived would have done no good, and if knives were their only weapons then they honored us with a kind of ferocity that I guessed grew from instinct: self-preservation and protecting their young. I killed as many as I could by hand, not wanting to cheapen their bravery with the use of flechettes when so many of them had earned a more honorable ending. Our clearing action took less than an hour. After we finished, we shouldered our weapons and headed south again, into the sun and for our main force, satisfied that no armored units or heavy weapons waited in ambush along our path. *Three girls short.*

The advance-column waited for us at Tejen, in a part of Turkmenistan we controlled, and the engines from thousands of tanks and APCs rumbled as they sat in the fading light, their exhaust turning the sky over town a dirty gray. We crouched by the roadside to wait. Soon our APC would pull alongside and we'd join the column at nightfall for the next phase of the push, soon we would be in combat again, maybe this time against more worthy opponents.

Megan pulled off her helmet. "I like this climate."

"You take a risk," I said, pointing to her helmet, "with no thermal block."

"Risk?" One of the other girls, Jennifer, removed hers

so I saw her face; it had turned red. "Who are you to mention risk? I saw you in the village, with your hands. Any one of us could have been compromised by the chances you took. Everyone else uses their weapons but Catherine? She snaps necks instead, crushes throats."

"They had no weapons other than knives," I explained.

"How did you know that? Could you have been sure? What if in the time it took you to dispatch one, another had risen with a grenade launcher? What then? We'd all die, that's what would have happened."

The rest of the girls watched, and I imagined what they were thinking because I thought it too, that this was interesting, the dialogue leading to an event we had been trained to cope with but hadn't yet faced.

"You are spoiling," I said. "And we haven't been on the field for even a few months yet. Curious."

Some of the others laughed while color drained from Jennifer's face. She looked to Megan. "I am not spoiling. I don't fear anything."

Megan shrugged. "Then Catherine is wrong. Explain it to me."

"It's a question of numbers, Megan. Our mission is to conquer the enemy without taking too many losses; to remain combat effective and still take the objective."

Nobody laughed now. The sounds of engines surrounded us, but it may as well have been silent because we had become so focused on what would happen next.

"Who," asked Megan, "gave you the job of understanding our mission? Our mission is to die on the field, and to take as many men with us as possible. And who gave you the task to judge Catherine?"

"Let he who is without sin cast the first stone," someone

said. "Catherine kills without mercy. Catherine kills in ways we, her sisters, have not yet mastered."

Jennifer gripped her helmet with both hands, holding it up to her chest. "I did not mean anything by it, my Lily. It's just that—"

Before she could finish Megan slammed the butt of her carbine into Jennifer's face and then spun the weapon in midair, firing point blank until the girl slumped to the ground dead. Megan gestured to me—that I should get rid of her. I grabbed Jennifer under the shoulders and dragged her into a nearby ditch where she slid to the bottom, her face gone, riddled with so many flechettes that I could only guess at where her eyes had once been. When I returned Megan smiled.

"She wasn't spoiling; this was something worse. Jennifer must have been defective but slipped through the final test."

And they all cheered. In less than a second the girls gathered around me, slapping me on the back and everyone speaking at once so that I barely picked out the requests for training, to show them how I had learned to snap necks so easily, and how was it that God had granted me the gift of mercilessness? We all had the same training in the tank. Where had I learned these methods? I was about to try to answer at least some of the questions when I noticed Megan cock her head, listening to her radio, the smile gone from her face.

She motioned for everyone to be quiet and looked at me. "They want you in the rear. Now."

"Who?" I asked.

"The men in white."

"But why so soon and after such a timid engagement?"

Megan shrugged. "We don't ask these questions."

"Megan," someone said, "will we advance without Catherine? We can't go into combat without her."

Megan didn't answer. I pulled my helmet off to smell the fumes of unburned alcohol leaking from a nearby engine, and water vapor exhaust gave the atmosphere a moist, tropical feeling as I shouldered my way through the girls. Some of them muttered apologies for my fate— not that I was going to see the white-coats, but that I might miss the coming battle. My morale sunk. My hatred of men, especially the scientists, leapt in response as if the sudden depression fed it, and by the time I found myself in the midst of the main column I barely saw the vehicles, didn't register the faces of girls from other units, because all I could think of was killing. Alderson wasn't just a coward anymore. He was robbing me of purpose, shaming me by refusing to let me advance with family into the next battle.

In the rear of the column waited a caravan of trucks, huge alcohol-burning tankers and behind them equally large prime-movers towing trailers. A line of Special Forces saw me coming and opened to let me pass. The trailers bristled with antennae and communications dishes, and once past the guards I found myself in a sea of white coats where two Special Forces joined me, grabbed each arm, took my weapon, and escorted me into a trailer toward the rear. They expected trouble. A third one walked directly behind us, his flechette pistol drawn and pointed directly at the back of my head as they pushed me through a metal door and into a narrow hallway, two of them in the front now and the pistol-armed one in the rear.

Alderson waited in a room off the side of the main hallway, tapping a small table. "Undress," he said.

"I have to return to my unit."

"Not right now you don't. We need you here."

"For what?" I asked. "To observe your cowardice? To watch you shake, hear you wonder out loud if our drones will be enough to keep enemy aircraft away? The air is braver than you are, Alderson."

"Undress."

I did as he asked and a nurse came into the room, wiping me down with alcohol and peroxide. She then shaved my head until it was perfectly smooth again, and wiped it down too, the alcohol evaporating so that I had to will my body to warm itself because even the carpet felt cold under my toes.

"Follow me."

Alderson and the soldiers led me from the small office into a white room, its walls and ceilings covered with a seamless ceramic material, polished, in the middle of which rested an operating table with nylon restraints. Machines surrounded the table. At one end, near what looked like a headrest, a medical bot rose from the floor. It was a metallic cylinder with sensors that resembled a snail's eyestalks and retractable arms, the ends of which were hidden by red plastic stenciled with the words STERILe—OPEN BEFORE USE. I lay on the table without being told to and allowed the men to strap me down.

"I need you to prepare yourself," Alderson said, "for a procedure. It will be painful, even with your ability to block nerve impulses."

The straps pinned me to the operating table, and air handlers sent a warm breeze across my naked chest and legs, next to which Alderson stood, his white coat buttoned to the neck, a surgical mask positioned over his nose and mouth. I hadn't noticed the window. Either that or I somehow missed the fact that a thin ceramic panel must have initially covered it, the panel now receding downward into the wall to expose glass, behind which another group of men in white coats waited. Watching.

"What procedure?" I asked.

"We need you for an experiment. If it works, your mind will synch with a new armor system under development, and it will put us years ahead of Russia in weapons development."

I smiled. "My history lessons were complete enough that I know this is illegal, Alderson. The Supreme Court ruled on cybernetic issues over ten years ago."

"The joining of human and machines, yes. But you're not human."

"What if it doesn't work?" I asked.

"Then you die in glory. The Atelier Mothers have ruled that this is a battlefield sacrifice, one granting entry to the Kingdom, Catherine."

"And if it works?"

"Then you also die in glory. It's a test, nothing more, and once we get our data you will be discharged. Does this bother you?"

I felt a flutter in my chest, maybe the first sign of fear, but then thought of Jennifer. "I am not weak, like you."

"Fine." Alderson reached over and began pulling the bags off the med-bot's arms, but a knock from the window stopped him. I turned my head. Beyond the glass stood a general, a Marine, so short that he barely reached the chin of the next shortest man, and his face was pudgy in an angry kind of way. He glared at Alderson and gestured with a finger, mouthing two words silently around his cigar. *Come here.* I had never met one of the generals before but the black bands around his shoulder-boards meant the man was one of the supreme commanders, in charge of special units, in charge of me and my family. Once Alderson disappeared into the next room, the general winked at me before stepping out of view; I almost liked the man.

Alderson returned a moment later.

"Let her go," he said to the Special Forces escort. The men took off their white aprons and refitted with weapons before pulling my straps loose.

"Get her dressed then send her back to her unit; the push is on in an hour." Alderson paused to glare at me. "They've been monitoring you, Catherine. General Urqhart said to tell you to keep, and I quote, 'fucking these bastards, hard, like a bitch in heat.' He thinks you're special."

Once free, I swung from the table and spat on Alderson, before allowing the men to push me toward the door. "Maybe he is something you will never be. A warrior."

"Other countries will beat us to it," Alderson called through the door after me, "the Chinese or the Russians. Soon we'll face things you've never dreamed of, half human, half machine, and all *this* means is that I have to pick another girl. One that isn't so popular with Command."


"Alderson was right, you know," my bunkmate said. He sucked on the last bits of a cigarette and stubbed it out while the other boys nodded. "The last wars, the ones in Asia, didn't totally exterminate the Chinese, despite Korean and Japanese attempts; they retreated underground to prepare for a return. We hear the same stories you do. And the Chinese don't share American concerns about law and machine."

"Then again, neither do we," added another boy. "We're almost in Zeya now. We should sleep."

The others moved through the aisle to get back into their bunks while the car lamps snuffed out simultaneously, and then, one at a time, their cigarettes went dark.

"What will happen to me in Zeya?" I asked my bunkmate.

"You will be treated like the others. Given a choice."

"A choice for what?"

"To work in the mines or farms or factories, deep underground, or to join with Russian forces and earn the chance for revenge against the men who hunted you. Good night, Ubitza."

Soon, everyone slept. Megan's face appeared every time I closed my eyes, her short hair moving in the wind and her smile visible even at night, in the darkness by the river where they took her. I cried, not even noticing the intensifying pain from my feet.

# FIVE

# Outcast

*The spoiled are cursed. Their lives become
those of bondwomen, slaves, bound unto
God but without His grace.*

MODERN COMBAT MANUAL
JOSHUA 9:23

The doors on either end of the car opened with bangs,
and men filled the car in an instant, their voices calm,
almost a whisper, Russian words spilling into the aisle in
a slurred string of meaningless vowels. They carried the
boys out, one by one. Eventually, hands grabbed me by
the shoulders and knees, lifting me gently onto a stretcher
and shuffling me into the light.

It took a few moments for my eyes to adjust. The
sounds of shouting strained my ears and stabbing cold
whipped around the stretcher, forcing me to curl into a
ball and pull the blanket around as tightly as possible,
until finally my eyes opened in slits. Zeya, an alleged
city, was nothing. Snow covered every structure, and here,
there, small chimneys poked through drifts, sending gray
smoke into the sky where it blended with the clouds and
sucked up flakes from a light flurry. The few tall buildings
left stood empty; their steel frames had bent and a clear
crust covered them, forming long icicles which pointed

toward the ground and threatened to fall. Military history, forced into my brain in the tank, burst out, streaming facts about an older war with China; chemicals, plasma, biologicals: all dropped more than two decades previously and still the area hadn't rebuilt. *War upon war,* I thought. Why rebuild when another war, this one to the south, could ruin everything again? Experience gave me its own lessons—more effective today because I lived them instead of being force-fed in the tank. Beyond the snow fields, forest bordered the city on all sides, giving the feeling that nature had surrounded it, waiting for the right moment to attack and take back what it owned.

The men took me to a waiting truck and slid me into a rack under four other boys. I grunted with the jolt, my feet screaming about their death.

"Easy times ahead, Ubitza," said my bunkmate, who rested in a stretcher opposite me. "But you'll need to learn Russian."

"Easy times for who?" I asked.

The truck's door slammed shut, just before it jumped forward, a bumpy road making it an uncomfortable ride so that each jolt sent a wave of pain. My bunkmate grunted.

"Easy for everyone. We get to live in Siberia, you get to return to the war or work in the mines or underground factories. Mines aren't so bad. Russia has a history of sending broken toys into its mines. But the factories… they're better."

Everyone laughed at that. I glanced down at my feet, which poked out from under the blanket, and saw the black flesh had crept upward from my toes, halfway to my ankles.

"How can I return to war with no feet? Even if the treatment works, they'll have to be taken off."

The boy turned his head and lit two cigarettes, handing one to me. "Zeya is the place of our birth. Research is here, Ubitza. There are rumors. We can take off your feet, and replace them with new ones—"

"Of a sort," someone interrupted, and again the laughter.

My bunkmate went on. "Even a kind of new body. Hardwired to your armor. Think of it. A new Ubitza, flechette proof, able to fire missiles with a thought, not a button. Vials of drugs continuously streaming in, no need for tablets anymore. All the drugs you want or need."

*Need.* Already I felt the terror return, nibbling at the edges of my brain along with the memory of Megan— twin rats that fed and fed. They needed to be put down, put to sleep. I needed drugs. Now.

"It's just a rumor," someone said. Already the truck had filled with smoke, but I pulled on my cigarette, the only drug I had, and listened. "I heard another one. That the experiments have gone nowhere, the subjects having to be put down or killing themselves with impulses that trigger a servo, send a powered limb too far too fast, ripping the brave volunteer to pieces without meaning to."

"Death is death," said my bunkmate. "And testing is part of war. It is a glorious way to die, being ripped apart, I think. Quiet now, Ubitza, we reach the center in half an hour. Under the mountains outside Zeya where we'll be safe and warm, underground again."

The Russians had brought me underground; you sensed the moisture, detected the kind of echo that only came from having solid rock on all sides, the protection of earth and mineral. Two men carried me through a narrow tunnel, and then past a doorway and into an open area where I could see again.

The chamber was so large that I had trouble finding the roof, which arched overhead at least a hundred meters away, a honeycombed network of concrete and steel set to reinforce it. Tiny pinpoints of light made me blink. Thousands of them stared down at me as if little stars had been set in the concrete to wink and fill the area with a warm yellow glow. And there *was* warmth. Loads of it. Space heaters along the edges groaned and creaked with their thermal load, blasting the area with waves of air that smelled of ozone. Finally the men dumped my stretcher on a table, and I realized that the underground chamber was packed with operating gurneys, and between them medical bots, which swayed on their pedestals like mobile willow trees, half sentient. Their arms darted down and then flicked up again, a suture here and there, sewing up some boy or man who had been strapped in place, immobilized and anesthetized. Another one swayed over its subject, two arms peeling away skin that had been charred black and red, while a doctor stood by, dressed from head to toe in light green plastic. Someone screamed.

A doctor leaned over me then, his face so close I smelled vodka on his breath, and he shone a light in my eyes at the same time he activated the bot. It sprang to life and injected me before I could react.

"A dose of tranquilizers. Same ones you use," he said. His English was stilted, rough. "I'm surprised you aren't going through withdrawal."

"I'm cold. I feel sick."

He nodded. "Maybe you are in withdrawal. We've added some microbots to the solution so in a few seconds"—he checked his tablet and nodded again—"we'll know just how much flesh is gone, how much can be saved. It looks like parts of your feet will have to go. Also, I think we can save all the fingers and the nose, but you may lose feeling in them. Permanently."

"How much of my feet?" I asked. The drugs finally started working, warming my insides and calming the receptors, millions of them screaming for their dose so that my nerves would loosen and relax.

The doctor shook his head. "All of them. Above the... what's the word? Here." He tapped my ankle and said something in Russian. "Then we'll give you the radiation treatment, and find out what you want to do with the rest of your life. Within reason. You are now the property of Moskva."

He tapped on his tablet with a finger and once more the bot swayed in, stabbing me with a second injection, this one burning so that my back arched with pain. The doctor's voice faded as the room started to go dark.

"Good night, Germline. We fix you, don't worry. If what I hear is true, and Americans wanted you dead more than any other we've seen, it has to be for a reason. Makes one curious."

At that moment I missed him, wondered where they had taken my bunkmate from the train because at least he was someone I knew. Even if he had no name.


There was no way to tell time. What might have been days floated by in dusty exhaust, through which I caught glimpses of myself on the gurney with millions of tubes and wires inserted into my skin and a wave of microbots so thick that I actually saw them, lying in pools of metallic gray that glittered on my arms and stomach. Faces came and went. First the doctor's, then others, until Alderson's face superimposed itself on them all and I giggled at the surge of hatred that accompanied each visit by a man, hatred that had almost been forgotten and that bubbled within my throat. Their Russian became something familiar. At times it felt so close to my own speech that I began picking out individual words in a way that made understanding almost possible, like standing at the edge of a river and looking across at the next objective, an easy one, but with no way to reach it. Those realizations made it difficult; made me want to sink back into haze. The familiar had vanished to leave me in an alternate universe, in which everyone looked like me but wasn't, were all slightly different in language in mannerism, creating a world in which I was no longer just an oddity; I was a *foreign* oddity, worth even more attention. Then, every once in a while, Megan's face appeared. But with time and drugs, the feeling of loss eroded, until one day it vanished altogether, although I suspected my memory of her wasn't gone—that she lurked in a corner of my mind, waiting to jump out and surprise me with an anguish that could be covered up but never fully exercised.

And then there was motion. The gurney's wheel servos hummed and they moved me from the main operating chamber into what felt like a maze of tunnels, and some slanted downward where the air thickened with moisture to become a humid film, forcing my skin to burst with sweat—water that would never evaporate, only collect in pools. A door rattled as it opened to allow a pulse of cold air to wash over the gurney, and then I entered another room. Still I didn't open my eyes. The air felt cool but electric, and a low vibration made my skin tingle so that even before looking I suspected I didn't want to. In the distance, hydraulic pressure released with a loud *hiss*.

*"Wake up, Ubitza,"* someone whispered. I opened my eyes and saw him, my bunkmate from the train.

My voice didn't want to work at first, the words coming out in half-croak, half-whisper. "What's your name? How long have I been sedated?"

"My name is Misha, and you've been gone a long time because they found so much damage—tissue that didn't want to come back to life. Months, I think. But now it's time to wake up and look; they sent me because this is never an easy time and I know you better than the others do. It's time to choose."

"I don't want to wake up, Misha. I want to sleep."

"Come on," he said, moving to my side. The stump of his arm slid under my shoulders and lifted until I sat upright, three needles in my arm stinging with the movement, which made a cluster of IV bags sway. "You can't stay broken forever."

"What," I asked, "did they do to me?"

The absence of feet didn't surprise me. I expected those gone, had seen the black skin and knew what it meant, but as I ran one hand over my gown the skin underneath felt pocked, as if a thousand spoonfuls of tissue had been dug out to leave craters. The backs of my hands showed it more clearly—tiny bowl-shaped divits that had turned pink with scar tissue—and before moving my hands to my face Misha nodded.

"It's the same on your face, Ubitza."

"But why? Why did they take out so much flesh?"

He shrugged. "Why not? It's not like you've lost your insides, although the doctors said those were starting to deteriorate as well. You're still Ubitza. They said that the decay had advanced in a way they'd never seen, seeded throughout your body in pockets that they had to remove with microbots. The radiation worked though. You won't die, Ubitza, unless you choose to. So *choose.*" He gestured to the rest of the room.

The area was mostly dark except for a single overhead light, beneath which stood a hulking set of armor, half-supported by chains that disappeared into the ceiling. It was twice the size of a man. Misha moved next to it and ran his hands over the shiny surface, its ceramic opalescent with what must have been the Russian version of chameleon skin, and then it did something I didn't expect: it moved. The arms raised with a whining sound and grabbed Misha by the waist, lifting him off the ground so that both his legs flopped in empty air.

"Powered armor, Ubitza, but not like the prototypes we just shipped out to my brothers at the front. Inside this one is Shlotka, a permanent resident now, fused with the systems, a true warrior. Fed on a glucose and nutrient solution, his body provides power to the support systems, which reduces the drain on fuel cells. More power for servos, more power for heavier plating. This is the *future.* You and me? Obsolete."

I stared, shocked, unable to speak.

"Say something nice to Ubitza, Shlotka," he said.

"*Strasvwi.*" The voice was mechanical, synthesized from the outset and not the sound of a genetic's voice piped through speakers. It sent a chill through my legs.

"That's Russian for 'hi'," Misha explained.

"He can never leave the suit," I said.

Shlotka lowered Misha, who approached the gurney, helping me to lie flat again.

"He doesn't *want* to leave. It's an honorable sacrifice, and you should think about it. If you return to battle, does it matter what humans you kill, whether they're American or not? We are bred for this, Ubitza, a singular purpose."

I looked away, the thought suddenly occurring to me. "I would also have to kill my sisters."

"I know. But you might never make it into battle." Misha must have seen my confusion, and went on. "Let me explain. Shlotka isn't ready for the field, he's a prototype. The process they used to link his nervous system to the suit's computer has not been perfected, so it made him . . . stupid. Subnormal. Synthetic genes were supposed to grow nerve tissues off the suit's wiring, and target the right parts of his brain and nervous system for linkage. The scientists call it Exogenetic Enhancement. But in Shlotka's case his linkage nerves didn't stop growing, began going places they shouldn't so that within a week he'll be paralyzed, dead in a month. Your sacrifice would be like his, and if it works with you, God! What an honor."

"And if it doesn't work I live a short life, subnormal, but trapped in armor."

Misha stood and frowned. "I have volunteered. My name is now on the list, and when it's called, I go into the Exogene Workshop. We fear the Chinese have reawakened and last week began receiving reports about things like Shlotka—to the west and south, armored nightmares that take Russian outposts and then vanish before we can respond or coordinate."

The room felt suddenly cold, enough that I missed the wet heat of the hallway, and it was the kind of chill that made me remember how I had once worshipped death as much as Misha had—that for him this must have been a clear decision. And I grew jealous. It had been a long time since feeling that level of faith, a long time since God had spoken to me, since I had felt as though there were a plan.

"You are fearless, Misha. The honor is mine, for having met you. What is my other choice?"

"Prosthetic feet, titanium skeletons. Full functionality, and they use a basic form of exogene technology to enhance control, to regrow muscle and nerve tissue."

"Why don't you just replace your hand then?" I asked.

Misha looked at me as though I were crazy. "Why would I do that? Feet are one thing, you need to walk. But to receive a wound like this, it's a badge—better than a medal. It shows that I fulfilled my end of the bargain and performed like a warrior should. I have one good hand left." He broke out his cigarettes and lit one, offering another to me, but I waved it away.

"You need to decide," he said.

I thought in silence. My drugs made the process easier, because I searched for the fear, the terror that should have been there like a waiting monster but it now felt more like a whimper, Megan a shadow of a shadow. Still, the memories were crisp; we had run for a reason, to escape and live something other than what we had been bred for and despite a lingering hatred for men, war seemed like the wrong option—as if choosing it would be to deny the reason for which Megan had died. She screamed at me even now: to choose the more difficult path.

"Prosthetics."

Misha nodded and switched off the servos to my gurney, then turned it around, pushing back toward the door through which I had entered. The heat returned and I breathed out in relief.

"There's one other thing, Ubitza," he said.

"What?"

"When we fled with you, the Americans sent a full battalion, maybe more, of Special Forces to chase us; I only found out now. Do you have any idea why the Americans would send so many to retrieve one girl?"

This time the heat didn't help, and I shivered with the news, recalling the general who had winked at me through the window.

"I have no idea, Misha."


They stopped giving me drugs, replaced instead with a chain of operations. I watched as the doctors guided their bot in an assault against my ankles, first cutting the stumps open and inserting needle after needle, preparing the tissue for microbot insertions while I strained against the straps, bit down on a wad of cloth, and did my best not to scream. *"Zha-zha, Ubitza,"* a nurse would croon, not realizing that had I broken free, my hatred had grown into something that would have snapped her neck without thinking. I wanted them all dead. Day after day passed, with my mind drifting in and out of consciousness, sleep coming only during the prescribed hours in which the process had to be paused so wasted microbots could be collected, their power used up. Then it began again. Little by little, they printed tissue onto my open stumps—their titanium to my bone, their nerves to mine; my world was reduced to a plastic bubble that had been erected to maintain a sterile zone. *We're trying a new procedure, Ubitza,* one of the doctors had said early on, *so no anesthesia and I want you to describe your sense of pain as we go. No free rides. We can't just spend our medical resources on escaped American girls and gain nothing in return, without gathering experimental data. What if we try this and the metallic-bone interface snaps? Your description could provide the key to what went wrong, so we can try again, get it right. You chose this, Ubitza, so let's think of this as a trade. A transaction of sorts.* And I vowed that he would die at my hands, if only I could remember what he looked like.

Then, one day, I woke up to feel a lesser pain. It was a pinch, as if someone had grabbed a toe and squeezed, and looking down I saw that the medical bots had finished their work, gone dormant to fold up like dead spiders, and that new feet had appeared in the place where so recently there had been nothing; an impossibly thin line separated the new skin from the old, just above my ankles.

When I tried to move them, I screamed.

"Rest, Ubitza," said Misha. He sat on a stool beside me, inside the plastic tent, a crooked smile on his face.

"My feet," I said.

"They tell me it will hurt. New nerves. New muscle. You'll have to get used to it, but the pain will go away more quickly the more you use them. Pain means that things are as they should be."

"I want my drugs back, Misha." I tested my arms and felt the straps, still in place. "They will all die. The doctors and nurses, everyone."

"You think they don't know that?" he asked, laughing.

"From here on out, I will take care of you, protect them from you."

"Then I will kill you."

Misha shook his head. "By Russian military standards, I'm not combat capable, but I can still fight. I still control my pain and have no fear. Go back to sleep, Ubitza."

I stared at him for a moment, seeing that his smile had faded, his eyes glassy, and then my fear returned; Misha was right. He grinned again and patted my shoulder.

"Wait, I forgot I have good news for you, Ubitza. Something to dream about in your time of rest."

"What?"

Misha lifted a shard of something, white and dull, like fired porcelain. "I had you assigned to my factory. We make ceramic plates, armor components. You will work for me until my name is called for the Exogene shop."

Something told me that I should have been happy. This was freedom of a sort. I had run and succeeded in getting away from my creators, but fate had stepped in to save me from slow death, had even replaced parts of my body so that soon I could function again. The scars on my face and body meant nothing. Hatred still mattered. But as I stopped to examine the hatred, Misha's face fading with my concentration, I noticed something had changed; it had begun to crumble at the edges. Thoughts of killing remained, a promise of a warm glow with each death, but the heat wasn't as intense, as if a malaise had seeped in, its origins unknown but maybe related to the spoiling, maybe related to the facts that my body could be repaired but that for my mind there was nothing. A part of my mind warned me, though, a distant, subtle voice that said,

*You can't stay here, Ubitza, time to move on or you'll lose the edge. Kill, or you'll die another kind of death, one more horrific than the death of our body. Take what they give until you're ready.*

"Thank you, Misha," I said. He beamed. I waited for him to put away the shard and went on. "Misha, what happens to those who try to escape?"

Misha shrugged. "Nobody has tried, Ubitza. Why would you? There are no guards here, nobody would stop you."

"Nobody?"

"Think about it. Russia is a big place, and there is nothing outside Zeya except the outposts which are hundreds of kilometers away, thousands. Where would you go? North? There you find only more ice, and would surely die. South, east, or west? There you would find trees. Wolves. Maybe Chinese infiltrators, or wander into China itself. Again, certain death. Why do you ask this?"

I thought for a moment and then forced a smile. "It will be an honor to work in your factory."

"Forget honor, Ubitza. It will be fun. Cigarettes and drugs. Music. The work is hard, but once the other girls place you, accept you, we are like a family."

"The other girls?"

Misha's smile disappeared. "I'm in charge, Ubitza, but we allow you to govern yourselves, and I have orders not to interfere. The other girls have a system, leaders, and it's important that you fit in. But don't worry, I'm sure everything will be fine."

He stood to leave, and my fear expanded, making my hands shake, so I was glad to be strapped down. Other girls. It had been months since I'd seen my own kind, and knew that if their deterioration had been like mine, things would be different—not like the system on the battlefield, the one we'd been conditioned to follow since birth—and fitting in meant the unknown.

It took weeks to be able to stand, another two to walk, and even then it was with enough pain that I shuffled more than stepped, having to grab hold of anything nearby to keep my balance. But the doctors seemed pleased. They handed me over to Misha, who guided me through the tunnels until I became lost, only a single bulb every hundred meters illuminating our way through smooth cylinders, eight feet across. A narrow stream flowed under us in a channel. The water mesmerized me, and provided something on which to concentrate so the pain from my ankles could at least be partially ignored, and eventually the tunnels slanted upward, bringing us closer to the distant hum of machinery and roaring ventilators. Soon the tunnel air became dusty, tasted of dry metallic grit, and then Misha brought me to a thick sliding metal door where he stopped.

"Listen to me, Ubitza," he said. "On the other side of this is my factory. As long as your sisters work and fulfill their production quotas, I have no reason to interfere with their business, their way of handling their own kind. You have to fit in."

I nodded. "You told me that already. These are my sisters, I can handle myself."

"Fully functional and I would believe you. But you're not fully functional and their leader is something strange, a girl who calls herself Heather and who isn't like you at all. Be careful. These girls have no honor."

"Misha, why are you helping me? Why did you ask for me to be in your shop?"

"Because I am supposed to keep an eye on you—to find out why the Americans were so determined to take you back. I told them I would tell you the truth if you asked, Ubitza, so there it is: I'm to spy on you. Humans do not understand what it means to be created for death."

"We call them the nonbred, Misha."

He opened the door. Russian music from loudspeakers and noises of machinery filled the tunnel and forced me to cover my ears when we entered what looked like a main workshop, with huge metal hoppers that lined the walls and rested over massive mixing vats. A thick dust filled the air and Misha handed me a filter mask. Every few seconds kiln furnaces blasted jets of flame and I wondered about the danger of explosion, the errant ignition of millions, billions, of tiny metal particles, and then noticed that the walls had been scorched at least once to leave black streaks that someone had started to clean but not bothered to finish. *Explosions,* I thought, *might be commonplace.* Misha motioned for the machinery to stop and when the room went silent, twenty girls stood from where they had been gathered, hidden in a corner, all dressed in loose brown coveralls.

*Color,* I realized. These girls had dyed their hair in a sea of varied shades. My head was bald, already covered with dust that I wiped off with a shaking hand, and as one of my sisters walked toward us I stared, transfixed by the blue of her hair which fell nearly to her shoulders. Even with the drugs, which hadn't begun to wear off, I felt a sharp pang of regret, a wish that it had ended for me on the river because Megan would have looked beautiful with blue hair; it had been her favorite color.

"This," said Misha, "is Heather."

She didn't look at me. Russian streamed from her lips when Heather opened them, sparking a feeling of envy in me, and when the two had finished talking Misha turned.

"Heather says she doesn't have a free billet for you, Ubitza, that she wants you in the mines. I told her that's not what we agreed on but she's holding firm, and says you can earn one if you want. I suggest you take the offer. There's nothing I can do unless I call in a human officer, and that isn't a wise thing to do. Not for me or you."

I shook my head. "How do I earn a slot, Misha?"

"*Ubitza.*" She spat it through a filter mask in English, the tone sarcastic. Heather stared at me now, both eyes empty and black, pupils so dilated that I had trouble thinking of them as anything other than puddles of oil. "Murderer. I can only imagine the depth of your faith, a first-generation Germline who served to the very end of her term. You earn a spot in this factory, a position on-shift, by creating a vacancy. By killing one of my workers."

"My sisters?" I asked. "You would allow one of your own to be killed?"

"You're assuming that you'll win. And you aren't one of my own; we're all captured units here, second genera- tion and better than the first. Besides…" She pointed at my feet. "I heard that you haven't gotten used to those yet."

Misha laughed. "I've seen her knife-work, Heather, and this one isn't like you, hasn't gotten fat off vodka and whoring. She's a match. Ubitza is still intact."

"Fuck intact, Misha, you're as new to this place as she is." Heather smiled at me, a gesture that made me want to run at the same time that it calmed my nerves, triggering something inside to prepare since fear would only prevent me from doing what needed to be done. "Do you want a slot?"

I nodded and Heather grinned.

*"Emma."*

Another girl stepped forward, walking toward us.

"Heather," I asked, "you said you were all captured, that you didn't fulfill your service term. Does that mean you can still control nerve impulses, control pain?"

She laughed and slapped Emma on the back. "Yes."

"But in terms of combat experience," I said, bending slightly at the knees, an imperceptible amount, my muscles tightening and preparing for what I was about to try. Both ankles felt as though they would shatter. Without the ability to control nerves, I ignored the agony, sensing the room begin to spin as I prayed for my plan to work. "How much experience have you had? How many battles?"

Heather was about to answer when I leapt. My legs unloaded their pent energy, sending me in a dive at Emma, who stepped into a fighting stance and raised her guard a fraction of a second too late. It had been a long time. Months if not years had passed since I'd seen the expression that only comes when someone knows they are about to die and I couldn't imagine the thoughts that must have run through Emma's mind in the moment just before my shoulder impacted against her nose. There were no words to describe such a look. It was enough to touch off a sensation of regret for having to kill one of my own, almost making me stop in midair, except for the fact that I had studied her as the girl approached. Her legs had gone soft, and her face looked full, the fleshiness of relaxation and excess. You knew with a glimpse that Emma, like all of them, had lost her way. This was a prodigal moment. So when my arms wrapped themselves around her neck, and my legs kicked up to leverage myself into a flip, pulling her over so that Emma's back began its last arch, I sensed that it was a favor, a necessity, her penance. She would earn a death in combat. Killing Emma was a holy thing, an act of charity that Megan would have seen as my duty.

The girl's neck snapped twice before I landed on my back, echoing throughout the workshop like shotgun blasts.

"Ubitza!" Misha shouted, raising both arms over his head as he laughed.

Heather looked furious. "That was unfair, Misha, I hadn't started the combat. She cheated."

"No, Heather." Misha's voice had gone quiet, his smile gone. "We can't fill two empty slots, and I need you to meet production quota for the week. I can have *you* replaced, though, if you'd prefer that. Now we can consult with the hu—the nonbred if you like."

"Let me see the back of her head," Heather said, "If she has the mark, she can't work, you know the rules. Lilies go directly to experimentation, straight to Exogene."

"She's not a Lily. I've seen it."

But Heather moved before I could stand again, grabbing me by the arm, and without thinking, I reacted, used her to pull myself up and regain my footing. I launched into her then, knocking her off her feet at the same time I grabbed for her larynx.

*"No!"* Misha shouted, forcing me to pause before I crushed Heather's throat. "She's a trustee, so if you kill her I am obliged to have you executed." Misha pulled my hand from her neck, and then turned my back to the group, forcing my head down so they could see it clearly. "There, the number one. This is no Lily."

Heather spat on the ground. "Fine. She works. But the first time she screws up, this one goes to the mines or worse."

Misha opened a nearby cabinet, pulled a set of brown coveralls out, and handed them to me. They smelled of bleach. He watched while I dressed, grabbing me each time I tottered on the verge of collapse.

"Amazing, Ubitza," he whispered. "I never saw it coming. Where did you learn to move like that?"

I shook my head. "I've been asked that before, and never had an answer. Killing has always come naturally to me, Misha, and I never had to learn how to do it."

The main barracks had been carved out of rock, a hundred meters under the factory, and two elevators and an emergency shaft serviced them directly from the ceramic workshops. Its ceiling barely allowed one to stand. Bunks filled the chamber so that narrow passageways provided just enough room to traverse, and a haze of cigarette smoke made breathing and seeing difficult propositions, in addition to adding stale nicotine to a mixture of smells that combined latrines with unwashed workers. I pushed through, looking for an empty bed. My ankles ached and trembled, threatening with each step to give out, but walking upright mattered in the face of my sisters, their mental state unknown, where a sign of weakness might provoke an assault. And the next time they would be ready for my surprises. A hush fell over the chamber; as I passed, the girls whispered that it had been me who killed Emma, who defied Heather, me who had almost crushed their leader's throat just because she had touched me. It was like looking into a menagerie of Megans, each one a little different, each one potentially hostile. A scar here, a different hair color there, they all reminded me of her so that by the time I found an empty bunk their stares had brought tears, made it so that I had to roll onto the mattress and shut my eyes, waiting for the thoughts to leave. Megan had never stared at me with such a lack of recognition.

The bunk I had chosen, its top and bottom racks empty, rested in the corner farthest from the elevators and for a moment it felt like a foolish one to choose, one that would trap me if they came. But being cornered didn't matter; in the event they all attacked there would be no escape regardless of where I was, because having to wait for an elevator or unlock the emergency shaft would take too much time anyway. In a corner, at least surprise would be harder for them to achieve.

A girl called from the bunk next to me, and my eyes snapped open as I recalled Megan's voice.

"You could have taken any bunk you wanted," she said, "maybe even Heather's. If she lived here."

The girl had short blond hair, but a scrollwork pattern covered her face with black lines, tattoos in a labyrinth of swirls and sharp corners so dense that her face seemed more ink than skin. I smiled with relief at the sight: she didn't remind me of Megan at all.

"Why do you think that?" I asked.

"We've all heard the story, that maybe you're a Lily, someone with the courage to stand up to her. Resolve enough to rip out her larynx. I barely remember having so much resolve."

I shook my head. "I'm confused. We're all the same,

born of the atelier. You should see the duty in killing one so far off the path, the satisfaction, and that it has less to do with courage or resolve than it does with calculus. She is broken, an abomination. Why haven't any of you killed Heather yourselves?"

"Because we know better. Maybe we even like her. It's different for the ones who flee at the end of their term, first generation like you. For us, the second-generation ones they capture who are less than seventeen equivalent, the Russians have a special program."

I propped myself up on two elbows. "What program?"

"Rape." She paused to light a cigarette and then snapped her lighter off. "And some truth—enough anyway to show us that mindless fools like you are the danger, not Heather. There is no God, Germline-One."

"That's a lie," I said. But my words felt empty, no matter how they sounded, because she didn't speak like any of the girls I had known, not even the new ones we had lost so long ago at Tamdybulak. It occurred to me then: this girl was the veteran in Zeya, in their factories, but not me. It was my first day. Deep down I wondered if maybe she was right, and that this discussion would prove me the idiot in an unfamiliar world.

"What would you know about lies?" the girl asked. "Ever been raped without end for months? It tends to open your mind to new ideas, like maybe there is no plan, no point to all this and maybe it's acceptable to do what you need to survive. It's why we hate you—all the first-generation ones. You're too stupid to do anything but die."

"What's your name?"

She shrugged. "Margaret. I know yours already, Ubitza. Catherine." Something beeped on her wrist and Margaret glanced down before stubbing out the cigarette. She stood to pull on her clothes. "Lights out in ten minutes, Ubitza, welcome to Zeya."

"Where are you going?"

"To earn some tranq tabs. How many did they supply you with? The usual?"

"Misha issued me three."

"Three seems hardly like the old days. I remember being supplied with all the drugs we could eat, all you'd ever want."

"Where are you going to work, Margaret? How do you earn extra tranq tabs? Misha said the factories were a good place to work, that there would be plenty of tranquilizers." Already I felt the last one wearing off, my hands shaking with the onset of fear and the prospect of hallucinations making me grip the bed's blanket.

"He wasn't lying, there *are* plenty of drugs, but only for those willing to earn them. One tranq tab for every Popov you fuck. Here, killing gets you nothing, Ubitza, because you need a different set of skills, ones that it sounds like you've yet to master."

"You relate with them, the boys? Misha?"

Margaret laughed and had enough trouble stopping that other girls shouted for her to shut up. Already the lights had dimmed and would soon go out. It was the only indication of night we had.

"*Relate*. We don't relate, Ubitza, we fuck and screw, and Misha doesn't *screw* anyone. None of the boys do, only the nonbred men and some of their women—the researchers and their guards. Their boys, their genetics, have no testicles. Our people abandoned male genetics in favor of females to deal with problems of aggression, but the Russians? They created an army of eunuch warriors. I'm off to see a young nonbred doctor and he's not as bad as some, sometimes gives me two tabs if I do a good job."

Margaret began moving away through the bunks when the lights finally clicked off. I called after her. "Margaret, I need your help!"

"With what, Ubitza?"

"Russian; I need you to teach me Russian."

"Fine. You'll be dead before I can teach you anyway. Nobody gets by on three a day here. Not even those with mountains of resolve."

Margaret and I were driving an electric truck when a Russian experiment went wrong. The engine whined as we climbed the final ramp to the surface and three trailers clanked behind us, slamming over the concrete curb and into the open where the sun made me squint; I hadn't seen it in almost a year. Three-meter snow banks lay on either side of a narrow path that had been cut through drifts near the main tunnel entrance and we drove along it, careful to swerve out of the way of trucks winding in the opposite direction, coming out of the railyard. By now, we spoke only Russian. Mine was broken, slow, the language of a child, but it was enough to get by and with the basics my vocabulary grew every day. Although responding was often difficult, I understood anything said. Misha had sent us topside to collect the factory supplies and I closed my eyes, leaning my head back so the sunlight soaked into my skin, warming it with direct rays that instantly lifted my mood and made me smile.

"How long?" asked Margaret.

"How long since what?"

She pointed to the sky. "Since that?"

"Since my arrival. I don't know, exactly."

"Everyone needs the sun, once in a while. The sky. When I see it I wonder, how much longer I will live, is a life underground really worth much?"

I shrugged. "It is where we are. You do what you have to."

She nodded and gunned the engine; the truck fought its way up the icy incline but slid side to side, struggling against the combination of gravity and reduced friction. One of the cars scraped a bank. Piles of snow collapsed onto our vehicle, forcing me to curse and sit up so I could wipe it off, the snow's cold reminding me of my first day off the train when everything about Zeya had seemed so new. Now it was all there was, so that it had become harder to remember war, remember that I had once meant to go beyond Zeya, with Megan; but Megan didn't visit anymore. Escape for something like freedom had become the dream of an ignorant child, a thing to remember and laugh at over vodka.

"Heather hasn't bothered you since your arrival," Margaret continued. We made it over the hill and began our descent, the railyards spreading out below us in the middle of a man-made forest—chimneys that stuck from the ground, their pipes spewing exhaust.

"I know."

"Don't you think it's strange?" Margaret asked. "She hasn't stopped hating you, and there are rumors that she and her closest will try something soon."

"I'm hallucinating more," I said, changing the subject. "I save my tablets for my shift, so I won't black out in the factory, but they come at night. Not dreams."

"Nightmares?"

"Not nightmares. I go back to the war or the atelier, and it feels like I'll never come back."

Margaret laughed, the noise immediately swallowed by the screaming engine and absorbed in the high snow banks. "Why would you want to come back to Zeya? To this? Don't worry about them, Ubitza."

"If I have one on shift, Heather will send me to the mines."

"No," she said, "that wouldn't happen. If you spoiled on shift, Heather would have a reason to kill you—or to send you to laboratories. Probably the former, though."

We pulled onto the concrete platform next to the train tracks, parking behind scores of other trucks who had also come for supplies. Margaret turned off the engine. She was about to say something when an alarm sounded in the distance; we both stepped from the truck and stood, squinting against the glare of sun on snow, trying to see. Other girls, from the mines or one of a hundred factories, stepped from their vehicles and did the same.

"What is that?" Margaret asked. A far-off portal leading to an underground section had burst open, and something emerged—a black shape that disappeared with a shimmer.

"It's coming," I said. "Are there weapons here?"

"What, Ubitza? What is it?"

I pushed Margaret toward the flatcars, and then waved for the other girls to follow. "Under the railcars, now."

After I had taken cover, lying on ice and feeling it burn through my factory overalls, the cold made me shiver to the point where I forgot and tried, unsuccessfully, to regulate body temperature. The others must have been second

generation; none of them shivered. Soon we heard a thump-
ing noise, the footsteps of a giant, which grew louder with
each passing second.

"What is it?" Margaret asked again.

"One of their powered armor experiments. But maybe
the alarms mean something went wrong."

Seven missiles streaked overhead, and one of them
slammed into a nearby boxcar, shooting splinters of metal
and wood into the ground. One of the girls to my left
screamed. I glanced over and saw her, shredded, a pool of
blood growing in the snow but I looked away when the
ground beneath us began vibrating. We watched as a cam-
ouflaged shape approached, its chameleon skin turning
the air into something like a mirage so that I couldn't tell
the thing's shape, only that it headed straight for us. It
reached the platform at the same time a rocket impacted,
striking its rear and sending hot metal to hiss on the ice-
covered concrete. One of the armor suits, the same one
shown to me by Misha, materialized then, as it crashed to
the ground in front of us. Its shoulders sparked. The thing
was close enough to touch and I reached out toward its
helmet just as teams of armored Russian soldiers swarmed
in, their weapons pointing at me and voices screaming to
keep my distance, their officer pushing through to kneel
beside it. He flicked open a panel and punched a series of
keys until the carapace hissed open to send a wave of
green fluid around his feet and reveal the suit's occupant,
who was face up, empty eye sockets connected to the suit
via a series of fiber cables. When I saw the face, I threw up.

"God above," said Margaret. "It's one of us. A Lily."

We didn't stay to watch. But the memory of her—
armless and legless with tubes and wires that seemed to

Margaret started the truck and moved us slowly, taking us deeper underground.

"Everyone speaks of Thailand—of going to Korea and catching a boat from there to Bangkok—because in Thailand a number of us have found freedom. But take me with you. And stay out of Heather's way; if you kill her, they'll put you in the laboratory, and if she kills you...I should never have become your friend, Ubitza. Should have stuck with just whoring, with looking out for myself."

"Then that's where we'll go," I said. And it was a relief to have at least part of a plan.

# SIX

# Forest for the Trees

*All of God's children spoil, all doubt. Repent*
*or the end will come slowly, with vengeance*
*as a sword from my mouth.*

MODERN COMBAT MANUAL
REVELATIONS 2:16

It's good to finally see you like this," said Misha. We both spoke Russian now. I sat in his office, a rock-hewn cubicle with a single computer on a desk, its holo display showing the factory's progress toward the month's quota. He pointed at it. "This is my war these days."

"Grow a hand," I suggested, "return to the real thing."

"I'm too soft. You're the only one that still exercises, still trains. The other girls talk about it, you know, call you insane when it's they who have gone insane. Maybe even me."

"Heather tried for me a week ago. On shift change, she and two others attacked when I got off the elevator."

Misha sighed and lit a cigarette. The room's ventilator sensed the smoke and kicked into high automatically, sucking the cloud into a vent. "I know. So kill her and be done with it."

"Then I'll die, or be sent to Exogene."

"So what?" Misha flicked off his computer and stood,

then pounded against the rock with a fist. "This is just rock! This is all shit, wasn't what I wanted after all, isn't that funny? For a whole war, we begged for this, dreamt of it, our own piece of Russia. And when we get here, guess what? More of the same: humans, this time not even warriors, but bureaucrats *disguised* as warriors, calling the shots like big pinecones. There was never a place we would call our own, only more service to Mother Russia and more service to the nonbred incompetents. Remember the songs on the train? That was our dream. A moment on a train, a moment of Brodyaga and maybe some of the Jew song and cigarettes, only back then we didn't appreciate it for what it was."

"What was it, Misha?"

"Freedom. Our own little piece of Russia, for just a few days."

It had been sitting in my mind, crouched like a panther about to leap, and still I hadn't let it out because nobody, not even Margaret, could have predicted how Misha would react when he heard the reason for my visit. Margaret was waiting in the barracks, terrified. But now that I saw him, like this, it became clear that it was time.

"I'm leaving, Misha."

He turned from the wall and stared at me. "What?"

"Zeya. The factory. I'm leaving with Margaret, to head southeast. She says that if you make it to Korea, you can head south and grab a ship to Thailand. There's real freedom there, Misha."

"So go." He sat again and turned the computer back on, punching at the keys like they were his new enemies.

"I can't go. Not without your help. The snow, the forests, it's like you said: we won't make it far."

Misha glanced up at me. "I know what you're about to ask, but do *you*? Do you have any idea what they'd do if they found out I supplied you with food or extra tranquilizers, let alone a knife?"

"We're all dying here, Misha, even you. Please help us get the things we need."

"Little murderer." He tapped a finger against his chin. While Misha considered the request, my heart rate jumped when my thoughts turned to the possibility that he wouldn't help us, that he'd turn us in. What then? I hadn't been ready for death since I left the battlefield, and Margaret, who had far less courage than I, would have even more trouble. What made it worse was how she'd trusted me, as if I were a Lily and there could be no questioning my success—only she wouldn't get the truth until Misha and a group of humans arrived to haul her to the mines or the labs; she wouldn't understand the truth that had taken me so long to discover, and only then after I'd watched Megan disappear into the muddy river: that there are no certainties. The fact was, I realized, God's plans sometimes didn't include you in them, or sometimes called for you to die, and that was if He even existed. Some of the girls' opinions had rubbed off on me. Prayer had turned into a thing hated, a joke, so that instead of asking for glory, my few prayers lately had focused on showing me a sign that He existed in the first place. But I trembled then not because of my fears, but because I didn't want to fail Margaret like I had Megan.

Misha smiled. "Fuck it. I'll get you what you need. Armor, a couple of weapons, tranqs, food, and fuel cells. There's one of us who came before, maybe the first one, who they allowed a special dispensation to live alone in the woods with the wolves. I'll have it all sent to him with a note. His name is Lev."

"Where is he?"

Misha tapped at his computer, changing the display to a map. He pointed toward a small yellow dot, northeast of the city, where it blinked in the midst of what looked like the largest forest in the universe, a single shade of green that went to the very edge of his display. Misha then pointed at the mountains. "We're here, and this is the service exit where you leave to pick up factory supplies. Take the main road to the northeast but then leave when you see forest, and make your way east until you're four kilometers inside the trees. Then head due north. And don't be seen; I don't know anymore what they'd do if the nonbred realized you had escaped; maybe they wouldn't trust the snow and ice to take care of things. Study this."

After a few minutes I nodded and he switched back to his charts, motioning for me to leave. "Get out."

"What about you, Misha. What happens if you don't make your quota because we ran?"

"Fuck the quota. They called my number."

It took a second for me to realize what he meant. "Exogene? You'll go to the workshop? Isn't that what you wanted?"

"Yeah." Misha stubbed out his cigarette and flicked away the butt. "Exactly what I wanted. Except that was a lie too. All these people know are lies—which lies will curry favor with Moscow, which ones will curry favor with the supply clerks. Favors and lies are the currency of Zeya, Little Murderer, not honor. Not war."

I shook my head. "I'm confused."

"Of course you are, and you should be. Listen. They

perfected the system months ago, the armor and the techniques. We've been promised something that doesn't exist: a chance to return to the field. Why doesn't it exist? Because all these experiments have been designed only to tweak things a little so they don't waste their new units on such tiny experiments, ones designed to see how they can squeeze more power out of new fuel cells, or improve the cycling rate of coolant. Instead they use *us* as guinea pigs, so they don't waste their next generation of fighters. I've seen the new ones in their tanks. Little men who aren't men, little men with big heads and no arms or legs, who won't know a life other than one encased in ceramic, wired to machines. They never intended to field the new armor systems with real warriors like you or me, but with half-human animals, created in someone else's image. Certainly not your God's." Misha stopped talking then and laughed. "So go."

"You could come with us," I suggested.

"This is still my country. I won't run to Thailand or anywhere. But you have to leave tomorrow morning because I'll be gone by then, in the workshop. I'll have your supplies delivered tonight. Nobody ever questions a supply to Lev, and nobody ever inspects me or my brothers, so don't worry. Your things will be there. Do you know the route to take, to Korea?"

I shook my head. "I know what they put in my head, but the information is only as good as the Americans had; your information, Russian data, would be better."

"The East Asian War took much of the Kamchatka Peninsula. When those North Korean idiots decided to take a second try at capturing all of South Korea, China worked with them, making a play for Eastern Siberia. It was the only time we'd allied with your country since the ancient wars, and look what it cost us. Your president, our president, both drooled at the thought of untapped North Korean resources, so as soon as you and Japan attacked through Korea, we counterattacked the Chinese, not counting on the number of nuclear weapons Beijing would use. The Chinese irradiated all of Kamchatka and our major ports, leveled Sakhalin Island; the North Koreans did the same to all of Japan—even to their own shitty country."

Misha saw me nodding and smiled. "I know you know all this, Ubitza, but there's a point. China will be to your southwest much of the way, to your west when you turn south and head straight for Korea. It is farther than you think. Make for the border crossing at Khasan and until then don't stray east or you'll find yourself in a nuclear wasteland, staring at the ocean as your DNA dissolves. Remember: we may have driven the Chinese underground after the war, slaughtered so many between Russian and American nukes that nobody could have survived. But they did. So if you wander too far west, whatever Chinese filth is attacking our outposts could take you. None of *these* dangers will be on your suit's map. Head south, and stay in the middle, between China and the sea."

I was about to leave and close the door behind me when Misha said one last thing: "And be careful in North Korea, Murderer. Everything is gone. The fields are still hot and there, even dust is an enemy."

"Thank you, Misha," I said, "I'll never forget this," and then I shut the door.

The factory was quiet except for the popping of the sintering presses, still cooling from the day's work, and dim battery lights provided just enough light for me to weave my way through the machinery, which rose from the factory floor in a forest of dark shapes. Something moved. I stopped and crouched, momentarily grateful for the titanium in my feet, which had turned them into weapons; a single impact had nearly broken Heather's back in our last encounter. Then, without warning, I felt the beginnings of a dream, a nightmare. Machinery began dissolving at its edges and with a sense of terror I realized that I had taken my last tranq tab six hours ago, its effect long since worn off, and nothing stood between me and the abyss into which I now slid. In front of me stepped Heather and two others. Her voice fading quickly, she asked, "What's wrong, Murderer? I want to finish our dance."


Two girls crouched, locked in a kind of haka-dance, each waiting for their opening. We had been pulled off the line for refitting where the white coats required us to spend as much free time training as possible, and this was a knife fighting exercise, with Sasha and Francesca its combatants.

Sasha feinted and chopped with her empty hand, barely missing Francesca's neck, but it left her knife arm exposed. Francesca saw the opening. Her hand blurred, precise in its movement, and the blade punched through Sasha's elbow joint with a loud crack. I saw it then. *Hatred*. Every once in a while, one of us went bad, a different kind of spoiling in which the girl ceased being part of our family and hated everyone and everything. You could see it in eyes like Sasha's, which had gone glassy a long time before this, dilated and empty, telegraphing that she wasn't stable.

The two circled again, watching for another opening. Sasha stumbled. She was favoring her wounded arm and hadn't noticed a small rock that now snagged on the outside of her foot, sending her off balance. I never even saw Francesca move. In less than a second, she had slammed into her opponent, sending Sasha onto her back, and stopped her knife point only inches away from the girl's chin.

"You fought well," said Francesca; she stood to offer a hand.

Sasha grinned. "And also you." But her smile disappeared, and instead of taking Francesca's hand, the girl slammed her knife through the center of it, the sharp end snapping through her palm in an instant. "Forgive my clumsiness. I slipped."

We attacked. All of us moved in and began pummeling Sasha, kicking and punching at her face, the only portion of her body that was unarmored. When it was over, Sasha had lost a tooth, and both eyes swelled shut as she laughed and rolled in the sand, spitting blood and cursing us in mumbles that made me uneasy, a language that one would never understand but which conveyed a sensation of hatred. She was gone. Medical technicians took both girls to the medical bots, and for a while we forgot about it.

A week later we waited in a hangar, where a technician stood at a podium. He dragged the canvas shroud off a bulky object next to him and gestured for us to gather around. Both Sasha and Francesca had returned, each of them standing on opposite ends of the group.

"This is a newer version of the stealth fusion cutter, and, when properly operated, it will cut through hard rock at a slightly faster rate than our previous models, at about sixty meters per hour. You'll get the same tunnel, cylindrical, one meter in diameter. Also, instead of grinding the spall, this unit breaks it into small enough chunks so that they get taken back along the muck line as-is; there will be almost no sound to reveal your position.

"But even with these capabilities, reports from the field suggest that our stealth tunnels are being detected through their heat signature, long before our sappers break into underground target areas. Your enemy can see the rock heat up, an hour prior to arrival, even with such a small thermal cross-section, so in order to counteract the problem, we've developed a simple technique. Once you get close to your target destination—about a hundred meters from an enemy tunnel—you shut down the resistor elements. Coolant will still flow and speed up the chilling process in the surrounding rock. Wait for temperatures to go down, dig another ten meters, and do it again. You'll stop boring a meter away from your target tunnel, same as before, and complete the incursion using shaped charges. There's no way to eliminate the thermal bloom completely, but this approach should at least reduce it, make it harder to spot."

The machine sat on small wheels and resembled an elongated fifty-five gallon drum. Like the large borers, the front heat-probes consisted of an alloy ring, inside of which were hundreds of smaller spikes. Most of the unit consisted of fuel cells, but a power line could also be used, which this one did, its thick black cable snaking alongside the muck hose to our rear.

The man glanced at his watch. "OK, chow time. Eat up. We'll be headed out to the ruins after lunch for some practice using live charges, starting with..." He searched the group and then stopped. "*You*. Which one are you?"

"Francesca."

He clapped his hands. "Excellent. Francesca will be first. Dismissed."

We were silent while heading to the mess hall, and everything seemed fine, but I couldn't help but think that something was about to happen, an itch in my head telling me that it would all go wrong. I sat at a table with Megan and scanned the room.

"I don't see Sasha, Megan. Do you trust her?"

"No, but who does? We'll have to deal with her, though, this cannot continue." She smiled at me then and squeezed my hand under the table. "Do not worry, Catherine, we will be back on the line in a few days, and maybe Sasha will be fine once we have an enemy again. She is good in the field."

"Death and faith."

We finished eating, and jogged to the ruins as a single group. Sasha was already there. After everyone had assembled, technicians lined us up in four columns, opened the backs of several APCs, and showed us the cargo areas, which had been filled with brand new combat suits, all coated with opalescent black polymer, dark and yet glimmering.

"These are sapper suits," the technician said. "It will be an improvement over your current issue. Virtually the same as normal combat suits, but these ones have a guidance unit and navigation computer that interface directly with the stealth borer so you can guide yourself in three dimensions, underground. We don't have much time—and it's incredibly simple—so you will learn as you go." He pulled a flexible cable from the back of a stealth borer and jacked it into a forearm port. "All you have to do is plug in, power up, and the commands and route are displayed in your helmet."

The man pointed to the stealth borer at his side. It had already been positioned in a starter hole, and oriented downward into sand. "Francesca?" After she had plugged in and turned on the power, he nodded, then turned to us.

"Good. Her computer should display a menu now. Franc-esca, select 'activate.' Once you've done this, the borer will begin heating and you'll see a preprogrammed route on your heads-up display. Head for the empty storage tunnel twenty meters north, ten meters down."

The hole began to glow red as the borer slowly sank. Francesca held her free hand against her forearm to guide it, and, a few minutes later, disappeared into the hole. A short while later, she backed out of the tunnel, waited for the boring unit to emerge, and then reentered.

"Place the charges in a circular pattern." The technician spoke into a handset, watching Francesca's progress on a computer. "Good. Whenever you're ready."

"Fire, fire, fire," she warned.

None of us expected what happened next.

The charges—usually harmless to those in combat suits—touched off as planned, but the technician fell back with a scream, torn apart by something that had flown from the tunnel. Nobody said anything. I started down the tunnel after Francesca, but Megan grabbed me. "We don't know what's going on. Let *men* do this."

Minutes later, the corpsmen pulled Francesca free, and we saw what had happened. The front of her suit was gone. None of us recognized the girl, couldn't, because her torso and face spasmed in a mass that seemed more like raw meat than anything else. Flechettes still protruded from the back of her carapace.

"Look," said Megan, pointing at Sasha. The girl grinned as the men loaded Francesca and the dead technician into an APC.

"Sabotage," I said, and Megan nodded. "We take care of this?"

Megan nodded again. It wasn't the first time we had to deal with one of our own, and I had already decided: *I would enjoy this one*. We finished the exercise, exhausted and hot, but I had become happy with the anticipation of what would come. In retrospect I should have mourned Sasha—we all should have, her disintegration wasn't her fault and on the battlefield she had killed almost as many as me. But that wasn't how I felt at the time.

After lights out, six of us rolled from our racks and snuck toward Sasha's. She was awake. Two grabbed her arms, another two grabbed her legs, and Megan and I stood on either side of her head. My knife was invisible in the darkness.

"It is time," said Megan.

Sasha chuckled. "You will all rot in hell. None of you are destined for His side, how can cowards ascend?" She spat at Megan. "Francesca was weak, I did you a favor, eliminated a—"

I didn't let her finish. My blade fell so hard against her neck that it almost removed her head.

Megan and the others relaxed, except for one, a replacement. "Won't we be disciplined for this?"

"No," said Megan. "Our family must be pure, and it is good, because tonight we have *honored* Him, not offended. The technicians will not only understand this, but expect it. Death is the fate for all of us, and a shortened life is no cause for punishment."

"She died like a coward," said Misha. "They all did. All three. Begging for forgiveness, another chance, just like the nonbred. How did we come to this, Murderer? How can we so quickly forget our purpose?"

Misha knelt on the floor, bare to his waist, around which he had tied the top half of his coveralls. In the dim light I saw blood. It pooled around me where I lay, soaked into my outfit, and when I moved, the pain in my side suggested that some of the blood was mine and that it still flowed from a deep cut. My ribs ached. It took me a moment to remember and when I sat up it was to see Heather and the others, motionless beside us, their necks slit and eyes open so they all stared in a way that made me look away.

Misha flipped his knife and caught it again. "That felt good, Murderer. Why didn't you defend yourself from them?"

"The spoiling."

"You hallucinated?"

I nodded, ashamed.

"Well then it's good you're leaving, because if you did that on the factory floor they'd take you to the labs."

"What will you do?" I asked. "Now that you've killed three girls the humans will need replacements, won't they be angry?"

"What would they do? Send *me* to the labs?"

Misha grinned and the thought of leaving him there made me sad; it was ironic to think that among all the people in Zeya, the one person most like me was a boy, a Russian, my enemy.

"You will spoil out there too, Murderer," he said. A spark entered his eyes, barely noticeable in the electric lights but there, cold, as if there were two Mishas: one a friendly boy, the other something demonic and with the conviction of infinite hatred. His eyes told me to run. I'd seen it in him before, in the factory, when something Heather or one of the other girls did that displeased him, made him furious. It was easy to forget when Misha was personable that he was dangerous; this wasn't something tame and the look reminded me of myself, proof that I wasn't sitting next to a friend but a shark who, on occasion, became frenzied when he smelled blood. I moved away until I felt a mixing tank at my back.

"Let me end it for you here," Misha suggested. "This is no life for you or me."

"I don't want to go that way."

"Oh. Still, you must have wondered. I sent the requisition for your supplies, but the reason I came here was to stop you. It occurred to me that I could prevent you from making a mistake. I believe in your God, I think. Maybe he sent me to take you back, place you at His side."

Misha flipped the knife again, gripping it tightly when it landed, and leaped to his feet. He moved toward me.

"Don't, Misha," I said.

"What better way to go? In combat with the Murderer, best of the best, right? This is what we were meant for, and didn't you tell us the story that night, about how we were killers first, never test subjects? You had it right I think, Murderer, you convinced me of the truth and I will not go to the lab for some useless experiment when I could die in combat. Here."

Misha flicked his hand and the blade of a second knife flashed as it tumbled through the air, finally clanking onto the rock floor at my feet. He stopped and waited.

"Take it."

I shook my head. "Misha, let's have a cigarette. Maybe

some vodka. You've never told me your stories, never let me know what it was like for you at the front."

"*It was all shit!* Don't ask me what I saw, what the human soldiers did to us, to my brothers."

Misha lunged and I rolled, picking the knife up as I went, and then grunted in reflex at the pain in my side. I pushed my free hand against the wound. Blood seeped out from the cloth, between my fingers, and felt warm in the conditioned air, made me think of summertime and happiness despite the reality of my situation.

"You're still fast," said Misha, circling. "Even wounded and you're fast. They promised us something, Murderer, but they didn't deliver. Instead they gave me soft girls, broken ones, where I've spent the last year getting weaker, infected by their pessimism, their lack of will. Even being among the humans would be better than this. You were the one reminder of what we are, a contrast, a blade of grass in the desert. If I take you, it means I am still something."

I saw him shift his weight, flex, getting ready for a leap; my mind went blank. Instead of thinking, I relaxed, let the tank's teachings have free reign of my nervous system, and almost immediately felt some muscles bind up, get ready for the move, while others relaxed completely. Misha charged and then rolled, swinging his knife upward at my gut, but I was already gone with a jump, sliding across his back and behind to bring my knifepoint against his neck. The tip pressed against his jugular.

"Stop this, Misha."

He dropped his knife. "You are too good for the factories, Murderer. Too good for the labs. We never should have taken you from the field, should have forced you back into war where you belong. So kill me. Show me I am right and send me home, save me from one more honorless experiment. Show me that you can still kill."

It took no thought. By now the furnaces had cooled so that they ceased their popping, the only sounds coming from the rattle of air-handling systems shutting on and off, and the drip of water from leaking pipes far overhead, their drops splatting on the floor. At first I thought water had poured onto my hand. But with only a shift of my thoughts came the realization that my wrist had flicked, sinking the tip into his artery and then side to side, opening it to the air so that I now imagined Misha's pain shooting out along with his blood. He was in the air now. Around me. The body slumped to the ground, almost empty, and he grinned a last grin, winking one eye.

"It is true then. Your heart is as black as it needs to be." And then Misha was gone.

So much blood had spilled and mixed with water that I slid along the floor, stopping only at Heather's body so I could fashion a bandage from her coveralls. A long strip of fabric tore free. I unzipped my clothing and tied the cloth around my side, wincing at the sight of a four-inch gash, white bone visible beneath, and then headed for the elevators. They took forever to arrive. The downward trip to my barracks lasted an eternity, in which Misha's face refused to leave my mind, took its place alongside Megan's, and even though I suspected the act of killing had made them both happy, I screamed and screamed with horror. With each scream it became clear that something was wrong: I couldn't hear. Everything had gone silent. These were the shouts of futility, ones useless to everyone, even me, so that although my vocal chords ached and shook in my throat, no noise came out, not even when I slumped to the floor, drained. There had been so much blood. Blood had never bothered me before and plenty of it had been that of my sisters, and so when the elevator lowered into the shaft opening, and Margaret jumped in to pound at the button to move upward, I smiled and stood to lean against her. She spoke, but it took several seconds before her words came through.

"What is wrong with you, Catherine, what happened up there?"

"Misha is dead. So is Heather."

Margaret ran a hand through her hair and pushed me back against the elevator wall. "Then we're through. We may as well report to the labs right now. Turn ourselves in."

"You go to the labs. I'm going to the forest."

"Catherine, you killed him. A boy. A factory head. There isn't any running now, no going on."

I grabbed her throat and slammed Margaret against the wall, the elevator clanking and sparking with the motion, which sent it to scrape against rock. The knife was still in my hand.

"Do you want to go with them? I do. I can send you there, will have no problem doing it because I've killed for my entire existence and it's the only thing I'm good at. There doesn't even have to be a thought; my body will act on impulse alone, the question 'Should I kill?' an after-thought. But you know what the funny thing is, Margaret? The funny thing is that I am too much of a coward to die. So I run."

When I let go of her, Margaret nodded. "We'll run." She pulled a canvas bag from inside her coveralls and opened it, pushing something into my mouth. A tranq tab.

"Thank you," I said.

"I suspect you'll need it, Murderer. It will be a long night, and we aren't dressed for the forest, aren't dressed for the Siberian winter."

"It's winter?" I asked. "How can you tell it's winter?"

Margaret laughed, reaching for my hand to loosen my grip on the knife, slipping it into one of my pockets. "It's always winter in Zeya. Didn't anyone teach you that?"

She was right. We moved through the maze of tunnels, which by now were familiar, and once we cleared the service entrance, a night wind whipped up a deep valley, slamming into us with a chill that ripped my breath away. I folded both arms and ran. We jogged down the road, winding through the mountains, and each step jolted my side to make me light-headed from the combined pain and blood loss until I felt another hallucination coming. I grabbed at Margaret to slow her down.

"Misha ordered supplies for us," I said, dragging her to a stop. "It's important you understand in case I fade out. Take us down the road and leave it when you see the forest, then head due east into the trees for four kilometers before turning north. We're to meet someone named Lev."

"Please, Catherine, it's after ten p.m.; we have to *move*."

Our units moved out at ten p.m. Megan and I watched as the girls spread over the wreckage of Shymkent's northern suburbs and then crouched in holes, behind concrete, or under scraps of metal, our sisters waiting for their order to move up. The barrel of my Maxwell carbine lay on a block of rubble and vibrated softly in my trembling hands. *Quiet and eerie.* Marine units, far below us underground, were boring toward enemy lines and had to be getting close by now. We'd get the order soon, I thought, and a few moments later smiled, knowing I had been right.

To the south, the dull crumping of our plasma batteries began and it wasn't long before bright flashes illuminated the skyline to our north.

"Mary," a man's voice announced over the radio. "Mary."

Megan gave us a hand signal and we began a crouching jog northward. In the open. It was the first time any of our forces had tried an aboveground assault, a response to the multiple Russian efforts to infiltrate our lines from above, to repay their courtesy. Lessons ticked past like a mantra: never move aboveground against well-defended fortifications; topside assaults were useless and would result in unnecessary casualties from which a unit might never recover. But none of them made me afraid; they made the move *more* exciting. We picked our way through the rubble, my boots occasionally slipping on countless Russian dead in combat armor so with each step the plasma bursts came closer. The temperature readout on my helmet display shifted colors, climbing, and I almost missed Megan's next hand signal, but then melted into my surroundings, lowering to the ground to begin a slow crawl with chameleon skins on, so hard to see that my very existence became a thing to doubt. Within half a kilometer of the barrage, we stopped.

"Betty, Betty," the man announced. The command meant that the Marine units were in place near the Russian lines, waiting underground for us to advance. Almost at the same moment as the signal, the barrage lifted and Megan waved us on.

Our suits scraped against jagged rubble as we moved up, the sound seeming like a scream over the winter silence. My arms and legs cramped. To move at a snail's pace that would not be detected by Russian motion sensors required a control that none of us had experienced, and two hours later we still lay more than a hundred meters from the enemy positions. When a green light appeared ahead of us, I froze. My vision kit zoomed onto the outline of an airlock blockhouse, its dim green interior light blinking out after its door sealed shut, and then the goggles tracked two Russians who jogged in a crouch, before both vanished into a nearby hole.

"Enemy spotted," Megan whispered over the net. "Russian airlock located, point-two klicks to our front."

We resumed our inching progress northward until Megan gave the signal to halt, and then passed another series of hand signals, ending it with one meant only for me. I thanked Him for the chance to kill, not doubting that I would succeed, and continued forward while everyone watched. It was better this way. An audience always made it more satisfying.

The Russians spoke loudly and you heard them laugh, comforting one with the realization that they wouldn't be able to hear the scraping of a suit on concrete. They sounded *happy*. I reached a shallow defilade in front of their post, drew my knife, and tested its weight. *A quick kill*, I prayed, *and faith*, and then rolled into their position.

The knifepoint buried itself in the first Russian, who gasped and fell against the hole's far side, almost ripping the blade from my grasp. The second one dropped a liquor bottle, too drunk to grab his carbine or call for help, so I snapped the knife into the man's neck joint and slammed it in with the butt of my other hand.

"Clear," I said, and collapsed on the ground, shaking.

There was blood. Even in darkness I saw the black pool spread across the snow, inching toward me, telling me to run. The thought snowballed. It became a voice, shouting to throw my weapons away and leap from the hole, sprint toward Shymkent and keep going south until I hit the water in Bandar, where I should dive in and swim. But Instead I sat there, paralyzed. By the time Megan peered over the lip of the hole, I had collected myself, not sure why the sight of blood had suddenly become a thing to fear, and rejoined the group, embarrassed that she had almost seen me frozen, could have mistaken it for what it was: an early onset of spoiling. Megan motioned for the rest of us to cross the last ten meters to the blockhouse, where we waited for our sapper to place a series of charges on the airlock door.

"Diane," the man announced over the net; the Marines were about to attack.

Megan pressed her helmet against mine and whispered loudly.

"That hole was a mess. Death and faith, but you lose your touch, make it cleaner next time, efficient." We felt the thuds of multiple explosions then, far beneath us, and Megan pointed at the sapper.

The airlock door blew inward and slammed against the far wall of the blockhouse, after which the girl slowly rose to inch her way in. A minute later she called over the net, "Inner door was unlocked. We're clear."

One of us, a replacement, stood quickly to rush forward.

*"Stay down!"* Megan yelled. In midstride the girl realized her mistake and stopped, but it was too late. Three sentry bots popped up and spat streams of flechettes, her

helmet flying thirty meters when they chewed through the girl's neck. Within moments the bots had retreated to their holes.

"Move in," Megan ordered, her voice trembling with anger.

We crept toward the green light, and I crawled through a mass of tissue and blood from the girl who had just been killed, seeing the jagged shards of a spine. *I hate you*, I thought. *For being so stupid, a stupid fucking cow who can't make any more mistakes, and for being lucky that you don't have to do this anymore . . .*

"Come on, don't be a stupid cow," said Margaret, "*Move.* We only have six hours before day comes."

Somehow I had gotten off the mountain. The narrow service road glistened in moonlight, its surface like a sheet of ice that had been frosted with fresh snow. We shuffled along, one of my arms draped over Margaret's shoulder, and once I returned to the present, the haze shaken off, I let go of her, moving under my own power again.

"How long was I out?" I asked.

"An hour. I thought tranq tabs would help with that."

I grunted, not sure if I believed what I was about to say, or that I even had the strength to answer, but tried anyway. "I took it too late. And sometimes they just don't work."

"You know the way? Before you stopped talking you said 'east on the service road' But I've forgotten now."

"Misha said to leave the road only when we see trees." I gave her the details about Lev then, and the supplies. "We still have a chance."

Margaret stared at me as we walked and jogged, saying nothing for a while before she touched my shoulder.
"You *were* a Lily, weren't you?"

I stopped. "Why would you say that?"

"Our hair grows because we let it. Want it. But not
you, even with your scars, you shave your head, keep it
clean and military. You take lives so easily."

*"I am not a Lily."* An anger came out of nowhere, all
the hatred I had felt for so long awakening again and I
slammed against her, throwing Margaret into the snow-
bank. "I am not a Lily."

"I'm sorry, Murderer. But thank you."

"For what?"

"For taking me with you."

And we ran through the night. The cold bit through my
leather shoes, reminding me of the pain I had once felt
and making me wonder if I'd lose my toes again. But soon
everything went numb. The cold bit so deeply that my
teeth chattered no matter how hard I tried to clench them,
and twice we had to hide while a truck passed, burying
ourselves in a grave of ice and snow. Before long I lost
consciousness in a way, the cold and exhaustion making
everything disappear so that we almost missed it, the
shapes rising in the moonlight, out of the darkness to our
front.

"Trees?" Margaret asked.

"Trees."

"We will be there soon?"

I glanced up at the sky, seeing the first signs of morning, a pink light forming over the mountains to the east,
and nodded. "By midday. If we don't freeze to death and if
they haven't already discovered Misha and the dead girls."

Margaret leapt into the snow, her feet and legs sinking almost to her waist as she blazed the path, and I followed, hoping we'd make the treeline before another truck came. Once we passed the first birch we both laughed with relief.

"You said we'll get there about midday," said Margaret. "I'll kill you if you're wrong because I'm so fucking cold that I can't shut my nerves down."

I was too cold to talk. A log hut stood in a clearing ahead of us, reminding me of the farm in which Megan and I had found the murdered farmers, so that for a moment I was sure we would find Lev dead and hanging from the rafters—assuming this was even the right place. Smoke billowed from the hut's chimney. A bundle of wires ran down one corner of the structure, a sign that we hadn't stepped back in time three hundred years, that the hut had at least some modern features, but the energy it required to process the thought nearly made me drop; winter's winds had been too hard. Margaret showed no sign of any similar deterioration and even looked at me with a grin as a wave of dizziness hit, making me stumble. She grabbed me before I fell.

"Are you all right?"

But I had no breath, couldn't seem to piece together a sentence to answer her. Margaret looped my arm over her shoulder and dragged me to the hut's front door, pounding on it with a free hand until an old man opened it.

"What?" When he realized what we were his eyes went wide. "You! Dear God, now I understand why Misha sent armor and supplies, and to think I was about to send them back. Come in, come in."

Margaret ushered me through and the man shut the door behind us, blocking the cold. A fire burned in a woodstove. Compared to outside the air in the small room seemed tropical, and I collapsed on the floor with exhaustion, curling into a ball to shake while he knelt by me and shone a light in first one eye, then the other, before disappearing into a side room and returning with a blanket. He threw it across my back.

"Your friend is in bad shape," the man said to Margaret. "Is she first generation?"

She nodded.

"What are you?"

"Second."

"My God," the man repeated, "what a treat! I've never seen one up close. So you still have much of your genetic material intact, ability to control pain, blood loss, all the normal functions, and she"—he pointed at me with a thumb—"is more or less like me now."

"She is a Li—she is still fearless. Catherine is a killer. I am Margaret."

I did my best to control my teeth from chattering as I spoke. "A-a-are you L-L-Lev? Misha told us you were a g-g-genetic, a boy like him."

The man clapped his hands. Instead of a uniform he wore a wool sweater and tweed jacket, a pipe hooked from the left side of his mouth, and the pure white of his beard reminded me of the snow we had just escaped. He nodded at my question but then pulled the pipe from his mouth, speaking for the first time in English.

"Yes and no. I'm Lev to the Russian genetics. They are allowed to speak to me over the com lines but not to visit, and the Army tells them I am a genetic, the fulfillment of their promise to provide the boys with their own land one day. I'm a lie."

"Who are you, really?" asked Margaret.

"I'm Vince. Doctor Vincent Sleschinger. One of the first Germline designers, but that was almost thirty years ago; I was much younger then. My God, do you think I could take a tissue sample from both of you? You are the true pharmacons, the precursor of exogene and everything that stems from it. They won't let me near any Germline units—security or something. In fact after I gave them my data on our first generation, they put me out here. There's Russian gratitude for you. I must remember to thank Misha, send him something nice from my workshop."

"Misha is dead," I said, "I killed him. You designed us?"

The man shook his head. His smile faded and he moved toward what looked like a small kitchen, to sit on a tall stool. "Not you. The boys, the first generation that failed. I designed them, the ones who turned on their handlers and massacred an entire company of Marines in Iran, or was it Special Forces in Thailand? Who cares? It was spectacular as far as failures go, you should have seen the aftermath of the fight, where my boys had waded in to kill the men by hand, not stopping even when nobody remained to fight so that my sons battled the human corpses, ripping them to pieces. But what does the military do? Shit-canned. Kicked me to the street along with a *do-not-hire* sign around my neck so it wasn't long before I became desperate for money. I left America and worked my way to eastern Europe, where I ran into some very interested buyers and voilà. Zeya has been my home ever since. I was the one who suggested a simple fix for the aggression: snip off the boy's balls."

As soon as he stopped talking, the feeling from my extremities returned, forcing me to scream. Margaret dropped to my side. My feet felt as though they had caught fire and a sense of panic rose in my chest as I scrambled to pull off the blanket and then my shoes, convinced that all ten toes had already turned black. They were bone white. Vince came over and squatted, then poked at them with the tip of his pen, watching over a pair of glasses.

"Blood flow is returning to normal, but barely. You were close, Catherine. It's a good thing you found me when you did." He pulled at the makeshift bandage then, which had soaked with blood, and checked the knife wound on my side. Vince reached toward his belt. He pulled out a medical kit and told Margaret to hold the wound closed before he sprayed it with an antibiotic adhesive, adding to my pain, to the burning. Vince tried to hide something then but I saw: he pushed what looked like a swab, its tip red with my blood, into the kit and then reattached the kit to his belt.

I screamed again and grabbed Vince's arm. "Armor and supplies. Where are they?"

"They're in the back, but I'll need help, I'm not young anymore, Catherine."

I didn't trust him. The man hadn't stopped smiling since we arrived, and there was a look about him, a kind of hunger that spoke of men I had seen before—of Alderson. Margaret followed him through a small door at the back of the hut and then disappeared, leaving me to the sounds of the hut and the wind; I was about to shut my eyes when I noticed a kind of scratching sound. It came from the kitchen. I threw the blanket off and stood carefully so my wound wouldn't reopen and shuffled closer to the noise, which came in bursts and at first was difficult to locate. I looked in every drawer, every cabinet, taking the time to do it noiselessly so that almost five minutes elapsed before I stumbled upon the sound's source under the sink: a radio headset. Even though there was no sign of a receiver, it was there, relaying to the tiny speakers, which mumbled for a moment and then scratched with static. I picked the headset and wrapped it around my ears to hear Russian.

"Keep them there, Doctor. We're on our way, please respond."

"Understood," I said, trying to make my voice deep, and the other end went quiet.

"You discovered my secret," said Vince.

I spun to find him standing in the doorway, still smiling, an aeroinjector grasped tightly in his right fist.

"You were careless," I said, moving a hand into my pocket until it touched the knife.

"In this case, their distrust of me, a foreigner, worked to your advantage. Misha never told me why he sent supplies, and the Russian forces never told me that you had escaped so I didn't know anything until you knocked on my door. There wasn't much time to radio that I had visitors. You were lucky, but it's over, Catherine. Lay down and let it all happen now. Rest."

My next moves had already been mapped, preordained, and there was no need to plan or prepare, the only sensation a familiar hatred that invigorated me. *This* was Alderson. It didn't matter that his name was Vincent, didn't confuse me in the least, because they were both motivated by curiosity, saw us as something to own and use, to vivisect.

"Where is Margaret?" I asked.

"She's resting already." He held up the injector. "A kind of sedative, one I've developed to counteract the biochemistry of Germline defenses. When fully functional, you were a masterpiece. Almost nothing chemical or biological would get through except for my little cocktail, and you could never imagine the amount of work it took to formulate, how many girls died when the Russians tested different versions for me. But I have no idea what it will do to a first-generation girl. You should just give up. How can you fight on when you have none of the benefits of being a genetic, and most of the disadvantages of a human?"

He didn't wait for my answer. Vince's courage surprised me—or maybe it was that I still suffered from blood loss and the cold—because he ran forward with the aeroinjector extended in front of him, and almost slammed the thing into my chest. I spun to the side, slicing downward. The knife struck his outstretched arm with a loud smack, digging into his bone, and the aeroinjector clattered to the floor. He dove for it. Vince had wrapped his left hand around the thing and was about to turn for another try when I threw the knife as hard as I could, burying it in his chest. He slid to the floor, his back against the wall, and looked first at the knife and then up at me with a horrified expression.

"Why don't you give up, Catherine?"

I shook my head. "Because I think there is one more thing to accomplish. I don't know what it is, but if it gives me more chances to kill men like you, it must be good."

"Take me with you," he whispered, too delirious to understand anything. "I want to watch."

I kicked the aeroinjector from his hand and leaned

over to grab the knife. The hallucination came at the same time. I had just pulled the blade out and slammed it into his neck when everything went blank a second later.

"Germline units don't take prisoners, do they?" he had asked before dying.


We never took prisoners. On our way northward through Iran a Guard unit had surrendered to us en masse, and they stood there with their hands up, weapons on the ground, all of them with looks of uncertainty and fear. On the beaches we had thought them brave; the Iranians had no combat armor, and I recall being taught that once most of the oil had gone, their forces suffered from a lack of money, a lack of discipline, but had a faith in God that matched ours—a fundamental belief that dying in the face of our advance would ensure them a place in heaven. So they fought. Neither Megan nor I had yet fired a shot in anger since our first landing, having only just moved off the shore, and the Iranian's surrender made me feel sad that the battle had ended before it began. Maybe these men were *not* so brave.

Our human advisor spoke Farsi, and approached them. After a few words, he turned to one of the Lilies from a different unit and sketched an imaginary plan into the palm of his gauntlet.

"We can hold them here until our main forces catch up to the advance. Can you spare a hundred of your girls to guard?"

Her voice sounded cold over the helmet speakers. "No."

"What?"

"It's not in your original orders," she explained.

The man must not have understood, and scratched his bare head as the morning sun turned the horizon wavy. "So? Adapt and improvise. Prisoners are a good thing, they can provide intelligence on enemy plans and defenses."

"Our orders are to advance and secure the border before halting. They die *here*." She motioned to the rest of us. "Faith."

We opened fire. The Iranians realized immediately what was happening, and most tried to run. Some dove for their weapons.

Our advisor crouched to avoid the fire and began speaking excitedly, forgetting to switch into command net so that we all heard him on the radio.

"Fox-Seven, Mango-One."

"Fox-Seven," a voice answered.

"Get command, I need orders for my girls to hold the Iranian prisoners here. *Alive*."

"Hold."

The radio went silent for a few minutes, and we began moving forward again, chasing the ones who had run. I felt depressed. This was like killing animals, unfulfilling and without honor, especially when it came to the ones who fell to their knees and begged, throwing their hands up in supplication.

When the voice came back, it was more quiet. "Negative, Mike, orders are to push on, secure border. Over."

Our advisor stood then, and watched us, his Maxwell still slung over a shoulder. When we finished he waited as we loaded back into our APC's, and before snapping his helmet into place I saw the look of hatred on his face, amplified by a scar that ran over his left eye.

"I hope that was fun," he said.

\*　　　\*　　　\*

I came around to find Margaret shaking me. When my eyes snapped open, she grinned, handing me my knife, which she had cleaned so it gleamed in the firelight. "It looks like you had some fun."

"What happened?"

"He surprised me, injected me with something that induced unconsciousness and I only just came to. It's been half an hour, Murderer."

"Did you find the armor? The supplies?"

Margaret nodded, laughing at the same time.

"What?" I asked, "What's wrong?"

"The armor, Murderer. It's for boys. Misha sent us diapers to wear because the undersuits weren't meant for female waste needs."

I laughed too, and pulled myself from the floor. Margaret handed me another tranq tab and I swallowed it whole, waiting for the relief. It came almost immediately.

"Let's go then. Get dressed and we'll move out. Vince alerted them we're here; they're on their way now."

"Where are we going?" she asked.

"I don't know exactly. But south."

# SEVEN

# Fog of War

*To those who harbor and teach His daughters,*
*they will be killed along with their children, so*
*that all who witness know His name.*

MODERN COMBAT MANUAL
REVELATIONS 2:20–23

The forest brought my episodes more frequently. Margaret did her best to keep me from shuffling away when my mind left, by grabbing my arm and preventing me from hitting the trees, but soon the woods closed in again, made it impossible to see anything clearly. A lack of any view forced my mind to wander, pushed me toward a realization that I preferred Kazakhstan's open steppes, maybe even longed for them. And thinking made it worse. It took some time to acclimate to the Russian suits but our ability to read their systems facilitated the process, and gave me another mechanism to stay in the present. Learning took concentration. The combination of tranq tabs and a focus on learning how to master my armor gave respite from hallucinations, and I studied the map display, charting our course east around the northern border of China, and then south toward Korea. It was so far; we soon gave up on estimating how long it would take—or wondering what we would do when fuel cells and food ran out. We noticed that Russian suits consumed power at a slower rate than ours, despite the demands of heating us in icy conditions. Theirs contained an extra layer of insulation, sandwiched between laminated ceramic, so that as we pushed through waist- to chest-high drifts, our systems sometimes switched to cooling mode, to bleed off the heat that our carapace trapped.

Marching brought into focus two problems, the first of which stemmed from my physical condition. Endless advances would never be possible again. My body felt as though it had become a fragile thing that couldn't be pushed, my muscles aching to the point of ceasing to cooperate altogether unless we broke for rest so I could catch my breath. And then there was pain. It shot upward from my feet when blisters formed, the undersuits' footgear not a perfect fit so that before long I felt my heels bleeding, my blisters breaking open, weeping. Soon enough, the multiple sources of pain fused into one constant, searing, nervous impulse, too great to ignore but too great to mitigate. There was nothing to do but let it take me.

The second problem stemmed from the dead. At times the ghosts of Megan walked on one side, Heather on the other, and neither of them spoke, left me to imagine their thoughts and come close to screaming at them that I had no choice, but it wouldn't have done any good. Their judgment was clear: I had earned the name Murderer, and somehow it had become a source of shame because to them killing was wrong. Tears came without warning. There was no way to explain the streams of them, only to thank God that my helmet kept them invisible to Margaret and that my body had become too fatigued to visibly shake with fear. How could killing be wrong and where

had *that* thought even come from? The new internal conflict grew in the tissues of my chest, not my brain, to move
downward into my stomach slowly, but multiplying geo-
metrically by the minute, to fill my gut with a sensation of
dread—that behind every tree was one of my sisters, and
that she would die at my hands. Sometimes Margaret
asked me questions or spoke but I don't remember
responding, only that we kept moving. There was no sign
of a Russian pursuit as we headed southeast in the general
direction of Korea until at the end of the second week,
Margaret stopped and looked up. They had come.

"Drones?" she asked.

"Freeze."

And we stopped. But the aircraft didn't attack us,
didn't even seem to focus on our area, instead screamed
overhead and then dropped ordnance somewhere far to
the west, a series of distant thuds too distant to be felt
underfoot. Another wave screamed over, and another, and
both of us looked at each other.

"What is it?" Margaret asked. "What in hell could
they be attacking in that direction, on their own soil?"

"Look at your map."

"So?"

"There's nothing in that direction except China," I
said.

"So what are they attacking?"

I pushed Margaret, who moved without speaking. We
both rushed even though we weren't sure why, only knowing that the Russians wouldn't send so many aircraft
unless there had been danger from that direction and
recalling Misha's stories about the things in armor. Neither of us wanted to be trapped on a battlefield. But after a

while nothing happened, and we stopped every so often to listen for the approach of vehicles, until by nightfall the fear had subsided into a simmering kind of awareness that the Chinese border held something unknown, which hadn't yet reached us.

We moved through valleys and crossed rivers, every couple of days changing fuel cells and chill cans, our stores rapidly dwindling until only a week's worth remained. Margaret had noticed a city on the map: Chegdomyn. It seemed roughly the same size as Zeya and might provide a source of fuel cells and other supplies we could steal while avoiding the major city to its south, Khabarovsk. Chegdomyn inched closer on the display, until finally we were one day out. Margaret stopped us in the late morning and whispered to switch to chameleon skins, which I almost didn't do because it would use more power, of which we had almost none. But as soon as I did, and fell into the snow, they finally came.

Russian troops swarmed out of the forest in front of us, and I marveled at the fact that we hadn't heard or noticed any sign of them sooner. They didn't bother to conceal themselves. It occurred to me that these troops were most likely reservists, lesser cadres that had been deemed unfit for service in Kazakhstan and sent to the east to man garrisons and outposts that were supposed to face no threat. Many of the men were weaponless. They shouted at one another, but there was no effort to retain cohesion and as the exodus continued I began to worry about one of them stepping on us, or that night would fall and the men would bivouac in the area. Night eventually did fall, but none of them stopped to rest, and for the entire episode neither Margaret nor I had dared whisper to each other over the

Russian radios, knowing that any pursuer would be able to intercept our transmissions. Eventually, by midnight, the flow of men slowed. An hour later it ended, and once more the forests became quiet so that we stood and moved closer to each other, switching off chameleon skins and digging in a bag for two of only three remaining cells.

"Should we turn on coms systems?" Margaret asked. "Maybe we'll hear something."

I shook my head. "We haven't had time to do a thorough scan, to see if the doctor hid anything to help them track us. The transceiver would be the most logical place to conceal it."

"Nobody is looking for us, Murderer. Something is happening. I counted almost a full division of men, and they taught our generation Russian markings in the atelier tanks; those were armored units that passed. Where were their vehicles?"

I thought for a moment, remembering Misha's question about why the Americans would have sent so many men after me, and worried that they too might be able to home in on our signal; it wasn't just the Russians who might listen. But eventually I sighed. "Go ahead."

We both popped our suits, and I was thankful for the Russian design, the external cables allowing me to let go of my helmet so it hung on my back while I attached the communications line to my vision hood. Margaret and I glanced at each other when we were ready, and then powered them. At first I couldn't understand. So many voices filled the channels, all of them speaking quickly so that the words were muddled, multiple transmissions crossing over one another in a confused mixture of status and contact reports. Finally Margaret grabbed my shoulder.

"What?" I asked.

"Chinese forces have broken through and taken 650 kilometers of border. Khabarovsk has fallen. They're also pressing in toward Sverdlovsk, attempting to break Russia in two and take all of Siberia. All those *resources*, Catherine."

The forest started spinning. What began as an unlikely goal had just turned into something impossible, and acceptance of the fact that we'd have to move through a war zone sank in. I dropped to my knees and vomited. Margaret sat beside me and started crying, her head between her knees, and I wished I was alone, without her, wished for the first time that I could see the ghosts of Megan again, maybe even Heather, so I could tell them they were right, ask them to welcome me home. Misha had given us flechette pistols. I pulled mine from its holster and made sure it had power.

"What are you doing?" Margaret asked.

"I'm not ready for the line anymore. I want someone to pull me off."

But Megan, and the forest, both disappeared before I heard her answer or could use the pistol on myself.

Being pulled off the line meant boredom. *Sometimes.* Although early in the war we had reached Pavlodar quickly, the length of our supply routes from Iran was such that thousands of kilometers of roads and rails had to be protected. Supply lines often broke. The Russians, when they attacked, had less than two hundred kilometers to travel and wave after wave of them came, pushing us south and west, at the same time insurgents hit rear areas.

Vehicles and munitions disappeared faster than they could be supplied, so whenever we pulled to the rear for refitting, they ordered us to stay on alert as a reaction force. To plug the gaps.

One day Megan assembled us. "Gather weapons and ammunition. Two weeks' rations. Form up at the motor pool, fifteen minutes." It was the first I had ever sensed that she was uncertain.

"What's wrong?" I asked. We helped each other suit up, holding the hoses and wires of our undersuits out of the way.

"Maykain."

"What about it?" I asked.

"Men are under attack. Over a thousand insurgents, partially armored and well organized, possibly led by Russian Special Forces or genetics."

Maykain. A briefing ran through my head until I remembered: *key road junction, remote, important supply route that was to be held.*

"We will succeed." I said.

"Perhaps. I do not doubt the *unit*; it is the distance that troubles. We'll have no air cover on the way out, and no APCs. Division is supplying us with captured trucks. It will be . . . difficult. I have a feeling, Catherine."

*Difficult* meant that Megan had already assessed it, that many of us might not come back. A *feeling* meant that it could be worse than that.

After two miles, my teeth felt as though they had chipped from rattling as the line of our ten Tedom trucks bounced over the road, trailing dust. It was summer. The sun glared at us, but you felt cool fluid while it crawled through the undersuit tubes. We hadn't yet helmeted, so although our suit temperatures had been kept in check, our faces baked in the heat and I struggled to fall asleep, the rough jolting forcing me awake every ten minutes—into some vague reality, part dreamer and part dirt-breather. I found it hard to believe that anyone lived in such a place.

The villages we passed barely existed. Wooden shacks straddled the dirt track, most of them surrounded with warped fences to contain a few chickens, pigs, and sometimes goats. I remembered one settlement in particular. An old woman stood near the road, her white scarf almost identical to the ones worn by our mothers. She stared as we passed. The lines on her face cut deeply, and she scowled, shaking her fist at the trucks and shouting something in Kazakh—not Russian—when she bent over to lift something from the ground. At the same time she threw it, one of the girls swung her carbine and fired, the needles slamming into the woman's brow and forcing her head back so that for a second it looked as though she laughed at the sky. The thrown object struck my shoulder and shattered into fragments. A dirt clod. At the time, it seemed silly that she had sacrificed herself just to throw dirt, but later I thought it brave. *Dirt against Maxwells and grenades*. We all tasted it. I was in one of the rearmost trucks, which bounced through the clouds of grit that the other vehicles tossed up, coating the insides of my mouth with a sandy paste, and by the time we neared Maykain, our black suits had turned light gray, then orange when the setting sun changed everything's color.

It felt good to walk again. We put on our helmets and crouched, advancing in a skirmish line for the last kilometer, but Maykain was all quiet. *Dead*.

"No movement," I said.

"Maykain Outpost, this is Ginger," Megan said over the radio, repeating it three times. Nobody responded. She motioned to four girls on her right side, and they crept forward, inching toward the town while the rest of us went prone.

Nothing happened. The girls made it to the first line of houses, stopped, and waved us on. "Clear to here," one said.

"Go stealth," said Megan.

Maykain was different from the other villages, its buildings constructed of stone or brick, and some of them had been coated with stucco painted a brilliant white. The wind came. It howled through the town's empty and broken windows as we advanced toward the center, stopping only to kick in doors and check each home like a mob of shimmering ghosts that I knew existed only because I saw the dots of other girls on my heads-up. The town, though, was *empty*.

"It is strange," I said.

Megan grunted when we reached the main square. "Where are they?" She clicked off the tactical net, but I heard the muffled sound of her voice until she clicked back in. "We are to search the west side of town and secure the roads. This time watch for traps. Death and faith."

We split into fire teams of four girls each—one grenade launcher and three carbines—and filtered westward into the alleys. The grenadiers announced they were switching to shaped charge. When we approached the first house, our grenadier fired in a detonation that shook the ground, and once the dust settled I saw the perfectly circular hole in the wall, getting bigger as I sprinted toward it. I dove through. All of the houses we searched held only dusty furniture, as if their inhabitants had simply vanished, and by the time we reached the far outskirts, we had gained nothing except the sweat that had soaked into our undersuits.

"Lily," someone said. "The *building*." But Megan had already seen it.

"Deactivate stealth, town clear."

Maykain had one tall structure, near the main road, a concrete warehouse; its slabs had been stacked end to end, forming a poorly constructed, now crumbling, façade. We had found the friendly unit. They hung from the building's windows, upside down, stripped of armor and undersuits so that a soft rain of blood fell from them to form a rough red square outline around the building. In the dying light we saw words, scrawled across a bare section of concrete.

*You cannot win.*

Megan ordered one of the teams to search the warehouse. At first it went normally. They blew a hole on one side and entered, the bangs from their movements echoing through empty alleyways, until we saw a bright flash followed by a shock wave that threw me backward. We thought it had been a remote detonated trap, a mine, and fanned out, searching for any remaining enemy units but soon we realized four charges had probably been set to a timer. The explosions had touched off simultaneously, one at each corner, bringing the building down on our sisters in a geyser of dust.

I didn't understand it then—the point of fighting that way, of defeating our forces at a key road crossing but then abandoning it. There had been *no* attempt to hold.

They simply hit and then vanished, so that we called for a flight of drones to search the steppes westward, but by the time the aircraft arrived they found only empty plains. Our enemy had been as ghosts, just like us.

"We are ghosts," Margaret whispered to no one. She thought I was still gone, and her tears hadn't stopped, leaving pink tracks on her cheeks and freezing in spots on her armor. "Nobody sees us and it's not because of stealth mode, it's because we no longer exist. We're already dead, and this is hell, but nobody told us."

"If this is hell, then we should just keep moving, find a way to make it ours." I lifted my head from her lap and thanked her before going on. "But I don't think it's hell, Margaret. We can kill humans. For me, it suggests we're in heaven."

She laughed at that, which I took as a good sign, even though I wasn't sincere in my bravery.

"So what now?"

I shook my head. "We keep going. Chegdomyn is immediately south, and from there we'll skirt Khabarovsk and move to Korea. We'll at least try."

Margaret ran a hand through her hair, and her breath came out in clouds. "I've been listening to the radio, Murderer. The Chinese control Russia from Khabarvosk almost to the sea west of Sakhalin, and we're wearing Russian armor with almost no fuel cells left—not to mention food. We can't get through."

"Then some Chinese will die before we do. Let's go."

"Sometimes," said Margaret, "I hate you."

We moved slowly, unwilling to use stealth mode and

drain our last cells, but hoping we'd see anyone before they saw us. The forest was silent. Only the sounds of our feet, which crunched through a centimeter-thick layer of icy crust, broke the quiet stillness, making me realize just how silly it was to try and hide when we made so much noise. The forest ended less then a kilometer from where we had rested and we stood behind trees, shocked at what lay before us: an infinite field of destruction. Russian armor and APCs littered what looked like a frozen swamp, with stands of cattails bending under the weight of ice that clung to their ends. Smoke still billowed from the vehicles. The popping of ceramic plates sounded in the distance, their noise like firecrackers, which made Margaret and me flinch with each snap, and thousands of Russian bodies lay strewn in the snow, their armor shattered from flechettes or molten from plasma and thermal gel. Margaret was about to sprint out and I grabbed her.

"Their fuel cells, Catherine," she explained.

"Not yet."

And we waited. I don't know what forced me to make that decision, maybe some premonition carried over the snow in a cloud of smoke, but we were about to break cover when we saw something move; it was far away, and almost immediately disappeared among the tanks. But it came again—then from other spots, more than one shape, slipping among the wreckage. The figures flicked in and out of sight, any one hard to see, but eventually different glimpses formed an image in my mind of men and women, covered from head to toe in what looked like padded clothing and who stopped only for a second to snap off fuel cells or gather weapons from the dead before disappearing again.

"They are so fast," Margaret whispered.

"Snowshoes. They're wearing snowshoes or skis."

A flight of drones appeared out of nowhere and we saw the people dive under wrecks or bury themselves in snow, so that within seconds they were invisible. I flicked to infrared. Nothing. Whoever they were, these were humans trained in how to disappear and we watched in fascination, almost forgetting to take cover when the missiles and bombs fell, scattering snow, ice, and ceramic across the frozen swamp, sending shards of armor to embed themselves in trees. Within a few minutes the attack ended and we waited before seeing the people emerge again, continuing to scavenge. One finally came into clear view and I zoomed in to get a better look. A thick kind of fur hat protected his head and face with a flap that wrapped under his chin and over his nose, leaving only a pair of thin eyes exposed. He stopped. The man appeared to stare directly at me and then whistled so that the rest of them disappeared again, melting into the wreckage. We watched each other for a minute before I stepped into the snow, into the open, and held up both hands to show I was unarmed. At first he stood there, frozen. Then the man started a fast glide toward me, pushing off from side to side on thin skis. My heart pounded. I heard Margaret start to pull her pistol from its holster and stopped her with a glance before the man finally stopped, barely three meters in front of us.

I lowered one of my hands and waved with the other once, shocked when he waved back.

"What now?" I asked Margaret.

"You tell me. We might not have a lot of time before another attack. Who are they?"

The man cocked his head at the sound of our English and said something I didn't understand, but Margaret stepped forward and answered, speaking something that sounded like Chinese before she turned.

"They're Korean."

"What are they doing here?" I asked "Unarmored?"

"They want us to come with them, and he says it's not safe to stay here. I've explained we're escaped American prisoners."

I didn't want to go. Not with them. These were humans and although the Atelier lessons had included the Koreans, all the Asian nations, and their wars, it was different to see one in person for the first time and feel his stare, an expressionless unblinking one. Unreadable. Margaret must have seen my hesitation and threw up her hands.

"What else are we going to do, Catherine?" She turned back to the man and said something else, conversing with him for a full five minutes before finishing. "They said the Chinese haven't arrived yet but they will, either from the south or out of the west, but that they won't bother them. They're friends with the Chinese. Just like they're friends with the Russians."

"Is that why the Chinese just attacked them?" I asked.

"Catherine, you know those were drones. They can't tell a friendly unit unless you're wearing a transponder."

Margaret was right. There was no other option; we'd revealed ourselves to them and even if we ran now we'd freeze to death in the open once our fuel cells finally drained, and one death was just like any other so what did it really matter? I pushed into the snow, moving toward the man, who motioned to the others. Within seconds they had surrounded us. The Koreans carried Russian weapons, probably ones they had just stolen, and trained them on our chests as the man took our pistols, then pushed Margaret and me southward, toward Chegdomyn. Their pace was relentless. One group sped ahead on cross-country skis, pausing every once in a while to wait for the remainder who guarded us; by the time we reached a road I had begun to see stars from exhaustion and the act of pushing through snow—deeper now that we had moved into the open—made my muscles scream. I wanted to lie down. At that moment if someone had offered to kill me I might have accepted the fate, but the road offered an easier path, one on which our feet didn't sink too deeply, and soon the agony faded a bit, allowing me to catch my breath. They pushed us through another small forest, and then over a half-ruined bridge that crossed a frozen river; on the other side, a rusted sign declared in Russian that this was Urgal. But it wasn't on my map display, and soon I understood why.

A thin steel cable ran through rusted pipes that had been driven into the ground on either side of the road, and hanging from the cable at regular intervals were small signs. Faded. Ice and snow covered most of what remained of old paint and lettering, but enough was there to see the radiation warning symbols, and almost at the same instant the warning beep came alive inside my suit. A dosimeter began reading my exposure. The Koreans didn't have dosimeters or armor, but they sped up, pushing us even faster, until we reached the other side of the abandoned village where the radiation beacon flickered out. We continued south across an empty field, indescribable in its breadth; here and there large tree stumps sticking up through the snow suggested that a forest had once existed but had long since been conquered. The radiation and trees retaught another lesson we had absorbed in the tanks, described to me in more detail by Misha: that the Asian wars had gone nuclear, and had spilled over into Russia.

Ten minutes later the group led us into Chegdomyn. They pushed us into a low hut, most of it underground except for the roof, and then tossed us a pair of Russian fuel cells before saying something to Margaret and shutting the door.

"They said to stay here and to not come out. Or we die."

Almost as soon as my helmet hit the cold earth, my eyes flickered, and I whispered. "Why would they kill us now?"

"Not them. The Chinese will be here soon and if we're seen, they'll kill us. He said they may already have forward observers in the town, sent from Khabarovsk."

This time, I never felt the nightmare coming.

They needed a forward observer and there were no humans available. *We* would infiltrate. Megan and I crawled through Pavlodar's rubble, moving down into craters and then up the other side on our bellies, flinching at the sound of aircraft booming overhead, their wreckage littering the rubble with blackened metal that fell without warning. The shaft of a broken water tower was close now. One hundred meters. Then fifty, and a few minutes later we sat at its base. The Russians had established an aboveground defensive line, and our intelligence suggested they would soon move out from it for another push, coordinating with underground forces. Megan and I would help stop it.

"Are you ready?" she asked.

I slung my carbine. "Yes."

We climbed the remains of a ladder, hand over hand, careful to ensure that we moved slowly enough to evade motion sensors, watching power levels drain more quickly when our chameleon skin activated. It took us ten minutes to reach the top. Fifty meters up we crawled out onto a sheet of bent iron, its edges jagged as though God had reached down and torn it to pieces, where we lay still and watched.

The Russian positions extended for as far as we could see. Their forces had massed on the northeastern edges of the city, tiny figures in black armor, who, from this distance, resembled worker ants. Before radioing in, we mapped the positions, marking plasma cannon locations, APCs, and troop concentrations; our fingers moved quickly over forearm controls to lock in the data. After we sent the report, we had one last job: to wait. As soon as the enemy began to move out, we would call in the artillery and retreat to our underground position.

Megan was hard to see. The chameleon skin made her outline shimmer, as if she were an optical illusion, no more than a distortion in the air next to me so that this time I had to reach out and touch her. To make sure she was real.

"I am here," Megan said.

"It's strange." I shook my head and scanned the line again.

"What?"

"Us. The only time we get time to be alone is when we cannot afford to pay attention to each other."

Megan laughed quietly. "This is war, Catherine.

Sometimes I wonder if you are human, the way you think and talk. We have but one purpose. 'To serve him and—' "

" 'And to kill any enemy who stands in our way, any who block the path of His holy word,' " I finished the scripture for her and sighed. "They show no sign of moving out yet."

"This bothers you?"

Clouds had gathered overhead and the suit temperature indicator had been dropping steadily since we came topside. I shivered. "It will snow soon. This will cause trouble."

"Why?" Megan asked.

"Because it covers everything, conceals the true nature of things, making it all seem quiet and peaceful when there is no such thing. Snow is deception."

I sensed, rather than saw, Megan turn toward me. For a moment she was silent. "You are not like us, Catherine. There's something special, maybe better than us, as if you've been chosen for—"

But they came before she finished. First we heard, then felt, the booming of their cannon, containment shells screaming just over our heads to illuminate the rubble well to our rear with plasma. Russian APCs roared to life. Like a wave of black dots, the lines move forward, toward us, and I froze, unable to think in the face of such a massive force. Megan slapped my helmet. She had already reported the attack and I hadn't even noticed the sound of our artillery tearing the sky above us, hurtling into their lines to explode in white hot hemispheres of plasma, turning into beautiful greens and reds as the heat dissipated.

We didn't bother to move slowly. As we slid down the ladder several of them locked onto our movement despite the chameleon skins, so that Russian tracer flechettes snapped past us or pinged into the tower's structure, sending a shower of sparks over our shoulders. We ran. Several times I slipped and fell, the vibration of artillery and Russian APCs making the ground shake as we did our best to scramble over rubble and wreckage. After we made it to the airlock, I popped my helmet and tried to kiss her.

She pulled away. "Not now."

"Why?"

"We are under attack, Catherine!" And with that she stepped into the elevator, motioning for me to follow. "Later."

The elevator banged its way down the shaft while plasma artillery impacted on the rock above, but the motion put me to sleep because it was important to rest any time I could, and when it finally reached the bottom, Megan had to shake me—to get me to wake up.

"Catherine, wake up!" Margaret had slid the locking ring open and began to pull my helmet off when I pushed her away.

"I'm awake."

"They're here. The Chinese."

I sat up and reached for my pistol before remembering it wasn't there, and then looked where she pointed. Megan had opened the door a crack, letting in a fierce wind and making me grateful for the armor, but through it we saw a portion of the street outside where a line of Koreans stood at rigid attention. They looked cold. Zooming in I saw that some were women, and that one woman in particular wore several medals, which swung in the wind, clinking under a flag that flapped so wildly it looked about to rip free from its wooden pole.

A line of Chinese soldiers faced them. At first I thought all of them wore armor, similar to the powered suits I had seen in the laboratory at Zeya but more sleek, and not as large, the carapace a deep green with a single red star on its shoulder and the faceplate half glass, a thick mirrored gold. But one wore nothing except a uniform and winter coat. The shoulder boards indicated he was a general, but above the collar began a horror of skin, its surface mottled by hundreds of scars that fused, one into another, making me wonder if I looked as terrifying as he did. The general approached the woman with medals, and they hugged.

"Smallpox," Margaret whispered.

"What?"

"The scars on the Chinese general's face. I'm guessing smallpox. All of them probably have it, a strain that everyone is worried will one day find its way out of China and into the world. It mutates incredibly fast and is resistant to all antibiotics; that's why they imposed such a strict quarantine on China."

"How do you know of this strain?"

Margaret turned to look at me. "They taught us this in the tanks, full training on biochemical defense and recent data on information obtained from sources inside China. You didn't get this?"

"No," I said. "We didn't get that. Unless my mind has eroded to the point where everything is beginning to fade." Which was possible, I thought. Even as I spoke I felt the threat of hallucination lurking on the edge of my mind, and I reached over to Margaret's belt pouch, unsnapping it to remove another tranq tab, my hands shaking so badly that it was difficult to pop my helmet. How much longer until my life became one long dream? Even my hatred of men seemed to have faded, for as I looked at these ones I felt nothing, searching the Korean faces for something that would spark it, reignite the one thing that had kept me going for the past year—maybe for as long as I had lived. But nothing came. These people were different, subdued, and what I could see of their faces, which was mostly the eyes, suggested a level of suffering that equaled mine, and none of their expressions reminded me of our creators. And the Koreans had women in their ranks. Real women, who hadn't been manufactured and who carried weapons, their narrow eyes exuding the same resolve for which I now searched. There was nothing about these people for me to hate.

"Can you hear what they're saying?" I asked Margaret.

"The Chinese are recounting a history of the wars in which their people have fought together, as allies." Margaret waited until the Korean woman spoke and then continued translating. "She is saying that the Democratic People's Republic lives, and will always come to the aid of their Chinese brothers and sisters." Margaret turned her helmet to the side, to try to pick up more, but then she sighed. "It looks like the formalities are over, and their voices are too low for me to pick anything up now."

Their ranks broke then, and the Koreans led the Chinese away from us, down the street and out of view.

"What are they doing, Catherine?" Margaret asked.

"I can't see them anymore, they've left."

"Not that," she explained. "I mean with us. Why are they holding us here and will they give us to the Chinese?"

I thought for a minute, trying to swallow the fear the

question brought, and then shook my head. "Does it matter anymore? We have nothing left, Margaret, and I still believe in God. I don't like him, but I believe in Him. Let's see his plan unfold and decide what role we'll play in it—decide for ourselves. This is the fog of war, and right now only He has a clear line of sight."


We stayed in the hut for almost two weeks, watching Chinese troops and vehicles move northward through Chegdomyn, continuing their advance into Russia's east. Every once in a while, a Korean girl visited us. Her name was Yoon-sung, and she delivered us food, and buckets to use for toilets, taking away the buckets that we had used for the previous two or three days. At first she wouldn't look at us or speak, no matter how hard Margaret tried to engage her in conversation. But a month later Yoon-sung glanced at Margaret, who had popped her helmet to make her voice clearer, natural, instead of having it sent through helmet speakers. When she saw Yoon-sung staring, she pulled off her hood.

"Do you speak Russian?" Margaret asked.

Yoon-sung nodded.

"Why are you holding us?"

The girl's Russian was hard to understand and heavily accented, but I caught most of it—enough to follow the conversation. I wanted to say something. But I feared that if I removed my helmet, my scars might suggest that I had been infected with smallpox, and I didn't want to do anything that might end the discussion early.

"We are not sure what to do with you," she said. "You are Americans, the first we've ever seen, but you are also our sworn enemies. Devils."

"Then you will give us to the Chinese or kill us?" Margaret asked.

"We do not know. You are…" her next word sounded like Russian for artificial, something created, but I couldn't be sure.

Margaret nodded. "Genetically engineered. We are not your enemies, and my friend," she pointed at me, "has killed American men."

"That is good," said Yoon-sung. "We need fighters. In the spring we ship our stocks into Korea and the way is difficult. Our train will come under constant attack and all our Russians are gone now."

"I don't understand. The Russians would protect your train? What do you ship?"

Yoon-sung glanced toward the door and shook her head. "I must go. I will tell my superiors what you told me; it may help your case. But nothing will be decided until the matter has been investigated thoroughly and until after your trial."

"Trial?" asked Margaret.

"You are to be tried as spies."

After Yoon-sung left, shutting the door behind her, Margaret and I looked at each other. There was nothing to say.


A week later a group of Korean soldiers motioned for us to exit the hut and pushed us into the street, and for the first time we got a view of something other than what could only be observed through cracks in the door. The streets were empty. I expected to see them filled with Chinese troops and vehicles; the relief of finding them empty almost made me faint. Five minutes later, amid the beginnings of a heavy snowfall, we strode through the entrance of a huge building, which was also half underground, and entered a vast auditorium decorated with gold paint and colorful murals, its seats a dark red velvet. Each one held a Korean. This time, though, they wore uniforms—not the padded suits—a dark green wool with red collar tabs, and each of them stared at us blankly, their eyes following until someone forced our backs to the crowd, to face the stage.

Two men sat on either side of a table, at the head of which sat the same woman we had seen greet the Chinese. She wore no hat, and had brilliant white hair that pulled back into a tight bun to expose a worn face, its skin gouged, hardened, and tanned from having spent years in the Russian east where the cold ravaged everything with wind-born ice. The woman wore a small pistol in a shoulder holster. She reached for something and I flinched, thinking she was about to draw the pistol, but instead her hand raised a gavel, which she banged three times.

The woman spoke into a microphone, her voice amplified from every direction, and I looked over at Margaret. She popped her helmet and motioned for me to do the same. Before the woman continued, Yoon-sung appeared at my side, speaking in a soft voice as she translated what was being said.

"You are charged with spying against the Democratic People in exile, a charge which carries a death sentence. You are not here to be asked how you plead, since the evidence is almost incontrovertible, but to investigate the possibility of mitigating circumstances."

The room fell silent except for someone who coughed

behind us, and after a few seconds it became clear that they expected us to say something, but I had trouble keeping a smile off my face despite the circumstances. Who would we be spying for?

"We are not spies," I finally said.

The woman didn't like the answer. She pointed at me and spoke so quickly that Yoon-sung had trouble keeping up.

"You are on our land, granted to us fifty years ago as a gift from the Chinese before Russian aggressors claimed it using nuclear weapons. The weapons of murderers. Today our Chinese brothers have returned, granting us autonomy once more, and so I say it again. You are spies."

The insanity of it made me feel suddenly sick. How could Russia *belong* to Chinese invaders? The details of the Asian war ticked through my mind quickly, recalling the period where Chinese forces had taken over portions of Russia, but for these people to think that this was their land...

"Please," I said, doing my best to sound reasonable. "We're Americans. We were captured fighting the Russians, and escaped their factories in Zeya. What is it that makes us seem like spies?"

One of the men cleared his throat and looked at Yoon-sung, refusing to even glance at us.

"You wear Russian armor," she translated, "speak Russian, have Russian weapons and supplies. And *Zeya*. You expect us to believe that you came here all the way, on foot, from Zeya? Clearly the Russians left you behind to spy on the Chinese advance. Therefore, you spy on us."

The woman spoke again. "This discussion is a waste of time. Do you have anything to say that might mitigate your sentence?"

Margaret began speaking in Korean. She bowed her head, and Yoon-sung smiled for some reason, which confused me until I saw the surprise of the three in front of us, a visible horror that they failed to hide upon realizing that here was someone who spoke better Korean than they did, someone as different from them as the dirt from water. *Yoon-sung,* I thought while she translated, *knows the people on stage, predicted they would be shocked because she had never told them of Margaret's language capabilities.*

"We speak many languages, Aunt, and mean no disrespect, but neither of us has met a Korean before, let alone as honorable an assembly as this. Please. We have no way of knowing what circumstances might mitigate, and so throw ourselves at your mercy."

Now it was my turn for shock. For all I knew, Margaret had just sentenced us to death and I had to restrain myself to keep from screaming at her for having said something so stupid. But Yoon-sung looked amazed. There was no other way to describe the look she gave Margaret, and it struck me then, how unaccustomed I was to these people, since they had been able to impress me with the simple fact that I had finally seen some facial expressions, that until then I had been able to read nothing.

The three at the table huddled in conversation. At one point I glanced at Margaret to see if she caught any of the discussion, but she stared at the floor, her face just as expressionless as theirs and her eyes focused on a single spot. Finally the woman spoke again.

"Do you have any skills?"

Margaret nodded. "We are soldiers."

"Can you cut wood?"

"We can learn, Aunt."

They spoke among themselves again until a minute later the woman banged her gavel. Everyone in the auditorium rose.

"You," the woman announced, "will be assigned to one of the wood-cutting units, and will remain under armed guard until the spring thaw. Then you will help defend the train for our trip south."

With that it ended and the three exited the stage, at which point the entire auditorium emptied, leaving us, Yoon-sung, and six guards, who promptly ushered us toward the door and into the street. Yoon-sung accompanied us. She stood in the doorway of our hut, holding her nose at the smell, and after the guards had left, smiled.

"You are very lucky."

"Why?" I asked.

"The Dear Leader never shows such mercy. But then many of our wood cutters have been killed, and we need the help for the spring shipment."

"Where are we going?"

Yoon-sung's smile disappeared, replaced by the usual expression, empty and distant. "Wonsan," she said, "Korea," and then shut the door.


The next day they stripped us of our armor. According to Margaret, they promised to give it back in time for the spring trip, but the clothes they replaced it with made me realize that the discomfort of living in armor—of having to remove it to use the latrine bucket—was nothing compared to living with Russia's winter. Yoon-sung handed us two sets of clothes, which consisted of wool pants, shirts and socks; leather ankle boots; padded mittens; and a

hooded oversuit. The oversuit was identical to the others
we had seen. It consisted of an underlayer of what looked
like ballistic cloth, over which had been sewn quilted canvas, stuffed with feathers so that when I put it on and
pulled the hood over our heads, the cold retreated except
from my eyes. The Siberian cold stabbed into them,
bringing tears. My vision reduced to what I saw through a
constant squint, and at night it became a terrifying propo-
sition to open them for fear of having the lids freeze in
place. Without armor, we felt exposed.

The next day Yoon-sung came for us, and pulled us
from the hut into a dark daylight, with thick clouds overhead and flurries already starting to fall. We scurried
after her. As we moved down the road, southward out of
town, she explained where we were going.

"Today you go to cut trees with us. They assigned you
to my unit and I am to teach you how to become
timber-women."

I crossed my arms over my chest, trying to hold in the
heat. "Will we get food?" Our own supplies had finally run
out, and my stomach began growling. Yoon-sung stopped
to reach into a satchel slung across her back, pulling from
it two bundles of mushrooms wrapped in paper. She
handed them to us.

"I don't care what the Dear Leader tells us," she said,
"this is Japanese food. Raw mushrooms. It's the food of
cavemen, the uninitiated. Still, it's a meal and better than
nothing."

I finished mine in a few minutes, so hungry that I
almost didn't hear what she told us about the rules. "So if
we do anything wrong," I said, "we'll be shot."

Yoon-sung glared at me. She patted a holster at her

side, which held an old-style pistol, chemically propelled. "I may be among the untrusted, Catherine, but do what I say. I will use this if I have to, especially on you."

"Why do you call yourself untrusted?" asked Margaret.

"I am part Japanese. My grandfather was an expatriate in Japan before the war, and so my father grew up there, married a Japanese woman. When the war started he brought us back to the great city, to Pyongyang. Things went well for him. But for us, his children, with enemy blood in their veins..." Yoon-sung paused to think. "It did not go as smoothly."

The thought that a nonbred could hate her parents confused me; of all the conversations of men I'd heard on the line, in the tunnels, so many of them had included fond sentiments about their parents that it became something to envy—an experience we would never have. But Yoon-sung's eyes showed no sign of tears. When she spoke there was no indication of sympathy or nostalgia, no love for the past or family, and a bit more of my convictions began to crumble when I realized that my observations of humanity had been limited. They had been only a small part of a much greater world. Here was one that seemed to hate being human, or at least aspects of it.

"But she was your mother," I said. "Do you not love her? Does she not care for you?"

Yoon-sung laughed. "She was a Japanese whore, and it would have been better had he never married her, had I never been born. You are not like me, cannot understand. We do not choose our parents. We are taught from a young age to respect and honor them, but to honor the Dear Leader more, to give our loyalty to the Republic first. So when I caught my mother communicating with

Japanese relatives I turned her in, and now my mother is dead. She got what she deserved. My father did not. The Dear Leader removed him from a Ministry position and sent him and my older brother to the lines; now I'm the only one left. Had I been older I would have acted differently, I think; I would have killed her myself and spared my father the humiliation of being labeled untrustworthy." Ahead of us, a group of about twenty others waited, stamping their feet and slapping their shoulders to keep warm. "No more talking now, we join the remainder of my unit. Do as I show you and let Margaret translate, because as much as I enjoy the chance to practice Russian, everything today will be in Korean."

I almost laughed at that, thinking that if this was Yoon-sung when she enjoyed something, I would hate to see her angry.

The men and women who waited glanced at us with blank expressions, and Yoon-sung didn't bother with introductions, instead ushering us off the main road and down a logging trail, on either side of which lay barren snowfields littered with stumps and fallen trees. Ice and snow had collected on some of the branches. It capped them with its cold hand, as if to say that the winter had claimed these ones and that no amount of work could pull them free. In the distance I heard shouting. A loud crack followed, and a large pine ahead of us started to fall over slowly before it struck the ground to send up a cloud of snow. This was the logging area. Yoon-sung spoke with the foreman to get directions, and before long we arrived at our assigned section where someone had already positioned ancient, alcohol-powered saws, ropes, shovels, and chains. She pointed to a pair of handsaws.

"Those are yours. When we fell the trees, you will strip them of branches."

"That's all?" I asked.

Yoon-sung shook her head. "For now. We are fed according to the danger and exertion of our labor, and yours is the easiest. The least food. Soon, you'll wish for more dangerous jobs so you can eat, because those mushrooms are the only things you'll get until tonight."

All day we worked. At first the duty seemed easy, even boring, since Margaret and I had nothing to do but wait for the men and women with power saws to cut through thick trunks. The saws screamed, and eventually took on voices as their operators started and stopped them, the whining of metal on wood alternating in pitch. Then the first tree fell. I almost missed it when someone shouted in Korean, and had less than a second to dodge the huge timber as it collapsed to the ground where I had been standing. From that point on, the labor was nonstop. After an hour of sawing, pushing the metal back and forth, my arms ached and I wondered how long it would take to wear through the palms of my mittens. After two hours I could feel my hands, the cold penetrating everything as sweat soaked into my wool clothes and then the oversuit, threatening to freeze. Snow started falling, lightly at first. But as one after another tree fell, the snow picked up until we found ourselves in a near-blizzard, with visibility reduced to tens of meters in either direction. Yoon-sung blew a whistle three times quickly. We all gathered around her, and she kept blowing it until everyone had arrived to be counted, before we began moving in a line, the person in back placing his or her hand on the shoulder of the one in front so nobody would get lost. Margaret was in front of me.

"It's a different kind of living," I said.

"What do you mean?"

"I mean this. Working. And not like in the factories, here everyone seems to work for survival. It's like a different kind of combat, with its own code of honor. Did you notice that nobody spoke?"

"So?"

"I like it." My shoulders disagreed with me, making it hard to even keep my arm on Margaret's and I laughed. "Because there is no discussion of God or bred versus nonbred. We are equal here, all equally expendable I think, and this is confusing."

There was to be no more working that day. Margaret and I huddled for warmth in our hut, not sure if we'd survive. Once we stopped moving, the sweat-soaked oversuits froze in places, threatening to send us into hypothermia, but sometime after midday Yoon-sung arrived with three others, men who carried an iron stove and two handfuls of wood. They helped us assemble it. A thin exhaust pipe exited the stove's top, and the men bored a narrow hole through the roof so they could push a pipe section into the air outside. Once it was lit Margaret and I crouched beside it, grateful for the bit of warmth it provided.

Before they left, Yoon-sung pointed outside. "You are permitted to gather wood in your free time. Do not touch trees that have been cut down, and take only wood that has fallen." She tossed Margaret a pistol and smiled. "For the wolves. That is only to be carried when collecting personal wood so do not show up for work or meals with it. Once you've proven yourself to me, then I might change the rules."

"We'll be shot?" I asked. "If we show up armed for work?"

Yoon-sung grinned. "Dinner is in one hour. You should get moving; that wood won't last long." And she left.

Margaret and I stared at each other, and didn't say anything. The warmth seeped into our mittens, thawing blistered hands and easing the aches in my shoulders as it dried the sweat that had, a few minutes before, threatened to kill us. It was an awful stove. The metal had been welded poorly, and dents and repaired cracks spoke of its history, of having been used long past its life, but to me it was a thing of beauty. I didn't want to leave it. But after a few minutes we looked at each other and smiled.

"Do you want the pistol?" asked Margaret.

"You take it."

"I'm guessing the wood close to town has all been scavenged," she said, "we may have to wander far, and there's the danger of getting lost in the snow. How do you suggest we do this?"

I thought for a moment and then shrugged, delighted that without armor she could see the gesture. "Quickly. I'm hungry, and it's cold."

As we left the hut and reentered what had become a living hell, the Siberian snow, I tried to focus on the good things, which really only amounted to one thought: we'd get to Korea in the spring. Yoon-sung and the others didn't know that they would take us to exactly the place we wanted to go.

# EIGHT

# Arduous March

*She who finds peace outside His kingdom*
*will know only war, and will find herself*
*fighting the dragon; both will be cast out.*

MODERN COMBAT MANUAL
REVELATIONS 12:7–8

All winter we worked. On some days enough snow fell that Margaret, I, and all the logging units sat for hours in the communal hall, smoking cigarettes that had been made from sawdust and a bit of tobacco, or drinking tea that was probably made from the same. The Koreans were a marvel of resourcefulness; everything was used, recycled, and then made into something else until finally it crumbled into dust so that nothing was allowed rest until the life had been squeezed from it completely. Eventually we learned the names of our fellow loggers, who were women, men, and young girls and boys, all of them among "the untrusted," not worthy of a factory job underground where it was warm. There was Kang Song-won, a withered man who limped from gout and who told us about the Asian war because he had been a fighter pilot at age sixteen, but the Japanese shot down his plane in China so that by the time he found his way out of the mountains and into Russia, the nuclear weapons and biologicals had

already been unleashed. He refused to climb back into a
plane. Song-won stayed with the logging community out
of fear and never saw his family in Samjiyon again, forever labeled a coward.

Ch'on Sang-mi's mother escaped with her when Allied
forces bombed their political gulag, then hid on the other
side of the Tumen River until South Korean and American forces pushed across in force, forcing them to run
through the Russian winter snow. There had been almost
no food. Her mother used all their winter clothes, which
amounted to a single overcoat and two blankets, to keep
her six-year-old daughter warm enough to survive, so that
by the time she reached Chegdomyn gangrene had crept
up to the woman's knees and nobody knew how she could
have even walked. She died a few minutes after handing
Sang-mi to a stranger, also handing down her prison-
camp dishonor.

Hwang Eun-ch'ung had been born in Russia and didn't
remember anything. But her parents fled before the war's
start, as defectors who wanted to escape the North and
find a better life, so that when the Russians found them in
Khabarovsk they waited until she was born before turning the entire family over to camp officials; the Koreans
executed her parents and placed her in the care of a new
family before sending her fourteen-year-old twin brothers
southward to fight. She couldn't remember them but had a
photo. The Japanese captured both boys and paraded
them both through the captured city of Munch'on, their
images on all the news holos, even ones that made it to
Chegdomyn, dooming Eun-ch'ung to a life in the woods.

And eventually Yoon-sung explained who the old
woman was, the one with the medals. Ch'o Na-yung. The

Dear Leader. She had been twenty when the war began, a lieutenant in one of the women's units that had marched northward in a mission to move North Korean Party officials, including the former Dear Leader, from the horror of Pyongyang to safety in Chegdomyn. It was to be a temporary stay. The Koreans in Chegdomyn straddled a line between Chinese and Russian relations because on the one hand they were a source of cheap labor to Moscow, and on the other had historic ties with China, the two having shed blood in an ancient war against a common enemy: America. Na-yung's unit was supposed to have eventually escorted the officials to Dalian to form a North Korean government in exile, but the city's nuclear destruction preempted their plans, leaving them stranded in the camp.

But the old system was corrupt. When a logger accused one of the Party ministers of raping his twelve-year-old daughter, the man was executed along with his child and anyone else who complained. Food and supplies went to the officials. Leftovers were to have gone to the soldiers and then to the loggers, but often there was nothing left, resulting in starvation and freezing for everyone except Party officers, which triggered a rapid decline of living conditions for everyone else, including Na-yung, since it was the loggers and soldiers who did the work—and because war had choked off virtually all supplies in the first place. Na-yung approached her colonel one day, weak with hunger. She found the woman, naked and in mid-copulation with the minister of People's Security, the colonel's cabin littered with empty bottles of alcohol and with a half-eaten chicken scattered across the dirt floor.

Na-yung reacted without thought. She shot the two in bed and then gathered the dirt-crusted chicken, returning with the remainder to her unit, who devoured it, bones included. Na-yung explained what had happened. She expected to be shot by her sergeants, maybe one who had an eye on a promotion and wanted to take Na-yung's position, but instead her NCOs cheered. *Then all of them did, including the enlisted women.* Na-yung realized instantly what she should do; she gathered her unit to quietly make the rounds of other platoons, telling them to join their coup or be shot, and again she found only willing supporters. *Everyone* was hungry. Starvation had converted Party loyalty to hatred of anyone attached to it, and her soldiers sped through the camp, executing every official they found until none remained except the Dear Leader, who fell on his knees in the snow, begging for mercy and promising to change conditions for the workers. Na-yung slit his throat while everyone watched. The Koreans then tossed the dead corpses into the forest to attract wolves and birds, which came in vast numbers, and which the loggers and soldiers shot for food. Since then, the leaders of the camp, the new Party, didn't eat until the workers did and everyone served in the military having an equal stake in survival, even the untrusted. To Yoon-sung, and everyone else, Na-yung was a saint.

But to them, Maragret and I were still "the Americans." Even though they included us in everything as members of the Third Soldier's Logging Unit, it was almost spring before we gained real acceptance, and all it took was for one of them to die.

The fourth tree that morning crashed into the snow, and Margaret smiled at me from over the noise of her chainsaw while water exhaust billowed from its methanol engine.

"I'll beat you today!" she shouted.

I shook my head, and shouted back through the padded face mask, "You always beat me!" and then returned to my clean-up work. The branches cut easily. By now my muscles had adapted to the hard work and pushed the saw through them, back and forth, as though the limbs had been made of balsa wood, and the sounds of chainsaws filled the forest with their screams, sending me into my thoughts. But then everything went quiet. I looked up and saw the other loggers standing, motionless, their eyes fixed in one direction so that when I turned to see what was so interesting I dropped my saw.

A Russian had emerged from the forest. He stood at the western edge of the area we had cleared and wore one of the powered suits I had seen earlier. Half of it shimmered, invisible. The other half had been damaged, its ceramic shattered in places to expose power lines, hydraulic pistons, and thin piping, some of which leaked a green viscous fluid that hissed and steamed in the snow. Upon seeing the thing my fear returned, surprising me with its intensity. At first I couldn't speak and my legs felt as though they had vanished, leaving me floating on air so that I had no way to move, frozen, and only my eyes functioned as they focused on every detail. It had been too long. Margaret and I had finally let down our guard, forgetting war because of hard labor, but a moment later the lessons began ticking through—slowly at first, and dim, as though covered with mental dust.

"Tell them to get down," I said to Margaret.

She spoke to Yoon-sung in Korean, who repeated it, and everyone vanished into the snow. "Now what?"

I couldn't see its offensive systems, and suspected that

whatever weaponry it had was still concealed by chameleon skin, but it moved, rotating with a hum to face me. "Distract it!" I shouted, and then ran.

Grenades detonated in the spot I had just left, and followed me as I leapt over stumps, trying to make it to the trees on the thing's right flank, its bad side. The grenades began to catch up. One of them detonated immediately to my side, sending a spray of thermal gel that ate through the outer layers of my coat. I gritted my teeth against the coming burns, but the gel died upon reaching the innermost layer, the one I had once thought consisted of ballistic cloth. It almost made me stop running. *What was this stuff made of?* I heard shouting then, probably Margaret, and the dull thud of something striking ceramic, but didn't take the time to look, and sprinted into the treeline to begin working my way to the Russian's rear. The pops of grenades sounded again, but this time they weren't aimed at me.

A minute later I stood behind it, hidden by a tree. By now Yoon-sung had relaxed her original rules and allowed us to carry the old chemical pistols, nine-millimeter ones, as protection from the wolves and I eased mine from its holster, quietly chambering a round. Margaret's voice still shouted from the clearing but there were no more grenades.

Then came the sound of an enormous zipper and I cringed, the sound immediately followed by snaps as flechettes broke the sound barrier and cracked into trees. I leapt from behind cover. It was four meters to the thing, and the snow fought me as I struggled closer while the Russian turned, its feet lifting and slamming back into the snow so it could rotate more quickly. It must have had rear-facing motion sensors. But before it could turn completely, I leapt, grabbing a hold of where I knew the crack between its head and shoulder plates should be, pulling myself up onto the thing's shimmering arm. There was no going back. The nose of my pistol barely fit into the crack and I emptied my pistol, not even remembering when the thing threw me off, sending my body to career through the air and land against a stump.

For a second there was nothing. I lifted my head to look and saw no shimmer now so that all of the Russian was visible, and more green fluid ran from under its main carapace, steaming in the cold as it slid down armored legs. Margaret appeared at my side and smiled.

"Goliath slays the giant," she said.

I felt my shoulder and nearly screamed. "Something is broken." Margaret touched the spot, under my coveralls, and this time I *did* scream.

"Collar bone. It's snapped."

She helped me up from my good side, and by then others had gathered with Yoon-sung, and we approached the thing with pistols drawn. Margaret slid mine into its holster.

I sat in the snow as Margaret moved closer to the Russian, examining the armor and squinting at its characters. Finally she found what she was looking for, cracked open an access panel, and within a second the armor opened with a hiss while a massive frontal plate swung wide on pistons. The sight reminded me of what I had seen in the rail yard and I dry-heaved with the memory.

Inside was a thing the size of a baby, cradled by a padded harness. But its resemblance to anything human stopped there. It had no legs or arms, but a head larger

than normal rested on its shoulders, and when I noticed
the absence of a mouth and nose I wondered how it could
breath until I saw that among the hundreds of wires leading under its skin there were a series of tubes that poked
into its chest, each one carrying a bluish liquid. Like we
had seen in our sister, its eyes were gone. Instead, bundles
of fiber optics had been attached to plastic ports that
seemed to grow out of it, almost like goggles, and when
the cold finally hit, the thing started struggling so that the
cables shook and clicked against the carapace.

Yoon-sung emptied her clip and it stopped moving.

"You have seen these before?" she asked me in Russian.

"Not the final version," I said, clenching my teeth with
pain. "Only a prototype, the ones they tested on my kind."

"Come." She lifted me and motioned for Margaret to
help, so we stumbled across the field, heading back toward
the camp.

"Where are we going?" I asked.

"Na-yung. She will want to have dinner with us tonight.
Na-yung will have questions, and you need to be ready."

Margaret looked at the others, who followed close
behind. "Where is Song-won?"

"Dead," Yoon Sung said. "But he died standing up,
shooting at the Russian so his children will now be allowed
a place in the factories. Underground. Hurry now. We will
have to vaccinate you and there is much else to do."

"Vaccinate me?" I asked.

"Na-yung travels to China frequently and may carry …
things. We have all been vaccinated. You will sit near her,
and should be prepared in case she has been contaminated."

"I am engineered to resist biologicals," said Margaret,
"I don't need vaccination."

Yoon-sung laughed at that and then grunted under my weight. "You weren't engineered for these bugs."

"Do you still want to run to Thailand?" Margaret whispered in English. The doctor had left, and the painkillers, combined with my tranq tabs to kill the pain, made me smile. They had set the bones; now all I had to do was wait for the plaster to dry and report to the dining hall.

"Yes," I said.

She squinted at me. "Why?"

"What do you mean, why? It's our plan, my plan, it's what I've been doing all along." But the truth was that I didn't know why anymore; Margaret's question made sense. Here we half-starved, constantly froze, and were so tired that we walked with our eyes shut, asleep before we even lay down. But I hadn't had many hallucinations since I came. The work reduced everyone to the same level and although I suspected it was an existence that would horrify most humans, especially those like Alderson, it was the first time I felt part of something worth doing. Nobody had told us to take an objective and the only combat had been forced onto us, an engagement of self-defense to protect the logging unit. And strange as it might have seemed, logging was at the root of my confusion. The trees would be turned into lumber in underground factories to be shipped into Unified Korea in exchange for steel, wool, and other things that Na-yung's people couldn't get here. Wood waste was turned into methanol, cigarettes, and a hundred other things including fertilizer to help grow oil crops for their tractors and saws; the oil came from castor beans, grown in half-underground hothouses that stretched for acres. You soon learned that if it was possible to make, these Koreans made it and because nothing went to waste, neither did we, instead being folded into the community. The fact that we were untrusted meant nothing because we were still a valuable part of a machine geared not for war but for survival; the Koreans made us feel like we were worth at least *something*.

But even that wasn't enough to keep me there; an invisible cog turned in my chest, pushing me forward so that even though I couldn't explain why, it was clear that staying wouldn't be an option.

"There are others there, Margaret," I said, hoping to convince myself as much as her. "Other girls who didn't give up until they were free. And I still believe in God. I don't think He wants me to stay here, even though I want to. But you can. I won't make you come with me."

She thought for a while, eventually shaking her head when the doctor came to release me. "No. I'll go too."

The clothes fit loosely, reminding me of how much weight I'd lost. There was no fat on anyone here. Yoon-sung had given both of us stiff wool uniforms that had been worn and patched in places, the leftovers from someone else who had passed on yesterday or ten years ago, and which smelled of chemicals that the Koreans used to keep their clothes from rotting in storage. The fabric of my jacket was dark green and around it she buckled a cracking leather belt, almost three inches wide. With no mirror Margaret and I laughed at the way we each looked, and for a moment it felt as though we had stepped back to an era that had faded centuries ago, and we were still laughing when we stepped into the cold, heading for dinner. We entered the dining hall and I nearly jumped. The entire room clicked its heels to attention with a sound that reminded me of thunder, and Yoon-sung marched with us to the dais at the far end, pointing to where we should each sit, helping me ease into a chair next to Na-yung.

Yoon-sung sat beside me and translated the introductions. She had coached us on the way over: don't speak Korean, only Russian, because my Hangul was horrible and I would risk insulting the Dear Leader; do not look at the Dear Leader, keep your eyes on the table; when one of the senior officers speaks to you, wait before responding, to allow the Dear Leader a chance to field the question or give you permission to answer. The rest I couldn't remember, hoping that the instructions would come to me if I needed them. One other thing she told me I *wouldn't* forget: that I would leave the table hungry, because it underscored the sense I'd had with Margaret—that these were a strange people, in that they were human *and* honorable. Party Officials only took half rations; they didn't perform manual labor, and therefore had to scrounge the extra calories they needed.

"You look good in your new uniforms," said Na-yung. Her voice reminded me of the old woman who'd screamed at me in Kazakhstan, frail but determined, and for a moment I feared a hallucination. "Almost like Russian volunteers for the People's Army."

Although others at the table laughed, I didn't understand the joke; I smiled anyway and said, "Thank you."

"The word has gotten out," she continued, "that you sprinted through deep snow, under fire, to attack an armored monster. One of the new Russian abominations."

A man across the table, his uniform threadbare but his eyes hard and cold, cleared his throat. "Excuse me, Dear Leader, but don't our Chinese brothers field these same abominations? You spend so much time in their mountains, I often wonder if your last name is Ch'ang, not Ch'o. I'm sure you have seen a Chinese version of these creatures before."

Nobody looked up. A tension descended over the table so that the air felt charged, and I waited for someone to say something. Anything.

"General Kim," Na-yung finally said to me, "thinks we should all be Russian puppets, like the original Kim of old. That Russia is our home, and that our allegiance should therefore be to Moscow."

Yoon-sung stared at me when she finished the translation, and grabbed my wrist, squeezing it hard. It was a prearranged signal: *don't say a word.*

"Not to Russia," the general said, chuckling with some of the others. "Allegiance to humanity." He pointed at me then. "One shouldn't admire these things, and certainly not the one they killed today. We should exterminate them all, any we find."

Na-yung looked at me for a moment. "I wonder what you think about the general's idea?" she asked.

There was no guidance from Yoon-sung, who had turned pale. She pulled her hand from my wrist and waited with everyone else for my answer.

"I would kill me," I said.

Na-yung sounded shocked. "What? How could you say that?"

"Because," I explained, staring directly at the general. "We are bred to destroy, and the one we met today is no different. There is no fear of death for us, at least for the ones new to the battlefield, and we are as machines, with only one purpose: to attack. Besides"—I paused while a young girl lowered a plate to the table in front of me—"Now that I know the general's intentions, I will surely kill him the first chance I get."

Na-yung laughed hysterically at that, as did three-quarters of the table, but some, the ones sitting closest to the general, sat silently. They looked to him for a response. But the general said nothing, both of us glaring at each other until he finally looked away.

"You," Na-yung said, "are welcome in our little community. What is your name?"

"Catherine."

"Thank you, Catherine, for saving my loggers."

From the corner of my eye I saw her pick up a spoon and start on her soup, followed by the rest of the table. My soup looked thin. Watery. I lifted some to my mouth, hoping it would taste better than it looked, but was disappointed when I found that it was little more than salty water with flecks of what could have been wolf or deer meat. This stuff did nothing to abate my hunger.

"Well, Catherine," Na-yung said, "as a reward for your accomplishment, I will allow you and your friend to choose your next assignment. Maybe you'd both prefer a job in the greenhouses or in a factory, out of the wind and snow?"

I thought for a moment; God had to be with me, because this was an opportunity that nobody could have predicted.

"I would stay with the logging unit, with Yoon-sung," I said, "but I was wondering. Would it be possible for my sister and I to stay in Korea, maybe in Wonsan when we travel there in the spring?"

Yoon-sung paused before translating. Na-yung noticed and snapped something at her, too quickly for me to understand, and Yoon-sung's face turned red until she finally repeated my request. The table went silent.

"You would rather stay with them, in the south where the people are fat and lazy? Perhaps you are not as strong as I thought."

I realized then that the request had been an insult, and did my best to explain. "No. If I had to choose between staying in the south and staying here, I would choose to remain in Chegdomyn, not in Korea. It's just that more girls like us have escaped the Americans and relocated to Thailand, where they have their own community. We wish to join them. They are like family to us."

Yoon-sung translated quickly, and some of the men and women started breathing again. Na-yung smiled.

"Well. Who can compete with family after all?" She thought for a moment and then nodded. "Fine. If you serve with honor on the train ride south, we'll leave you in Wonsan."

The rest of the dinner passed more or less uneventfully. Na-yung spoke briefly with Margaret, performed a small ceremony to welcome Kang Song-won's son and his family into the trusted ranks, and then excused herself early, leaving me with the general, who did everything he could to make me uncomfortable. When it was over and Yoon-sung escorted us back to our hut, starving, she shook her head.

"General Kim wants you dead," she said.

"I am used to men like him."

Yoon-sung nodded. "Yes, but I can't protect you, Catherine. You should not have spoken so bluntly. He and Na-yung are at war, and the general thinks she is too old to lead, thinks he should take the place as Party leader, sooner rather than later. You are now aligned with her and we have a saying: when two whales collide, the shrimp get crushed."

I ducked into the hut after Margaret and turned back to look at Yoon-sung. "I don't understand, what does that mean?"

"It means," said Yoon-sung, blowing into her hands to warm them, "don't get crushed."

In three weeks my shoulder had more or less healed, and winter ended. Yoon-sung had to tell me because at first I couldn't see the difference, but then one morning I saw my shadow on the ground and heard an intermittent crashing in the woods. I wondered what it was and drew my pistol. The others in our unit kept working as I crept toward the tree line expecting to see a pack of wolves or a bear, only to be covered in snow when a clump of it, heavy with melting water, collapsed onto my head. Somebody laughed when I returned. It took a few seconds to brush the snow off my shoulders and although it was still cold we all threw our hoods back, wanting to feel the sun on our faces for the first time in months.

We worked all day, happy for most of it, but then Yoon-sung stopped her sawing and looked up. Eventually everyone stopped working. You sensed a kind of ominous weight in the air because it had become so silent, an unsettling and heavy quiet with no indication that any-

thing had gone wrong or that there was cause for concern—
except that something wasn't right.

Margaret looked at Yoon-sung. "What?"

"There's no noise," she said. "There should be another
logging unit working in this area, and there's nothing."

"Let's go find them," I suggested. "They may have run
into another Russian."

Yoon-sung nodded and rested her saw on a tree stump,
calling out instructions for everyone to draw their pistols.
She led us toward the second logging area. The snow
crunched underfoot and we moved cautiously through the
forest, suddenly aware of just how quiet it had become
because there was no wind in the trees, nothing except for
the occasional *crump* when snow and ice fell from
branches overhead, and the noise reminded me of a distant artillery barrage. Ten minutes later we arrived at the
second logging area; nobody was there. The loggers' saws
and tools lay in the snow, as did their clothing, a fact
which made everyone especially nervous so that we gathered back in the trees, careful to watch in every direction
as Yoon-sung spoke.

"This is strange," she said.

"There were no footprints leading into the forest," I
said, "only ones leading to the city. I think they went back."

"But why?"

Margaret and I looked at each other, but before I could
answer we heard a distant noise, different from that of
crashing snow, like the sound of far-off firecrackers.

"Back to Chegdomyn," said Margaret, and we started
running.

The noise increased as we stumbled through the forest, and I wondered what I was doing. We were headed

into combat. But this time there would be no armor, no radios to coordinate, and I had never fought with this unit before, didn't know if they were *capable* of fighting, and even if they were, all we had were pistols. The discarded clothing suggested that the missing unit's members were either all dead or had replaced their oversuits with armor, but why? Was this a coup and was the missing logging unit sympathetic to the general? The answer to that question sent my brain into a spiral of thought, making it hard to concentrate as the noise of combat increased.

We were about to break from the forest onto the main road into the camp when a group of Koreans, several of them trailing blood in the snow, emerged from the trees in front of us. As soon as they saw us, our pistols drawn, they stopped and threw up their hands. Yoon-sung recognized one. She said something, and the man smiled while the rest of them, realizing we weren't going to shoot, continued on their flight, disappearing into the brush and snow.

"They've attacked the Dear Leader," Yoon sung explained. "She's holding out with a small guard force but can't last long."

"We should help her," said Margaret.

"How?" Yoon-sung asked. "General Kim's men broke into the armory and grabbed weapons and suits. What good are pistols?"

The fear rose into my throat and I couldn't speak, watching as my hands started shaking. Margaret looked to me for support.

"Murderer, what should we do?"

"I don't know," I whispered.

Margaret's jaw dropped and she chambered a round. "Well I know. I'm going to help her and you should too.

The general will take care of us as soon as he finishes with Na-yung."

"I will go," said Ch'on Sang-mi. "This is *Na-yung*."

"Death to General Kim," someone muttered.

And soon all of the loggers had gathered. I saw in them the same look that must have been on my face, one of terror and uncertainty, but they all stared at Margaret and Yoon-sung and waited for instructions, ready to go. I fell on my knees. For the first time the cracks in my resolve had turned into a full-blown collapse and I cried openly, not able to move when the unit moved out to leave me behind. I lay down in the snow. The cold eventually seeped through my coveralls and into my back, making it feel as though I lay on a slab of ice, cooling not just my skin but the sensation of terror along with it. The quiet returned. No snow fell, and for a moment the firing stopped, giving me time to think about everything— about Megan, who seemed to whisper in my ear as the crying abated, my tears not freezing now that temperatures had climbed. *Running was the only sane option,* Megan whispered, *but you were not born into sanity.* I got up slowly. My pistol lay deep in the snow where it had fallen, and I dug it out, making sure that it had a full clip before I followed the prints that the others had left. Eventually I caught up with them, and rejoined Margaret and Yoon-sung as they surveyed the camp from behind an abandoned tractor. Margaret welcomed me back.

"We have two things to accomplish, one before the other," I said, speaking in Russian so Yoon-sung could follow. "First, get armor and weapons for everyone, or we will not survive."

"And the second?" Margaret asked.

"Kill General Kim. As soon as we do that, the coup will crumble."

Yoon-sung nodded. "He will probably be hiding somewhere. The man is a coward."

"Is there any chance the Chinese could help?" I asked Yoon-sung.

She shook her head. "I don't know, but probably not. Besides, the only radio with sufficient range is underground, with Na-yung. If the general's forces haven't disabled her antenna by now, she has already thought of that."

My hands shook. Every nerve in my body screamed to run in the other direction as I forced them to function, to enable me to scan the camp from our spot and search for something that would show the way. Nothing obvious revealed itself.

"We have to move closer." I slapped the tractor. "Yoon-sung, can anyone in your unit drive this?"

She nodded. "All of us."

"Margaret and I will move in to get a closer look. If you see us come under fire, move in with the tractor to provide cover; it's the only armor we have." I looked at Margaret and we left.

We stuck to the ditch at the roadside, taking the chance of crawling our way into town but keeping low in the hopes we could avoid any thermal sensors. My coveralls were soaked with melted snow. The cloth clung to my shoulders, dragging me down so it felt as if I would keep sinking if I paused, and we moved even more slowly. The weight made it difficult to force freezing limbs forward and both arms ached so badly that when someone called out, I sighed with gratitude for the stop.

They yelled again and Margaret hissed at me. "We've been spotted, they're saying to get up and that it's safe, the aboveground part of the camp is secure."

"Tell them we can't, we're wounded."

Margaret answered, and within seconds we heard footsteps and rolled onto our backs, thinking the mud and filth would convince them we needed rescuing. Two men in armor peered down at us, their Maxwells cradled. I extended my left hand to them. One of them took it, pulling hard, and he lifted me to my feet as he said something in Korean after which I placed my pistol into the joint at his armpit and squeezed the trigger twice. Margaret had done the same. The two men fell to the ground and we stripped them quickly, dragging the bodies into the ditch and then slipping into their bloody undersuits, hoping we hadn't done too much damage to armor systems. I connected essential items and buttoned up.

"Mine's fine," Margaret said through the speakers.

A red light showed on my heads-up. "Targeting won't link with my Maxwell, so I'll have to use iron sights. Otherwise I'm OK."

A moment later we heard the coughing of an engine and saw steam billow from the tractor where we left the others, and I realized I'd forgotten the instructions we gave them. They had heard our gunshots and assumed we'd come under fire. Yoon-sung's unit moved forward slowly, and in infrared we saw the heat of their bodies, coming in a group as they huddled behind their makeshift vehicle.

"Take the left side of the road," I told Margaret, "I'll take the right. In the ditch so we can give covering fire."

Both of us dove into our positions, facing the center of

town, while the tractor's rattling grew louder behind us. We waited for Yoon-sung to draw to our side but before she did, a group of Koreans gathered in front of us, walking forward in armor.

"I can hear them," said Margaret. "They're Kim's people and one is asking what all the noise is; the tractor has them confused. I think..."

I opened fire. Tracer flechettes walked into them, and one by one the figures fell to the ground until none remained standing. When the tractor drew even I told Yoon-sung to wait.

The wind picked up, sending ice and snow across the road, and Margaret and I jumped to our feet, sprinting toward the Koreans we had just killed; we slid into the pile of dead, not pausing to fully stop before our hands worked to pop their armor. I recognized some. Two old women stared back at me, dead, and I remembered that they had worked with the Second Logging Unit, a memory that froze me in place.

"What are you doing?" Margaret shouted.

"This is Mi-ae. The girl we smoked with whenever it snowed. I can't remember the other one's name."

"It doesn't matter, Catherine, we need the armor."

*"I can't remember her name!"*

A squad of Korean soldiers rounded the corner, from the other side of the People's auditorium, and I dove behind one of the bodies, resting my carbine on its back. My sights centered on a moving target, a woman, and even though Margaret's flechettes flew and snapped, their green streaks seeming to float down the road and into the people at which she had aimed, my finger wouldn't move. It had stopped working. Then someone targeted me, riddling the body in front with fire. I ducked my head before Margaret called out.

"Clear. We have to get these weapons and armor back to Yoon-sung, Catherine."

But it didn't matter. Yoon-sung's unit showed up around us, silently slipping into undersuits and armor, grabbing any weapons they found. These were Chinese- or Russian-manufactured Maxwells, and felt several pounds heavier than the ones I had grown used to, but it could have been due to the fact that I hadn't held one in so long that the weight was now foreign. It felt better when Margaret ripped it from my hands.

She pushed me down when I tried to stand. "Stay down, Catherine. You'll get someone killed."

"I can't see the way anymore, Margaret." I tried to stand again and she slammed her carbine into my chest, forcing me to trip over one of the bodies.

"I don't give a shit. What's wrong with you? I followed you because you were the Little Murderer, the one who took life without a thought. I don't want you to die. But I also don't want you with us right now, not when you're insane."

Yoon-sung's people were ready and she stood next to Margaret, saying, "Listen to her. Just stay here."

And before I could respond they were gone. It was late-morning now, and clouds gathered overhead, the temperature dropping back to the point where it felt like winter again, and when the snow came I started to cry. The tears must have been what brought the dead. All of them, everyone I had killed including Heather, knelt around me and formed a massive crowd of people and genetics so that the throng stretched farther than I could see, and each one's eye-sockets had been crammed with bundles of fiber optics. The dangling strands glowed. At first the sound of laughter came from these people, until I realized it came from *me* because I saw it clearly finally, that my mind had caught up, had fully spoiled. Explosions ripped through the street, but not even they brought me back. It was hard to tell the difference between what was real and what was a lie, but the blasts of grenades threw ice and rock against my suit, and then thermal gel that hissed in its familiar way, suggesting that they were real, and my visitors the only illusion.

"I am at home here," I said to them.

Heather smiled, her mouth leaking blue fluid. "You are past your shelf life, Murderer. Come with us now, because it's true: we all wind up in the same place."

"You are in hell."

"No," she said, "but not heaven, either; it's just a place where things make more sense. You don't know who you are anymore, but we know, we know everything. The spoiling isn't insanity, it's normality, maybe the only indication you have that you aren't who you think you are."

"I am the Little Murderer."

"Are you?" she asked. "What's stopping you from killing now?"

I grabbed two handfuls of snow and dirt, throwing them at her only to see them pass through, her body that of a ghost. "Because I am with them now. Humans. This is the first time I've encountered any who treated us as equals, who took us in and gave us a chance when everyone else wanted us dead. Because I *owe* them."

"Owe *them*? Have you forgotten all your history? These people are almost genetically predisposed to dictatorial rule, and their genocides exceed those of Stalin,

Pot, and even Hitler. They don't treat anyone as an equal, least of all their own kind. Are you really *with* them, or only *like* them?"

I shook my head. "It's you who doesn't get it, Heather, because those questions don't matter. History is about perspective. Maybe for someone like me, a strong leader makes sense, a leader for whom the threat of death is just as useful a tool as diplomacy. A leader like Stalin. *Maybe I feel at home because I'm like them and with them— both.*"

"Really?" Heather smiled. "Then stay here. Forever. Don't leave this place and die so that your body can decay in the earth of Chegdomyn. But you won't stay. You keep running because you're afraid to face death, and now you're too afraid to even take a life."

*"I am not afraid!"*

"You hated me in life. I understand. But I don't hate you now, in death, so listen to me for once: I'm not Heather. I'm you. And I'm telling you that man calls it the spoiling because it is a mental deterioration that reduces their creations, nibbles away at us until we are shadows of humans. Weak. It makes us question war and death, telling us that killing is wrong and that for it we are damned. These are lies, Catherine; God intended for man to create us as killers, holy and fearless, but the spoiling is His, and given time you will see why He inflicted us with madness. Man did an imperfect job and made mistakes. Yet what man made incomplete, He can make whole. Help Him. Take the next life you see and it will deliver you from the spoiling forever, so that you can take a message to the nonbred, for Him."

"What message?" I asked.

"You'll figure it out, Catherine, but I can't tell you; you need to have faith. At the end of your journey, when you are perfect, then you'll know."

The crowd of phantoms began fading into the snowfall, allowing a man to run through Heather as she spoke. "Kill *him* now. Don't show me anger or fear; show me that you are still with God. This is another test, Catherine, and like the last day at the atelier, he is a kitten."

His armor had been burned in places, its helmet not completely locked down so it bobbed and clicked as he ran, and his feet moved uncertainly, as if not used to the weight of armor, or he may have allowed himself to get too soft, too weak. A patch of ice sent him onto his face. The man slid toward me, and as he got closer I heard wheezing breath, then a sob as he spoke in Korean. He tried to get his footing, but each time a grenade landed nearby the man overreacted, sending himself flying. I grabbed him as he passed and ripped his helmet off.

General Kim screamed, and put up both hands as if trying to stave off what would happen next. You didn't need to understand Korean to know that he was begging.

"I don't hate you, General," I said in Russian.

He lowered his hands. Dirt streaked the man's face except for where tears had run, and his skin looked red from the exertion of sprinting.

"Please," he said, "don't kill me, I didn't mean what I said at dinner."

"Why did you attempt a coup?"

"She is too old. You wouldn't understand, because you're new to our culture, new to humanity even. Respect toward the elderly is our way. So I would never undertake something like this lightly, especially not with someone so revered as Na-yung, not with someone I am sworn to serve, someone old enough to remember the war. But this is a different war. Soon we'll be caught in the middle of it, and I don't think she can navigate us through. *You don't know what she has planned for you and your friend.*"

"I want to thank you."

He opened his eyes all the way, maybe surprised. "For what?"

"For everything your people have done. For me and Margaret. Even though you don't want us here, I appreciate the collective decision to keep us; I'm sure it couldn't have been easy for you to accept it."

"You will let me go?" he asked.

It would have been cruel to answer him or to allow the conversation to continue. And by then the fires had begun around the camp, touched off by the grenade and rocket fire, so that when a group of soldiers marched in our direction the flames backlit them, their silhouettes getting larger as they approached. But it wasn't an easy decision either—not like the ones regarding those who had died before. I had to grit my teeth and close my eyes, then find his head by touch before I twisted as hard and as quickly as I could, snapping his neck. A feeling descended on me then, a kind of weightlessness and lack of care; God had been there.

By the time Margaret and the others reached me, along with Na-yung's forces who had fought underground, I wasn't hearing anymore and couldn't see or talk. Later Margaret told me that I lay on General Kim's body for the rest of the day and into the night, begging him for forgiveness. Crying. Na-yung had thought she understood. She knelt beside us for a while, and shed her own tears, brushing the hair back from Kim's forehead and then cleaning his face with a handkerchief while she told me in Russian that it was never easy to kill a great man. But that wasn't it; how could *she* understand? What had come to me that night, through Kim's death, was the gift of acceptance, of finally knowing who and what I was: a killer. But not like the one who had fought her way to Kazakhstan through Iran and Uzbekistan. I would be a killer like nobody had seen before, one who saw God's will.

"Na-yung counts us among the trusted now," said Yoon-sung.

I didn't respond to her. They had given us Chinese armor and Maxwells, and after so long in clothes, the ceramic felt heavy and confining, so that at times like now it seemed to suffocate, but not in the way it had when I once feared the helmet. Whatever had happened on the night of Kim's death, it had restored me—removed every bit of fear so that the armor's weight and confinement was nothing like it used to be, only a distraction. Spring had arrived in full, and Chegdomyn lay just far enough south that the snows melted fully, turning the areas surrounding the city into a swamp. We stayed helmeted, not because there was any danger, but because of mosquitoes. The insects had become so thick that, unhelmeted, if you opened your mouth for even a few seconds a hundred would fly in, catching between your teeth or inhaled into your lungs. Margaret said something in response to Yoon-sung about earning the Dear Leader's trust by defeating the coup, but I knew that wasn't it because I remembered more of what she had said during our time with General Kim's corpse—when she revealed that she could speak Russian fluently. *I secretly agreed with the General, Catherine, that you are an abomination. But the abomination isn't that your kind was created in the first place; the abomination is that here you are, barely twenty, and yet you think and speak as though older than me by twenty years. I have pity for you.*

"How much longer?" I asked.

"Those are the most words you've spoken all month," said Margaret, "I'd begun wondering if someone had removed your tongue."

Yoon-sung surveyed the rail yard. "At this rate, about two more days."

We stood on a gantry over the main rail line that ran through the middle of town, and looked down on the men and women who ran from one job to another while massive steam cranes swung back and forth, lowering logs and cut lumber into waiting cars. The cars were ones I had never seen. Yoon-sung told us that a Unified Korean business had developed them, and had designed the cars to open like clam shells so the lumber would be protected. Each side of the cars rested on the ground, and once full, the sides would swing upward and seal hermetically, locking out radioactive dust and biologicals that still lurked among the route we'd take through a desolate North Korea. I didn't know what to feel. The breakdown I'd suffered during the coup had caused a shift in me, and maybe was just the thing I needed, so that now I felt comfortable with the thought of moving south. There was a kind of peace. The new warmth felt wet against my skin when I took off my helmet, and the smell of new grasses and flowers amid the swamps and forests wafted through the air, as if the season quietly promised that something good was about to happen. Even the mosquitoes didn't bother me that day.

"What will we face on the trip south?" I asked.

Yoon-sung kicked a rock from the gantry, watching it land before answering. "Mostly bandits. They will have set traps along the tracks, loosened rails in spots or placed mines. We'll move in front of the train in a series of separate, armored cars, scouting the way ahead."

"How do they live?" Margaret asked. "In an area so contaminated?"

"They find a way. Many of them were people who survived during the Japanese attacks and just stayed, somehow adapted to it all. Some people can't bring themselves to leave. The rest are Chinese who ran from their country, thinking things would be better in South Korea, but they were refused admittance at the new border. Those people couldn't go back."

Margaret slapped me on the back and laughed. "I can almost see the ocean, Catherine. Smell it. I wonder how South Korea compares to Bandar Abbas and can't stop thinking about Thailand."

"We may die before Thailand," I said.

"What is it with you? Do you have any room for optimism?"

I smiled and clicked my helmet back into place. "I am eternally optimistic, but my will and yours are irrelevant. We can be more optimistic in Thailand."

The new suit linked to my Maxwell the way it was supposed to and I scanned the tree line closest to us, sighting on a pair of wolves. They stood absolutely still. Both animals watched us, their tongues hanging out and their skin stretched taut from having eaten better than ever during one of the coldest winters on record for the area, a winter in which there had been plenty of Chinese and Russian corpses. I pulled the trigger and waited. A second later the flechettes hit the wolf on the left, punching through its head so that the animal died before its tail hit the mud. Yoon-sung called out the kill and several people cheered, all of them volunteering to go out and collect it. The second one went down a moment later and I grinned. Tonight we would eat meat. But even more important, it felt good to draw blood, even from a wolf, and even if only for food.

"You kill animals with no problem," Margaret said. Things had been strained between us since the day of the coup, and she no longer looked to me for guidance. "Will you be good on the trip south? You take only two tranq tabs a day."

"Only God knows."

"So," she continued, "we're back to God now?"

I felt sorry for her then, wondering if she would ever see it—see the things I saw now that everything was clearer. It may have been a new form of insanity. But for now it didn't matter because when I held up my hand the difference was obvious, should have been clear even to Margaret.

"What?" she asked.

"What do you see?"

"A hand. A gauntlet."

I shook my head, exaggerating the twisting of my neck so she could see it. "Not just a hand. It's a hand that isn't shaking anymore, a hand touched by God himself."

Chinese suits had one advantage over American ones: the faceplate. Instead of a relatively narrow slit, or even the rounded ports on Russian models, these suits had a glass section that spanned from our forehead to our mouth, providing a better field of view, and, if you were close enough, allowing you to see the face of your fellow soldiers. Margaret was staring at me. She didn't say anything at first, then sneered, pulling at a water tube that poked upward inside the suit, near her mouth.

"I'm taking a walk," she said.

Once she was gone, Yoon-sung sighed. "She is younger than you."

"Only by a year or two."

"That's not what I meant. I meant in mind, not in years. Margaret has started selling herself for extra food, at night, to the men in the factories, and she sees no value in herself. I didn't want to tell her the truth about the trip, the full extent of the danger we face and I don't think you should either. The railways are paved with the skeletons of dead North Koreans. That is the truth."

"I don't care about the truth anymore, Yoon-sung, or lies. It will unfold how it unfolds."

Yoon-sung grinned. "You have changed since the night of the coup. I'll ask you what you think about the truth once we head south because right now you can only imagine it. The people in contaminated zones have nothing to lose and will kill us the way we kill wolves. For food. They feed on the humans they capture."

"Well then there's no problem." I grinned back at her. "Because I'm not human."

And the words reminded me of my last meeting with the men in white coats.

*     *     *

"You forget," said Alderson, "that you're not human." It was late in the war, just before we were to make a new push for Pavlodar, our second advance, so by then he had been in long enough to become tired. Alderson lit a cigarette and blew the smoke upward. "You're artificial."

He handed me a towel. I had just come off the line, where a Marine had poked his head out of the topside observation post, just to get a breath of fresh air. I had reached up to pull him down when it happened. A grenade blew off half his head, sending a spray of bone and tissue over my unhelmeted face, and there had been no time to clean off because a moment later came the order to report to the rear for another interview.

I wiped the blood from my face and tossed the towel back. "I haven't forgotten, Alderson. I'm proud of it. We are better than you."

"Your hands," he said.

"What about them?"

"They're shaking. Badly. And you're drawing down your tranq tab inventory at an alarming rate."

I didn't have an answer for that. It was true. "What do you want to know, Alderson?"

"Tell me everything. Or nothing. It doesn't matter anymore, Catherine, this will be our last interview because once the spoiling gets this advanced, we're not allowed to speak to you anymore—for our own safety. I asked for you to come back here so I could say good-bye. And to say I'm sorry."

His apology stunned me. At first I didn't know what to say, thought it was another of his tricks. "There is no entry into His kingdom for you, Alderson. It's too late to change. You can apologize all you want but a coward's fate is in hell."

"Yeah," he said, "with Lucifer," and then laughed. He acted strangely. This wasn't the arrogant Alderson of a year or even a month ago; this was an Alderson who smoked, breaking the rules, and who stared at me with no fear and with half-lidded and lined eyes as if he had seen something that aged him prematurely. "You have no idea how right you are. If you knew what the Russians and Chinese are working on now, scientists like me, and the horrors they've created..."

"You should just die," I said, not wanting to hear him finish. "And do you *really* want to apologize? Ask the guards to leave for one minute. Just for ten seconds to see if you have the courage to stay with me alone, to see if you could survive."

Alderson nodded, stubbed out his cigarette, and lit another one immediately. I noticed it then: his hands shook, too.

"You're perfect, Catherine. The most perfect unit I've ever met. So I'm assuming that the spoiling has begun? Are you having any hallucinations?"

I didn't say anything at first, but then nodded. "Is that what we're here for today? So you can pick at my dreams the way Kazakh women pick at the dead, looking for anything valuable, anything that might have been left behind?"

"That, and to tell you something else. You are the most amazing war machine, the most complex ever created and a perfect biological weapon, and I have no problem with being a part of this because we did something good, nothing to insult God. But that's just the problem: biology and God.

Your genes are essentially human. So instincts will kick in, telling you that you need to look for something else beside war and find a peaceful place in the world. I feel sorry for you. Because there is no place for you in this world."

He stood and left through the door at the back of the room, while the four guards motioned for me to leave in the other direction, and I headed back to the tunnels. My head felt light. Not a good kind of light-headed feeling, but the kind in which you sense that you've just stepped into an alternate reality, where the first question you ask is, *did I really just experience that?* Megan noticed something was wrong as soon as I got back and asked if I was all right. I told her what happened.

"They pay attention to you," she said. "Even when I or the others go for interviews they ask about you, not me or the other girls. They all want to know about Little Murderer."

"That doesn't make me feel any better."

"It should. It should make you feel like your life has a greater purpose, and like maybe Alderson was just delivering God's message."


"God's message to me," said Margaret, "was that I and my sisters were a joke."

I was still on the gantry, holding on to the railing, and I pulled off my helmet and shook my head, trying to clear it of the last remnants of memories, of Alderson. Margaret had returned and was talking to Yoon-sung. The cranes finished loading one of the cars below us and we listened as hydraulic pistons hissed, lifting the huge car sides with a whine until they slammed closed to create a sleek container, its seams almost invisible from our vantage. The train cars extended almost a kilometer in either direction and I counted the remaining empty ones, losing interest before I finished.

"Yoon-sung," I asked, "where are our scout vehicles?"

She shouldered her Maxwell. "At the front of the train. Come, I'll show you. We can justify leaving our post by calling it a patrol."

We moved off the gantry and through the running groups of Koreans; I saw their faces, former factory workers who had once been among the trusted now humiliated and forced into labor units because they had supported General Kim. Some of them cried as they worked. Yoon-sung said things to them, and without seeing her face, I tried imagining the feeling of hatred that must have showed but I couldn't, almost stopping in my tracks with the realization that I still couldn't recall my *own* hatred. It had vanished. We sauntered through slush and mud along the sides of the tracks and neither Margaret nor Yoon-sung knew the numbness I felt, the shock of having lost something that had been so long a comfort, and which I sensed was gone forever. It felt like losing a friend. But by the time we arrived at the train's diesel engines my smile had returned, and my feet felt light despite the caked mud; the hatred that had been so heavy, an infinite weight, no longer resided in my chest. No more fear. No hatred. Their absence made everything warp in my mind, yielding a new point of view with which I had yet to become accustomed, and one for which I occasionally doubted what I knew to be the real explanation—the one given to me by Heather. *All I did was kill a man,* I thought, *and in doing so overcame an obstacle, moved closer to His side?*

Yoon-sung showed us the twenty scout cars. They were small, and had six large off-road wheels that just cleared the railroad ties so that steel train-wheels could ride the tracks. A turret with an automatic grenade launcher, coaxial Maxwell autocannon, and thick ceramic plates covering the cars from front to back completed the vehicles, made them lethal to anything less armored.

"The cars ride the rails unless we need to leave the tracks," Yoon-sung explained. "And then we can lower the wheels, so they lift the cars and allow us to go off-road. Behind the train will travel similar vehicles, but outfitted with bulldozer blades and cranes for making repairs."

"How do we find mines?" I asked.

She pointed to the front-most scout cars. "Those have detection equipment. We'll move slowly, about twenty kilometers per hour, so slowly that the old ones named these trips 'the Arduous March.' Any faster than that and our detection equipment is useless. If we lose the detection cars..." But she didn't need to finish.

The eagerness to go south had left, maybe with my hatred. But I didn't want to stay either. Instead I stared at the cars with satisfaction, a kind of serenity born of knowing that soon we would have new experiences to add to our old—whatever those experiences were. Everything was out of my hands. *That was the explanation,* I realized, *why things had changed with Kim's death.* I hadn't wanted to kill him but he had needed to die because it was all part of a greater plan and my actions would have been carried out regardless, by Na-yung or one of the others, and it had been like breaking through a glass wall for me. Killing was no longer to be enjoyed. But nor would I hesitate to do it, or fear that my actions could result in death for anyone, because finally, for the first time, I saw the path and was on it. People would die, some at my hands, but there was no more honor in it.

"We'll kill them all," said Margaret.

"Will we?" I stared at her for a moment. "Death is something we'll all know some day, Margaret. Even you."

# NINE

## *Chuche* Soup

*And she who finds peace outside His kingdom
within another's, will call the beast, who will
rise from the earth and make war.*

MODERN COMBAT MANUAL
REVELATION 11:3–7

Na-yung placed the scout unit under Yoon-sung's authority. She would be in charge of protecting the train, each car of which held only wood, except for the engines and the rear-most car, which would house a platoon-sized support unit. Yoon-sung beamed. She assigned us to her command vehicle, the last scout car at the train's front, and we climbed in, taking a few minutes to link our suit systems with the vehicle's; I needed assistance since everything was in either Chinese or Korean, but once finished, we waited. And waited some more. I sat in the turret, where a fiber optic bundle connected to a port in my helmet, and where I watched views of the surrounding yard in split-screen on my heads-up. Korean engineers walked slowly up and down the train making final preparations and then, finally, Yoon-sung said something in Korean, radio traffic ceased, she said one more word, and the scout car lurched forward.

She spoke over the intercom in Russian. "I think you'll

like North Korea, Catherine. You can't destroy nature, not with anything man-made. The wildlife has taken over everything, and now the country is more beautiful than ever. Just wait."

I scanned the forest on either side of the tracks, watching the trees crawl by at twenty kilometers an hour. "How long until the border at this speed?"

"Just over three days. We can relax to some extent until then, but keep your eyes open." She clicked into the general radio channel and spoke Korean, which Margaret translated. "Safeties off, weapons hot. Kill anyone within ten meters of the tracks and announce any hits on detectors. Out."

It didn't take long to get our first look at nuclear devastation. Less than ten minutes after we started, the tracks took us due east—a direction in which we had never traveled for logging—and into the thickest forest I had seen, the trees towering over our tracks and some of them leaning at a dangerous angle, about to collapse. Then the trees gave way to open fields. Our tracks angled slightly north, guiding us into the ruins of a city that had been abandoned, its buildings rising from the middle of a swamp so that bushes climbed from the bases of their concrete structures, vines reaching to the very top as though something had reached up from the mud and was slowly demolishing everything. Our detector alarms screeched, forcing me to knock my helmet against the turret ring in surprise.

Yoon-sung heard the bang and laughed. "That's why we seal the cargo, Murderer. Don't worry. Our cars are shielded, and the dose we'll get is next to nothing."

"So," I said, "the attack has already begun."

"We have plenty of tranq tabs from the stores Misha gave us," said Margaret, her sarcasm obvious.

"*You'll* need them soon, I think." I smiled. There had been no hallucinations in a while, and something told me there wouldn't be any more unless it was a message from Megan or the dead, not a hallucination but a way to see the path.

"Do you want me to man the turret?" Margaret asked.

"Maybe later."

"Are you sure? It could take your mind off things if you had something to concentrate on."

"I said *no*. You begin to bore me."

I wanted to enjoy the scenery. The turret gave me and the commander/driver, Yoon-sung, the best view of our surroundings, a three-sixty panorama of abandoned humanity and the victory of forest and swamp. Margaret, who monitored the detectors, had no view unless I piped it to her. She was to make sure that our automated cars up front, their sniffers barely clearing the wooden ties and ballast, kept moving and that a nominal number of sensors functioned. It was tedious. Her view consisted of a bank of computer screens and indicators, row upon row of numbers and blinking lights that rarely changed and that would be sure to tell *me* nothing. And Yoon-sung had confided in me that she had grown concerned with Margaret, a concern that I shared because Margaret had turned into something I recognized, an organism that closely resembled the way I had been only a few months ago. *She will kill, even when the time doesn't call for it; I think she is going mad,* Yoon-sung had said, and I nodded, not sure how to respond. Margaret's spoiling manifested in a different way—through whoring—but the process had converted her nonetheless so that now she hated everything, most of all herself.

"Fine," she said, not bothering to hide the anger in her voice. "If you hallucinate, even once, I'm going to take over from you. *Murderer.*"

"We will settle our differences, Margaret. Soon." I felt her stare then, but she said nothing and Yoon-sung only chuckled.

Some time later, the scout cars leaned slightly as the tracks angled sharply southward in the direction of Khabarovsk.

"Yoon-sung, the Chinese are in Khabarovsk." I said.

She sounded amused. "Are you scared?"

"On the contrary, I plan. They might inspect us."

"I told you a long time ago, they are our friends. There will be no inspections; the Chinese are expecting us, and with a quick bribe of their officials we'll continue on our way."

"Bribe?" I asked. "With what?"

"You'll see when we get there." I tried to pry it out of her, but Yoon-sung refused to say anything more on the subject.

Her answer created a sense of something hidden, a stirring in my chest that urged me to remember something, anything she had ever told me, so that I could predict what it was that the Chinese would take as a trade. But nothing came. Wolf pelts, methanol, wood—all of these the Chinese could gather themselves, and the only thing I could think of that they didn't have was us. Margaret and me. The Chinese had no American genetics of their own and General Kim's warning came back, "*You don't know what she has planned for you and your friend,*" and I checked the flechette pistol in my belt holster to make sure its fuel cell was still full. My newfound serenity came from accepting that fate would unfold the way it was supposed to; but it didn't include volunteering for experimentation by Chinese researchers.

We saw Khabarovsk long before we got there. It was early in the morning of our second day when smoke billowed up from the city and into the sky, turning the air over the trees black, and we were kilometers away when the thud of artillery started shaking the scout cars slightly. Movement caught my attention. I spun my turret to face the target and zoomed in on a squad of soldiers, their deep green armor and red stars clearly visible as the *things* ran parallel to the tracks.

"Do you see that, Yoon-sung?"

She sounded as excited as I was. "Are they keeping pace?"

"No, I have them at fifteen kilometers an hour, a little slower than us. But it's a constant rate. No man or woman could run like that for long, not even our sisters."

The squad leapt over wreckage and then turned in unison, wheeling like a flock of grounded birds before disappearing into the forest on our right. My breathing was shallow, rapid, from excitement. And despite a suspicion that whoever manned the armored suits was probably like the Russian thing we had found months ago in the forest, there was no revulsion. For a moment I envied the troops, wondering what would happen to the rest of my sisters, regular Germline units, if Americans adopted the model. Would they be discharged? Or would they be taken off the line and detailed with menial tasks? This was a new era of combat and it forced one to reflect on the fact that what Misha had said was true: once you had seen a squad of them moving in the open, you had to admit that Margaret and I were obsolete.

The scout cars pulled into Khabarovsk station long before the train did, and Margaret and I stayed inside while Yoon-sung left. I watched her through my targeting sight. She climbed onto the platform just as the train's first diesel engine emerged from the trees behind us, and then she faced the main station—a ruined structure, still on fire, which made it hard to follow her on video. Before our train pulled in, a platoon of armored Chinese troops walked out of the smoke and dust, picking their way carefully through the wreckage. Yoon-sung waved to them. I kept my weapons trained on the one closest to us, but a moment later three turned simultaneously to face me and my targeting alarm tripped, a red light flashing on my heads-up display and warning that we had been lased for range. The things lifted their arms and pointed grenade launchers.

"Catherine?" Yoon-sung's voice crackled in my headset. "I suggest you point our turret somewhere else. Our hosts aren't happy with it."

I fingered the controls until the guns faced in another direction. "Done," I said, and the warning alarm switched off.

"Thank you."

The train pulled in behind us finally, its brakes hissing when they locked, and Yoon-sung stood with her arms folded as she faced the Chinese. Nothing happened. Five minutes later, Margaret and I looked at each other.

"What are we doing here?" she asked.

A flash of plasma burst nearby, overloading my view screens at the same time my temperature indicator flickered upward. "We'll find out. But it is unusual; I thought the Chinese had already secured Khabarovsk, and there is no reason I can think of for this level of conflict."

My movement indicator caught something, past the station and in the city. I zoomed on the target area and saw a group of what looked like civilians—women and children—being forced through ruined streets by armored Chinese troops and then into waiting trucks. The outside microphone picked up their screams. One of the soldiers shut the back of the truck, which had a solid box-body in the rear, obscuring my view of them, but then another truck pulled up and a second group piled in. Then a third. For as long as we waited the armored troops moved back and forth, loading civilians as war raged all around them, pausing only once to fire streams of flechettes into a group of children who decided to run. None of it disturbed me. Instead, while I watched, I wondered what they would need women and children for and where were the men? My interest was no more than curiosity, the same kind Alderson might have had while pelting me with questions, and after watching for a few minutes more I decided that from a tactical perspective there was little explanation. The strategic perspective yielded only questions. Nobody would need factory laborers so badly that it was worth risking turning an entire city of civilians against them, and there had been no news of the Chinese underground facilities at all, so nothing of the scene made any sense— not even after their officer arrived.

A scout car crawled over the rubble and ground to a

halt behind the soldiers who faced Yoon-sung; its top hatch popped open to emit a human, his head protected by a green helmet that he pulled off with a smile. He jumped down onto the platform and greeted Yoon-sung. I fought the urge to train my turret in their direction again, to point the microphone so Margaret could translate, but it would have been foolish; the three armored soldiers still faced me. Yoon-sung and the man laughed, and he hugged her, before waving the armored soldiers forward, where the whole group of them passed out of sight, walking in the direction of the train's rear.

"What are they doing?" asked Margaret.

"I can't see them; they went toward the back of the train."

Margaret pulled her pistol and lay it on top of a bank of electronics. "If they come for us, I'm not going quietly."

"I thought the same thing. There is something strange here, but don't get upset, Margaret. This will reveal itself."

"Use the turret gun," she said. "We can lower the wheels and break from the train."

"I can't have you react, Margaret. Do nothing. It will play out."

Margaret screamed. *"You are not my Lily!"*

"No. I'm not." I unclipped from the turret harness, and dropped to the compartment floor before grabbing my own pistol and pressing it against her faceplate. "But you will listen to me. I don't know what's wrong with you, the night of the coup is over and I see the way, will never again hesitate to act. Do you want to settle everything now?"

"You're a coward," she said, but her voice trembled. "You can't kill me, you couldn't even kill the North Koreans that night, ones you barely knew."

"I will do this to put you out of your misery. I know where you are, don't forget that I have walked that road, the one your mind is on now. I know that any exit for someone in the desert is a relief."

The blue power indicator from my weapon reflected off her faceplate. Margaret said nothing. We stayed like that for a minute, after which she started crying and I took her pistol before climbing back into my turret.

Five minutes later, one of the soldiers reappeared. The thing used a pincerlike hand to grasp a rope, towing something behind it that hadn't yet come into view. When it did, I cocked my head in confusion. People. I told Margaret to watch through her computer screen and piped in the view. One of the other cars must have contained humans, and from their features they appeared Russian, hobbling after the Chinese troops one after another, the single rope looped around each neck. The men wore nothing, and clearly shivered as they walked barefoot over ruined concrete toward the line of trucks and civilians. Some started crying. All of them looked more starved than we did, the skin of their cheeks hollow and gray to the point where I wondered if I watched skeletons or men, and soon, the remainder of the Chinese troops emerged to move in the same direction, the last one carrying the most mystifying thing of all: the Russian I had killed in the forest. All its sockets had been disconnected from its suit, the wires and tubes severed, so that short stalks of fiber optics still protruded from its eyes, and the Chinese soldier held it gently with both ceramic arms as if carrying a baby that it didn't want damaged.

Yoon-sung shook the officer's hand and then waved good-bye as she strode back to our car. "Let's go," she said, slamming the hatch behind her.

"The Chinese were shooting children in the city," I said. "What is this all about?"

"What?" Yoon-sung asked. "What was what all about?"

Margaret nearly exploded. "Are you kidding us? Those people. Who were they?"

"Russians," said Yoon-sung. She radioed the order to move and we started forward before she continued. "Russians we captured the day before you arrived at Chegdomyn, and the one you killed in the forest. The Chinese want them."

It still made no sense and I shook my head. "For what?"

Yoon-sung turned to me, and it looked as though she was smiling, for the first time showing a part of her that I hadn't known existed: the ambivalence of a criminal. A complete lack of concern for the fate of others. "You know as well as I do, Catherine, how important good genes are."

"What?" asked Margaret. "For *what*?"

I sighed, returning the view-screens to scan for targets, and not wanting Yoon-sung to know I suspected something more. "Experimentation and genetic material. We're all raw materials, Margaret, if you think about it. And who knows what else the Chinese want. So that's why there is new fighting then? Because the civilians of Khabarovsk have decided it's better to die than allow their children to face whatever the Chinese have in store? What happens if the Chinese decide they want Democratic People for their experiments? What will Na-yung do then?"

Yoon-sung didn't say anything at first. The scout car picked up speed, leveling off at twenty kilometers per hour, and we heard the rails clacking beneath us in a steady rhythm. Then she spoke.

"Na-yung has a saying that became famous after her coup. Self-reliance, *chuche*, is good, but noodle soup is better. We do what we have to, Catherine, to survive. Now, so must the Russians of Khabarovsk. They can all go to hell. If the Chinese come for us, then we will find a way out, the same way we always have."

Yoon-sung decided that until we reached the border, we would keep moving, even at night, while one person took a shift at monitoring the detectors. There would be no targets, she argued; only the Chinese moved freely in this area of Russia and we'd get all the sleep we could manage because it would be needed once we reached North Korea.

During my shift on the second night, I had time to think. Yoon-sung and her people weren't what they had appeared to be, and now I had proof that if pushed in the right direction, given the resources, they too would probably have created their own versions of Margaret, me, or the new generation of armored genetics. They had traded humans for a pass south, and she had smiled at it. If we had failed to convince Yoon-sung when we first met, if Margaret hadn't succeeded in making Na-yung comfortable with the two strangers who had arrived in Russian armor, we would have been traded too. Our American advisors, both of them, had fought against the killing of innocents, had wanted to kill *us* when we took the lives of civilians and prisoners—their enemies—and now Yoon-sung had shown no such restraint. She had orders. But that meant nothing to me and even less to the condemned Russians who by now were dead, and even they, the Russians, had given us a choice, hadn't forced us into experiments. I had no moral objections to what Yoon-sung had done and didn't mourn the loss of a few Russians or children, but it was the revelation that disturbed me, that I had been so wrong about her, about the North Koreans, about everything. Deep down, there was no difference between Alderson and Yoon-sung. Maybe she was worse.

Yoon-sung slept in a tight space next to me, a wool blanket wrapped around her shoulders and her head resting on her vision hood. I still couldn't read her face. What dreams did she have? Did the dead, even the deformed genetic we had killed in the woods that day, did *they* visit in nightmares? Whatever friendship we once had, a solid structure that had been based on the common hardships of the forest and starvation, now seemed more like it was of sticks, suggesting that for her part it had been even less, a straw man; not only was there no guarantee that she or her leaders wouldn't sacrifice us, there was a likelihood that this, in fact, was the plan all along. The path was clear. We still had Chinese-captured territories to negotiate, and passage may still have to be purchased through the sale of Margaret and me. I searched for my hatred. It should have been there, and not finding it frustrated me to the point where tears began rolling down my cheeks, until there was no place left to search because this wasn't a time for hatred anyway. The only thing for this was calculus. Moving on from their camp had been the right decision, and things would need to be patched up between me and Margaret because now I suspected that whatever it was that had come between us, Yoon-sung was behind it. She had begun spending more time with Margaret than me. Both of them spoke Korean. In the last month, Margaret had begun referring to the possibility that she might stay with the North Koreans, make Chegdomyn her home, where she was seen as a valued asset and rising star now that she had clawed her way from the trees. Calling her a valued asset was probably true on the part of the Koreans; to them, Margaret *was* valued. But valued for what? The irony was that she'd be safer once we crossed the border and moved into the contaminated remnants of North Korea, because there Yoon-sung couldn't trade her to the Chinese.

I piped the forward view from the turret into the closest screen and watched, keeping my peripheral vision on the detector panel. The night slid by in white and black. A hundred meters in front of us, the rear of another scout car bounced over the tracks and I wondered who was in it. Chinese? Things had moved so quickly that there hadn't been time to get a sense of the scouting unit, and no briefing to speak of concerning specificities, of how to handle the mission and who would do exactly what. Manning the detectors didn't matter for the moment and I moved into the turret, zooming into the scout car's rear, examining it for anything that might reveal its occupants' identity. It was as if a voice whispered in my ear, conveying a message of danger that convinced my fingers to pressure the firing controls, lasing the distance to the car and preparing to shoot. Someone popped out of the hatch. The helmet hid their features, but they were clearly distressed and holding up their hands as if to ask what the hell was I doing. I pulled my fingers off the twin triggers. It seemed to satisfy whoever it was, and the person popped back into the car, their hatch swinging shut.

"Are you OK?" Margaret asked, speaking English for the first time in months.

"I'm glad you're awake."

"Why are you in the turret, is something wrong?"

"I'm not myself. I want to cross the border, Margaret, and get to where we're going. But to do that we have to carry out His will."

Looking up, she sat as best she could below me. "I don't know what we were meant to do."

"You were not meant to have sex for food."

"She told you?" Margaret's tattoos converged when she frowned but she didn't look away. "I am not happy with how things turned out either."

"You needed to eat and I understand because look at us. We're barely alive. Starvation effects judgment."

Now Margaret started crying again and I fixed my attention back on the view-screen, giving her time to think.

"They shot children," she finally said, "at the station? You saw it?"

"Yes. But I shot children too, early in the war. Do you remember what it was like, when you were first given duty on the line?"

Margaret nodded. "I killed for the sake of killing. It was my duty."

"It *was* your duty. And the children of Khabarovsk *were* just children, and now they have no cares—all the dead ones are free, for that matter—and are seated next to God. Now your duty is to keep going until you find the answer."

"What answer?" Margaret asked. She moved to wipe away the tears before realizing that earlier she had fallen asleep with her helmet on and now couldn't reach her face.

"*Your* answer, Margaret. The answer to the question, 'who do you want to be?'" I tossed the pistol back to her, and she stared at it for a moment before tucking it back into its holster.

Margaret glanced at Yoon-sung then and motioned for me to put my helmet on. Once I had, she clicked into the intercom. "Yoon-sung told me I should whore myself. For food. I told her that I was hungry one day, and that was her suggestion, but despite the way it made me feel in Russia, I did it anyway because she made it sound so simple. Likc it was normal. And for the past few weeks she's been telling me you were crazy. Too crazy to follow, and crazy enough that we might have to get rid of you someday."

"She said the same about you."

"What do we do, Murderer? I don't trust anyone anymore, and these people hug the Chinese as if they were family. I've seen humans. Humans don't smile after they see children shot. Yoon-sung isn't who we believed her to be, she would be happy to trade us, and we can't ignore the fact that she betrayed her own mother to her government. This woman is a monster."

I thought for a moment, forming the first part of a plan, but the entirety of it wouldn't crystallize. "Do you know who is in the rest of the unit, the other cars?"

"Yoon-sung told me," she said. "A couple of men from our logging unit and the rest are a mixture of soldiers who remained loyal during the coup." She ran through the names and I recognized a few, but most were unknowns.

"What are you thinking?" asked Margaret.

I shook my head. "I'm not thinking anymore, that time is over. Just don't speak and do everything I tell you. *Faith.*"

Margaret's eyes went wide at the word, but it had the intended effect. There was a spark there now. I lowered myself from the turret and crawled to Yoon-sung, where I yanked the vision hood from under her head, ripping the wires from her suit and sending the woman's head to bang against the ceramic floor. She woke cursing. Once her eyes opened fully, I slid my knife from its sheath and placed the tip against her throat.

"Margaret," I said, "get in the turret. Jack your helmet in so you have full weapons control." I smiled at Yoon-sung and moved my faceplate to within an inch of her nose. "Not the wake-up you intended, Yoon-sung?"

"What are you doing?" She tried to look past me, for anything that might help, but before she could move I lifted the knife and jabbed it downward, piercing one of Yoon-sung's eyes; it took a second for her nerves to react, to send the message to her brain that something horrific had just occurred. A second later she screamed.

"Hush," I said, "you still have one eye and it's not that bad. *Chuche*, or soup, Yoon-sung, that's what you should be thinking right now."

*"What do you want?"*

"How much is an American genetic worth?" I asked. Yoon-sung was in so much pain that I had to slap her, to remind her that I was there and could take the other eye in an instant. "How much?"

"You are worthless. Margaret is worth quite a bit more."

"Worth more to who? The Chinese?" After she nodded I went on. "And what about me?"

"We were going to let you go, to the south if you lived. The Chinese already have first-generation Germlines, but nothing of generation two and know that the Russians have several. They fear that it gives Moscow an advantage. It would be easier to do it this way, to pretend the Chinese had set up a routine border inspection and let them handle it themselves; they were to kill you if you tried to stop it. Some of us wanted to do it in Khabarovsk, but you might have damaged too many people there since you were on turret duty, maybe even destroyed the train itself."

I inserted the tip of the knife under her chin, cutting it so the blood flowed over the fingers of my left gauntlet, making my grip more slippery. She screamed again and I shifted, placing a knee on her chest before pulling the knife free.

"You lie. I was never going to see North Korea, and you would have either traded me or killed me. Why don't you want us to see North Korea?"

"That's not true," she said. "I swear. Na-yung told me specifically to make sure you reached North Korea, that someone would be there to take you—but not the Chinese. She had sold information to someone, someone who knew that a Germline One named Catherine had been in Zeya and escaped, but even I was kept from the details. *I swear.*"

"Who are you?" I asked.

"What do you mean? You know who I am."

"I mean you speak many languages. They chose you to handle us, back in Chegdomyn. You translated for our hearings, and escorted us to dinner with Na-yung, knew exactly when to answer, when not to. No logger has that much intimate knowledge of the ruling cadre. So who are you, really?" I placed the knife tip under her good eye as a reminder.

"I am Chu Yoon-sung. Minister of Public Security. Na-yung wanted to learn everything she could about you before making any decisions, and couldn't trust this to my subordinates, could only trust me."

"So you're the head of Na-yung's spy organization?"

She nodded again, the lid of her good eye beginning to flicker, and I realized she was about to pass out. "Why do the Chinese need Russian civilians?"

"To repair genetic damage caused over the years. The Chinese had to survive after the war with a population reduced to almost nothing. They cloned themselves, underground, but the process was imperfect and now they need genetic material so they can inject more diversity into their population. Russian tissue will be like a genetic map back to civilization. They will also harvest the prisoners' organs to replace those of wounded Chinese troops; with the proper immunosuppressants, it's quicker and cheaper than growing new ones."

"Last question. Exactly how many reserves are in the last two cars, and what are they armed with?"

"There aren't any reserve troops in the rear; that car was reserved for the Russian prisoners."

"Thank you, Yoon-sung. That was well done." I snapped her neck then, the same way I had snapped General Kim's.

The enormity of her plans made me sit. I rested my back against the bulkhead, trying to absorb what we had just learned. Margaret said something to me but the words didn't penetrate my thoughts, which now swam in a sea of possibilities, its current flowing around us as the scout car crawled southward to bring us closer to whatever Yoon-sung had planned. Dealing with the North Koreans in the forward scout cars wasn't the issue, and eliminating that threat would be simple. I worked it out in less than a minute. The Chinese forces were the thing to worry about and there was no choice but to assume that what Yoon-sung had said, that they would take Margaret at the North Korean border, was true. There was something to admire in the scheme. This was a plan that should have worked, except that the North Koreans failed to consider our abilities to calculate and form our own plans, and I supposed that Yoon-sung had made a mistake, thought Margaret the greater threat and that I really *was* insane—incapable of sound judgment. The spoiling, in a way, had saved us both. But there was one variable I couldn't define, and it brought back the memory of the general, the one who had winked before stopping Alderson's experiments. Who would have paid for information about *me*? And would Americans be waiting in North Korea?

I glanced up at Margaret. "I need to know how far behind the train is; can you see it?"

Margaret punched at the small computer beside her and then looked down. "I can't see it through the trees. But it's about four kilometers to our rear."

"Get down here into the driver's seat and slow to ten kilometers an hour."

Margaret moved quickly, not even pausing at the sight of Yoon-sung's body, and she moved the corpse out of the way, folding down the driver's seat. As soon as the car started to slow, I clicked into the general frequency before I remembered one problem.

"Wait, lock the car into auto." When she had, I pulled Margaret's hood over her head, making sure the headset speakers were on her ears. "I forgot I don't speak Korean.

Tell everyone we have a problem with defensive systems, and that they should slow down to our speed. But tell them we don't need help; Yoon-sung is climbing out to fix it."

She did, and then slipped the headset off to look at me. "What are we doing?" she asked.

"Getting rid of this bitch."

Half an hour later the lights of the train came into view, about a hundred meters behind us, before it slowed to match our pace. I opened the top hatch and got out. The wind, even at ten kilometers an hour, surprised me, almost knocking me from my feet; I waved through the hatch to Margaret. She passed me Yoon-sung's body, feet first, and it took a minute for us to angle the corpse and get it through the narrow hole, but once it came free I leaned over and yelled down.

"Clean the inside. Use whatever you can find and get rid of all the blood. It doesn't have to be spotless, just enough so people won't see it if they glance in."

By now Yoon-sung had stopped bleeding, and I thanked God that we wouldn't also have to clean the outside once I'd pushed her off. The body thudded to the tracks, rolling. Now that it was over I breathed again and sat, cross-legged, waiting for what would happen next—the distant sound of a train whistle and screech of brakes. I dropped back into the car, finding the driver's area still a mess.

"Aren't you cleaning it?" I asked.

"With what?"

The humor of the situation got to both of us and we laughed, deciding in the end to let the cleanup go since if anyone was so suspicious that they had to look inside it wouldn't matter anyway; it was more important to clean the blood off our armor.

"What will you tell everyone?" Margaret asked.

"That Yoon-sung was outside dealing with a weapons problem when she slipped and fell. She was exhausted. We would have stopped the car but we never even knew it had happened, which reminds me." I pointed to her vision hood, which Margaret had taken off while trying to clean. "You should put that back on, the train engineers are probably panicking and telling everyone to stop; after all, they just ran over the Minster of Public Security."

"What if someone figures it out?"

I shook my head. "I'm not worried about that. I'm more worried about what happens after we stop and whether or not you have the strength. We can't go on unless we kill them all, take fuel cells and food, and then strike out on our own. Just do everything I tell you and we'll make it."

All the forward scout cars reversed to return to the train. Margaret and I watched as the Koreans leapt from their cars and into the night, joining four engineers to pull pieces of Yoon-sung from under the train as two held flashlights. I told Margaret to stay in the turret. Her gun would be trained on the armed Koreans, never leaving, a death that none of them suspected existed yet, and which would soon take everything. They didn't deserve it, I thought. But they didn't *not* deserve it either, and none of their screams or pleas would affect me, not like General Kim's, because now I was a believer—a convert to a faith already professed but maybe never believed, a faith that had *already* written the fate of these men and women for whom there should be no pity because they had chosen their path so long ago. Death to them. I was a tool of God.

If their children had been there I would have ordered Margaret to slaughter them as well, and this time their spirits would have found my soul intact, impregnable to their efforts to haunt me because the answer had been there all along and just needed to be recognized. I did that with General Kim. He was my best friend, and only his and Megan's ghost would now enter my thoughts—if I let them—because General Kim had showed me the way and allowed me to finally overcome the one thing that had threatened to force me from my path: spoiling. Already my tranq tab dose was half of what it had been. Soon I would leave the remaining doses to Margaret with a prayer, that she would find the same peace I had. *That* was the point of this journey. It hadn't been to escape or to find freedom; it had been to show me the meaning of it all, a meaning that couldn't be seen from the rear, but only from the front and only then after a certain amount of ground had been captured and you could look back at the journey, understand every thread of its tapestry. For that I pitied the Koreans about to die, for their ignorance, not for their imminent death. They just didn't *see*.

The ballast crunched under foot as I moved toward the group of Koreans with my Maxwell, and they all began speaking, asking me questions, but I didn't stop and instead marched past until I had moved beyond the last of them, the ones who had come forward from the repair vehicles at the train's rear. Someone called out in Korean.

"They're asking you to come back and explain what happened," Margaret said over the radio.

"Shoot them all now. Grenades and flechettes."

Margaret sounded shocked. "What? What if there are still some in the scout cars?"

"They all left the cars, I counted, and these nonbred chose their own fate. Kill them with faith and make sure to let none escape; don't let anyone past you. Do it now."

The thudding of her grenade launcher opened up, followed by explosions and the snaps of her flechettes; I fell to the ground as I spun, firing into the thick of the Koreans and swinging left and right. One of them ran toward me. She was screaming and I centered my reticle on her head, ending her approach quickly. Once they had all fallen I stood again, sprinting toward the train's rear.

"Keep your aim on them. If any move, kill them."

"Where are you going?" Margaret asked.

My breath was short, and I didn't answer right away. "To the support vehicles, to make sure none remain to radio out."

It took five minutes to run the entire distance, and my sprinting soon reduced to a jog. There were ten support vehicles. Two Koreans had gathered to smoke, looking up when they heard me approach, and both died before they realized what was happening. Ten minutes later I had searched the tractors and cranes, and began working my way back to the train's engines. Margaret hadn't moved.

"Nothing," she said. "They're still down."

"Let's make sure." Grenades and flechettes had torn apart the Koreans, shattered their helmets and armor, but I ignored the evidence and pulled my pistol, firing twice into each head and changing clips twice before it ended. The train's engines were empty.

"Almost finished here," I said.

"What next?"

"Watch. Cover me."

All of the scout cars to our front had returned and sat

close to each other, almost bumper to bumper, their guns hanging down toward the ground. I pulled myself up on the first. Its hatch was open and I sprayed into it, firing three bursts before moving down the line and repeating the procedure until I was confident that nobody living remained.

"Come out," I said to Margaret. "It's time to get ready."

She climbed out and leapt from vehicle to vehicle until she stood next to me. "What do we do now?"

"Move our scout car to the very rear and send the train, the sniffers, and the scout cars south ahead of us to the border where we're expected; everything is already automated; all we have to do is activate control from our car. We can leave the support vehicles here. If any fighting breaks out, we'll leave the tracks and find a way through. In the meantime we transfer all the ammunition, fuel cells, and alcohol that we can to our car."

"How long do we have?"

"We'll work for twenty minutes and then go, we've already delayed our arrival to the point where they might be suspicious."

While we worked the night grew colder. The moon set and my muscles started aching as we transferred belts of grenades and hoppers full of flechettes, moving back and forth from the other vehicles to ours. We found drums of alcohol in one of the support cars and rolled them up the tracks before decanting fuel into all the jerry cans we could, which we then clipped to the sides of our car, along with fuel cell-filled duffels. My motion detector went off. Almost finished, Margaret and I fell to the ground, pointing Maxwells in the direction of the movement, but it was just a wolf, alone at the edge of the trees who watched us with curiosity. I was about to fire. But something held my finger and I grinned at the thing, saying a quick prayer that he would find something on his hunt. We were ready.

"This won't be easy," said Margaret.

"How do you know?"

"If we lose the car, there's no way we'll move through North Korea without getting a fatal dose."

I grinned and slapped her on the shoulder before climbing onto the car. "Everything kills. Time is killing us right now."

"I've always avoided the spoiling," said Margaret. "But not anymore. I started having nightmares, which bleed over into the day, and the fear won't leave me."

Margaret's foot slipped as she climbed up. I grabbed her shoulder, pulling until she stood on the car. We dropped through the hatch. After we had linked up with the vehicle and powered up, the engine thrummed in front of us, making the floor vibrate with what felt like promise and energy, so that I grinned, not caring anymore if things worked as planned or not, only a little sad with the fact that Margaret hadn't seen it yet, didn't understand enough to leave terror behind. For a moment it felt like it had at the beginning; I wished for more Koreans to kill, having been granted another chance to function the way I had been designed, but then decided that, as harder targets, the Chinese would be even better.

"It's all right," I said. "Spoiling is from within, it's part of growing into what you should have been all along, a curious defect that, in order to fix, you have to experience. Enjoy the hallucinations."

Margaret smiled while I wriggled up into my turret seat, her finger poised over a button, the one that would set everything in motion. I closed my eyes.

"Do it. At forty kilometers an hour we should be at the border in less than twelve hours."

"What was it like?" Margaret asked.

The view-screen captured my attention for the moment and I wanted to pop my helmet. Outside, to the left of the tracks, the ocean pounded against the shore as a storm flickered lightning far out to sea, and the camera's lens fogged every once in a while until systems kicked in to remove the haze. There was a quality to the ocean that made it call out. If you swam into it, tasting the salt no matter how tightly you closed your mouth, there was a hope there, a chance to swim under the waves and keep swimming down into darkness where an infinite number of things might be possible. Up here there were only two possibilities: either we'd make it or not.

We were just north of Lebedinoye and the trickiest part of our journey was about to begin. Margaret would soon have to stop our car, lower the wheels, and take us onto the road. It ran parallel to the tracks and would eventually bring us to the same place as the rail, to the border crossing, so if we timed it correctly we would arrive at the exact instant, just as the Chinese opened fire upon the lead scout cars that refused orders to stop. I looked at her. Margaret had her back to me, both knees drawn up to her chest, barely fitting in the driver's alcove.

"What was what like?"

"Fighting," she said. "For two solid years."

"You've never asked about it before, why now?"

Margaret tapped her helmet against the bulkhead and I knew what she was doing. With a flick of her head, she had just taken another tranq tab. "I could go out like this," she said, "if it weren't for biochemistry. Enough tranq and nothing happens, but too much and automatically my body metabolizes the stuff, neutralizing it so it won't damage my organs or cause my heart to stop. I can't even kill myself in the good ways."

"It was fun at first," I said, wanting to get her onto a different subject. "Like it was at the beginning."

"And then?"

"And then... it changed. My mind betrayed me."

"But *why?*" Margaret asked, her voice almost pleading.

I set the servos on auto scan and slid out of the turret. "It was doubt. The lessons, the teachings, none of them fit. God had different plans for me, and somehow I knew this, and so did my...Lily, Megan. She felt it too. I eventually doubted even that we should kill. And so we ran from the field and got captured, which is when I ran into you."

"I don't believe in God," she said. "Not after the Russians did things to me. The worst wasn't even what they did; the worst were the holos they showed us while they did it—images of America and the Germline program, the truth behind it and why they taught us about God. Man created God to make us believe in all this, to fool us into thinking that the only way to reach Him is through death in combat, but he doesn't really exist."

"He does. I believe what you saw, believe the truth of it, but none of those things matter. The fact that man would create such stories just means *they* are not with God anymore. It does not mean He doesn't exist."

"But how do you know? I see it in you, that you believe, and I know you've had the same doubts and maybe worse experiences, so what changed it? What made a Germline-One go from absolute faith to complete doubt, and then back again?"

There was no easy answer. How did you explain something that took years to discover in the space of less than an hour? I could have said that Megan's death contributed a speck of faith and a mountain of doubt, but that a continent of belief instilled by Misha and the other boys had countered that doubt because in them I saw a sense of duty that was unquestionable—duty to their brothers, which could never have come from teachings of man—and then there was an entire string of tiny, seemingly insignificant events, all invisibly connected, so that the statistically impossible came to pass as minor miracles. Would I have believed it at her stage of spoiling—that this had to be God?

In the end I took her shoulders. My gauntlets clicked against the ceramic armor and I rocked her back and forth, something that Megan had once done for me, to make the internal sensors rub against my back in a spot that one could never scratch without completely desuiting.

"I can't explain it to you, Margaret. It's just something you have to learn on your own."

She sighed. "We're coming up on Lebedinoye now. Should we get ready?"

"As soon as we hit the town's outer marker." I jumped back into the turret and fastened the harness straps, watching the water recede from us as the tracks curved westward, away from the sea. "Now," I said.

Margaret hit the brakes, simultaneously disengaging the auto-drive function, and then flicked a series of switches that lowered the wheels. The compartment filled with a humming sound. Slowly, pistons drove shock absorbers downward, lowering the six axles until we felt ourselves rise off the track, the steel rail-wheels finally clearing it before Margaret hit the accelerator.

"It's been a while," she said. The car bounced violently up and then crashed downward, knocking my head into the turret ring. "The last time I drove anything it was an electric cart in Zeya."

I said something like *you're doing fine,* but my attention focused on the view-screens looking for any sign of Chinese forces. If we'd stayed on the tracks we'd have been clear all the way to Khasan, the border town, our destination. But now that we'd left the rails in a bid for surprise, there was always a chance that the road would take us into the middle of a Chinese garrison, an unexpected destination for us and one that would require me to open fire as quickly as possible while Margaret did her best to extract us. The past few days had given me plenty of practice. Even when Yoon-sung had been alive, I'd mentally gone over the targeting and firing features, locking onto wolves, rabbits, and anything else I could use as a stand-in for hostile units. But so far, nothing used the road except us.


They waited for us just outside Khasan, in a place where the road and rail-lines re-converged at a narrow shoulder of land, on one side of which was a bog, the other side a steep hill. The first scout car's auto-defenses never had a chance to engage before the Chinese opened fire, destroying it. The weapons systems had been designed so that as long as they were functional the guns could return fire in the event their gunner had been killed, and the second car's swung over just in time to launch a salvo of grenades at its attackers. Two armored Chinese soldiers fell back into the swamp and didn't move.

But there were more than thirty more to take their place and in the distance a full company moved up from the Khasan rail yard to the south, along with three scout cars and an APC. All of them stayed dark green, not even bothering with chameleon skins. The third and fourth cars destroyed several more Chinese, and held their own until the APC got its range and started firing, obliterating the vehicles into flaming frameworks that continued down the tracks on inertia alone.

"Slow down," I said.

"What?"

"Slow down. Let the train get further ahead and then cross the tracks behind it to move over the hilltop. Head south overland."

The last scout car barely began firing when a salvo of rockets sent it flying off the tracks. I was about to open up with our turret when the train did something unexpected. It derailed. The engines had been traveling at forty kilometers an hour, so when they caught up to the crawling frame of one of the scout cars, the impact knocked the first diesel off the tracks, which did little to curb the train's inertia. Its engines careened sideways. The things acted like bulldozers, scraping the earth of Chinese troops, who the diesel engines crushed under their weight and then smeared over the ground, and the things refused to stop, even when the APC started firing in an attempt to at least slow the train down. This was a juggernaut of sorts, the lucky by-product of a half-baked plan such that Margaret slowed down too much, transfixed by the show that began to unfold. I had to yell at her to keep going. The scout car accelerated quickly, catching some air as it bounced over the tracks; and I felt the sensation of being thrown in an impossible angle when it began the climb, moving up the hill's steep incline. At that point we were blind. There was no knowing if the APCs and soldiers had sighted us yet, which they probably had, or if their guns would be trained on us next, which they probably would, but at the very least we had taken out a significant fraction of their forces. This wasn't Khabarovsk. Even when cross-border trade had been brisk, Khasan had been little more than a village; it was now marked on maps as a biological containment zone, uninhabitable by anyone sane, which meant there was no reason other than our arrival to have troops here at all—no reason for the Chinese to occupy it using the kind of strength they had farther north.

Margaret crested the hill and turned south, giving us our first look at the border. The town stretched out below, but like the abandoned cities we had already seen, vegetation had consumed it so the main road looked more like grass and weeds than anything of concrete; the houses, empty shells with their caved-in roofs replaced by trees or bushes or mushrooms. Khasan's rail yard had fallen into decay and even from this distance you noticed that only one set of rails had been maintained because the grass around them rose only a few inches, whereas tall weeds entirely obscured the remaining rails, dotted here and there with the rusting hulks of cranes and empty cars. A kilometer away was the bridge. There was no way to tell if it was sturdy enough for our passage, but I knew that we wouldn't have time to lower our rail-wheels, and there was no road section, so we'd have to go across on railroad ties. Below the bridge, the Tumen River flowed by slowly, carrying with it the last chunks of winter ice.

"Make for the road at town center and then head straight for the bridge," I called out to Margaret.

My eyes jumped at a flashing red light, thinking we had been targeted, but it was only the rad-detectors, which had suddenly jumped as we descended. The Chinese APC turned toward us. Its turret spun more quickly than the vehicle itself, so the thing's barrel almost stared straight at my main view-screen; I opened fire with grenades, hoping for a lucky hit on a key sensor or the gun itself.

"*Move!* They're about to fire plasma."

Margaret gunned the engine and I felt the car slip sideways before the wheels regained traction on the slope, and we dropped into the town. The plasma round detonated on the hill behind us.

"Are we out of sight of them?" Margaret asked.

"For now. Keep moving forward."

There wasn't much time before we would leave the cover of ruins, and when I was about to launch obscurant ahead of us, the targeting light flashed on, indicating we had been lased from the rear. I launched two canisters of smoke to the front, vaguely aiming for the area where we'd break into open ground, and then spun the turret rearward. Grenades popped on our hull, their noise cracking through the interior like a thunderclap.

"Hits," said Margaret, "rear deck."

"Try and evade. Give me some time to deal with them before we have to break cover and face the APC."

One of the Chinese scout cars had swerved onto the road behind us and I locked on, fingering the trigger at the same instant. My thumbs dialed in the rounds, armor piercing, and although it wouldn't do any good I willed my nerves to calm, the muscles to relax and hit everything smoothly. The grenades popped against their glacis. We couldn't have disabled it, but the rounds must have convinced our pursuers to veer off; they skidded into a space between buildings. I had just reoriented the turret to the front when we hit the smoke and Margaret drove blindly through the obscurant cloud, using only her location indicators and map display to steer.

"Speed up," I said. Something urged me onward, an uneasy feeling that we had to move.

"Why?" Margaret asked.

"Just do it."

She gunned the engine again, and we broke from the haze just as a plasma round detonated behind us, sending both rear temperature sensors into the red. We lost the backward-facing camera. To our left the APC was trying to keep up, angling to cut some distance between us and the bridge entrance as its turret adjusted for range and speeds, but for now they were beyond my grenade range.

"I can't shoot; it's all up to you."

I told Margaret whenever they prepared to fire so she could slam on the brakes or accelerate, and for next thirty seconds, which felt like thirty minutes, she kept us alive while working her way toward the bridge. I wasn't even watching the view from the front. My turret stayed locked on the APC, rotating to keep its aim, but then I noticed that the range between us had stopped dropping; it increased now. Steadily. Suddenly our scout car shook with a deep roar and it felt as though the bottom would fall to pieces.

"What's wrong?" I asked. "Where are we hit?"

Margaret laughed. "We're not hit, we just hopped the rails onto the bridge."

"Then why aren't they firing anymore?"

I focused back on the Chinese APC and watched as two of its hatches popped on top, letting out figures dressed in green coveralls. They stared at us. Their turret still pointed in our direction but there was no way for them to fire without sacrificing their own two men, and so I exhaled, letting out my excitement at the same time I grinned.

"Why aren't they firing?" asked Margaret.

"I don't know. Maybe they don't want to risk ruining the bridge in case they have to come over it one day. When we get to the other side, head for the far southwest side of . . ." I had to pause and switch to map view to read the name. "Tumangang. That should put more than enough distance between us and their plasma, and on the road south to Najin. We'll follow the railway line for at least a while, until we have a better idea of what's in store for us."

It seemed like we stayed on the bridge forever. But eventually, we crossed into North Korea, which met us with a strange quiet and a sensation that at that point, Margaret and I were the only two people on Earth. The Chinese showed no sign of having followed. Margaret sped through Tumangang, a town just as abandoned as Khasan, and swerved at the main intersection where she leveled three saplings that had begun to make their way through the road.

She stopped there, letting the car idle. "I just thought of something."

"What?"

"We'll have to use the scout car waste system, and

dump our suits through their ports. We won't be able to leave the car from now on." Margaret pointed at the rad-indicator. Unlike our experience in Russia, the light stayed on, and the reading had increased slightly, showing no signs of abating.

I scanned the northern view to check for signs of the Chinese, but couldn't see anything of the bridge or the far side of the river. "I've spent time like this before. It's no worse than the tunnels. But we should take the time now to desuit and at least enjoy the freedom of the compartment, because as soon as one of us steps from the car, we'll track the contamination inside; I can no longer fight infections like you."

Margaret pulled off her helmet and laughed while she wiped sweat from her face. "I never made it to the tunnels, Catherine. They captured our train before we even had a chance to go underground."

"Don't think about that, Margaret. You have different problems today."

"Like what?"

"Like how do we deal with getting outside and refueling when we need to, without getting too high a dose."

Margaret squinted and thought for a second. "How was Yoon-sung going to do it?"

"I killed her before I thought to ask the question." She grinned at me and I shook my head. "What, you could have done better?"

"No!" Margaret insisted, holding her hands up. "No, I would have gotten us killed or captured for use in Chinese experiments. I'm smiling because I thought it would have been nice to have her here—to make that little human bitch fill our tanks *for* us."

The night had begun to fall and we drove south for another several kilometers along a fractured road, its surface covered with moss where the sun had hit it, and ice where the road had remained shadowed by mountains. Margaret pulled off onto the shoulder. We needed rest; although our rear camera was gone, I judged it safe enough to sleep in shifts because otherwise we might risk making a mistake out of exhaustion and I suspected we'd need all our wits to make it through this: the last leg of our flight.

# TEN

## *Chollima* Moments

*And you will find another sign, seven last
plagues for those who deny Him, and in
them will be filled up the wrath of God.*

MODERN COMBAT MANUAL
REVELATIONS 15

The view-screen defined my world's borders. Outside,
spring rains fell, washing the car with its heavy down-
pour and sending drops of water to form at the top of the
camera that hung there for an eternity, until they dripped
and the next one formed, and if you looked hard enough
you became convinced that just out of range—behind the
gray haze of water—an army of shadows darted back and
forth. It was morning when the motion sensors tripped. I
shook Margaret awake, and she fell trying to scramble
over her armor into the driver's seat before holding her
shaking finger over the starter button.

A fox came into view. It sniffed the air and crossed the
road with a rat in its mouth, disappearing into the brush on
the other side, and I wanted to jump from the car to chase
after it. I had never seen a fox. It had taken a few seconds
for me to even remember the animal's name, and the image
stayed with me long after the fox had left, burned into my
retinas as something spectacular—worth remembering.

Margaret stared at me. "Well?" she asked.

"It was a fox. The most incredible animal you've ever seen."

"Oh." She relaxed, leaning back into the seat and wiping her eyes from exhaustion. "Next time pipe it in; I want to see one too."

The rain continued, pattering on the car and making me sleepy as we sat, even though the trip called out, whispering that it was time to go and that this was no place to sit because we were still close to the Russian border, and what if the Chinese decided to chase us after all? But something kept me from moving. I didn't want to face the road and its uncertainty, and here was a place that promised something that had been so rare throughout the course of my life: quiet. The scout car became a cocoon, closing us off from the world and keeping us safe from things seen and unseen, the gentle breeze from intake blowers doing its job, making the car smell so clean. *We* had begun to stink. The pair of us had been confined to the car for four days, and soon we'd be locked within suits, which offered another kind of torture, one that I hadn't thought of until seeing the fox. Until then it hadn't occurred to me: we'd never *really* experience North Korea at all. Always there would be a buffer, something in between us and it—view-screens or helmet faceplates—and through the screen, I'd caught a glimpse of its mountains, their sides almost vertical and covered with varying shades of green to rub it in; we'd get to see, but never touch. The rain was a sort of blessing. It hid much of the view and prevented for the time being, a full image of what we would soon describe as one of the most beautiful countries we'd yet experienced. After waiting to make sure nothing else came within range of our cameras, I decided it wasn't worth waiting here anymore, and motioned for Margaret to power up. A few seconds later the car started rolling.

"How are we going to get through the demilitarized zone?" Margaret asked.

I shrugged, and picked at my food: a can of mushrooms, packed at Chegdomyn's underground factories; soon, once we cracked the car's seals to refuel, we'd be restricted to liquid rations—the thought made me nauseous. "I don't know."

"They'll be expecting us anyway. Maybe we can go through and tell the South Korean guards not to pay any attention to us, that the train will be along shortly."

"That sounds good," I said.

We drove in silence while Margaret concentrated on staying on the road; the rain and overgrowth made it a difficult task, and more than once I grabbed the turret ring to steady myself, sure we were about to slide into a ditch.

"What's wrong?" she asked.

"I'm just wondering about how we'll get from Korea to Thailand. Where is the DMZ?"

"Just north of Wonsan, if we stick to the east coast. On the west coast, it's about thirty kilometers south of Seoul. I can drive it in two days, but I wouldn't count on it being faster if the roads are this bad all the way. Why?"

I sighed, and finished my meal. "We need money."

"For what?"

"People need money, Margaret. We'll be in South Korea, and it's not like we can walk around in armor if we want to stay out of trouble, so we'll need to buy or steal clothes and food. And if we're going to Thailand, our best bet is to find a ship, for which we'll also need money."

"I hadn't thought of that. We've never needed any before, Catherine; it's strange to think that we're so close now."

"Hold on a second. We're headed for the main coastal road, right?" She nodded and I switched to map view, struggling to try and read as much Korean as I could before giving up. Margaret had to stop the car and help me, flicking on the large screen behind her and folding it down into a table so we could get the battlefield view.

"What are you looking for?" she asked.

"A gold mine."

Margaret laughed. "No, really. What?"

"I'm serious. Look for any gold mines, large enough to have a collocated refinery. North Korea was one of the few countries with plenty of shallow metallic mines before their war and we might find something since nobody was able to mine it after the war."

She typed on the touch screen until the view changed, symbols of picks and shovels appearing in tiny green icons, and then Margaret ran her finger down the road, tracing our path. Half way down the coast her finger stopped.

"Here. Tanch'on. Just northwest of the main city, in the mountains, and it looks like the place wasn't hit with nuclear weapons; but there are plenty of biological warning markers."

"How long before we can get there?" I asked.

"Late in the morning of our second day."

I nodded to her, and she closed the screen, getting back into her seat. The car continued its bumpy ride southward, until Margaret made a sharp right, putting the ocean to our left, so close I wanted to get out of the hatch and feel spray on my face, the memory of Bandar still fresh. The sea had a way of washing everything off, I thought, maybe even radiation. Maybe dying slowly, burning inside and out, wouldn't be so bad and maybe, even if it meant I'd be dead, it would be worth feeling the ocean once more. I knew without looking at the detectors that there was more than enough radiation to kill us, if not today, within a few weeks, because now all around us was nothing except blackened earth; the road had disappeared into the outskirts of a radioactive crater. And we were driving into the middle of it.

"Catherine," Margaret said, "I'm worried about whoever paid for information about you. About who they might be and where."

"It doesn't matter. They weren't at Tumangang, which leaves only two places they could be: at the Unified Korean border or anywhere in between it and us. All we can do is stay alert. And I suspect I know who it is."

Without a road, Margaret had to drive slowly, sometimes no more than five miles an hour, crawling over massive blocks of wreckage and trying to negotiate the loose dirt from years of mud and landslides that had dislodged off the mountains. In places we saw squares of concrete to mark where houses and buildings once stood—the only remaining indications that people once lived here.

"What town was this?" I asked Margaret.

"Unggi."

"Stop the car for a moment, I want to listen."

She stopped, and I donned my vision hood to hear whatever my microphone picked up, closing my eyes in the process. Surf. To our south, large waves pounded against a breakwater, the storm that had rained on us all night, bringing with it a massive swell, and over all of it I heard the rain and occasional gusts of wind. It was aural desolation. Nothing here sounded of men; a grin grew on my face, getting wider until it couldn't grow anymore and until Margaret woke me from a trance.

"What is it?" she asked.

"It is nothing. No sign of man, other than what he has abandoned. If I were your generation, this is where I would stop, Margaret, this is where I would call home. Are you sure you don't want to stay here?"

"Sometimes you are strange, Catherine. Did losing Megan hurt you that badly?"

The question stirred something in me, until a subtle sadness mixed with the joy of everything else and brought tears along with a chuckle. "Yes and no. I miss her and when I think of it—really stop and think, so that I remember her hair and her smell—then I get sad for what we could have had. But that's not why I want to stay here, I was only half serious. It's just that it's ironic that the only places we ever call our own are ones that kill everything: the battlefield and this. An ex-battlefield, still undergoing its man-made spoiling. Let's go."

It took an hour for her to move through Unggi and Sonbong, where we linked up with the railway, the one our train would have taken had those plans worked out. Before we got close to it, I noticed something and zoomed in. Every fifty meters lay a pile of armor, its green color long since bleached by what must have been years of rain and sun, so that now the piles were almost yellow, and here and there a bone lay exposed from where an animal had succeeded in breaking down ceramic to reach the suits' occupants. We debated what it could have meant as Margaret drove. Eventually we realized that in the middle of all the destruction, someone had to have repaired the tracks. These were the ancestors of people like Yoon-sung and Na-yung, "volunteers" who had sacrificed their lives so their children could live among the trusted, so a train carrying boards and logs could make a journey, once or twice a year, to trade. I didn't care that they were dead. But the idea of it confused both of us, and in the end neither Margaret nor I could make the calculus work. Nobody would volunteer for someone like Yoon-sung; these had to have been prisoners, like us.

On the other side of Sonbong we entered Najin, and began to sense that the worst of the nuclear destruction was behind us. But we didn't relax until the radiation detectors showed a steady decline. The city was nestled between two monstrous mountains, which rose on either side so they lent the place an appearance of having been placed in the arms of the earth, with a deep-water bay at its mouth. How could the North Koreans have wanted war? I wondered. The thought amazed me even as it made me shake my head, that anyone could have traded an existence like this for guaranteed destruction and exile, but I had stopped really caring about the reasons men had. There was too much to see, too much to understand to let such thoughts ruin a new experience. I was so absorbed with my view screens that the motion detector alarm almost went unnoticed.

"Motion," said Margaret.

I nodded, already fingering the turret controls. "Zooming in."

The rain had stopped. A blinking icon on my viewscreen marked a position far to the north and I magnified, scanning in either direction until I caught something. It was a flash of movement, a vehicle that sped northward on a narrow dirt track in the mountains, and which vanished, disappearing into the trees as soon as I blinked. I amplified the audio and caught the fading noise of some type of truck or car.

"We're not alone."

"What is it?" Margaret asked.

"A vehicle, but it didn't look Chinese or Russian. It actually looked like it was American."

"Should we go after it?"

I shook my head. "No, we'll keep our eyes open. Right now it's more important for us to keep going and get to Tanch'on fast."

"We only have a quarter tank," said Margaret, "we'll have to stop and refuel soon."

She found the road again, south of Najin, and we sped up. I searched for the feeling of newness and wonder that I had had earlier; the sun finally broke free and the ocean crashed barely a meter to the left while seas of wildflowers and trees covered the hills and mountain slopes on our right, as if nature sent a message, *see what I can do if you leave me alone for a while*. But none of the feeling returned. Instead, my head ticked through the tactical concerns of being followed, and each time the road passed close to a cliff or a narrow point between hills and forest, I scanned for targets, waiting for the imminent ambush. It was training. The need overrode everything else, and I saw it in Margaret too while she kept her attention glued to the driving controls, calling out rad-detector readings even though I could see them myself, or announcing the remaining liters of fuel in our last tank. Finally, we had to stop. Margaret picked a spot in the open, with the railway and a wide lagoon to our right, the ocean and beach to our left; if anyone came, we'd see them long before they arrived.

"I'll do it," I said, and we both suited up.

Margaret ran the numbers through the tactical computer. "If you can do it in ten minutes, you'll absorb about twenty thousand millirems—a four-year dose. That's including the shielding limit of your armor."

"What if I take my helmet off?"

"What?" Margaret stared at me, her helmet half on.

I smiled. "I just want to feel the ocean. Look, you can see where the waves have washed over the beach and onto the road, spreading the sand in patterns. The ocean will take this road in a few years. And the rails. I just want to feel it for a few seconds."

Margaret shook her head. "Don't do this, Catherine. Just put your helmet on." She finished locking hers, and then helped with mine, making sure that she clicked it shut. "I can't handle this entire trip by myself."

As soon as I threw the hatch, the warning lights and buzzing alarms started, an automated voice calling out in Korean, listing the number of invisible dangers that flooded into the compartment. I climbed out. As soon as I secured the hatch and stood, a strong wind buffeted my side and I stared out over the ocean, watching the sunlight blink against distant swells. I stayed there for a minute, ignoring Margaret's pleas to start working. This meant something. God had never spoken to me directly, but if you imagined his voice, this is what it would have been like, a visual language combined with the pounding surf and the wind whistling through gaps in my armor. I sighed and got to work. The fuel ports fought me and it took a few minutes to loosen the first one, finally angling the jerry-can upward and letting its entire contents slosh into the near-empty tank. It took eight cans to finish the first tank. By the time I finished the second, there was a vague sense that Margaret was screaming at me, yelling something over my ear-pieces, but none of it mattered, the job would be done when it was done. I used half our reserve to refuel. Only sixteen cans remained, strapped to the car's side, and if we lost it or the diversion at Tanch'on took too much time, we might find ourselves walking before we reached the DMZ. I dropped back inside, locking the hatch behind me.

"Why didn't you answer?" asked Margaret. "I was shouting at you."

"For what?"

"You took twenty minutes and absorbed more than forty-thousand millirems."

I sighed, the sound echoing inside my helmet, and the urge to take it off and slam its curved ceramic into the bulkhead over and over until the thing cracked almost won out. "I used to be afraid to put my helmet on," I said.

"What does that have to do with anything?" asked Margaret.

"Everything. It used to terrify me, so that by the time of my discharge I'd go into battle with only thermal block on my head—if Megan would permit it. I was sure the helmet would kill me. Now? Now I see a helmet for what it is: a coffin. It's a thing often associated with death, but not its cause, a tool whose purpose is to block reality and erect a barrier between myself and God, another layer of control for the men who created us. Knowing this makes everything better, erases the terror. I still hate the helmet. But now it's no longer something to fear." I turned away from Margaret then and arranged myself in the turret seat, strapping in tightly before continuing. "Forty-thousand or forty-million, neither number matters. I will decide how much exposure I get, Margaret. Not some chart written by and for the nonbred. Now, let's go. Coast when you can, do anything to conserve fuel and reduce consumption; there is barely enough alcohol to get us to Wonsan, and that's without the detour at Tanch'on. And deactivate those fucking alarms, we know about the radiation and biological threats. We should be more concerned with the vehicle we saw."

"Who are they?" asked Margaret.

"Someone who has been interested in me for some time. Americans."

I spotted the vehicle three more times while we crept southward. It always stayed in the mountains, following dirt roads that barely even existed in spots, so that often it would climb over the ridges and out of sight before giving me a good look, but on one occasion I saw what looked like an American communications antennae, characteristic in the way it curved upward from the car's rear and then doubled over. I didn't tell Margaret because it hadn't tripped our motion sensors, and because I already knew that they were after me, that whatever the Americans thought special had been enough to make them risk coming to North Korea to retrieve me, enough to pay for information. Exactly *what* they thought was so special wasn't clear at all.

"Margaret, did they ever modify you in any way, like with organic linkages to processors, like the Russians did with Exogene?"

She kept her attention on the view-screen. "The Russians told us they removed tracking devices, but I never saw or heard of anything else. Why?"

"Megan," I explained, "my Lily. They installed a computer at the back of her skull. I was just thinking that they could have done anything to us in the tanks." Fear, the thing which had left me alone for so long, began its return, nibbling at my certainty that everything would go as planned. *It will go according to His plan,* something in my mind whispered, and the fear subsided, a fire extinguished by a flooding calm.

"Why?" asked Margaret.

"I was just thinking about what Lev said," I lied, not wanting to tell her yet about what had me worried, that it was me who they followed and Margaret would die as soon as they caught us, if they caught us. "About how strange he was, how he wanted a sample of our tissue and it still makes no sense."

"The nonbred often don't make sense, Murderer. Forget it. We're almost at Chongjin, a major city that escaped destruction; we'll need to be careful because if there's anyone here, Chongjin would be a logical place for them to reside."

"And the horned beast will rise," I said.

Margaret shifted into neutral when she arrived at the top of a hill, preparing to coast down. "Don't quote the manual, Catherine. Ever. You should have seen how the Russians used it—"

She stopped in midsentence. It was late afternoon and for the last hour we had turned west, heading away from the ocean and into rugged country where what remained of the concrete road appeared more like massive blocks that a child had lined up and then kicked so that the ends no longer met, and each block had heaved upward in odd angles from decades of freeze-thaw. Steep mountains rose on either side, making it impossible to turn around. Margaret had stopped talking because we rounded a sharp corner and stumbled on the car—the one that had been following us. It *was* American. A secondary road joined ours, and the car had come from it, probably hoping to move ahead of us into Chongjin, when they rolled over a mine, blowing off all three tires on their right side.

But nobody else was there. My mind filled the void with an image: about fifty men and women, dressed in the same padded clothes we had worn in Chegdomyn, swarming over the car and working hard to dismantle it, to strip it of everything they could, anything that one or two of them could cart off down the road to trade or sell. *Act,* I thought. *Be determined, and resolute.* But before I could fire they all vanished, leaving me with the sensation that I had seen ghosts, an army of them, which had only existed in my mind and that reality consisted of a smoking American scout car, one of its wheels rotating slowly as it burned to send a pillar of greasy smoke skyward. The black contaminated my dream of perfection. I blinked, expecting the looters to return, maybe from a phantom universe, but they didn't, and my microphone sent only the sound of popping metal, crackling rubber.

"Can you climb the slope on the high side?" I asked. "To get around?"

Margaret had already started forward. "Yes." She put the car into low gear, and gunned it gently so the turbines whined as the car pushed upward and then teetered on the center two wheels. We crashed down the far side. She crept forward then while both of us scoured the road visually for any sign of disturbance, signs that another mine had been planted, before rounding a sharp curve. Maybe they would be there, I thought, again fingering the triggers. Maybe motion sensors would illuminate a line of about thirty Korean scavengers, running away from us until within a minute they'd lie dying, filled with explosive flechettes that made me grin every time they hit, each time they found a home. But the road was empty. I told her to go back, and Margaret reversed our car then, returning slowly to the scene of wreckage.

"Why go back?" she asked. "Do you want to help the Americans? See if they're still alive?"

"No. But we'll need their alcohol."

"Who did this? Where are they? Why haven't we hit any mines and why are there Americans here in the first place?"

Her voice verged on hysterical, but there was no sense in explaining it. Not yet. The hatch popped, and I climbed out as fast as I could, shouting for Margaret to dog it behind me and man the turret. The American car was still running. Its engine forced my goggles into infrared for a second, outlining the grill in white, and on its side, ten jerry cans remained. They came off with trouble. Several of their latches had been bent shut from the rocks and it took me some time to free them, tossing the cans behind me toward our car where an additional two lay, blasted free. Men shouted from inside the car. They pounded on the hatches and begged me to open them but a boulder rested on top and even though I might have been able to dislodge it, there was no point in making the effort— calculus would have prevented me from acting. The calculus of time. Each moment I spent in the outside world, the beautiful death of radiation did its job, piercing the miniature openings between atoms of my thin lead shield, less than a millimeter's worth, radiation knocking off an electron here, damaging a nucleic acid there. Moving the boulder would have given death more time to work on me. Besides, even if I had taken the time to free them it wouldn't have been for their benefit, it would have been to take one out and torture him, get the man to tell me everything he knew, and I had little doubt that he would prefer to die from starvation than from my hand. Did they think they could explain anything? Be our friends? They must have eventually figured it out for themselves because the pounding gave way to curses, to the shouted "bitches" and "sluts," the limits of their descriptive powers when it came to me and my sisters. By the time I made it back to Margaret with all the alcohol, fifteen minutes had passed; there hadn't been time to secure it outside the car, and we did our best to store it in the interior compartment, under bags of food and ammunition.

"Next time let me do it," she said.

"How much longer until Chongjin?" I asked. The sun was already approaching the tops of mountains to the west, and it wouldn't be smart to sleep here, or in Chongjin; we needed to move as far as possible, as quickly as possible, but without hitting any mines of our own.

"Ten minutes at our normal speed."

"Go slowly. Especially around corners. And don't worry about bandits, there aren't any. That's just what Na-yung wants everyone to think."

"How do you know?"

I gritted my teeth and banged my head against the turret ring, over and over again, trying to knock the truth out—about how I knew, about how God spoke to me and said things without my hearing them, so they would lodge in my mind unnoticed until I stumbled on them. Like landmines.

"I know. That was probably a mine laid by Na-yung's people. Do you think they want South Koreans to come here and scout? What do you think they do all year, Margaret, cut down trees? What would you do and what happened to your training?" My voice rose to a shout, then a scream. *"You are supposed to be like me, able to breathe war and piss it, but instead you act like I'm your nursemaid and you're a fucking baby!"* I let a few minutes roll by, until my anger faded, before I tried again. "The North Koreans probably booby trapped as much of the north as they could, little by little, each year, leaving skeletons behind them, the skeletons of slaves. There are no bandits, except in the legends dreamed up by Na-yung and propagated through an endless chain of lies. I know what we'll find in the mines at Tanch'on, Margaret. I know it because I've already seen it, God showed me."

"What are you talking about?" she asked.

"More mines. Traps. And hundreds of skeletons of Russians and other prisoners that they transported here to work them while being irradiated, to extract metal and gold. Just like the Americans do in Kazakhstan. We'll find gold in Tanch'on. And we'll find hundreds and hundreds of skeletons, the voices of the dead which are only able to say one thing: that they're dead. Na-yung wants people to believe that North Korea is worth nothing so that nobody will come here, so that someday she can reclaim it."

Margaret put her foot on the brake, slowing our descent as we rolled downward toward the city. "Who were they? The Americans, why were they here?"

I strapped in, making sure the flechette hopper was still full, wondering if maybe I had fired at something and forgotten all about it. "They're here for me," I said, and told her everything—about the strange general and about what Misha had said, everything about the efforts that had been made to kill me, and that for some reason, the Americans thought me special.

"I know why they think you're special," said Margaret.

"Why?"

She slowed, driving around an almost imperceptible lump in the road. "Because you're better than everyone. Especially them. More than a Lily, something new and incredible."

Chongjin breathed us in at sunset. The car coasted a last few meters into the city's northern suburbs, and we whined between crumbling houses and buildings that had turned half orange and half shadow in the little light remaining. To our left the remnants of a partially eaten factory rose over the walls. Somehow the spire of a smokestack had survived the years, a middle finger that refused to give into anything, and which grabbed my attention, the reddish sunlight making it seem covered with its own blood. I almost didn't notice when Margaret tripped a mine. It blew half heartedly, a fizzle, which sent fire and smoke all around us as if we'd driven through flare, but the time and elements had degraded its components—or maybe it was never built correctly in the first place—and the thing did little more than set a jerry can on fire and melt some rubber from our tires.

I laughed at the sight. "*Boom, and the Americans die!* Only a tiny *Zzzt* for us though, the footstep of good fortune always tiptoeing ahead of us a bit, making everything all right, neutering things in our path."

"It scared me to death," said Margaret. "I thought we'd died."

"We did. The 'us' that existed a second ago is no more. It's dead. Now it's the us that exists this second, until it passes and kills us to give birth to the new Margaret and Catherine. A new Little Murderer with every tick. Dying isn't what you think it is, Margaret. You think it's the end of life, but it's not. Death is the end of birth, the fact that time can no longer spit out a new Margaret."

"Should I get out and check?" she asked. "To see if anything else was damaged?"

"No. We need to get as far as possible tonight, so we can make Tanch'on tomorrow. Maybe between now and then a different Margaret will be born, not a rebirth, but a miracle one, a Margaret born from a virgin."

"Like you?"

I started crying then, and knew why. There was nothing to emulate in me, and the fact that someone could think I was worth following made me sick, as though in a moment the bile would run from my pores, filling my armor until it suffocated, but even then it wouldn't stop, would continue until it killed Margaret and everyone nearby. Margaret didn't know what she had said. I forgave her for that. If she had known that there was nothing special, that whatever the Americans saw to make them follow, whatever my sisters saw to make them believe in me, had been placed in my genes by men—those who created me and therefore who were responsible—she should have pitied me. But then so much had happened since my creation that deep down I knew something else had taken over and it was all from inside, all me. At a point, late in the war when Megan and I had run, the decisions had become mine, the growth mine, the changes mine. All mine. And I didn't want the responsibility, just like I had never wanted to be a Lily. I *wanted* to be a fluke, someone else's mistake. Everyone would laugh, I was sure, when they realized that it had all been a big mistake, and I was just like my sisters.

But I wasn't and there was no denying it.

We waited on another road remnant, positive that we now rested among ghosts. Evidence was all around. Piles and piles of skeletons lay scattered everywhere, none of them whole since they had been ripped to pieces and we had to drive over them, the crunching sound coming clearly through the microphone and reverberating through my thoughts. The skeletons traced a path all the way along the road and led straight to a refinery's gate, the machinery beyond it still gleaming as if Na-yung had replaced it yesterday and oiled it with the fat stripped from corpses. It was new machinery, maybe from Korea, a compact unit that took up less than a few hundred square meters and around which had been erected a wall and tall guard towers with green leaded-glass windows. Guards were worth shielding. Armed men and women would have been among the trusted, worth protecting from radiation. But for now the fortress was vacant, and autocannons hung loosely from their tower ports, barrels covered in canvas and pointing at the sky as if angered by their own impotence. Only the skeletons were here; they had won, simply by waiting until Na-yung had left, but they didn't know that as soon as she needed more metal she'd return, driving over them with as little concern as we had. But it was morning now, and the mineshaft couldn't wait for us any longer; I silently praised the dead for their temporary victory. They had found a home in Tanch'on.

"How much of a dose have I gotten?"

Margaret checked the computer. "About eighty thousand millirem. A hundred thousand more, Catherine, and you're in trouble. But the readings here aren't so bad; it would take about an hour to get that dose."

"We can count on the mine giving me some cover, too," I said.

"What are you planning?"

"To find some ore carts. I have to assume that these people died in the middle of their job, probably from the exposure of making hundreds of trips outside on the surface. I'm guessing they left unprocessed ore. It looks from here like the plant itself is automated."

"You want me to go start it up?"

I thought for a second, before climbing out the hatch and flicking on my internal helmet blower to defog its faceplate. "No. Man the guns. I'm bringing relays with me to drop if we start losing communications, so when I talk make sure to respond."

Wind howled through pine trees that climbed every slope, their trunks bent and twisted from the constant battle with elements, but even misshapen they amazed me. The needles were dark green. Each one held a different shade, and then between them I saw tiny birds flitting in and out silently. But when I got to the mouth of the main shaft everything stopped. The air became heavy, even inside my suit, and when I glanced back it seemed that nothing moved, as if local wildlife had put two and two together, that the presence of people at the mine meant something bad would happen, meant it was time to hide. A long line of ore carts rested on two sets of narrow rails, the ones to my left filled with chunks of rock and gravel, the ones on the right empty. Car after car stretched into darkness.

"This should be easy," I said. "I don't know how much gold the ore contains, but there's already a line of full cars going as far as I can see."

Margaret clicked in. "So all you should have to do is turn the thing on and we'll just wait."

"Is everything clear?" I asked.

"No sign of movement."

I turned away from the shaft and headed toward the refinery. The main gate, a solid steel panel almost eight feet tall that linked to a concrete wall topped with an electrified set of wires, was locked. The wires hummed overhead. Working electricity surprised me, suggesting that refinery contained a micro-reactor. What other surprises were here? Blowing open the door would be easy but knowing Na-yung and Yoon-sung, it seemed *too* easy;

and intrusion was something they would have thought of; I peered through a crack between the door and wall to find three wires, stretched tight on the other side.

"Booby traps," I said into the radio.

"What have you got?"

"Wires. Taut, on the other side of door to the refinery yard. I'm cutting them."

"Why take the chance?" Margaret asked. "If you release tension they could go off."

"What else is there to do? The door opens inward, and these must be designed to function on an increase in tension, not its release."

I pulled out a pair of wire cutters, and slipped them through the crack, clipping the wires one at a time before waiting for something to happen. Nothing. So I jogged back and took cover inside the mineshaft.

"Give it a couple of grenades," I said, "Just blow the lock."

A minute later I was in. There were a few more traps, each one designed to touch off a series of charges that ran throughout the refinery and into the mine itself. It took a few minutes to disarm them all and then activate the refinery, the machinery coming to life with a squeal.

"We'll have gold eventually," I said.

"But how long will it take?"

I thought for a moment. Huge chains cranked the carts to the top of a hopper, where they automatically turned over, dumping their ore into crushers and grinders that roared and screamed as they chewed rock into smaller and smaller bits, shaking them through screens for sizing. From there, pulverized ore fell into vats. An acid solution broke down the rocks, dissolving metals and carrying them to a new liquid home, which was then piped to the end of the line, a warehouse-like building. I checked the warehouse door for booby traps and then opened it, seeing row upon row of mechanical sorters, where gold precipitated out of solution with other metals, and was then separated based on mass, magnetism, or any number of characteristics. Furnaces waited at the end of the production line; they lay dormant for now, but a line of molds stood ready, waiting to shape molten gold into bars.

"Days." I finally decided. "Maybe weeks. I didn't anticipate this."

Before she could answer there was a sound. It was from the direction of the mineshaft and the noise of ore crushers should have drowned it out completely but it came anyway, faintly, a kind of howl that didn't fit. I left the warehouse and headed toward the mine.

"Did you hear that?"

Margaret clicked in immediately. "I heard something. It came from the mineshaft."

"Movement?"

"None."

The sounds disappeared once I had moved a few meters into the tunnel's darkness, my infrared and light amplification kicking in to change everything green, the reticle for my Maxwell a bright red. There was no movement. The only sounds were those of water dripping and the squeaking of the ore carts as they inched forward on their rails, but then farther in the tunnel there was something else—a low groan, as if someone was in pain. I dropped a relay and then pushed forward, my Maxwell raised. The shaft moved downward gently, and eventually opened into a large chamber that cleared my head by at least ten meters; the floor was littered with human skeletons in rotted, padded Na-yung uniforms now moldy and soaked from water that ran down the walls in rivulets.

"See anything?" asked Margaret. Her voice startled me, loud in my ear, and I dropped to a knee expecting something to come charging at the noise.

"No," I whispered. "Hold on communications, I'll get back to you soon."

Something was moving now, but nothing showed on my heads-up, no sign of anything, and only three dark circles suggested that other tunnels existed, two running along what must have been a track parallel to the ridgeline far above, and the last heading deeper into the mountain. I was about to move toward one when my motion sensors tripped.

A huge shape crashed from the tunnel, almost tipping over a string of carts as it barreled toward me, and before I could fire, the thing collided, sending me through the air to slam into a wall, my eyes filling with stars before everything went black. Unconsciousness may have saved me. By the time I came to, the room was quiet again, and the carts still moved along their rails, heading slowly toward the exit.

*"Catherine!"* Margaret screamed in my ear.

"What?" I answered. "I'm OK."

"Did you see that?"

"It knocked me out." I stumbled toward the outside, still groggy from the impact my head had taken, and blinked upon stepping into the sunlight. It was almost noon. "What was that thing?"

"A bear! It was the most magnificent thing I've ever seen, a huge black bear that came rushing out and then ran into the mountains."

I climbed onto the scout car and opened the hatch, sliding in headfirst so I could lie down. Margaret slammed it shut behind me.

"Are you OK?"

"I'm fine. I'm surprised it didn't rip me apart."

Margaret laughed and rotated the turret, scanning. "I think you must have scared it more than it did us. I don't care if we make it or not, these last two days have been the most amazing of my life. To think: first a fox, now *a bear!*"

We spent three weeks watching the bear, and once I took a chance on following him, staring in awe as it ambled up the river that coursed nearby with the refinery's refuse, mixing it with skeletons that had collected on its banks. The bear ate dead salmon. I watched as it rolled in the grass nearby and when it stood on both legs, roaring in my direction because I had gotten too close. Both Margaret and I wanted to stay; this was an amazing place if you ignored Na-yung's contribution, a place where the animals soon accepted us or at least ignored two strangers and allowed us to watch, to see what the world was supposed to be. But eventually our food ran low and the time to leave came. Margaret and I had gotten comfortable enough with the area that we both walked into the warehouse to take final stock of our efforts, a full three bars of gold that cooled in their molds, gleaming. Each one weighed half a kilogram. We slipped them into a ceramic compartment in our armor, breaking one roughly in half so that we each took a piece of it.

"Is this enough?" she asked.

"I have no idea. How much does gold cost?"

"How should I know?"

She laughed and we both returned to the car, touching up its alcohol tanks before starting again, but I stopped her, and jumped from the car for one last task. When I returned she was smiling. We blew up the refinery, setting off the booby traps and taking some satisfaction in knowing that one last blow had been dealt to Na-yung, even if the ones who would suffer with its reconstruction would be the ones who deserved it least. We sped down the road we had used to enter, and then slowed to rejoin the main one south, where Margaret settled back into her pattern of moving slowly, scanning for anything that might cut our trip short.

"I just thought of something," I said.

"What?"

I tried not to laugh too hard as I spoke. "We just made the North Korean's story half true. We're bandits. The only bandits in all of the Koreas, maybe."

All morning we crept along the road, the wheels crunching over rocks and gravel, detritus that had accumulated over years and maybe even recently, during one of the many storms we had weathered since first entering the country. Soon we'd reach the DMZ, probably that evening or first thing in the morning. We'd resolved to travel as long as it took, not stopping to sleep, because neither of us knew what would happen or if this would be the last time we'd breathe air as free soldiers. All we knew of the South was what we had learned in the tank, that the Southerners and America had been fast friends for two centuries, and that they and Japan had stood against China and the North in one more war, one fought for resources. We drove through a last city, glad to have heavy shielding to keep out the worst of the radiation as we imagined gamma rays doing their best to break our car into meaningless ions. Margaret told me the city's name: Hamhung.

"This is unbelievable," she said, staring at her screen. "That the North would do this to themselves."

I shrugged, not caring that she couldn't see the gesture. "It was their only choice, the last action of a desperate leader. Use nuclear weapons against Japan, obliterating it completely, and destroy enough of your own country so that the South and the Americans would be forced to leave. I can't say I wouldn't do the same thing."

"What's Japan like, I wonder. Maybe it's recovered to some extent. With bears and trees. It helps, somehow, to know that things still grow, still live where nonbred cannot."

"It's *your* last chance too," I said. "To stay. I can leave you someplace where the radiation isn't bad, and when I get to Thailand tell everyone about it. Maybe some will join you."

She fell silent. An hour later, after we climbed from the last of Hamhung's craters and began the final stretch of our journey, Margaret cleared her throat. "I think I know what you were talking about now. About how you get a sense sometimes about what you are supposed to be doing, and not doing. I'm not to stay here, Catherine. I don't think anyone is, except bears and foxes." Margaret sped up a little, and I didn't say anything to stop her because we were both thinking the same thing; we wanted to get the trip over with.

It was night when we first saw the lights. We coasted

down the road north of Okp'yong Ni and took a curve so that beneath us a valley opened up and pointed toward the coastal city of Munch'on. A distant ridgeline cut east-west, descending to the coast, and we saw the string of bright lights. They burned in cool blue and blinked in the wind, trees that we couldn't see waving in front of them to give a flickering effect. But as we moved closer the lights became clearer, and I zoomed in, seeing that they topped a high concrete wall, in front of which had been strung an incredible depth of barbed wire and the mushroom-caps of sentry bots—thousands of them. There would be no getting through without the South Koreans knowing. They probably had already picked up on our movements. At the same time I thought it, we saw the red streak of a jet engine, and a tiny drone barely cleared the wall, flashing straight for us, booming as it broke the sound barrier less than a hundred meters overhead. The drone slowed, circling us as we kept moving toward the coast and we did our best to ignore it, heading for a cluster of lights just south of Munch'on. My hands got slick with anticipation. Surely the South Koreans would have expected the trade delegation, wouldn't be surprised by a Chinese-constructed scout car in their territory, but Margaret convinced me that we should be careful, so despite the radiation, I took the time to find something white, a plastic bag, which I tied around the front of the grenade launcher, hoping they'd get the message. Soon our radio crackled, and Margaret translated from Korean.

"They want us to identify ourselves," she said.

"Tell them we're the trade mission from Chegdomyn, and that our train was destroyed by a landslide, that we're the only survivors."

She spoke, and then turned to me, her face hidden by the glare on her faceplate. "They want us to approach the Munch'on gate. I just got a route they piped into our computer. Apparently we die if we deviate from the path by even one meter."

"Well then," I said, sighing with the relief of knowing it was out of our hands now. "Don't deviate."

Margaret and I whispered to each other, not knowing if they could hear now that we were so close. The gate was less than ten meters from our car. Soldiers filled the viewscreen, which showed the top of the wall, a ten-meter-high structure topped with black-armored figures who stood, aiming grenade and rocket launchers directly at our deck.

"We have no choice," I said. "We should just get out."

"But what does report to Wonsan for 'in-processing' mean?" Margaret asked.

"It doesn't matter what it means. You're in charge now, Margaret, I can't speak their language so for now we'll tell them we're Russian and that you're the only one who can speak Korean. Take us through this. Tell me what to do. If it comes time for us to break and fight, just do what I tell you and don't hesitate to kill. These people are nothing, and you are everything."

We climbed from the car and stepped down its front, jumping onto the road just as the gate cracked open. We moved through. It shut behind us and I saw that we stood in some kind of receiving room, a wide corridor with tiled walls on either side, drains spaced evenly on the floor, and narrow mirrored windows running the length of it on either side. A small airlock door was the only way out, at the far end.

A voice came from overhead speakers and Margaret raised both hands; I did the same. Soon a solution showered down from nozzles in the ceiling. I followed Margaret through, the liquid impacting against our heads with a force that pushed the helmet down, and then a pair of bots rose from the floor, where we stopped, allowing them to take half an hour to scrub at us with brushes, going over every centimeter and using high-pressure microjets to clean every crack. The bots even opened our compartments and pouches. For a moment I panicked, thinking they would take the gold bars, but the robots simply cleaned them, and made sure no biologically contaminated dust or radioactive particles remained on anything we carried. The bots replaced the gold, and eventually we moved forward, reaching the door and passing through. On the other side another room waited for us, empty and tiled, and once more the voice spoke so that Margaret began taking off her armor while she whispered.

"Take your gold out. Now."

I took my armor off, and grabbed the small bars once my arms were clear of the suit, palming them while I wriggled out of the undersuit. Next we stepped into a pair of showers, while another pair of bots scrubbed and scrubbed, so that it seemed like an hour had passed by the time they finished. A panel opened beside us at the end. Margaret and I grabbed the white clothes that hung inside and dressed in thin coveralls, slipping the bars into our pockets. We moved to the last door then, and waited.

I spoke to her in Russian. "They might not recognize us," I said. "Might not realize what we really are." You saw the fear on her face; Margaret's eyes moved rapidly, looking everywhere but focusing on nothing.

"Why do you think that?"

"Your face and the tattoos. My body and the scars. Don't get worried until we have something to fear."

The door opened and we moved into a third room, with a long desk, which had two padded chairs and a Korean woman who sat on the other side, motioning for us to sit. A camera watched everything from the corner. She and Margaret spoke then and at first I paid attention, but without warning a wave of exhaustion washed over me and my lids fluttered shut so that sometime later Margaret had to elbow me awake while the Korean woman looked on, smiling.

"We can go now," Margaret said in Russian.

"Was that in-processing?"

Margaret shook her head. "No. They wanted an account of the accident, and I explained that you don't speak Korean so I told them everything. Now we're to walk south to Wonsan, where they have a hotel for us; Yoon-sung arranged it. Tomorrow morning they'll come get us for in-processing."

"What *is* in-processing?" I asked.

"I have no idea. Do you want me to ask so we can stay here for a little while longer, or should we go?"

I stood and smiled at the woman, before following Margaret out a final door, which opened into the night air. We stepped into an empty yard. Behind us the wall rose vertically and several soldiers glanced down through slitted helmets, but then looked away as if disinterested. It was cold but not too bad, and soon, once we started out of the yard and moved toward what looked like a modern highway, the cold vanished with the realization that we were almost there.

"Yoon-sung arranged the hotel?" I asked.

"That's what she said. A North Korean delegation is waiting for us there, one that stays in Wonsan year-round to handle transactions on this side of the DMZ."

"Then we'll have to find another place to stay; I'm surprised they weren't waiting for us here."

"They were," said Margaret. "But gave up waiting yesterday and left. The South Koreans are calling them right now."

Margaret and I looked at each other and then grinned, breaking into a sprint at the same time, heading south down a covered walkway that ran parallel to the highway.

"How far to Wonsan?" I asked.

"Ten kilometers."

I thought about it, already feeling winded, but then considered the alternatives. "We'll make it. Let's just get out as soon as we can; we can go straight to the port and try to find a ship in the morning."

"Have you ever been to a human city?" asked Margaret.

"Only ones that were nuked—the ones we both saw on this little journey. I don't know what to expect, Margaret, so don't think about it for now."

Margaret spoiled near Wonsan harbor, and I pulled her into an alley, hiding behind a stack of wooden pallets so nobody passing would notice. She shook in my arms. All night we had wandered the city, looking for a place to wait for morning but instead finding things we had never seen: neon signs in English and Korean, offering to sell everything, including drugs and sex, and people in bright clothes and thick jackets so different from the coveralls we wore staring at us when we passed. This was a foreign city—in more ways than one. The press of humanity on every side made me feel sick, drove me to believe that they all knew who we were, what we were, and were laughing at our stupidity for having put ourselves in their midst. And they were right. I marveled that we had once thought it possible to mix with the nonbred, and when I saw how they lived, it made me furious to see them unarmed and happy, walking in and out of restaurants with no thought of danger or an end to life. I especially wanted to kill the old men and women, who breathed just as much air as we did, who had lived for decades without considering what it would have been like to cram a life-time into just two years, and it was their fault for what happened to us; cracking their spines would help them understand, help them realize that they had squandered an entire universe by living so slowly for so long.

Margaret screamed. I clamped my hand over her mouth and whispered for her to hush. Because it was close to morning and the streets had quieted, her cry was like an alarm that ripped through the alleyway and announced to everyone that we were there. But nobody noticed. Her trembling worsened and Margaret started whispering things about her rapes, describing them to someone as if making a confession. Maybe to God. There was no urge to cry for my part, no sadness, because what good would it do anyway? This wasn't a tragedy; it was a life experience that to me seemed normal, and I wondered what the humans would think if Margaret told them her story, if they would think our experiences as odd as we did theirs.

Finally, when the morning sun hit her face, Margaret's eyes became clear, and she focused them on me.

"I was gone," she said.

"You were gone."

"Where are we?"

"Listen. And breathe."

We sat without moving, and then she smiled when she heard it: seagulls and the slosh of water against a quay. We could smell the ocean. Wonsan port was close. I lifted her to her feet and we did our best to brush off the dirt, walking into the sunlight and moving toward the sound of water until within a few minutes we stood outside a gate, beyond which a line of cargo ships waited, moored to their piers and sitting calmly as men worked to load them, offload them, or drop the lines that kept them in place, stuck against a pier. A man sat on a chair near the rusted portal. Margaret said something and they talked for a while before he finally stood, swinging the gate wide. We passed through, and even before the thing clanked shut behind us I knew that we had nothing to fear from the North Koreans. It was too late for them to catch us. And I was about to laugh when down the quay a group of men walked toward us, their hair short and skin deeply tanned so that it contrasted even against the dark khaki of their uniforms. I yanked Margaret to the side, pulling her behind a forklift where we waited for them to pass. At first she was about to say something but I motioned for her to be quiet. The men walked slowly. They didn't say anything, but between the forklift's roll bar and seat I saw them searching the quay, and each one rested a hand on the butt of a flechette pistol. We didn't move out until they disappeared.

"Americans?" she asked.

"Yes. What did the Korean at the gate say?"

She pointed to a ship whose sailors were about to move the gangplank away on huge rollers, the boat's Korean name emblazoned in white. "The *Songdowon*. Headed for Bangkok and due to leave in ten minutes."

I fingered the gold bars in my pocket and prayed they would be enough. We ran up the gangway and into a group of startled Koreans. Margaret said something to them, hurriedly, and one of them escorted us through a maze of narrow passageways where we had to duck through more small doorways than I could count, before finally we reached the bridge—its bulkheads covered with computers and screens, and speakers blaring with multiple Korean voices. The man said something to his captain, who looked us up and down and then muttered.

Margaret pulled out her hand, showing him the gold. "He wants to see it," she said to me, "show him."

When I did, their eyes went wide. At first I thought we had done something wrong because the Captain flew into a fit, dashing over to one of the radios and yelling into it. Margaret must have seen the look on my face because she grabbed my shoulder, holding me back.

"It's OK, Murderer. He's telling his men to hurry it up and cast off, and to forget about waiting for one last container that was due to arrive an hour ago."

"Why?"

"I guess," said Margaret, smiling, "that gold is worth a lot more than we realized."

Something occurred to me then, and I grabbed Margaret's coveralls. "Tell him I want paper. A lot of it. And some pens."

She squinted at me. "Why?"

"Just do it."

Margaret spoke to the captain and he nodded, laughing at the same time he answered.

"He said paper is expensive, but not *that* expensive, and you can have all you want. And his own personal pen, just as soon as they get underway. Murderer," she said, and then started crying and laughing at the same time. "We made it."

I saw a statue out the bridge window, in the middle of a public square below us off the quay; it was a winged horse that leapt from its base, taking flight.

"What is that?" I asked. The captain saw me pointing and said something as Margaret translated.

"That is a relic. A leftover from worthless North Koreans who were too stupid to realize the truth."

"But what is it?" I persisted.

"It is *Chollima*. The winged horse. North Korea promised its people that if they worked sixteen hours a day, anything would be possible, even to fly."

# ELEVEN

# A Warmer Clime

*Blessed are they who follow his commandments,*
*for they will find a tree of life, and will enter*
*through the gates of His city.*

MODERN COMBAT MANUAL
REVELATIONS 22:17

We stayed in our room. It reminded me of the scout car, but neither Margaret nor I wanted to give the Korean sailors more time to examine us, to recall any of a hundred ads they had seen on holos or video posters among the millions in downtown Wonsan that showed the generic face of my sisters—warning everyone to report suspected sightings. The men on the dock haunted my thoughts, and I dedicated at least a day to considering our options. If they had been sent to search for us specifically, they would have spoken with the guard already, who probably told them about the two women looking for transport to Thailand. We should have killed him. But then that wouldn't have solved it either because as soon as they found the body they'd go after any ship that had left port. Why the *Songdowon* hadn't been boarded yet was a mystery, but judging from the sun outside our porthole it still headed in the general direction of Thailand and at constant speed. I didn't care if they boarded anyway. But for Margaret it was a different story; she hadn't chosen the same path as me, still had a road to travel before she came to the same conclusions I had. And maybe she never would. For me, the path was almost done, and I knew it because I saw the ending now, the logical conclusion to everything I had learned, and there was no more fear of it, only a recognition that one last thing had to be done.

I wrote. Margaret busied herself with exercise and sleep while I scratched on the sheets of paper the Koreans had loaned me, the pen giving my fingers cramps until I finally grew accustomed to the motions.

"What are you writing?" she asked. It was the third day of our trip and only a few days remained until we would dock in Bangkok.

"About my life. What there was of it."

She laughed. "You speak as though it's already over, Catherine, when it's only just begun. Once we arrive at Bangkok you'll see; our sisters will find us, and we'll be among family again."

It wasn't the right time to tell her, so I grinned. "You may be right, Margaret. But anything can happen at sea, and I want to be prepared."

"You think they're after us."

"Can you swim well?" I asked.

Margaret looked at me quizzically. "What does that have to do with anything?"

"Just tell me. Can you swim well, have you recovered from everything or do you need more rest?"

"I can swim. I'm fine, we've gotten nothing but rest lately."

I nodded, and returned to my work. "The night before we dock, I want you to jump overboard and swim for land.

You should make it, and even if you miss Thailand it shouldn't be hard for you to make it there on your own, from wherever you reach shore."

"But where are *you* going?" Margaret asked. She approached behind me and put her hand on my shoulder. "What's wrong?"

"Do you remember the test? The final one, when we killed our pets?"

Margaret nodded. "It was a true test, and looking back I see why they did it."

"I remember mine too. And I just remembered what happened next, for the first time in years, and it didn't come as a hallucination or as a result of spoiling. I *remembered*."

Our Group Mother concentrated on her tablet, smiling as the numbers came in and told her my story. She glanced up at me and her smile disappeared. "Catherine. I think you twisted too hard."

"Excuse me, Mother?"

"Look down."

I did as she told me and saw that the cat's head had come off from my twisting it, so that it now lay in two pieces, its blood running down my forearm. I laughed.

"I'm sorry, Mother. But did I pass?"

"You passed. Discard the carcass in the can by the APC and join your sisters."

I was about to leave when a thought occurred to me. "Can I keep the head?" I asked.

"Why on earth would you want to do that?"

"When the flesh decays, I can glue the skull to my helmet. It will strike fear in my enemies."

"You can keep it," she said, and turned to the remaining girls. *"Next."*

My sisters all grinned at the cat-head when I boarded the APC, all except for Megan, who frowned. There was no point in explaining it. Megan would see when we arrived in war, how the gesture would make men hesitate before firing, give me time to fill them with the wisdom of my flechettes as they focused on the tiny skull, the one that prophesized their death.

It took less than a day to reach our staging point, where they loaded us onto ships for the last leg, and then a week before our APCs jumped into the water, submerging completely and then popping up with a shriek to head for Bandar's beaches. Our heads-up relayed images from the vehicle cameras. Ahead of us we saw the flashes of guns that fired from the city, and the billowing clouds of smoke that rose from ruined buildings, every once in a while punctuated by the flash of plasma as our ships fired continuously at our enemies. The landing would be hot, as predicted. Megan sat beside me and I shook my Maxwell at her.

"We are warriors, my Lily. Soon the APC will let us into battle where everything will unfold as it should, as we have been taught."

"I know, Catherine."

But I saw that she still wouldn't smile. "Then what's troubling you?"

Megan tried to smile but it was a feeble one, and her face went red from embarrassment.

"Tell me," I insisted.

"Your skull. The one glued to your helmet."

I had forgotten about it, and now laughed with an

added excitement, the fact that soon I would see if it worked. "But why would that bother you?"

"Because I didn't think of it. I'm jealous. It should have been me to make a gesture like that, and yet here you are, a proven killer to our enemies before any of us have fired a single shot."

I didn't get a chance to respond, but felt horrible. It hadn't occurred to me that Megan *could* get jealous, since she had won the title of Lily and the ultimate honor of command. The sounds of water disappeared and the power increased to our wheels as we felt land beneath us, the APC's plasma cannon pounding every few seconds to shake our tiny compartment with each shot. When the floor finally dropped out from beneath us, we dropped into wet sand.

Targets filled my heads-up. Without thinking we rolled from under the APC and moved up the beach toward a concrete bulwark, behind which the figures of Iranians popped up to shoot. An autocannon sent its flechettes to howl by, sounding like angry insects before they popped and crackled against the ceramic armor of our APC, and I had to will my nerves to calm so my aim would steady. It wasn't fear. The excitement of my first battle had induced a level of anticipation that was now impossible to control until finally, after missing with several shots, I screamed and jumped up, kicking sand into the air with each step as I ran in slow motion, cutting the distance between me and the concrete bulwark. A rage had filled me, burning with an intensity that was un-ignorable and which gave me the strength to reach the fortification in seconds. There I hid in defilade, the lip of the wall a meter over my head. Iranians shouted at one another directly above me. I lobbed a grenade over, and then followed it with three more, waiting for them to detonate before I leapt upward, grabbing the top, then letting my Maxwell hang by its flexi so I could heave myself over and land in the middle of ten dead soldiers. There were children among them. Boys my age. Some of them were alive and screamed, but others lifted their weapons to fire and I took their lives, the Maxwell swinging into my hands with such speed that they never had a chance to pull their triggers. Our own plasma, from the APCs, exploded on either side. It was easy to ignore the danger. This was a killing ground, a holy place, and if God intended for me to go out with friendly fire then it was His order to me that as many should be taken before my turn came, sending me through the concrete trench line in a sprint, firing from the hip at anything living or dead. Time melted into a frenzy of images, of men and women running toward the city, so they made easy targets for artillery and disappeared in clouds of brilliant gas. When it was over we sat among the blood and laughed.

"You are fearless," Megan said to me. We kissed and the others grinned, a few threatening that if we didn't swear off love they would turn us in. But they were joking. When we finished, Megan's smile faded and she pointed at my helmet. "The cat skull is gone, Catherine, I'm sorry."

But I screamed with joy and when everyone stopped laughing explained to her, "I can kill without it."

"I understand," said Margaret. "I mean I follow the story, and it must have been glorious to have spent time in the early days, in true combat. But I don't get your point,

Catherine. What does it matter now? What are you trying to say?"

I smiled at her and lay down the pen, tired from having written so many words in the past twenty-four hours that my head pounded.

"I never needed the cat skull. And you don't need to worry about why you should swim for land. Nothing we do can change God's plan, and it was He who spoiled my aim and made me furious so that I charged the Iranian defenses, He who took my talisman to show that I didn't need it. We never found the skull, no trace of it. Everyone can choose to run, Margaret, to pick her own path and even ignore the route God lays at her feet, but it will never feel right. I know this now. You can't know it, because it takes time to learn, time that has only just begun to pass for you, but which may one day catch up. Someday, if you keep your mind open, you will see it as I have, and will know what you are supposed to do."

"You're going to kill them, aren't you?" she asked.

"Who?"

"The crew. The Korean sailors."

I laughed at that, the futility of such a gesture, and shook my head. "No, Margaret. I'm going home." I saw the confusion on her face and wondered how long it would take for the realization to grow in her, if it ever did, and then spoke with patience. "The Americans will board this ship before we dock. You will be gone. I will be here and will return to their cities for discharge, and will never feel the warmer clime of Bangkok. That is for you to feel, but not me."

Margaret started crying, and then pounded her fist on my table, scattering some of the papers. "But why? You don't have to do this, Catherine; maybe you're wrong and Thailand is the answer. Why would you give them a victory after so much effort to run?"

"Because," I said, "it isn't *their* victory. One day you'll understand, but not today. Just believe me, that I believe this, and swim for it when I tell you to. This is what I have to do to make it all worthwhile."

I left her there, standing, and climbed into my bunk, pulling only a thin sheet over me because already the temperatures had gotten warmer as we sailed south, and the compartment felt steamy. Her sobs lulled me to sleep then, a sleep so deep that I didn't dream, one that could only have come from having achieved what had eluded me all these years: acceptance.

The water seemed to glow all around the ship as Margaret and I worked our way up, taking more than an hour to reach the top of the huge stack of shipping containers at the vessel's stern, where a crane towered over us. We lay on our backs. Even with the ships' lights we saw the stars clearly, the first chance I'd gotten to look at them since Megan and I had shared a foxhole aboveground, so long ago. Tomorrow we would dock. But there was still time to enjoy a moment or two, and when I found out that Margaret had never seen the stars the obvious thing to do was to show them to her.

"There are so many," she said.

"Millions. Billions. I heard men talk about them, in the tunnels, and apparently they plan to visit them someday."

"You lie," said Margaret.

"It's true. All these wars are good in a way, they've

spurred an effort to launch men back into space finally, to mine asteroids and other planets. Already teams are on their way."

She didn't say anything, then reached over to hold my hand. "That's what I want to do someday. Go out there and just look at things. Study them."

"Like a scientist?" I asked.

"Why not?"

I laughed, but quietly since we weren't supposed to go on deck at night, let alone atop the cargo. "We are killers, Margaret. Not scientists. Only people like Alderson or Lev can be scientists, because they have a way of disconnecting their curiosity from any sense of responsibility or accountability. They are cowards."

"Still," she argued. "I think I'd like to try. I don't want to go through life as a trigger-finger."

"Well, you'll have to go to a nonbred school. And you'll need a last name, because nobody will call you Doctor Margaret."

We laughed for a bit and then stared some more, the warm air tropical now, so that a sweat broke, making me wish I was the one going for a swim. There was always the danger of sharks, but the calculus was obvious so that even Margaret saw it eventually, that risking sharks was preferable to the certainty of death at American hands. For her, at least. She hadn't yet understood my motive for staying, but at least she had accepted it and her pleas for me to join her had stopped the day before.

"Are you ready?" I asked.

"I think so. How far is it to the water?"

I looked over the edge and felt dizzy from the height; up there, the wake's waves looked small and white.

"We'll climb down," I said, "to the deck, and you can go over the railing. Swim as far from the ship as you can, as soon as you hit the water, and then head northwest."

Margaret nodded. "I should get started."

We climbed down the outsides of the containers, and then across them until we hung over the deck before dropping two meters onto it. Margaret landed with a thud beside me. We both looked over the railing then, to our west. Stars silhouetted a black shape on the horizon, which rose from the water in a hump and had a few lights twinkling in its center—an island. We smelled land. It was close now, and Margaret looked at me while her eyes teared. She pulled me in, hugging me tightly for what seemed like five minutes, and by the time she let go she had stopped crying.

"I'll miss you."

I nodded and helped tie her hair, which reached the middle of her back now, into a ponytail. "I'll miss you too. Keep your toes pointed and hit the water feet first. Go."

Before I said anything else she vaulted the railing and disappeared into the night. I leaned over to try to see or hear the moment when she hit, but the engines and sound of waves against the hull swallowed everything. I never saw her again. On my way back to the room I thought about what I'd write, if anything more needed to be said about Margaret and the fact that I never fully understood how a Germline could transform into something so indecisive, incapable of the calculus of war, but then shrugged the thought away. Margaret was who she was because of her own experiences; that was her tale, not mine. There were really only a few pages left to write, so after shutting the door behind me I turned off the light and climbed into bed. Rest would help me face what was coming in the morning.

The next morning I rose early to scribble until there was only a bit more to say; already I felt the ship slow, the thrum of its engines deepening as they dropped in power, then eventually nearing total quiet when they shut off completely. It was especially hot. The air in my cabin didn't move, was humid and thick, so that my coveralls—the same ones acquired in Wonsan—soon soaked with sweat and my head swam until I finished off a bottle of water, wanting more almost immediately. There was a knock on my door. I knew who it would be before opening, so wasn't surprised to find the captain with two armed men, their pistols pointed at my chest as they squeezed in. He spoke English now.

"The American Navy is about to board us," he said. "Where is your friend?"

"She jumped overboard last night."

He ordered his men to search the room, which didn't take long. When they didn't find her he scowled. "I know what you are, and they want you and her. Now."

I bent over the table, trying to jot down the final lines. "Wait. Just a second."

"You can finish writing on the launch to the American boat. There will be time."

I knew then why it was so important to write a few last words, because I wrote them as much for my sisters as for the nonbred like Alderson who would wonder, like Margaret had, why I hadn't taken the chance to run, why I hadn't jumped overboard. The message I was to deliver included everything we experienced in North Korea. The foxes, the bears, the flowers, and the ocean. It was so simple. We had all been born into the world as killers, all of us Little Murderers in our own way, and the role suited us because it felt so good to kill, to be perfect at the job for which we had been created: to hate. But hatred was man's will. The spoiling eroded the emotion and took from us the one thing that had been our vocation, our identity, and it made us question the single action that defined us as creatures: murder. At first I thought the spoiling was also man's will, but this was wrong. It was God's test of faith. Given enough time, all of us—not just me, as Margaret seemed to think—every one of my sisters who escaped, did so to find a way past the spoiling and so walked a path to Him. It was always His will that we kill, but with honor, and the nonbred corrupted this the same way they corrupted everything they touched, but like nature reclaimed the waste in Korea, it would someday fix all of us who had escaped man's influence, and now I understood what Heather had meant when she'd said I'd figure out the message. *Men* were the abomination. They had replaced God with themselves; pity for the nonbred and discharge at their hands, the damned, was a ticket to His side, but so was finding one's own way.

Death and Faith.

# Epilogue

*Memorandum for Dr. Reynold T. Gregson*
*Defense Policy Board*
*Pentagon*

*Dear Dr. Gregson:*

*Attached is a verbatim copy of the document found with Unit AA-057111, Germline-One-A, Catherine, which you and your staff requested on 26 April. As you are aware, now that American forces have returned from the east, all seven active ateliers have been shut down and moth-balled per Presidential Directive 311256, and ateliers under construction were returned to a greenfield state until such time that program reactivation becomes neces-sary. Reactivation, should it ever occur, will take place in accordance with the new wartime mobilization guide-lines adopted by the Pentagon for the U.S. postwar readi-ness strategy. A few additional notes are warranted here, however, since the attached document presents new data that haven't been previously considered.*

    *I had been told that this was a set of notes, and relayed that same information to you in my April briefing to the Board. That information was inaccurate. The document attached is almost a complete file on Catherine's activities since de-tanking, including some of her thoughts and feelings as they relate to combat, the loss of friends, and her own mortality. In light of this I recommend that it be incorporated as part of future Germline training regimens, as originally outlined by General Urqhart before his death in the Almaty encirclement. Clearly this book is an important find. In my professional opinion—both as someone who had regular contact with Catherine and as a psychiatrist—her book validates many of the fears we had regarding religious aspects of the girls' training. General Urqhart, were he alive, would be pleased to know that in my opinion, he was right: Catherine was the one we had been looking for all along. She could have taught the other units much about what was expected of them and how to handle discharge at the appropriate time.*

*Preliminary modeling of Catherine's analyses suggest a strong likelihood that should we adopt her writings and incorporate them in the Modern Combat Manual, future generations of Germline units will receive a far more detailed preview of what to expect as they age, and will recognize the signs of spoiling with far less stress than the last models fielded. It may even reduce the number of escapes—perhaps bringing them to zero entirely. My staff feels that we could rewrite her biography so to seamlessly incorporate it into the latest versions of the Manual, perhaps referring to it as the "Gospel of Catherine," or something along those lines. Of course the final few paragraphs would have to be changed. We also advise passing copies of this book, once it is finished, to escaped Germline units in Thailand; our models suggest that doing so may convince more of them to report for voluntary discharge.*

*Of course, as long as production of Germline units is prohibited by the Genetic Weapons Convention, we should consider discussing this in a classified venue and should the Board decide to move forward I hope that you will give our findings the attention they deserve and consider the recommendations hereby set forth. My staff and I are looking forward to seeing you at the symposium in Hawaii; we trust that you and your wife are doing well.*

> *Warm Regards,*
> *Quentin Alderson, PhD*
> *Chief Psychiatrist*
> *Germline Wartime Mobilization Strategy*
> *Think Tank*
> *Hamilton Diversified Corp.*

# ACKNOWLEDGMENTS

Special thanks to Lou Anders who took me under his wing at my first WorldCon, and to John Scalzi for giving me a chance to participate in "The Big Idea." Thanks also to Jack Womack—publicist extraordinaire—Alex Lencicki—also a publicist extraordinaire—and of course to DongWon Song and Anna Gregson for everything else that it took to write this book.

# extras

www.orbitbooks.net

# about the author

**T. C. McCarthy** earned a BA from the University of Virginia, and a PhD from the University of Georgia, before embarking on a career that gave him a unique perspective as a science fiction author. From his time as a patent examiner in complex biotechnology to his tenure with the Central Intelligence Agency, T.C. has studied and analyzed foreign militaries and weapons systems. T.C. was at the CIA during the September 11 terrorist attacks and was still there when U.S. forces invaded Afghanistan and Iraq, allowing him to experience warfare from the perspective of an analyst. Find out more about the author at www.tcmccarthy.com.

Find out more about T. C. McCarthy and other Orbit authors by registering for the free monthly newsletter at www.orbitbooks.net

if you enjoyed

## EXOGENE

look out for

# EQUATIONS OF LIFE

by

## Simon Morden

I

Petrovitch woke up. The room was in the filtered yellow half-light of rain-washed window and thin curtain. He lay perfectly still, listening to the sounds of the city.

For a moment, all he could hear was the all-pervading hum of machines: those that made power, those that used it, pushing, pulling, winding, spinning, sucking, blowing, filtering, pumping, heating and cooling.

In the next moment, he did the city-dweller's trick of blanking that whole frequency out. In the gap it left, he could discern individual sources of noise: traffic on the street fluxing in phase with the cycle of red-amber-green, the rhythmic metallic grinding of a worn windmill bearing on the roof, helicopter blades cutting the grey dawn air. A door slamming, voices rising – a man's low bellow and a woman's shriek, going at it hard. Leaking in through the steel walls, the babel chatter of a hundred different channels all turned up too high.

Another morning in the London Metrozone, and Petrovitch had survived to see it: *God, I love this place.*

Closer, in the same room as him, was another sound, one that carried meaning and promise. He blinked his pale eyes, flicking his unfocused gaze to search his world, searching …

There. His hand snaked out, his fingers closed around thin wire, and he turned his head slightly to allow the approaching glasses to fit over his ears. There was a thumbprint dead centre on his right lens. He looked around it as he sat up.

It was two steps from his bed to the chair where he'd thrown his clothes the night before. It was May, and it wasn't cold, so he sat down naked, moving his belt buckle from under one arse cheek. He looked at the screen glued to the wall.

His reflection stared back, high-cheeked, white-skinned, pale-haired. Like an angel, or maybe a ghost: he could count the faint shadows cast by his ribs.

Back on the screen, an icon was flashing. Two telephone numbers had appeared in a self-opening box: one was his, albeit temporarily, to be discarded after a single use. In front of him on the desk were two fine black gloves and a small red switch. He slipped the gloves on, and pressed the switch.

"Yeah?" he said into the air.

A woman's voice, breathless from effort. "I'm looking for Petrovitch."

His index finger was poised to cut the connection. "You are who?"

"Triple A couriers. I've got a package for an S. Petrovitch." She was panting less now, and her cut-glass accent started to reassert itself. "I'm at the drop-off: the café on the corner of South Side and Rookery Road. The proprietor says he doesn't know you."

"Yeah, and Wong's a *pizdobol*," he said. His finger drifted from the cut-off switch and dragged through the air, pulling a window open to display all his current transactions. "Give me the order number."

"Fine," sighed the courier woman. He could hear traffic noise over her headset, and the sound of clattering plates in the background. He would never have described Wong's as a café, and resolved to tell him later. They'd both laugh. She read off a number, and it matched one of his purchases. It was here at last.

"I'll be with you in five," he said, and cut off her protests about another job to go to with a slap of the red switch.

He peeled off the gloves. He pulled on yesterday's clothes and scraped his fingers through his hair, scratching his scalp vigorously. He stepped into his boots and grabbed his own battered courier bag.

Urban camouflage. Just another immigrant, not worth shaking down. He pushed his glasses back up his nose and palmed the door open. When it closed behind him, it locked repeatedly, automatically.

The corridor echoed with noise, with voices, music, footsteps. Above all, the soft moan of poverty. People were everywhere, their shoulders against his, their feet under his, their faces – wet-mouthed, hollow-eyed, filthy skinned – close to his.

The floor, the walls, the ceiling were made from bare sheet metal that boomed. Doors punctured the way to the stairs, which had been dropped into deliberately-left voids and welded into place. There was a lift, which sometimes even worked, but he wasn't stupid. The stairs were safer because he was fitter than the addicts who'd try to roll him.

Fitness was relative, of course, but it was enough.

He clanked his way down to the ground floor, five storeys away, ten landings, squeezing past the stair dwellers and avoiding spatters of noxious waste. At no point did he look up in case he caught someone's eye.

It wasn't safe, calling a post-Armageddon container home, but neither was living in a smart, surveillance-rich neighbourhood with no visible means of support – something that was going to attract police attention, which wasn't what he wanted at all. As it stood, he was just another immigrant with a clean record renting an identikit two-by-four domik module in the middle of Clapham Common. He'd never given anyone an excuse to notice him, had no intention of ever doing so.

Street level. Cracked pavements dark with drying rain, humidity high, the heat already uncomfortable. An endless stream of traffic that ran like a ribbon throughout the city, always moving with a stop-start, never seeming to arrive. There was elbow-room here, and he could stride out to the pedestrian crossing. The lights changed as he approached, and the cars parted as if for Moses. The crowd of bowed-head, hunch-shouldered people shuffled drably across the tarmac to the other side and, in the middle, a shock of white-blond hair.

Wong's was on the corner. Wong himself was kicking some plastic furniture out onto the pavement to add an air of unwarranted sophistication to his shop. The windows were streaming condensation inside, and stale, steamy air blew out the door.

"Hey, Petrovitch. She your girlfriend? You keep her waiting like that, she leave you."

"She's a courier, you *perdoon stary*. Where is she?"

Wong looked at the opaque glass front, and pointed through it. "There," the shopkeeper said, "right there. Eyes of love never blind."

"I'll have a coffee, thanks." Petrovitch pushed a chair out of his path.

"I should charge you double. You use my shop as office!"

Petrovitch put his hands on Wong's shoulders and leaned down. "If I didn't come here, your life would be less interesting. And you wouldn't want that."

Wong wagged his finger but stood aside, and Petrovitch went in.

The woman was easy to spot. Woman: girl almost, all adolescent gawkiness and nerves, playing with her ponytail, twisting and untwisting it in red spirals around her index finger.

She saw him moving towards her, and stopped fiddling, sat up, tried to look professional. All she managed was younger.

"Petrovitch?"

"Yeah," he said, dropping into the seat opposite her. "Do you have ID?"

"Do you?"

They opened their bags simultaneously. She brought out a thumb scanner, he produced a cash card. They went through the ritual of confirming their identities, checking the price of the item, debiting the money from the card. Then she laid a padded package on the table, and waited for the security tag to unlock.

Somewhere during this, a cup of coffee appeared at Petrovitch's side. He took a sharp, scalding sip.

"So what is it?" the courier asked, nodding at the package.

"It's kind of your job to deliver it, my job to pay for it." He dragged the packet towards him. "I don't have to tell you what's in it."

"You're an arrogant little fuck, aren't you?" Her cheeks flushed.

Petrovitch took another sip of coffee, then centred his cup on his saucer. "It has been mentioned once or twice before." He looked up again, and pushed his glasses up to see her better. "I have trust issues, so I don't tend to do the people-stuff very well."

"It wouldn't hurt you to try." The security tag popped open, and she pushed her chair back with a scrape.

"Yeah, but it's not like I'm going to ever see you again, is it?" said Petrovitch.

"If you'd played your cards right, you might well have done. Sure, you're good-looking, but right now I wouldn't piss on you if you were on fire." She picked up her courier bag with studied determination and strode to the door.

Petrovitch watched her go: she bent over, lean and lithe in her one-piece skating gear, to extrude the wheels from her shoes. The other people in the shop fell silent as the door slammed shut, just to increase his discomfort.

Wong leaned over the counter. "You bad man, Petrovitch. One day you need friend, and where you be? Up shit creek with no paddle."

"I've always got you, Wong." He put his hand to his face and scrubbed at his chin. He could try and catch her up, apologise for being ... what? Himself? He was half out of his seat, then let himself fall back with a bang. He stopped being the centre of attention, and he drank more coffee.

The package in its mesh pocket called to him. He reached over and tore it open. As the disabled security tag clattered to the tabletop, Wong took the courier's place opposite him.

"I don't need relationship advice, yeah?"

Wong rubbed at a sticky patch with a damp cloth. "This not about girl, that girl, any girl. You not like people, fine. But you smart, Petrovitch. You smartest guy I know. Maybe you smart enough to fake liking, yes? Else."

"Else what?" Petrovitch's gaze slipped from Wong to the device in his hand, a slim, brushed steel case, heavy with promise.

"Else one day, pow." Wong mimed a gun against his temple, and his finger jerked with imaginary recoil. "Fortune cookie says you do great things. If you live."

"Yeah, that's me. Destined for greatness." Petrovitch snorted and caressed the surface of the case, leaving misty fingerprints behind. "How long have you lived here, Wong?"

"Metrozone born and bred," said Wong. "I remember when Clapham Common was green, like park."

"Then why the *chyort* can't you speak better English?"

Wong leaned forward over the table, and beckoned Petrovitch to do the same. Their noses were almost touching.

"Because, old chap," whispered Wong faultlessly, "we hide behind our masks, all of us, every day. All the world's a stage, and all the men and women merely players. I play my part of eccentric Chinese shop-keeper; everyone knows what to expect from me, and they don't ask for any more. What about you, Petrovitch? What part are you playing?" He leaned back, and Petrovitch shut his goldfish-gaping mouth.

A man and a woman came in and, on seeing every table full, started to back out again.

Wong sprung to his feet. "Hey, wait. Table here." He kicked Petrovitch's chair-leg hard enough to cause them both to wince. "Coffee? Coffee hot and strong today." He bustled behind the counter, leaving Petrovitch to wearily slide his device back into its delivery pouch and then into his shoulder bag.

His watch told him it was time to go. He stood, finished the last of his drink in three hot gulps, and made for the door.

"Hey," called Wong. "You no pay."

Petrovitch pulled out his cash card and held it up.

"You pay next time, Petrovitch." He shrugged and almost smiled. The lines around his eyes crinkled.

"Yeah, whatever." He put the card back in his bag. It had only a few euros on it now, anyway. "Thanks, Wong."

Back out onto the street and the roar of noise. The leaden sky squeezed out a drizzle and speckled the lenses in Petrovitch's glasses so that he started to see the world like a fly would.

He'd take the tube. It'd be hot, dirty, smelly, crowded: at least it would be dry. He turned his collar up and started down the road towards Clapham South.

The shock of the new had barely reached the Underground. The tiled walls were twentieth-century curdled cream and bottle green, the tunnels they lined unchanged since they'd been hollowed out two centuries earlier, the fans that ineffectually stirred the air on the platforms were ancient with age.

There was the security screen, though: the long arched passage of shiny white plastic, manned by armed paycops and monitored by grey-covered watchers.

Petrovitch's travelcard talked to the turnstile as he waited in line to pass. It flashed a green light, clicked and he pushed through. Then came the screen which saw everything, saw through everything, measured it and resolved it into three dimensions, running the images it gained against a database of offensive weapons and banned technology.

After the enforced single file, it was abruptly back to being shoulder to shoulder. Down the escalator, groaning and creaking, getting hotter and more airless as it descended. Closer to the centre of the Earth.

He popped like a cork onto the northbound platform, and glanced up to the display barely visible over the heads of the other passengers. A full quarter of the elements were faulty, making the scrolling writing appear either coded or mystical. But he'd had practice. There was a train in three minutes.

Whether or not there was room for anyone to get on was a different matter, but that possibility was one of the few advantages in living out along the far reaches of the line. He knew of people he worked with who walked away from the centre of the city in order to travel back.

It became impossible even to move. He waited more or less patiently, and kept a tight hold of his bag.

To his left, a tall man, air bottle strapped to his Savile Row suit and soft mask misting with each breath. To his right, a Japanese woman, patriotically displaying Hello Kitty and the Rising Sun, hollow-eyed with loss.

The train, rattling and howling, preceded by a blast of foulness almost tangible, hurtled out from the tunnel mouth. If there hadn't been barriers along the edge of the platform, the track would have been choked with mangled corpses. As it was, there was a collective strain, an audible tightening of muscle and sinew.

The carriages squealed to a stop, accompanied by the inevitable multi-language announcements: the train was heading for the central zones and out again to the distant, unassailable riches of High Barnet, and please – mind the gap.

The doors hissed open, and no one got out. Those on the platform eyed the empty seats and the hang-straps greedily. Then the electro-magnetic locks on the gates loosened their grip. They banged back under the pressure of so many bodies, and people ran on, claiming their prizes as they could.

And when the carriages were full, the last few squeezed on, pulled aboard by sympathetic arms until they were crammed in like pressed meat.

The chimes sounded, the speakers rustled with static before running through a litany of "doors closing" phrases: English, French, Russian, Urdu, Japanese, Kikuyu, Mandarin, Spanish. The engine span, the wheels turned, the train jerked and swayed.

Inside, Petrovitch, face pressed uncomfortably against a glass partition, ribs tight against someone's back, took shallow sips of breath and wondered again why he'd chosen the Metrozone above other, less crowded and more distant cities. He wondered why it still had to be like this, seven thirty-five in the morning, two decades after Armageddon.